PENGUIN BO

Zodiac

Sam Wilson was born in London and moved to Zimbabwe as a child before settling in South Africa. In 2011 he was listed as one of the 'Top 200 Young South Africans' and is now a TV director based in Cape Town. *Zodiac* is his debut novel.

Zodiac

SAM WILSON

PENGUIN BOOKS

PENGUIN BOOKS

UK | USA | Canada | Ireland | Australia
India | New Zealand | South Africa

Penguin Books is part of the Penguin Random House group of companies
whose addresses can be found at global.penguinrandomhouse.com.

First published 2016
001

Copyright © Sam Wilson, 2016

The moral right of the author has been asserted

Set in 12.5/14.75 pt Garamond MT Std
Typeset by Jouve (UK), Milton Keynes
Printed in Great Britain by Clays Ltd, St Ives plc

A CIP catalogue record for this book is available from the British Library

ISBN: 978–1–405–92164–0

www.greenpenguin.co.uk

Penguin Random House is committed to a
sustainable future for our business, our readers
and our planet. This book is made from Forest
Stewardship Council® certified paper.

For Tony, Diana and Kerry

Welcome to San Celeste . . .

Capricorn

Earth

22 December – 19 January

They may be the smallest group in the city, but True Capricorns are its brightest stars, controlling most of its wealth and institutions. The 'Neo-Caps' – born to parents of other signs – are rightly despised by True Capricorns.

Aquarius

Air

20 January – 18 February

Liberal hipster types: creative professionals, designers, architects, freelancers with laptop bags and vinyl collections. Despite being gainful members of society, they consider themselves separate from the mainstream.

Pisces

Water

19 February – 20 March

Hippies and intermittently productive 'free-spirits'. Many of them are artists, addicts or self-professed psychics. They are not widely considered employable, but have strong family networks for support.

Aries

Fire

21 March – 19 April

The city's underclass: violent, uncontrollable and unemployable. They mostly live in the large, dangerous slum area known as Ariesville.

Taurus

Earth

20 April – 20 May

Loyal, reliable and down-to-earth – they keep the city moving. A very large number of them work for public sector institutions such as the police force.

Gemini

Air

21 May – 20 June

The fast-talking, fast-living yuppies of San Celeste. With their silver tongues and moral flexibility, many of these city-slickers have made a killing in advertising and sales.

Where the stars always shine.

Cancer

Water

21 June – 22 July

Society's largest group. Sensible folk that uphold the status quo and fill many different management positions as they are considered naturally trustworthy.

Leo

Fire

23 July – 22 August

Hear them roar! A small but highly vocal group closely aligned with the Cancers. Also conservative, they often fill the role of entertainers, politicians and pundits.

Virgo

Earth

23 August – 22 September

Tend to be introverted and obsessive. Typical jobs include engineers and system administrators, and they have an extensive science fiction and fantasy culture.

Libra

Air

23 September – 22 October

Known to be 'people' people. They are employed largely in the service industry. Any job that requires a smile without a hard-sell is given to a Libra.

Scorpio

Water

23 October – 21 November

Could Scorpios be the new elite? Sharper and hungrier than the Capricorns, and well known for being control freaks, they are fast accumulating status and power.

Sagittarius

Fire

22 November – 21 December

Along with the Aquarians, they form the other half of the left-leaning middle-class. Often found in the education or charity sectors, they claim to have hearts of gold.

'True Signs in Harmony' ®

Chapter One

Rachel was going to be late for her first day of work, but it wasn't her fault. The laundromat on Gull Street didn't open until eight in the morning, and the manager at Jiffyclean Maid Service always insisted that their uniforms should be spotless, even though each of the maids had only one set each. She'd worked late the night before at a fortieth birthday party at a Sagittarius house in West Skye, and a drunken straggler had accidentally tipped some guacamole down the front of her white apron while making a half-hearted attempt to hit on her.

'Lucky you're wearing that,' he had said to cover his embarrassment. He didn't know that she couldn't show up the next day at a new client's house with a soiled uniform. After four hours' fretful sleep she had woken just before the laundromat opened and raced to clean the uniform. She sat in front of the washing machine and watched the clothes slosh around inside as the time ticked down to nine a.m., when she was meant to be at the new client's house.

She waited as long as she could bear, then cancelled the drying cycle early and went to the laundromat's bathroom to put on the uniform. She didn't realize how damp her clothes were until the heat faded, leaving her checked blue dress sticking to her legs, clammy and cold. She bundled up her warm morning clothes into a plastic bag and got on a bus heading to Conway Heights. Every few minutes throughout the trip she double-checked the time. When it got to nine and she still hadn't arrived, her heart sank. She didn't like letting people down. She was a Libra.

Conway Heights was a fancy district out in the southern suburbs of San Celeste. Rachel stared distractedly out of the window at tennis courts, trimmed trees and fake Tuscan villas. Everything was clean and expensive. She felt like an interloper.

The bus stopped on the corner of Morin Road. Rachel's plastic bag full of dry clothes bounced against her leg as she ran three blocks uphill to Eden Drive. The houses she passed all had front yards with palm trees and manicured flower beds.

Her client's home was a wide, single-storey building with beige walls and a low-sloped roof. She mentally prepared her apology as she walked up the brick path to the front-door alcove. Her finger was on the intercom button when she saw that the door was already open a crack.

She tapped it with her knuckles, opening it a little more.

'Hello?' she called. 'Jiffyclean Maid Service!'

There was no answer.

A splinter of wood was sticking out halfway up the door frame. She touched it experimentally. It was the length of her finger, torn off opposite the lock. The door had been kicked in.

'Hello?' she called again, and pressed the intercom button. A speaker buzzed somewhere deep in the house, but there was no reply.

Rachel shivered in her damp dress. She stepped backwards into the sunshine and looked up, then down the road. There was no sign of life and no sound except distant traffic and barking dogs.

She clenched her jaw and took her pink and purple phone out of the plastic bag.

It connected after two rings.

'911. What is the nature of your emergency?'

'Hello?' said Rachel uncertainly. 'I'm outside . . . um . . . 36 Eden Drive in Conway Heights. I just got here and the door's kicked in, and no one's answering when I call inside.'

There was the faint sound of fingers clicking on a keyboard and the operator spoke again. Her voice was warm and calm. There was a Libra lilt to it, which was reassuring.

'All right, I'm sending a patrol car to you. Can I have your name, please?'

'Rachel Wells.'

'And is it your home?'

'No,' said Rachel. 'I work for Jiffyclean. I'm a maid.'

'All right, Rachel. It'll be about eight minutes until the officers get there. I just need to ask you a few more questions, OK, hon?'

Hon? Definitely a Libra.

'Yeah, sure,' said Rachel.

'OK. Can you tell me what you look like, so the officers will recognize you when they get there?'

'Sure. I'm about five-eight, five-nine, I've got blonde hair and I'm in a blue checked dress with a white apron. Is that enough?'

She waited, but there was no response.

'Hello?' she said.

For a moment she thought she'd been cut off, but she could hear a distant voice. She lowered the phone and could still hear it. A man was speaking nearby.

On the left side of the house was a garden wall covered with climbing flowers and an ornate cast-iron gate with peeling white paint. She heard the man's voice again coming from behind it and felt a flood of relief. Of course. The client was in the backyard, which is why he hadn't answered when she called. Everything was fine. She pushed down on the gate's latch and went through, touching her hair to make sure her ponytail hadn't come loose.

'Hello?' she called again. 'Mr Williams?'

She followed a path around the side of the house, through a wicker arch covered in dying vines. The house was built on a hillside and the lawn sloped down to give a view across the city, all the way to the WSCR Tower.

Behind the house was an empty swimming pool. There was a trench dug into the ground next to it, and the paving slabs on one side had been pulled up and stacked against the back wall of the house.

'Hello? Rachel?' said the operator on her phone.

Rachel brought it back up to her ear. 'Hey, sorry, I thought I heard something.'

'From the house?'

'No, from the backyard, but there's no one here.'

'Rachel, listen to me,' said the operator. 'I need you to go to the front of the house so the officers know they're at the right place.' Her voice was firm and Rachel was good enough with people to detect something else. It was fear.

As Rachel turned back to the gate she heard a new noise. It was a straining, choking sound just on the edge

4

of her hearing. She froze and listened. After a few seconds it came again, from the trench by the pool.

'There's someone here,' she said.

'Rachel,' said the operator sharply. 'Please go back to the road.'

But Rachel was already running to the side of the trench.

'Oh, God,' she said. 'Oh, God. Oh, God. Oh, God.'

'Rachel?' said the operator.

The man at the bottom was about fifty years old. He had short white hair and was wearing black trousers and a long-sleeved white shirt that was stained with mud at the back and blood at the front. His eyes were able to focus on her for only a second before they rolled back in his head. His mouth was taped closed and one of his nostrils ran with blood. Rachel dropped her plastic bag and ran to the side of the trench, looking for some way to help.

'Ambulance!' she shouted into the phone. 'Oh, God. Ambulance!'

The operator's voice stayed calm. 'Who's injured, Rachel?'

'He's an old man. He's been cut open across the belly. His guts . . . oh, God, I can see his guts. I thought they were a hosepipe or something. They're in the mud –'

Rachel caught the smell of it and gagged. The intestines were punctured. She took a step back from the trench and took a deep breath. She'd always told herself that she would be able to handle herself in an emergency. She knew her priorities. People first. She breathed in the clean air and stepped forward again. The man was squirming and his breaths were short and shallow. His wrists and ankles were bound in duct tape.

'Hon! I need you to stay with me, OK?' said the operator.

'It's OK, I'm here. He's been bound and gagged. There's so much blood.'

'OK. Keep talking to me. I'm going to help you through this. I need you to slow the bleeding until the paramedics arrive.'

'I've got a bag of clothes here.'

'Are they clean?'

'No, but I just washed my apron. I'm wearing it now –'

'Perfect. Take it off and fold it into a long strip. I'll tell you where to hold it. The ambulance won't be long, but you're going to have to stop that blood.'

Rachel untied her apron and unhooked the strap from over her head. As she was folding it, a movement caught her eye. It was dark inside the house, but it looked as if someone was standing behind the cream-coloured curtains behind the sliding door. She froze.

'Oh, God.'

'What is it, Rachel?'

'I think there's someone in the house.'

The operator was silent. The only sound was the warbling static of cellular reception.

'Hello?' said Rachel.

The line clicked, as if the operator was switching back from talking to someone else.

'Rachel, I need you to go back to the street.'

'But the man –'

'Now, Rachel!'

There was a rumbling from the direction of the house. A man in a tan jacket was pulling open the sliding glass doors. He was wearing a baseball cap and a black scarf hid the lower half of his face. Rachel dropped her folded apron and ran.

'He's coming!' she shouted into the phone. 'Oh, God!'

The side gate had swung closed while she was in the garden. She ran up to it and pulled, but it wouldn't budge. The man was only a few steps away. She dropped her phone and tugged with both hands, popping the latch open. She ran through the gate and slammed it behind her just as the man caught up. For a moment she was face to face with him. His eyes were bright blue. She turned and ran. Almost immediately, the latch clicked again and the gate swung open again.

A black car was driving down the street ahead. Rachel ran out in front of it with her hands raised. It braked immediately and came to a stop in front of her. The driver, a middle-aged man in an elegant jacket, looked up at her in surprise. She ran round to his window.

'Help me!' she shouted. 'Let me in! Please!'

She could hear the feet of the man who was chasing her getting closer. The driver saw him coming and made a decision. He pressed a button on the door next to him and Rachel heard a clunk as the central locking disengaged.

She opened the back door and threw herself on to the seat. As she tried to slam the door behind her, the man chasing her grabbed it and held tight. Rachel lay on the back seat and kicked at the man's hand.

'Drive!' she shouted. 'Just drive!'

'Shhh,' said the car's driver. She looked up into the silver barrel of his gun.

'Stay very still, please,' he said.

Rachel froze. The man with the scarf over his face pushed her legs off the back seat. He squeezed in next to her and closed the door behind him.

'Do you have the tape?' said the driver, keeping the gun on Rachel. His hair was flecked with silver. To Rachel, he looked like a bank manager or an actor playing a CEO on television.

'Yeah,' said the other man.

'Tie her wrists.'

Sirens wailed in the distance, getting closer. Rachel felt a moment of hope.

'Shit,' said the driver. 'Take this.'

He gave the gun to the man with the scarf. As he passed it, Rachel kicked again, trying to knock it out of his hands. The man next to her was quick, though. He grabbed the gun and brought it up to her head in a single swift motion.

'Uh-uh,' he said.

The car pulled off and the man in the back kept the gun on her. Slowly, with his other hand, he took a roll of metallic duct tape out of his jacket pocket. He pulled up his scarf to just over his mouth and tore off a two-foot length of tape with his teeth.

'Wrists,' he said.

Rachel didn't move. The man dropped the tape. He leaned in to her and with blinding speed punched her on the side of her jaw. Her eyes watered in shock.

I've got to get out of this.

She held her arms forward with her wrists together.

8

The man grabbed them firmly with one hand. He dropped the gun in his lap and bound her hands with the tape.

The sirens outside the car grew louder and the tone dropped as an ambulance passed by. Rachel looked after it, but it showed no sign of slowing down. They hadn't seen her. The 911 operator was probably still on the line, on her dropped phone. No one was coming for her.

Rachel was on her own.

Chapter Two

Chief of Police Peter Williams's face was thinner than Burton remembered it, with fine wrinkles radiating out from the corners of his eyes. Burton hadn't noticed them any of the times Williams had stood on a podium in front of a room full of cops. A long strip of silver tape was stuck over his mouth, wrapping around on one side of his head and sticking to the fine hairs at the back of his neck. The same brand of tape bound his wrists and ankles. There was one cut on his abdomen, horizontal, through the navel. The Chief's intestines spilled out through the laceration.

'Shit, that's messy,' said Detective Kolacny.

Burton looked up and shielded his eyes from the morning sun. Kolacny was standing at the edge of the trench, biting the side of his lip. He was wearing sunglasses.

'Have you found anything?'

'Not yet,' said Burton. 'There might be some DNA if the killer tore this tape with his teeth.'

Kolacny winced. The stench was bad. The Chief's large intestine had been punctured and was spilling its contents into the bottom of the trench. Whoever had cut him open had gone out of their way to make sure he wouldn't be stitched up again.

'Don't forget to wipe your feet,' said Kolacny.

Burton looked at him coldly. Morbid humour was a

regular feature of most murder scenes when there weren't any civilians present. It made the job bearable. But this was the goddam Chief of Police.

'Sorry,' said Kolacny. He took off his shades and looked ashamed.

'It's fine. You're new. Did you get a photo of the soil?'

'What soil?'

Burton climbed out of the hole and pointed. There was a circle of soil scattered on the grass, about five feet in diameter. A lot of it had fallen between and under the blades of grass. It wasn't easily visible.

Kolacny knelt down for a closer look. 'Who made this? Did it spill out of a wheelbarrow or something?'

'I don't think so.'

Burton went to the middle of the lawn and stretched out his right arm. He turned around, miming scattering soil and matching the pattern on the ground.

'Weird,' said Kolacny, and frowned. He leaned in closer. 'It looks like there's some more scattered here . . . and here.'

There were another two lines, a foot or so long, extending from the circle at about forty-five degrees from each other. Burton hadn't seen them.

'Significant?' said Kolacny.

'I don't know,' said Burton. 'They could have just been kicked up when someone walked over the circle. Point it out to the photographic unit anyway. Any sign of the maid yet?'

'Nothing,' said Kolacny. 'I called the cleaning company. They gave me her mother's address and phone number.'

'You call her?'

'Haven't had a chance.'

'You'd better do it quick, before she finds out from the TV.'

The media were gathering at the front of the house and the cops guarding the crime scene were starting to bristle at them. None of the cops liked reporters poking their noses into police business. A lot of them, including Burton, had known Williams personally.

'Hey,' said Kolacny. 'There's something inside you should see.'

He took Burton through the sliding glass doors at the back of the house and into the sunken living room, three steps lower than the rest of the house. It took a moment for Burton's eyes to adjust to the darkness. There was less furniture than he remembered since the one time he had visited, back before the Chief's divorce.

Kolacny led him up the steps and along a short corridor to the front door. He pointed out the splintered wood where the door had been kicked in.

'It must have been loud,' he said.

'Have we spoken to the neighbours yet?' said Burton.

'Kallis and McGill are on it now.'

Burton pushed open the door with a gloved hand and looked outside. Vans from the major networks were setting up out front and reporters were talking into cameras, using the building as their backdrop. On the other side of the road Burton could see one of the uniformed cops, McGill, talking to a group of gawping neighbours. A zoom lens pointed at Burton from next to the news vans.

As Burton turned away, he spotted a small plastic rectangle at the top of the door frame. It was a magnetic strip, part of the home security system. He pointed it out to Kolacny.

'Why do you reckon the alarm didn't go off?'

'Maybe Williams only turned it on at night.'

Burton followed the wires up from the strip and along the top of the corridor wall. In a recess around the corner was the hub of the security system – a number pad with an UrSec logo and a metal box containing a battery on the floor underneath it. The wire between the two was cut. Kolacny craned in over Burton's shoulder.

'Oh, shit,' he said.

'Yeah,' said Burton.

There was a clatter from the living room. The Crime Scene Investigation unit were coming in with their white coveralls. Kolacny showed them the front door and the severed security system cord, and they dutifully dusted for prints and searched for DNA evidence while Burton scouted through the rest of the house.

It was interesting that Williams had chosen to stay in the same house after being promoted to Chief of Police. It was big, but far from the biggest in the neighbourhood. Then again, Williams was Taurus, like most cops. He didn't want things to change.

The bedroom was tidy but sparsely furnished. The bed was neatly made, which was a little surprising considering that Williams had called a cleaning service. But the room wasn't spotless. There was dust under the bed and an old laptop on the bedside table. Maybe Williams was the kind of person to tidy up before the maid came, so he wouldn't feel judged.

There was a golf club lying on the floor. Burton checked

the closets. Half of them had Williams's uniforms and weekend clothes neatly folded or on hangers, and the rest were empty, as if he was leaving space for his ex-wife to come back. Or maybe he just liked things arranged the way they had always been.

In the corner of the room, behind the bedroom door, Burton found a panic alarm button. There were a few dark red dots on the wall beneath it. Blood. He called the CS team.

While they were busy taking photographs and samples, Burton walked through the rest of the house and checked it methodically. Everything seemed lifeless. The only room with any colour in it was the small second bedroom, which had purple walls and boy band posters. It was Williams's daughter Ashleigh's room, whenever she came to visit. She had to be ten or eleven years old now. Burton hadn't seen her since she was three.

At the time, it had meant a lot to Burton to be invited for supper with the Captain of the Homicide Department. He and Kate were newly married and living in a cramped flat, and Williams's life had seemed like a promise of the future. But it had been an awkward evening. Williams had asked Kate a lot of questions and stared intently at her while she answered, which was uncomfortable, and a few too many of his jokes were at his wife's expense. But Burton and Kate had wanted to make a good impression, and Williams plied them with single malt. By the end of the evening they were all talking so loudly that Williams's daughter had toddled down the corridor rubbing her sleepy eyes and told them to 'pipe down', which made them all laugh.

That was years ago.

The house had already been half-dead before Williams was murdered. If this was the future that lay in wait for Burton – if he kept fighting with Kate, or their daughter was born in the wrong sign and their marriage didn't survive it – he doubted that he would hold things together as well as Williams.

Chapter Three

The day that Daniel Lapton discovered he had a daughter, he was meant to be in a meeting. The Vice President for Asia and Australia had organized a meeting with potential Korean investors, and although Daniel wasn't exactly needed there, it had been strongly hinted that having someone with the Lapton name at the table would be good for appearances. Daniel knew that it was high time that he started paying attention to the family business. His father had passed away a year ago and the company had been on autopilot ever since. But on the day of the meeting, he woke up late. He stared at the wooden ceiling for fifteen minutes, then took the phone from the bedside table and called the VP's secretary to make his excuses, citing an 'unforeseen medical emergency'. He wasn't fooling anyone. Everyone in the company knew he wasn't his father.

He put on a silk dressing gown and went down to the kitchen. Breakfast wasn't waiting for him. He had told the servants to take paid leave – now he was back home, he didn't feel like having other people around for a while. He scoured the pantry until he found some reasonably fresh bread, which he dunked into a bowl of taramasalata from one of the refrigerators.

When he'd had as much as he could handle, he went through to the downstairs entertainment room and dropped on to a black leather couch. He turned on the television and watched a few minutes of a war documentary. Guilt built up inside him. If his father had been alive he would've told him that the world was full of people hungrier and more desperate than Daniel would ever be, and that they'd gnaw their way through his empire like woodworms through this mansion. True Capricorns didn't leave their decisions to subordinates. They were wealthy because they deserved to be. They weren't quitters.

The month after his father died, Daniel left the family home and travelled the world, checking in at all the Lapton hotels. Lapton Europa. Lapton Pacifica. Lapton Afrique. He felt like a prince in a fairy tale, pretending to be a commoner just to see what life was really like in his empire. He wasn't deluded, though. He knew he was checking into the nicest suites and he wouldn't have been surprised if the main office had quietly warned the hotels that he was coming.

In truth, he wasn't inspecting his empire, he was running from it. But escape was impossible. He wasn't going to be leaving the beaten path at this stage of his life. He wasn't going to go base-jumping, or do ayahuasca in the jungle, or sleep on the dusty floor of a monastery. And he wasn't going to connect with anyone or anything new. So after ten months of travel he returned to his nest, middle-aged and flightless. There was no other place for him. He considered talking to an astrotherapist, but he was enough of a Lapton to distrust therapy. His problems were his own and only he had the right to know or fix them.

He wandered through the corridors of the house that he still thought of as his father's, past a generation's worth of antiques and trinkets – shelves of leather-bound books, pool tables, astrolabes and oak-framed barometers. On impulse he entered a passageway with a black-and-white tiled floor that led to his father's private study. As a child the area had been off-limits, although he had explored it in secret many times. The faint feeling of forbidden territory came back to him as he walked in.

The study was the same as it had always been. It wasn't a big room. There was a desk against the far wall, with shelves above it holding stacks of books and files. An antique swivel chair with a leather seat and wooden arm-rests sat in front of the desk, with a filing cabinet on the right-hand side. The walls and carpet were dark brown. It was the kind of room that was never meant to be exposed to sunlight. Daniel turned on the desk lamp and noticed a stack of papers that looked as if they hadn't been touched since his father died. Out of curiosity he started flipping through them, and after a while found himself sorting them into piles of things worth dealing with and things to be shredded. It was the kind of job he might have got a company lawyer to handle, or one of his father's former assistants, but it felt like an opportunity to get some perspective on the old man.

After sorting the pile on the table, he went through the documents in the filing cabinet. They were endless. Contracts. Tax forms. Decades-old dot-matrix printouts, faded to near-invisibility. He found a folder of old newspaper clippings and political cartoons featuring his father. He remembered as a child being furious that anyone would dare to mock his family. His father was a hard-working man and deserved no disrespect. It was only when Daniel was in his late teens that he started to question this.

He dropped the folder in a pile that he'd mentally marked 'keep' and picked up another. It turned out to be a series of letters between his father and the head of the hotel chain's security company, back from when Daniel had been about seventeen and living with his mother on the other side of the country. His parents had divorced when he was six, but their lives and businesses were still intertwined. At the time, his mother was trying her hand at being a restaurant owner. The Greenhouse was a converted penthouse suite at the top of one of the family hotels, the Lapton Celestia. It was a glass-fronted lounge that served cocktails and tapas, with a view looking out over the harbour. It was never well attended and had closed in less than a year. His mother had gone on to start a fashion collective.

Daniel was about to put the folder on the 'shred' pile when a name at the top of one of the pages caught his eye.

Mr Lapton

Further to our phone call last week regarding the situation with Penny Scarsdale, first we went to the hospital's obstetrics unit, where they did a paternity test via amniocentesis that confirms her claims. As the predicted birth date is early March, the child will probably be born a Pisces, so the family are

```
turning down your offer and keeping it
themselves.
    I delivered your subsequent offer and it
looks like they'll accept. I spoke to Dennison
directly about this and he's drawing up the
contracts now. He will contact you when
they're ready.

    Tyrese B. Coleman
    West Coast Regional Manager
    UrSec Group
```

The rest of the folder was filled with medical reports and pages of dense legalese. Daniel skimmed through it, then started again and read every word. Halfway through, his hands began to shake. He barely noticed.

He had a daughter.

Chapter Four

Burton tried to call Rachel Wells's mother, Angela, but she wasn't answering her cell phone or her landline. Her address was in Westville, which was close to the San Celeste Central Police Station, so on the way back from the crime scene he made a detour to visit her apartment.

The streets in Westville were narrow but clean. The Libras were part of the lower middle class and often lived in the same areas as Cancers, who shared their sense of civic pride. There were no visible gardens and all the ground-floor windows were barred, but for the most part the fronts of the houses and apartment buildings were painted and free of graffiti.

It seemed like a nice enough place to live, Burton thought, if the worst came to the worst and his family were forced to move after his daughter was born. It was just a road away from the Pisces market that Kate sometimes visited on Saturday mornings. It could be worse.

He parked his old brick-coloured station wagon outside Angela Wells's apartment building and went up to the third floor. Her door was varnished pine. He knocked, and there was a shuffling noise on the other side.

A voice said, 'Who is it?'

'Detective Jerome Burton, SCPD,' said Burton. 'Are you Angela Wells? I need to speak with you about your daughter.'

The door opened a crack and a woman's face looked out, marbled with age. Her hair was dyed dark orange and she was wearing a floral-print dress. She eyed Burton.

'I know you,' she said to him. 'I saw you on the news a while ago.'

'That's possible,' Burton admitted.

'What did you do?'

'I solved a murder,' he said. Giving her the details wasn't a good idea.

But it seemed enough for Angela Wells. She unhooked the chain and opened the door.

'Come on in.'

He stepped into a small living room that smelled of potpourri. There were two armchairs with crocheted covers facing a small television. An elderly fluffy dog sitting in one of them huffed at Burton as he entered, not having the energy to bark.

'Humphrey, no,' said Angela.

The dog looked away and started licking itself.

A reality show was playing on the screen. Members of every sign were being made to live together in the same house, wearing different-coloured T-shirts to make it really obvious who was who. Angela turned it off.

'What do you want with my daughter?' she said. 'She's at work at the moment, but she said she'll be back at three.'

Burton searched for the right words. It was hard to thread the needle between despair and false hope.

'Mrs Wells, I'm afraid your daughter has been involved in an incident.'

He explained the situation as calmly as he could. While

he went on, Angela Wells's eye wandered around the room, looking everywhere but at Burton.

'We don't know where she is,' he said. 'But we're doing everything in our power to find her. And if you hear anything on your side — anything at all — please call me. All right?'

He gave her his card. She took it without looking and stared out of the window, absent-mindedly rubbing the top of the dog's head.

'Mrs Wells?'

'Hmm?' she said. She seemed surprised he was still there. 'Oh, yes. I'm sorry. It's a bit of a shock.'

'I know, ma'am. I'm sorry.'

'Rachel's a really good girl,' she said earnestly. 'Of course I would say that, but it's true. I'm on a pension and I get a small grant for my arthritis, but it's never enough, so she's always working . . .'

Her voice petered out. A few years ago, Burton would have offered her the city's counselling services, but due to cutbacks there were now strict limits on what was considered trauma. All he could do was say, 'I'm sorry.'

'Well, then,' said Angela, giving Burton a small, brave smile. 'Thank you for stopping by.'

'It's my job, ma'am,' he said. 'And if you need anything, call that number. I'll do whatever I can to help.'

'Thank you.'

She showed him out, then slid the bolt and chain in place behind him. He waited for a moment in the corridor, but there was no more sound from inside the apartment. The television wasn't turned back on.

Chapter Five

The Central Police Station was one of the oldest buildings in San Celeste. Over the years it had expanded to fill a city block, with brutalist concrete wings bursting out from the original stone-faced structure. The traffic around it was always bad, and as Burton's car crawled the last few blocks he called up the home security company on his hands-free set.

He explained the situation to the call desk and asked to talk to someone with technical knowledge of Chief Williams's home security alarm system. They bounced him from person to person in the company, and he could hear the fear in the voices as they realized their involvement in a high-profile murder. But Burton was patient and they eventually put him through to a Virgo-sounding engineer, who had clearly been briefed to admit nothing.

'If the cord's cut, then the system won't work,' said the engineer. 'But you have to be in the house to cut the cord. So it's probably the house owner's responsibility.'

'Are you saying that the Chief of Police deliberately broke his own security system?'

'Uh, sorry,' said the engineer. 'I don't know what to say. No one could cut that cable unless they were already in the house.'

'Call me back if you figure out how it happened,' said Burton, and hung up on the engineer, who was probably scared for his job.

He parked in the underground garage, took the elevator up to the third floor and followed the corridors through the Personal Crimes Division to the Homicide Department. It was a long room with tall glass windows that reminded Burton of a train station, and which constantly smelled of coffee and cleaning products. He walked between the rows of white-painted desks to the door of his office, where Kolacny was waiting for him with a manila folder.

'Hey,' said Burton. 'Have you informed Williams's ex?'

'Not yet,' said Kolacny. 'We called his brother, though. He's the official next of kin. She's probably seen the news by now anyway.'

'Come on, Lloyd,' said Burton. 'She deserves a proper call. She's the mother of his child.'

'I'll do it, I'll do it,' said Kolacny. He handed Burton the envelope.

'What's this?'

'It's from CS. They say the blood in the bedroom is almost definitely from Williams, and it was fresh. Oh, and Mendez says he wants to see you.'

'Mendez? What does he want?'

Neither of them got on with Captain Ernesto Mendez, the head of homicide. He was in his late forties, with pockmarked skin and black hair sculpted like a politician's. He was a good policeman in many ways – fit, efficient and motivated – but he constantly shat on the officers below him, just because he could. Every cop needed to blow off steam once in a while, but Mendez wasn't exorcizing anything. He revelled in it.

Burton went back through to the central hub of the

station and up to the top floor. The door to Mendez's office was closed and guarded by a plain-clothes policeman, who looked Burton up and down.

'Name?'

'Detective Jerome Burton. Homicide. And you?'

'Special Investigation Services. What do you want?'

'Captain Mendez sent for me. What's happening in there?'

The plain-clothes cop opened the door for Burton. Inside, Mendez was in the middle of a conversation with two other men. One was Deputy Chief Killeen, head of the Personal Crimes Division. The other was Bruce Redfield, the mayor of San Celeste.

Burton had only ever seen the Mayor on television. He was taller than Burton, whippet-thin, with medium-length hair brushed back at the temples. He looked the way Burton imagined a violinist or an art dealer to look, elegant and a little oily. Mendez saw Burton and waved him into the room, interrupting the conversation.

'Burton!' Mendez said cheerfully. 'How's my star detective?'

'Good, thank you,' said Burton warily. Mendez's compliments always sounded close to sarcasm.

'Mr Mayor,' said Mendez, 'this is the detective I was telling you about. Burton spearheaded the investigation into Senator Cronin's murder. He's the one who caught the culprit.'

'I heard about that,' said Mayor Redfield, offering Burton a thin hand and smiling. 'Well done.'

'Thank you, sir.'

They shook. The Mayor's grip was firm and cool.

'I hear that you knew Williams personally.'

'Yes, sir,' said Burton. 'He was my first captain when I made detective.'

The Mayor nodded. 'I knew him too. He was a good man. A servant to the city and a friend to me. If there's anything in my power that I can do to help your investigation, let me know.'

'We're taking this one personally,' said the Deputy Chief, cutting in. 'We can't allow people to think the SCPD is an easy target.'

'Exactly,' said the Mayor. 'Let's show the city how swiftly and effectively we can deliver justice.'

'We've already found a promising lead,' Mendez said, taking the opportunity to look good in front of his superiors. 'Burton found a symbol drawn on the grass next to the body. A Taurus sign.'

'Is that true?' the Mayor said to Burton.

Burton frowned. The symbol had been barely visible, if it was a symbol at all. It could easily have been a random scattering of dirt. But this wasn't the time to appear uncertain.

'That's right,' he said. 'A circle with two lines coming out of it.'

The Mayor looked at Mendez. 'It's sign-related violence?'

Mendez nodded. 'That's what we're investigating, sir. I'd say it's almost certain that whoever killed Chief Williams is a member of Aries Rising, drawing that sign to taunt us.'

Aries Rising was a militant Aries rights group. It was fighting what it claimed was rampant signism in the justice system. Ninety per cent of police officers were Taurus and the people they arrested were disproportionately from the 'lower' signs, mainly Aries and Pisces. The group had been around for decades, but it had become a lot more prominent in the last few months after a spate of alleged police brutality. Their leader, Solomon Mahout, was becoming a regular face on television, and an irritation to everyone in the room.

'Bastards,' said the Mayor. His political mask dropped for a moment, revealing surprising vitriol. 'They're fucking animals. What can we do to tie them down?'

'We're already giving Burton the full support of Personal Crimes,' said Mendez.

'That's right,' said the Deputy Chief. 'This investigation takes priority. And I'm getting a trusted astrologer to assist in the case.'

Burton wanted to protest. He didn't have much experience with astrologers, and it didn't seem like a good time to be bringing in anyone new.

Mendez must have seen his expression because he said, 'We need to guarantee a conviction, Burton. Having an astrologer as a state witness could fill some important gaps in the case.'

Burton didn't like the implication that he couldn't be trusted to make a watertight case, but he understood. He'd seen guilty suspects go free because of partisan juries. Astrologers were a great way to swing them. Decades of TV shows about astrological profilers and forensic astrologers had convinced the public that they were the most trustworthy agents in the war on crime.

'Do you have anyone in mind?' the Mayor asked the Deputy Chief.

'Yes, sir. Her name is Lindiwe Childs. She's worked around the world training different security agencies how to profile travellers based on their birth date. Right now, we've got her in San Celeste working for the Airport Bureau. I'll send Burton her details.'

'Great,' said the Mayor, and offered his hand to Burton again. As Burton shook it, the Mayor gripped his upper arm for emphasis.

'Catch this bastard, Detective,' he said. 'We're counting on you.'

Chapter Six

Lindi was making coffee in her kitchenette when the doorbell to her apartment rang. She went to answer it, tightening the cord of her dressing gown. In the hallway outside was a serious-looking man, tall and clean-shaven, with short blond hair. He was wearing a suit and shirt with no tie.

'Good morning. Lindiwe Childs?'

'Lindi, please. And you are?'

'Detective Burton.'

'Of course! Hi.'

Lindi shook hands with the man, letting go of the cord around her waist. She worried that her gown might come loose. She wasn't naked beneath it – she had on a pair of shorts and a white tank top that she'd bought at a duty-free shop in Spain – but it was a question of vulnerability.

'Is this an OK time?' said Burton. 'You said after ten o'clock.'

I did, didn't I? thought Lindi. Shit.

'Yeah, no problem, come in,' she said, standing aside to let him past.

She was still feeling fuzzy from the night before. Megan, her only friend in San Celeste, had taken her out to meet new people and show her around the gay scene. She'd met a couple of interesting girls, but overall she'd found it a lot more segregated than most other cities she'd been to. Even in Cape Town, sexuality had trumped race, religion or sign, but the clubs Megan had taken her to in San Celeste were exclusively filled with the professional creative signs – Aquarius, Sagittarius and Gemini – and they tended to stay in cliques of their own kind. Lindi had begged Megan to take her somewhere a little different, and they'd ended up at a hard-core Leo dyke bar. One game of pool later, the regulars were making fun of Megan's hipster tattoos and Lindi agreed to call it a night. After it all, Lindi had completely forgotten about the policeman.

'I hope I didn't wake you,' he said.

'Not really,' said Lindi, and pointed at her dressing gown. 'Sorry about this. It's what I wear when I'm writing. I lost track of the time.'

Her apartment wasn't ready for visitors. There were piles of research books and loose notes scattered around the living room, a stack of dishes next to the sink in the kitchenette, and a rumpled blanket on the couch after a binge-watching session from earlier in the week. She had moved in recently and had only just put out her books and collectible toys on to the shelves. On the desk next to her laptop were a plastic astrolabe and a deck of cards called the Emoji Tarot. The only paintings she had managed to put up were of cartoon characters doing dark, inappropriate things, like begging on the street or queuing in a government office. She loved them because they reminded her of her graffiti artist friends in Barcelona. Burton would probably think they were childish. She cleared a pile of papers off a chair for him.

'Coffee?' she said. 'I've just boiled the kettle.'

'No thanks.'

'OK. I won't be long.'

She went to the kitchenette and poured herself a mug, topping it up with milk and two sugars. When she got back to the living room she saw Burton looking over the shelves of Japanese plastic figurines that she had collected in her twenties. As she'd expected, his expression was deadpan.

'All right, Detective,' she said, sitting on the sofa. 'What's this about?'

He sat down on the wooden chair and put his hands on his knees. He seemed like a bit of an odd Taurus. He was very focused, and repressed. She wouldn't have been surprised if his ascendant was in Virgo.

'I'm heading a murder investigation,' said Burton, 'and it has an astrological angle. I was told that you'd be a useful person to have on the case but that you wouldn't do it unless we met in person. Can I ask why?'

'Yeah, sure, sorry,' said Lindi. 'I wanted to see if we're compatible. What's your date and time of birth?'

Burton told her. She turned the laptop on her desk to face her and opened her main astrology app.

'And what do you need me to do?' she said.

'Help with the investigation,' said Burton. 'You'll get an enhanced consultancy fee. We think we know who did it, but we need you to back us up with astrological evidence, and testify in court, when it comes to it.'

Lindi typed the details in and loaded her own information for a synastry reading. She checked the resulting chart, going over the important areas one by one. It didn't look good. There were a lot of negative aspects and planets in detriment. She closed her laptop and shook her head.

'I'm sorry,' she said. 'I can't right now. I have to finish this manual. The Airport Bureau wants a standardized way to screen travellers as possible terrorists.'

She picked up the draft contents page from the top of a printed stack and showed it to him.

1. Introduction
2. Indicators of violence
    a. The Sun or the ascendant in Aries
    b. The position of Mars in a birth chart
    c. Negative aspects with Jupiter
3. Saturn as a positive or negative indicator
4. Houses
    a. Death: The eighth house
    b. Hidden secrets: The twelfth house
5. Horary prediction of violent events

'It's pretty intense,' she said. 'They want me to turn complicated astrological readings into a checklist that a computer could follow, which is ridiculous. There are too many variables. At some point, a human has to step in and make a judgement.'

'So you're too busy?' said Burton, obviously controlling his irritation.

'For the next month or so. I'm sorry. I'll be free again from early June.'

'OK,' said Burton. 'Fine. Sorry to have wasted your time.'

'Wait,' she said as he stood up. 'I have to ask. What case is it?'

Burton frowned. 'I'm not allowed to tell you more than our official statement.'

'Which is?'

'The Chief of Police was killed in his own backyard.'

'That's the case? Chief Williams?'

Lindi had heard about the murder, but hadn't thought about it much. It was just one of those events that got people riled on social media.

She looked Burton up and down again. His chart had been inauspicious, but . . .

'OK,' said Lindi. 'Listen. If I do this, I'd like to do it properly. I'll need access to the case files.'

'Under the standard restrictions of privileged information and confidentiality,' said Burton.

'Agreed.'

'So you're in?'

Lindi bit her lower lip. Damn it. She had promised a draft of the document in twenty days. But for the murder of the Chief of Police? The Airport Bureau couldn't object. And there was that missing girl they were looking for. She was good with missing people. And, although she tried to avoid jobs based on the prestige, she had to admit to herself that this one could be big.

'OK.'

She opened the laptop again and created a new chart showing an abstract representation of the sky. It was a spoked circle, with glyphs around the outside standing in for the planets and constellations. Lines connected them in a way that seemed haphazard and messy to the uninitiated. To Lindi, they held a great and beautiful significance.

'Tell me everything you know,' she said.

Chapter Seven

Penny Scarsdale had been the youngest of Daniel's mother's waitstaff, the one who took away the wooden boards that the food was served on after the customers were done. Daniel had met her while he was working at the restaurant, before he went off to university. He could have gone anywhere and done anything in the world, but he had decided that he needed to work for a living, the way people were meant to. So his mother had given him a bullshit 'supply management' position to keep him busy, and he spent his summer months living a parody of responsibility.

He was meant to order resupplies. On his first day the call to the wholesalers took him less than five minutes, followed by five hours of sitting in an office with nothing to do. Since no one was keeping an eye on him, he went wandering through the hotel. It was the kind of thing he used to do as a small child when his parents were in meetings. The back corridors were a maze for him to explore, filled with monsters like the cleaning staff and hotel security, whom he had to hide from for fear of terrible punishments from his father. As a young adult, there was no danger or wonder any more. He knew what every corridor and room was for and what every sign meant. He went to a back stairwell, intending to make his way down to the hotel foyer and find a magazine to read. On impulse he went up the stairs instead, and found a fire door that led on to the rooftop.

The top of the building was both loud and beautiful. The surface of the roof was dark grey and slightly spongy, criss-crossed by strips of metallic tape. Huge silver air vents stood up out of it, roaring like aircraft engines. Between them were blocky structures which Daniel guessed held elevator motors and air conditioning. The sky above was the bright orange of a seaside sunset.

Daniel explored and found a makeshift cage extending from the side of one of the blocky structures. It was made from four large squares of black-painted metal grating and contained all sorts of whimsical things – Christmas trees, sun-bleached plastic banners, the remains of a giant styrofoam turkey that had been displayed in the hotel foyer for Thanksgiving. Nearly everything in the cage was covered in glitter. It was the kind of discovery that would have overjoyed him as a kid, but in his late teens all he could see was waste and decay.

He walked around the cage, letting his fingers flick as they ran over the grating. On the other side he saw Penny Scarsdale.

She was sitting on the ledge at the edge of the roof, looking out across the sea with a half-smoked cigarette between her fingers. She had blonde hair dyed with streaks of red, a round face and high cheekbones. He had never seen her before, but he recognized her waitress uniform: black trousers and a dark green blouse to match the restaurant decor.

She must have seen him coming out of the corner of her eye, because she quickly stubbed out the cigarette. She shouldn't have been on the roof. He could have scored points with his mother by telling Penny to get back to work. It would have been the expected thing to do. But Daniel sat down a few feet further down the ledge, letting his legs dangle over the terrifying drop. He gave her a quick smile and looked out across the sea.

They didn't talk. The roar of the hotel's air conditioning made it impossible. Despite the noise, it was a strangely peaceful moment. They watched the sun set together. When it was gone a cold wind picked up and Penny stubbed out her second cigarette. She returned to the kitchen, giving Daniel a smile as she went.

For the rest of the night, Daniel couldn't think of anything else.

He made sure he was sitting on the ledge the next evening, and after an embarrassing half-hour wait, she came up to join him. When she had finished her cigarette, they went back down to the restaurant together, and they finally talked.

She was a Pisces. He knew what everyone knew about the Pisces – hippies, spiritualists, layabouts. He'd seen Pisces movies on TV and they always seemed to be about stoned, bearded idiots and spaced-out ladies, with dumb jokes and non sequiturs and no kind of plot. Penny wasn't dumb, though, and when Daniel got over her Pisces drawl he realized that she was surprisingly insightful.

One evening after work, while she was doing the final clean-up of the restaurant and he was counting the takings, he questioned her choice of career and advised her on how to get trained up for a job in banking or the housing market. The kinds of jobs that made Capricorns rich.

'What makes you think I want to be a Cappy?' she said, resting her hands on the top of her broom.

'Everyone wants to be a Capricorn,' he replied, as if it was the most obvious thing in the world.

She looked at him, amused.

'You're full of yourself, aren't you? We don't all want to spend our lives on stress medication and dying of a heart attack on the stock exchange floor. Most of us just want to be happy in the lives we've chosen.'

Daniel thought that she wasn't taking him seriously and his cheeks burned. He hadn't yet learned that there was no maliciousness to her smile. Pisces didn't care about status the way Capricorns did.

'You'd rather spend your life clearing plates off tables?' he said.

She laughed.

'There's a middle ground between that and this, you know,' she said. 'I'm doing this because I have to. It's not a career.'

He was angry with Penny for the rest of the evening. He thought that she was deliberately teasing and belittling him. It took him a while to realize that she was just stating a fact. He was so used to playing status games that it hadn't occurred to him before what it must look like to people who weren't playing.

He was lucky that she was patient.

The next evening he apologized. 'You must think I'm a money-crazed jerk.'

'We can't all think alike, can we? Otherwise we'd all make the same mistakes.'

She smiled at him. And Daniel realized that he didn't

have to say anything for a while. All he needed to do was listen.

Penny told him about her day, and her life, and the efforts that she and her mother were putting in to keep themselves and her extended family afloat. His first instinct was to tell her that her family was taking advantage of her. He wanted to say that she was being overly generous, and that her cousins were selfish to rely on her and she ought to be looking out for herself first. But she spoke about them with such affection, and about their losses with such pain and their successes with such pride, that Daniel began to lose certainty. His world view might be the way to power and success, but that didn't, ultimately, make it true.

On her side, Penny didn't seem to be having any self-doubt. Daniel was just someone her own age she could talk to.

When she first kissed him, he asked her why. The question confused her.

'Don't you want to?'

'Of course I do. But why? I'm . . .'

. . . weak, he thought. Average-looking. In a different sign.

'You're cute, and different, and you talk funny, and you're so serious about everything.'

When she said that, a weight lifted off him. She was right. He kissed her back, awkwardly at first, but with growing passion. They found a back room lined with empty shelves, stripped off each other's clothes and made love, stifling their moans and giggles.

The next day was a Friday and the kitchen was busy. Daniel barely saw Penny, but when their eyes met she grinned. He booked one of the smaller hotel rooms downstairs, hoping he could share it with her after their shift, but at the end of the evening Penny had to go home and look after her mother, who had twisted her ankle falling down the stairs at the post office. Daniel was scared that Penny was finding excuses not to see him, but the next night she dragged him into the storeroom again halfway through her shift.

The relationship continued for the next two weeks, with moments of passion and tenderness and confusion mixed in with the drudgery of life. Daniel was conflicted. She knew he was a Capricorn, but he didn't know if she knew what his surname was, or who his parents were. He told himself that if she found out it would ruin everything. He imagined giving her a gift, a few hundred thousand dollars, enough money to clear all her family's debts and get them back on track. How would she react? Would she think that he was buying her? He imagined telling his parents that they were together and bravely facing his father as he disowned him. But some deep, weaselly part of Daniel knew that a relationship with Penny would mean facing more fundamental problems. What future could they have? There would be a thousand little moments when they didn't quite understand each other, because they didn't have the same background. A thousand little moments when they couldn't share a joke. A thousand sideways glances and forced smiles from former friends. A thousand times they would look up at the stars and know that they weren't meant to be together. A thousand acquaintances who would look down on him for being *that kind of man*.

And then it was summer and Daniel had to head back to the West Coast for university. They both cried and promised to keep in touch.

The next few months were filled with travel, classes, new friends and new ideas. He joined the rowing team, although he didn't have the enthusiasm to last in it for long. He tried calling Penny, but her phone number had changed. He wrote letters, but he didn't get a response. He thought about her often, partly from desire and partly from growing shame. Over time he started to date other girls. Every few months, and then every few years, he tried to contact Penny. He never succeeded.

And now, looking at the letters in his father's dark office, he finally knew why. When he left San Celeste, Penny Scarsdale had been pregnant with his daughter. She had gone to Daniel's father, who had covered it up. He hadn't even let Daniel know his disappointment in him. He had taken it to his grave.

Chapter Eight

Burton went back to his office in the Homicide Department and about half an hour later Lindi came to join him. She had changed into more suitable work clothes. Her Afro was tied back under a burgundy scarf and she was wearing a dark green jacket that she'd put on over a flowing flower-patterned dress. It was a weird combination that seemed, to Burton, like a mixture of professional and bohemian, which summed up most other Aquarians he knew pretty well.

His initial irritation with her was fading and he had to admit that she was an interesting person. Lindi was in her mid-thirties, with dark skin and an easy smile. She had a transatlantic accent with some posh Capricorn, some West Coast Scorpio valley girl and something completely unplaceable. She said that she'd grown up in southern Africa but had spent years travelling around Europe and South-East Asia. Of course, like everyone else, she was raised on American movies.

He showed her through the Homicide Department to his personal office, which had a frosted-glass window in the door. Someone had stuck strips of black tape on to it, spelling out the words 'Jerome Burton, Super Detective' in a pretty good approximation of a private investigator's office from an old movie.

Lindi chuckled. 'Did you do that?'

'No,' he said, keeping his face wooden. 'This department is full of jokers.'

He opened the door and showed her into his spartan office. There was an L-shaped table that took up two of the walls, two empty plastic trays marked 'OUT' and 'IN', and a swivel chair in front of a small computer. He brought in a second chair for her, while Lindi looked up at the framed newspaper front page on his wall: 'SENATOR CRONIN MURDER SUSPECT CAPTURED'. The picture was of Burton pushing a handcuffed man in a rumpled business suit into the back of a van.

'What's this about?'

'They didn't tell you?' said Burton. 'I'm the one who caught Senator Cronin's murderer.'

'Who's that?' said Lindi. 'Sorry, I've only been in the country a couple of years.'

Burton breathed in through his teeth. He'd be reliving the case until he died.

'Cronin was spearheading Proposition 51, which would have made it illegal for businesses to refuse to serve people based on their sign. It took me three months to track down his killer, who turned out to be a member of the Thunderhead. You've heard of them? The reactionary Cancer group. You know how Cancers can get if they think someone's going to upset the status quo. They protected him by giving him a false alibi and by threatening the witnesses. I got him in the end, though.'

'Well done.'

'Don't throw a parade for me just yet. The media went crazy. They said it was a set-up and that I was hounding an innocent man. A lot of people believed the

Thunderhead's claims over the evidence and said I was part of a conspiracy against him. There was a big internal investigation. It caused a stink and we lost some funding. Everyone here knows I did the right thing, but they still give me a hard time.'

He pointed to the 'SUPER DETECTIVE' sign on his door.

'Sorry,' said Lindi. 'I didn't know. Did he end up going to prison?'

'Yes. I got that, at least.' He sighed. 'Anyway, I think the other cops framed this article just to remind me to be more careful.'

Lindi Childs spent the rest of the day sitting next to Burton, catching up with the case and making astrological notes while Burton kept the wheels of the investigation turning. He went through the forensic accounting reports of Williams's financial records and the DNA test of the duct tape, both of which had come back negative. Kolacny had checked the CCTV footage from all the street cameras in a five-mile area, but short of investigating every single vehicle in the footage, there were no leads. Burton had sent out every available detective to interview Rachel Wells's family and friends, but there was still no sign of her. Short of dredging the river for her body, Burton didn't know what to do.

Once in a while, Lindi would look up from her laptop and interrupt him with a question.

'So, right now, who's your main suspect?'

'That's kind of cheating, isn't it?' said Burton, raising an eyebrow. 'Isn't your chart meant to tell us that?'

'Sure,' said Lindi. 'But one configuration of planets can mean different things. Everything that happens, good or bad, is a result of those planets. That's why you can't get accurate automatic horary software. You need a human to interpret the data. Preferably a human who knows as much as possible about the situation.'

Burton had heard that before, but it made the same kind of sense to him as explanations of quantum mechanics. He wasn't an expert in the area, so at some point he had to just nod along and accept what he was hearing on trust. After all, the experts had spent years studying it. It couldn't be nonsense.

'The thing is,' said Lindi, 'you told me the security system was taken out. So the killer had to know about the alarm and do some planning. This wasn't a crime of opportunity. This was premeditated.'

'That's what I figured,' said Burton. 'I have to assume a professional killer.'

'And you said Williams had problems with Aries Rising?'

Burton nodded.

'Huh,' said Lindi.

He watched her as she typed out her notes, focusing intently. Her screen was covered in a massive grid of glyphs. It reminded Burton of the old computer games that he had played with his friends back in middle school, where numbers and symbols stood in for monsters and swords and magic potions.

By mid-afternoon, Lindi was confident enough to start making predictions. She showed Burton a spreadsheet of symbols.

'This is the sky at the time of the murder,' she said. 'And as you see, we've got an imbalance of the elements.'

'OK,' said Burton. 'This means nothing to me.'

Lindi looked at him dubiously.

'Didn't you study astrology in high school?'

'No. I went to a Taurus school. It was good, but the emphasis was on vocational training.'

'OK,' she said. 'Well, the main thing you need to know is that you've got the four elements – earth, air, fire and water. The zodiac signs are each a different kind of expression of one of those elements. So Aries is cardinal fire, meaning it's got all the energy and potential destructiveness of a newly started fire. Taurus is fixed earth, meaning it's stable, steadfast and loyal, like the ground under your feet.'

Burton nodded. 'And?'

'And in this chart we're seeing a lot of activity in earth signs, which is what I'd expect, because we've got a dead Taurus cop who was literally murdered in a hole in the ground, next to a Taurus symbol made of earth. And our eighth-house ruler is in Taurus. I think it pretty much guarantees that earth is important here.'

'Metaphorically or physically?'

'There isn't always a difference,' said Lindi. 'Ask yourself, why was Williams murdered in a trench in the ground? Maybe because the trench had some significance to them both. Or maybe the killer was the man who dug the trench. It would give him time to scout out Chief Williams's property. And which sign is most likely to be employed as a ditch digger? Aries, right?'

Burton thought about it. 'It's worth a shot.'

He opened the browser on his computer and searched for the pool installation and repair companies in Williams's area. One by one he phoned them and asked if any of them had been doing any recent work at 36 Eden Drive in Conway Heights. He succeeded on his fourth try.

'Yeah,' said a bored-sounding man on the other end of the line. 'We're putting in a new pump and replacing the overflow system.'

'Do you have the name of whoever dug the trench?'

'I don't know. We normally just find someone looking for work and pay him by the hour. I'll check and call you back. What's your number?'

Burton gave his number and went back to the reports while waiting for the return call.

After a few hours, his shift came to an end. He got to his feet and picked up his coat.

'Where are you going?' said Lindi over her shoulder.

'Home. I need to pick up a few things for my wife. She's pregnant.'

'Congratulations!'

'Thanks. Turn out the light when you leave.'

Outside the station it was already evening. The sky was overcast, slowly changing from grey to dark grey to black. Rain began to splatter down as Burton got into his car. There was just enough to make him turn his wipers on, but not enough to let them glide smoothly over the glass. They juddered back and forth, leaving dirty lines from a week's worth of dust. Still, Burton enjoyed driving. It gave him time to think.

He tried to play out the murder in his mind. The killer

had kicked in Williams's front door, breaking the frame. He had surprised Williams in the bedroom and fought with him, causing the blood spatter. He probably had a gun, or Williams would have fought harder and spilled more blood. The killer took Williams outside, bound his hands and wrists, cut him open and threw him in the trench. Leaving him for dead, he made a Taurus symbol, then went back inside and cut the cord on the security system. Or had he done that before? The maid had arrived and found Williams, and the killer had surprised her and taken her away just before the patrol car arrived. It all just about fitted together, but it wasn't very satisfying.

His phone rang. He answered it on the speaker.

'Detective?' said the man from the pool company. 'I found the ditch digger who worked at the Williams house. His name's Luke Boysen. The last address he gave us was a homeless shelter in Warburg. It's a place called the United Skies.'

'Do you have a description of this guy?'

'Sure. Aries, about five foot four, brown hair, brown eyes, with tattoos on his neck and forearms.'

Burton thanked the man and hung up. He pulled over and used his phone to look up the shelter's contact number. The line was engaged. Warburg wasn't too far off his route, though, and he had some time before Kate was expecting him back home. He called it in and pulled off into the traffic, turning right on to the bridge into Warburg.

The district had once been a slum. About thirty years before, some upwardly mobile Aquarians had bought up

the empty warehouses and converted them into apartments and offices. The gentrification wasn't total, and
there were still pawnshops and cheap takeaways and
second-floor charismatic churches along Warburg Main
Road. All the organic markets and design studios had
security guards at their entrances during the day and were
barred up and dark at night.

Burton drove around a corner on to one of the side
streets and pulled up in front of the United Skies shelter.
It was a bare brick building with an illuminated sign that
showed a starry sky held up by a pair of cradling hands.
One of the neon bulbs in the sign was flickering, making
an intermittent dark brown streak in the milky plastic. He
hunched over to avoid the rain and went into the
building.

The entrance hall stank of disinfectant. The walls were
dark green and peeling, covered with the torn remains of
old posters. Up ahead, the corridor was almost completely
dark, and the light fittings in the ceiling were empty.
Voices echoed from deeper in the building.

The reception office was a rectangular hole in the wall,
framed in varnished wood that looked like it had once
held up a window. A man in a white long-sleeved shirt
was sitting at a narrow desk, reading a tabloid newspaper
and not paying Burton much attention. He had thin blond
hair and a face that would have looked young if it wasn't
for his sunken eyes.

'Good evening,' said Burton.

'Sorry,' said the receptionist without looking up. 'Full
again tonight. Try Fourth Street.'

Burton held up his badge and cleared his throat. The

man looked at him and the backrest of his chair knocked into the rear wall of his tiny office.

'Sorry, Officer,' he said, getting to his feet hurriedly. 'What can I do for you?'

He ran his tongue over his upper lip. Burton was used to the nervousness. Most people got shifty when the cops turned up.

'You got a guy called Boysen staying here?'

'Maybe,' said the receptionist. 'We don't ask for names.'

'Can I go in and ask around?' said Burton.

The receptionist hesitated. It looked like he was choosing his words carefully.

'I wouldn't recommend that,' he said. 'It'll cause problems unless I'm with you.'

'Please,' said Burton. 'It's important.'

The receptionist pushed open the door of the small office and came out into the corridor.

'You're going to have to keep it quick,' he said. 'This way.'

He led Burton down the dark corridor and deeper into the building.

'You been working here long?' said Burton.

The receptionist nodded. 'About three years. It was a lot worse when I started. Trash everywhere. You know we set up a new shelter on Duke Street, just for women? You can imagine what it was like when they were still in the same building, with all that Aries machismo.'

'What's your sign?' said Burton.

The man looked insulted that Burton couldn't tell. 'Cancer, sir,' he said. 'Seventh generation. I'm just volunteering here for my church group.'

Burton could see it. The man's shirt was ironed and his trousers were pressed, and he had a hairstyle that was neat but not stylish. And he was volunteering for charity like a good Cancer boy. Burton doubted that was all there was to it, though. Under the piety, the receptionist had a desperate look about him. He was either paying off a debt to society or doing something on the side that was going to get him in trouble.

He pushed a pair of swing doors open into a large, echoing room that was filled with about a hundred beds laid out in a grid. The blankets and sheets were all dirty grey. Groups of men were sitting around on the beds, using them as sofas and card tables. Along the walls were trestle tables covered in big metal pots and urns – the remains of the shelter's free evening meal. The floor was wood, with lines of paint that were worn down but still visible embedded between the planks. It must have been an old basketball court.

Unsympathetic eyes turned to them as they entered. Burton was very aware that he wasn't carrying his gun, which was locked away at the station. He hadn't expected to end up here.

'Let me handle this,' said the receptionist. 'A lot of these men don't have the best relationship with the police. Some of them have PTSD.'

Burton thought that the man would make an announcement to the hall. Instead, he went across to one of the groups and spoke to a big man with a red beard. The man listened, glancing over at Burton. When the receptionist finished talking, the big man shrugged. The receptionist came back.

'No one called Boysen in here. Sorry.'

'That's all?' said Burton. 'You're asking one man?'

'That's Grint. He's the big man around here. We have to go through him.'

'What?' said Burton. 'Why?'

'There's a lot of ex-cons in here,' said the receptionist. 'They've got a hierarchy. You don't mess with that. It's not exactly prison rules, but it's close.'

He started walking back towards the double doors, expecting Burton to follow.

Fuck it, thought Burton. He had a job to do. He turned and addressed the room.

'Excuse me, gentlemen, if I can have your attention,' he said loudly, holding up his badge. 'San Celeste Police.'

The room quietened a little. Dozens of hostile eyes turned on him.

'I'm looking for someone called Luke Boysen. He's stayed here before.'

He looked at the men nearest him. They turned away from him, unwilling to make eye contact.

'Has anyone seen Luke Boysen? It's important.'

Burton caught a couple of them glancing to a door at the back of the large room. A man in jeans and a white T-shirt was walking out, not looking back. Burton got a glimpse of a tattoo on his neck.

'Hey!' he shouted. 'Stop!'

He ran down the gap between the beds towards the back of the room. He was almost at the rear door when the corner of one of the beds was shoved into his path, shrieking across the floor. Burton was going too fast to avoid it and the metal frame cracked against his thigh.

He looked around, trying to see who had pushed it. A row of faces looked back at him blankly. It could have been any one of half a dozen men. He didn't have time for this. He limped until he could run again, out the back and into another corridor.

It was smaller and better lit than the one at the front of the building. Burton stumbled as the floor unexpectedly dropped a half-step down – it looked like the shelter had been built from two buildings with mismatched floor levels and the dividing walls torn down. He landed on the side of his foot and his shoulder rebounded off the wall. He was fucking this up.

He ran past an open door, catching a glimpse of shower cubicles and toilet stalls. Around a final corner Burton almost ran headlong into Boysen. The rear exit of the building was chained and padlocked, and Boysen was trapped.

He turned from the door and faced Burton, hunching defensively. Burton sized him up. He had been chasing Boysen the way a dog chases a moving car, but now he had him cornered, he realized he had no weapon and no back-up. He had come to the shelter expecting to find Boysen's name on a register. He wasn't expecting to face down a suspected murderer.

Boysen was slightly shorter than him, but he was muscular and looked like he was used to working outdoors. His jeans were splattered in mud and frayed at the bottom. His white T-shirt had an 'SC Pools' logo across it, with a picture of a sun rising over rippling water. He was sizing Burton up too and from the way he held himself it looked like he knew how to fight.

But Burton had a script to follow: 'Luke Boysen, you're under arrest for the murder of Police Chief Peter Williams.'

Footsteps clattered in from the corridor behind him. He half-expected an ambush by the men from the shelter, but it was the receptionist, carrying a black metal nightstick. He saw Boysen and raised it defensively.

Boysen relaxed his fighting stance and showed his palms. He wasn't going to fight them both.

'Do you have any handcuffs or cable ties?' said Burton.

'Don't you?' said the receptionist, keeping his eyes on Boysen.

'In my car. Watch this guy, he's a murder suspect. I'll be right back.'

The receptionist grabbed Burton by the upper arm.

'Don't. Don't go back through there.'

'I can handle myself,' said Burton.

'Trust me,' said the receptionist. He had beads of sweat on his temples. 'Just wait here and call for back-up.'

Burton hesitated, then took out his phone and called dispatch. When they confirmed that a patrol was on its way he turned back to Boysen, who was watching them both warily. His palms were still raised.

'Why'd you run?' said Burton.

Boysen clenched his jaw, but stayed polite.

'Sorry, Officer.'

'That's Detective. Turn around and spread your legs,' said Burton.

Boysen turned slowly. Burton shoved him into position against the door and Boysen winced as his elbow hit the jutting-out padlock.

'Why did you kill Williams?' said Burton.

'Who's Williams?'

'Why did you run?'

'I was scared.'

'I'll bet you were,' said Burton. 'Down on the ground.'

Burton frisked Boysen, then stood over him and waited, hoping the back-up would be quick. Every so often he'd hear a clatter or a raised voice from the main hall, and the receptionist would look at him nervously. Then there were distant sirens, screeching and doors slamming. After another minute there were shouts from the main hall.

'Clear a way! Make a hole! Move!'

Boots stomped down the corridor and a group of heavily armoured cops came around the corner carrying assault rifles. Their suits were black and their visors were down. Burton knew them well. They were the specially trained SWAT team that had been operating in Ariesville for the last ten years, combating the kind of gang violence that regular cops weren't equipped to handle. Unofficially, they were known as the Ram Squad.

'This him?' said the one at the front.

Burton nodded. He stood back as they cuffed Boysen, pulled him to his feet and hauled him along the corridor. In the main hall, the conversations dipped and the men stood aside as the Ram Squad shoved Boysen through the rows of beds, with Burton and the receptionist following behind. The big man with the red beard stared at them coldly.

When they were out of the front of the building and

had loaded Boysen into the back of a black van, the Ram Squad visibly relaxed. The receptionist stayed tense.

'What's the matter?' said Burton.

'Nothing,' he said. 'Are you done?'

'Yes. Thank you for your help.'

The receptionist nodded sourly and headed back into the building.

'He's pissed off that you broke the agreement,' said a gravelly voice behind Burton.

He turned to see Vince Hare, the captain of the Ram Squad, coming around the corner of the van with a helmet under his arm. Vince was tall and broad-shouldered, with a flat-topped astronaut haircut. He gave Burton a toothy grin and went back to wiping his visor with a rag.

'What agreement?'

'The way I heard it, Mendez's men used to come here on the last day of the month and take the first guys they could lay their hands on back to the station, so they could fill their quota. The guys in there threatened to burn the place down if it kept happening. The charity running the place filed a report and Mendez put a stop to it.'

'So the receptionist just broke some kind of deal by letting us in there.'

'Probably,' said Vince. His half-smile said it wasn't his problem. 'Hey, are you here for the Williams investigation?'

'That's right,' said Burton.

'And this guy's the suspect?' said Vince, pointing a thumb over his shoulder at the rear doors of the van.

'At the moment.'

'Nice work,' said Vince. 'Listen, if you need us to get him to talk, you let me know. We can't have cop-killers walking around, am I right? I can give you a private room. Just you and him, no cameras. Or we can do it for you. Anything you want. For Williams, right?'

Chapter Nine

Simple math told Daniel that his daughter would be seventeen years old. A young woman. He imagined her with her mother's cheekbones and dyed hair. The thought that he might meet her within the next few days was incredible.

His father had always kept a tight control on the family and the family name, but it was still staggering that he had kept her birth quiet. He must have considered the situation so shameful that he couldn't even confront Daniel about it. Or maybe he thought he was doing Daniel a favour. An illegitimate daughter would have had severe repercussions, socially and financially. The tabloids would have crucified him. It would have ruined the life that Daniel's father had planned for him.

And what life was that? Daniel had flopped from one management position to the next, never caring enough to stick with anything, and failing at business and hedonism equally. Wealth was wasted on him. But now, he had a daughter.

That very evening, Daniel flew to San Celeste by private jet. He was on the phone throughout the first half of the flight, talking to people at UrSec, trying to track down Penny Scarsdale or his daughter. It was surprisingly hard to dredge up any information. Most of the security company's office staff were at home or out on the town, so they had to be called in on emergency overtime. Even then, any records the security company had on Penny Scarsdale were confidential and hidden in locked cabinets or encrypted with forgotten passwords. The company had to call up former employees and board members and lawyers, and organize a dozen private negotiations. Meanwhile, Daniel had nothing to do but stare out of his airplane window into the night.

He arrived at the airport at three a.m. and was greeted by Ian Hamlin, the current general manager of UrSec. He was a San Celeste local, Scorpio, well built, and he looked faintly uncomfortable wearing a business suit. Even though it was late, Hamlin was fresh and alert. As they left the arrivals hall, he brought Daniel up to date with the progress of the investigation.

'Here's what we know. Your daughter's name is Pamela. Brown hair, brown eyes. All the medical records we have show that she was happy and healthy at birth and through infancy. Unfortunately, my predecessor only kept records on the Scarsdale family until your daughter was five years old, which was twelve years ago.'

'What happened? Why did he stop tracking her?'

'The Scarsdales broke a confidentiality agreement with your father. Penny Scarsdale's uncle tried to take the story to *The Buzz*. When they called your father for a comment, his lawyers intercepted and killed the story, and cut off Penny Scarsdale's allowance for raising your daughter.'

'What?' said Daniel.

If Hamlin noticed his anger, he showed no sign of it. He kept calmly leading Daniel through the parking garage.

'As far as I know, your father considered the allowance to

be a courtesy. The legal threat imposed by the confidentiality agreement was more than enough to keep them quiet.'

'She was his own granddaughter!' said Daniel.

Hamlin nodded.

'From what I understand, if he showed that she was valuable to him in any way, the Scarsdales would have had the upper hand. He said that putting money into her wasn't a good investment.'

Daniel grabbed Hamlin by the front of his shirt and shoved him against a pillar. Hamlin was taken by surprise and his head thudded into the bare concrete. Some other late travellers who were loading their luggage into a hatchback nearby turned to stare.

'Investment?' said Daniel. 'She's my daughter!'

Calmly, Hamlin took hold of Daniel's arms and pulled them off his body. He did it slowly, but Daniel felt the bones of his hands grinding together. Hamlin looked him in the eyes.

'Sir,' he said, 'I understand that you're tired and upset, and I personally must apologize for my company's role in your pain. Please realize that we were working for your father. Now we are working for you. We do what you need us to do. Do you want us to continue?'

He let go and Daniel backed away.

'Yes,' said Daniel, rubbing his hands. He tried to recover his dignity. 'Thank you. I'm sorry.'

Hamlin blinked at him slowly. 'No trouble at all,' he said. 'We haven't located the Scarsdale family yet. Their lives are surprisingly poorly documented, but we have an excellent investigative team. Don't worry, Mr Lapton. We will find your daughter soon. I guarantee it.'

Chapter Ten

Boysen sat in the interview room opposite Lindi and Kolacny. His fingerprints had been found all over the crime scene – on the handles of the gardening equipment in a shed around the side of the house and on the sliding glass doors. A background check showed that he had an arrest record for petty theft and public drunkenness. Burton watched him through the mirrored glass. After his night in custody, Boysen had dark rings under his eyes. Burton had told the Ram Squad not to get involved in the questioning, but he wouldn't have been surprised if they had given him some personal attention during the ride back to the station.

The walls of the interview room were covered in soundproof tiles and the carpeting on the floor was institutional brown. There were two cameras on tripods set up at opposite ends of the interview table, one pointing at Boysen and the other at Kolacny and Lindi. Her grey laptop was open in the middle of the table.

'Chart reading beginning at 11.08 a.m.,' said Kolacny into the camera. 'Present are myself, Detective Lloyd Kolacny, as well as astrological profiler Lindiwe Childs, and the suspect Luke Boysen. Mr Boysen, do you consent to a professional horoscope reading? Be aware that information gathered in this method is admissible in a court of law.'

Boysen looked from one of them to the other. 'Do I have a choice?' he said.

'Always,' said Kolacny. Which was true to an extent, but refusing wouldn't look good if Boysen made it to court.

'Fine,' said Boysen, folding his arms. 'I consent.'

'OK,' said Lindi, looking at the laptop screen. 'Luke Michael Boysen, exact time of birth, 7.24 p.m., 14 April 1985, at San Celeste General Hospital. I am now creating your birth chart.'

Lindi Childs's fingers tapped the keys of her laptop and a circle appeared on the screen. It was divided into twelve segments numbered by Roman numerals. Around the outside were the symbols of the zodiac, and on the inside were the glyphs for the planets, unevenly spaced around the circle and connected by a network of green and red lines.

'All right,' said Lindi. 'This is a representation of the planets and constellations as they were at the exact moment of your birth. As you know, the energies released by the planets at a particular moment in time will be imprinted on anything that begins in that moment – in this case, you. So this chart gives me an accurate insight into the energies that shape your very nature and, by implication, into the likelihood that you committed the crimes you're accused of. Reading this properly will take some time, and I'm going to need to ask for further information from Detective Kolacny to confirm my understanding of the chart, but we can get an overview immediately. Your sun is in Aries, which ties your identity to the fire element of destructive energy . . .'

Lindi continued the explanation about orbs and applying aspects and other things that Burton had no experience with. He tried to follow along but was interrupted by a tap on the door behind him. Detective Rico leaned into the room. He was in his mid-twenties, dark-skinned and good-looking. The sides and back of his head were shaved, and the rest was gelled in a way that Burton thought of as uncomfortably trendy.

'Burton? Mendez wants to see you.'

'What about?'

'Some lawyer's arrived. Says she's representing Boysen.'

'State-appointed?'

'Uh-uh,' said Rico, shaking his head. 'Definitely no. You'd better come and see the Captain.'

Chapter Eleven

The horoscope reading was going well. After weeks compiling manuals, it felt good to get her hands dirty with a real chart reading. The cops were listening, Boysen looked scared, and Lindi had caught some features of his chart that a less experienced astrologer might have missed. And it didn't hurt that she was being allowed to work her skills on such a high-profile case.

It felt like clouds were parting in her life. Moving to a new city hadn't been easy, and knowing that she wouldn't be staying didn't make it easier. She wasn't putting down roots. While everyone she knew seemed to be having long-term relationships or accumulating memories, Lindi was staring at computer screens in the back offices of the world. But with this case, it was finally paying off. At last she was doing something worthwhile.

By lunch she felt sure she had the evidence that Burton needed. She left the interview room and asked some uniformed cops hanging out by a vending machine if they'd seen him.

'The Super Detective?' said one of them. The others grinned. 'No, not for a couple of hours. He might be having lunch across the road.'

They turned away from Lindi and continued their conversation. She went downstairs and out of the main entrance. After some searching in the street, she spotted

Burton through the window of a takeaway restaurant called A Taste of the Punjab.

The door chimed electronically as she entered. Bollywood music played through tinny speakers. There was a list of curries and prices on a long chalkboard hanging over the counter, with an empty glass display case to the side topped with a row of achaar jars. Burton was sitting at one of the three tables in the restaurant, wedged in next to a drinks fridge. He had a chicken curry with rice in front of him and was eating slowly with a fork, lost in thought. She stood over his table.

'Can I join you?'

He looked up, surprised to see her. He hesitated for a moment, then said, 'Sure.'

She sat down opposite him. 'I didn't think this would be your kind of lunch place.'

'Why not? It's run by a good Taurus family.'

'You mean Vrishabha. If they're Hindu, they use the Vedic system.'

'They've been in this country for two generations. They're Taurus. You want to order?'

Lindi looked up at the menu over the counter while Burton went back to eating. When the waiter came in from the back room, she ordered a chicken tikka masala with garlic naan.

'Good choice,' said Burton, wiping his mouth. 'How did the reading go?'

'Good. There's lots of fire in his chart, but also some water, which makes him manipulable. And he's got a weak Jupiter, which makes him antisocial. All in all, I'd say his chart paints a solid case against him.'

'And the stars don't lie,' said Burton. He scooped another forkful of rice into his mouth.

Lindi watched him, suddenly wary. 'What's wrong?'

Burton chewed and swallowed.

'I just had a meeting with my captain and a lawyer representing Boysen,' he said. 'He's got an alibi. When Williams was killed on Saturday morning, Boysen was at the Westville market.'

'That's what he told me,' said Lindi. 'But it's not very convincing. He hasn't got any witnesses and he won't tell me why he went there. Also, he didn't strike me as the type of guy who spends his Saturday mornings buying dream catchers.'

'No,' said Burton. 'But it's quite possible that he was panhandling or pickpocketing, which would explain why no one noticed him. It's easy enough to check his story, though. If he went to the market, then the CCTV at the Westville bus terminal will have caught him coming and going. We've requested the tapes to check and the lawyer is confident that he'll be there. If he is we've got the wrong guy.'

Lindi ran her thumbnail down the yellow plastic tablecloth.

'Shit,' she said.

'Exactly,' said Burton. 'And if we'd just done the police work and not been chasing the stars, we might have saved ourselves a false arrest.'

Lindi frowned.

'Well, my reading's still accurate. All I was doing was looking at his true nature. Even if he's not responsible for this particular murder, that doesn't make him a good person.'

'Don't worry,' said Burton. 'I'm not blaming you.'

The waiter came and put a plate of curry and the naan bread down on the table. Lindi tore off some naan and used it to chase a piece of chicken around her plate.

'How did Boysen afford a lawyer?'

'He didn't,' said Burton. 'The case is big enough to get the attention of an Equal Signs group. He's a charity case.'

'So, what now?' she said. 'I think the best thing we can do is a horary reading. You can ask a predictive question and it'll give you some idea where to look next.'

Burton shook his head. 'No thanks. I'm going to stick to the basic grunt work for a while.'

'But I'm still on contract to you,' she said. 'I'm a valuable resource.'

Burton pushed his plate to the side.

'Did you catch many people when you worked for the airports?'

'Oh yes. Dozens.'

'Terrorists? Smugglers?'

'No. Mostly people carrying liquids or items which could be used as weapons. A hunting knife one time.'

'OK,' said Burton. 'And did you get many false positives?'

'Sure,' she said. 'But it's better to be safe than sorry, right?'

'Right,' he said, heavy with scepticism. He wiped his hands on a paper napkin and got to his feet. 'Listen, I have to get back to the station. It was great working with you.'

'You're going?' said Lindi. She wanted to argue, but this wasn't the time or the place. 'Will you let me know if you need anything else from me?'

'I will,' he said. 'Thanks for your time. Enjoy your lunch.'

Chapter Twelve

There weren't many public records on the Scarsdale family. Whatever they had been up to since Daniel's father had cut off ties with them, they weren't making it easy for the authorities to track them down. Daniel waited in the UrSec offices while Hamlin chased up their leads.

The boardroom was on the top floor, with a long window looking out over the city centre. Daniel sipped Earl Grey tea and watched the light of the rising sun reflecting off the glass-fronted buildings.

After half an hour, Hamlin came to the doorway, looking sombre.

'I'm sorry, Mr Lapton,' he said. 'There's no easy way to tell you this. Penny Scarsdale is dead.'

'What?' said Daniel. 'How?'

'It was ten years ago. She was getting off a bus and didn't check the road. The driver who hit her was a young Scorpio. He was found guilty of manslaughter and received a suspended sentence.'

Daniel stared down at the polished top of the boardroom table.

'And my daughter?'

'She was seven at the time. She wasn't present. We have no idea how it affected her.' Hamlin reached for the door frame as if he was about to turn, then said, again, 'I'm sorry.'

Sympathy didn't seem right coming from Hamlin.

'Thank you,' said Daniel.

Hamlin nodded, then returned to his hunt. Daniel rocked back in his chair and looked up at the dimpled soundproof ceiling. Losing Penny was strange and painful. Over the last seventeen years, whenever he had thought of her, it had been of her as a teenager. His memories had been of fumbling sex, repeated over and over in his mind until they were distilled fragments. Meeting her after all these years would have been sobering, he knew, but it would also have been a chance to find out what she was really like, without youth and hormones to cloud things, and a chance to apologize for what his family had put her through. Knowing that he would never see her again, and that those memories and desires were now attached to nothing, was disturbing.

A few hours later Hamlin came back with a new update. His investigators had finally tracked down Penny's mother, Marjorie, who lived in an apartment block in the Westwood district, and she still owned a connected landline. Hamlin had called her personally, but she hung up on him twice and then left the phone off the hook. When he tried calling an hour later, one of the Scarsdales called Cooper answered and said that if anyone working for Daniel Lapton called again, they would be dredging Daniel's body out of the harbour by the end of the week.

'They want nothing from you and they don't have any reason to be polite,' said Hamlin. 'They think your father treated them unfairly and they seem to have a bad history with UrSec. They said they'll speak to her and no one else.'

'Who's "her"?' said Daniel.

'He didn't say.' Hamlin sat down at the boardroom table opposite Daniel and locked his fingers together. 'This company has two ways to handle antagonism. The first is with our lawyers, although they work best with people who are concerned about their business. We also have a more physical approach.'

'No,' said Daniel. Threats and intimidation would backfire, and he was getting impatient. 'This is a human situation. This has to be one-to-one.'

'I can send a representative.'

'I want to go in person.'

Hamlin frowned and tapped the boardroom table with his fingers.

'I'd like a risk assessment. Westwood isn't a great neighbourhood and we have to be prepared for the worst from the Scarsdales. Violence, extortion, kidnapping . . .'

'Let me put this another way,' said Daniel, fixing Hamlin with an unblinking gaze. For a moment he knew what it was like to be his father. 'I'm going there, right now, with or without you. This is my business and I'm taking it from here. Bring your security team if you want, but I'm getting my daughter from those people.'

Chapter Thirteen

The local news channel's theme blared as Burton opened his front door. The sweeping music was full of drama, making the chaos of the world sound like a fantasy, with heroes and villains and a coherent story. Burton knew several journalists personally – he'd had so many run-ins with them that they were almost friends – and they were as flawed as anyone, piecing together the jigsaw of truth based on whatever they were fed by press releases and social media and their own politics. And they were as happy as anyone else to throw away the pieces that didn't fit.

The living-room door was open and Kate was lying on her back on the couch. On the TV was a news story about a couple of Gemini reality-series stars and the Libra baby they had adopted.

'She's adorable,' said a lady with long straight black hair, as her muscular boyfriend in a half-unbuttoned white shirt coddled the baby in his arms. 'We're going to raise her in a Gemini household, of course, but we'll make sure she gets lots of exposure to other Libras. We don't want to get in the way of her expressing her true tendencies. We want her to be all she can be.'

'That kid'll have a rough time in the playground,' said Burton from the doorway.

'Oh, hey,' said Kate. 'Come here.'

He went over to the couch, and she reached out and hugged his legs.

He looked down at her. 'Is that comfortable?'

'Nope. You try and get comfortable when someone glues a bowling ball to your belly. Did you pick up the shopping?'

'We've got supper in the deep freeze. I'll get everything else tomorrow.'

He went through to the kitchen. The pots and dishes were still stacked up from the night before. He took an old ice cream carton full of frozen stew out of the freezer and put it in the microwave to defrost. He'd made it over the weekend as part of their plan to have real food once in a while.

'Don't forget we're visiting Hugo and Shelley next week,' Kate called out from the living room. 'We need a present for Ben. It's his second birthday.'

'I hadn't forgotten,' he said, watching the carton turning in the microwave. Stew was far from his favourite food. He didn't enjoy the way you had to pick out the bones. One of the first things he'd seen as a cop was an old man who had died in his flat alone during a heatwave. The neighbours only discovered his body three months later. In the heat, the old man had decayed so badly that he'd basically melted and become fused to the carpet. When they'd tried to lift him, parts stayed attached to the ground, like the tender meat falling off a bone. It was terrible how a memory like that could taint something innocent.

As he loaded the dishes into the dishwasher, he heard a sob.

'Kate?'

He went back to the living room and stood in the doorway. She was facing away from him on the couch, but he could see her shoulders heaving.

'Hey,' he said. 'Hey.'

As he approached, she turned her head away from him. He knelt down next to her.

'What's the matter?'

'Why are we bringing a life into this? What were we thinking?'

'Oh. Hey, now. Come on.' He ran his fingers through her hair, trying to comfort her.

On the screen there were people throwing Molotov cocktails. Drone footage showed a crowd of Aries protesters clashing with police somewhere in the Midwest. He used the remote to turn down the volume.

'Shhh,' he said. 'It's all right. She'll be fine. She'll have an amazing mother, won't she?'

She looked at him and smiled through a tear-streaked face.

'You're a bullshit merchant, Jerry Burton.'

She draped an arm around his neck, drawing him in. He tried to hug her back, but there was no way to get his arm around her, so he patted her on the forearm.

'It'll be OK,' he said again.

Kate sighed deeply and let go of him.

'Hormones,' she said. 'Ugh.'

'Want a bath? I'll put your towel and pyjamas into the tumble dryer. Get them warm for you.'

'All right.'

She kissed his forehead and pulled herself upright.

'Oof,' she said. 'I'm like one big boob. And no, it's not amazing.'

She got up and waddled to the bathroom, closing the door after her. Burton heard the pipes humming and the water splashing into the tub.

He went to the bedroom and fished through the laundry basket until he found Kate's towel and her blue cotton pyjamas. He took them through to the kitchen and threw them into the dryer mounted over the washing machine.

While they were warming, he went back to the living room and sat down on the couch. The title on the news said 'San Celeste: City on the Brink'. Solomon Mahout was waving his fist in front of a crowd of angry red-shirted men. Burton turned the volume back up again.

' . . . call us violent. How can we not be violent, when it's the only way to be heard? How can we not be violent, when we're met by violence at every turn? Peace is silence, and we can't be silent any longer. We will be heard!'

Burton turned it off.

Chapter Fourteen

That night, Burton woke up in the darkness. Kate was twitching in bed next to him.

'It's OK,' he said, reaching out and putting an arm over her. 'Shh.'

Her body slowly relaxed and her breathing quietened. Burton stayed awake and watched the light through the gap between the curtains growing and fading as cars drove past outside. He could hear drunken people down the street having an extended argument. He wanted to move and get comfortable, but he didn't want to wake Kate so he lay still, at the mercy of his exhausted mind.

It was all planned. They had booked the appointment at the hospital. They were going to induce the birth of their daughter on 19 May, making her a Taurus just like them. They should have been more cautious with the conception, but neither of them was as young as they used to be, and when they had found out that Kate was pregnant after three years of trying, they decided to take the risk and keep it.

But it meant that their daughter would be born six weeks premature.

He got out of bed and went to the kitchen for some water.

If they left their daughter to be born naturally she would be a Cancer, which would mean she would have to go to a Cancer school. That meant either they'd have to move to a predominantly Cancer district or she would have to go to a boarding school and grow up parentless.

The pipes sang as Burton poured the water. He cursed himself silently and turned down the flow. When the glass was half full he turned off the tap and gulped the cold water. From the bedroom he could hear the sheets rustling as Kate turned over in bed. He put the glass down by the sink and felt his way back to the bedroom. As he pulled up the sheets, Kate stirred again.

'What's wrong?' she said.

'Nothing. It's all fine.'

He put his arm back around her. He knew what all the other signs thought about Tauruses, but they looked after their own. They might be stubborn and set in their ways, but the schools worked and the fees were affordable. The pass rate was high at the local school because the teachers were diligent and methodical, and the community supported them. All his and Kate's friends had kids there, so their daughter would have play dates. If she was born Taurus, she'd have a community. She'd be secure.

But if she was born early she might be sick. And she might die.

Chapter Fifteen

Roland Terraces was an old apartment block in the middle of Westwood in downtown San Celeste. It was covered with peeling yellow plaster, the same colour as the dead grass on the long, thin traffic island down the middle of the road. Most of the windows of the building were grey from accumulated grime. On the other side of the road was a strip of failing businesses: a takeaway, a hairdresser's and a shop selling cheap phones. The sidewalk was littered with empty cans and shredded plastic bags.

The sky was cloudless and the city was cooking. Heat haze made the asphalt look like simmering black oil. Hamlin parked opposite the building. As Daniel climbed out of the air-conditioned company car he was blasted by heat and the smell of rotting seaweed from the docklands.

A black van pulled up behind them and a team dressed in military gear clambered out.

'Who are they?' said Daniel to Hamlin, who was getting out of the other side of the car.

'Insurance,' said Hamlin.

'The Scarsdales don't trust me. How do you think they're going to feel about me arriving with a SWAT team?'

'We won't interfere,' said Hamlin, deadpan. 'Don't worry. You can talk man-to-man with Cooper Scarsdale. We'll only be there when things go wrong.'

Daniel looked around. There was graffiti on almost every wall. 'GOATS FROM $HEEP'. 'FUK DIS PLACE'. 'AREEZ STEEZ'. A group of young men were watching them sullenly from the shade outside the takeaway.

'OK,' he said. 'But be discreet.'

The security team split up. One guard stayed at the vehicle and two went to scout out the nearby street corners. Daniel and Hamlin crossed the road, with the fourth guard leading the way.

It took a moment for Daniel's eyes to adjust to the building's foyer. The floor was bare concrete. The lower halves of the walls were decorated with small, square blue tiles that had mostly peeled off to leave an indented grid in the plaster.

The advance guard headed up the stairs. He didn't have his weapon out, but Daniel saw a hand hovering at his side.

'Wait for him to do a scan of the building before proceeding,' said Hamlin. 'Please.'

'Fine.'

After a few minutes, the guard came down and waved them up. Daniel and Hamlin followed him back up the stairs.

They came out on the third floor, through a propped-open door on to a walkway around the building's inner courtyard. The ground far below was cracked concrete. Laundry was hanging from lines stretched between walkways.

The doors to the apartments had metal security gates over them. Some were bent back at the corners like dog-eared pages and others had been torn out completely. Above, the underside of the fourth-floor walkway was cracking and stained, as if it was slowly dissolving.

'What the fuck is this?' shouted a voice from ahead.

A man stood halfway along the walkway. He was heavyset, with a beard and short blond hair. He was in a white vest that showed off a pair of heavily tattooed arms.

'Are you Lapton?' he said.

Daniel nodded. The man strode closer.

'Who the fuck do you think you are, coming here? And who are these people? You think you can bring your thugs here to intimidate me?'

Daniel felt a surge of fear turn to anger. He wanted to shout, 'Who the fuck are you?' right back, but being aggressive now would be a mistake. He could feel Hamlin and the guard bristling next to him. He stepped forward and stretched out a hand.

'I'm sorry for this,' he said. 'Are you Cooper? I needed to meet you in person. I wanted to –'

Cooper punched Daniel across the jaw. The crack echoed off the far side of the courtyard. Daniel was silenced, more by disbelief than pain. This was the first punch he'd taken since school. He had to struggle against the urge to run or fight back.

Hamlin and the guard didn't share that struggle and both pulled weapons from their holsters. Daniel felt a moment of relief, immediately followed by fear. This was exactly what he was trying to avoid.

Cooper kept his eyes on Daniel, but pointed at Hamlin and the guard.

'Tell your dogs to point their water pistols somewhere

else. I don't care who you are, you don't mess with my family. Turn around and don't fucking dare come back. Ever!'

He was talking louder than he needed to. Daniel realized that the speech wasn't only for his benefit. Some of the other residents of the building were watching. There was a young woman hanging out washing in the courtyard below, and a pair of old men were looking down from the fourth-floor walkway opposite.

Daniel touched his jaw and tentatively opened his mouth to check for damage. All the while, he kept his eyes on Cooper. This was a show of power and Daniel had learned enough to recognize that it was hollow. If Cooper Scarsdale had been in a gang, or if he'd had a weapon to back up his threats, he wouldn't be blustering. He was like a cat with an arched back and a puffed-out tail. Daniel had the real power, but Cooper needed to show his authority. And if Daniel wanted to win this, he needed to back down.

He lowered his eyes. 'I know,' he said, 'I was wrong. Please. I just wanted to meet my daughter.'

Cooper gave a choked laugh. 'Yeah, well,' he said. 'You got her.'

Daniel risked looking up at Cooper.

'Please,' he said. 'Where is she? Is she here?'

'What are you talking about?' said Cooper, sounding genuinely confused. 'You took her!'

Daniel's back tensed. He was too far outside his comfort zone for his experience to be any help. Maybe this was a scam. He almost hoped it was. He could understand a scam.

'I only just found out she existed,' he said. 'My father kept her from me. I didn't expect you to forgive me or my family, but I just want to know she's safe. I want to see her.'

The anger drained from Cooper's face.

'You're kidding,' he said.

'I swear I'm not. Please.'

Cooper Scarsdale looked over his shoulder to the open door of the apartment. He scratched the underside of his beard.

'Shit,' he said, so quietly that Daniel could barely hear.

'Don't you know where my daughter is?'

Cooper snapped his attention back to Daniel.

'OK, we need to talk. You can come in, but only you. Your watchdogs stay outside.'

Hamlin looked at Daniel and gave a tense nod. Daniel followed Cooper into the apartment alone.

The air inside smelled of smoke and incense. The entranceway was tiny, too small to be a room and too wide to be a corridor. It was empty except for a hockey stick propped up next to the door, which was presumably the Scarsdales' security system. The walls were painted green and the floor was covered in a dark blue carpet worn through to the concrete beneath. There was a tiny open kitchen area through a door on the right, with a bucket full of water to the side of a metal sink. Two closed doors faced the apartment entrance and a floor-to-ceiling batik banner of the zodiac covered the corridor's left wall. Droning music came from out of the left door.

'Wait here,' said Cooper flatly.

Daniel nodded.

Cooper pushed open the door and the music got louder.

'Hey,' he said quietly to someone on the other side, and squeezed in. The door closed behind him.

Daniel waited. He heard a woman's voice, and Cooper, but he couldn't make out their words. They talked back and forth for a while, then there was nothing but the music. Daniel wanted to lean in closer but didn't want to be caught eavesdropping.

He shifted his weight from foot to foot. Finally, Cooper opened the door again.

'Don't upset her,' he said, and stood aside.

Daniel looked in. The room on the other side was smoky and almost impossibly cramped, like the inside of a storage container. A queen-sized bed took up most of the floor space, with a dressing table squeezed against it and no room for a chair. There was an old television set, a cupboard and piles of clothes and open-topped boxes full of knick-knacks. An elderly lady was sitting on the only patch of bare floor, just in front of the cupboard. She was skinny, with grey hair dyed reddish-brown, and her clothes were brighter and thinner than Daniel would have expected. Her face was a mask of sadness. She was staring down into a bowl filled with burning incense that was resting on her crossed legs. Daniel recognized the pungent smell of marijuana mixed in with the incense.

'This is Marjorie,' said Cooper.

The woman lifted her head. It seemed to take a while for her eyes to focus on Daniel.

'You're the Lapton boy?' she said slowly. 'I thought you'd be younger. It was a long time ago, I suppose. What happened to your face?'

Daniel touched his already bruising jaw.

'This?' he said. 'I deserved it.'

He wasn't sure that he did, but he wasn't certain of anything much any more. Better to be open with them.

'Let me get you some ice,' said Marjorie. She stood up and waved him past her into the room. 'Come in and sit on the bed.'

She pushed her way to the small kitchen, leaving him with Cooper. Daniel sat obediently.

'She looked after Pam after Penny died, you know,' said Cooper accusingly. 'She raised her.'

Daniel began to feel light-headed. He wished they could get some air inside here, but the window looked like it was glued shut.

'Where is Pamela? Why did you think I had her?' said Daniel.

Cooper didn't answer. Daniel had the paranoid thought that he was coming into this situation thinking like a Capricorn. He was being strategic, but these people were Pisces. What he thought of as being straightforward and businesslike might be insultingly rude. He didn't know enough of their culture, though, to act any other way.

Marjorie came back in with a blue plastic cooler block from the fridge and handed it to him. He held it to the side of his jaw while she sat down next to him. Cooper stayed standing, leaning on the edge of the dressing table.

'Mrs Scarsdale, I'm sorry about coming to you like this, and I'm sorry for what my father did to your daughter and your family. I didn't know about any of it before yesterday. I didn't know about Pamela. All I'm trying to do is meet my daughter.'

'My dear, we haven't seen her since she ran away to join your family,' said Marjorie. 'Three years ago.'

'Shit,' said Daniel under his breath.

'Shit is right,' said Cooper firmly. 'We want her back too. And we're going to find out who's been fucking with us.'

He tensed his arms, ready for a fight, but Daniel stayed calm.

'Why did she leave?'

'She was rebellious,' said Marjorie. 'She didn't want to be stuck in this little apartment. Then she found out that her father was a Capricorn businessman and she became certain that she was meant to join you. We warned her.'

'So what happened?'

Marjorie picked up her bowl from the floor and put it on her lap. She looked down into it.

'She tried calling the Lapton One Hotel, but they said they didn't know what she was talking about. They got their security to block our number. But Pam was a stubborn one. She had to go there in person. She was certain that if you saw her, you'd know she was your daughter. So she stole some money from my bag and bought a bus ticket.'

She stopped, lost in the strands of smoke. Cooper took over.

'We didn't hear from her for a week,' he said. 'And then we got a lawyer's letter. It said that you weren't going to legally acknowledge that she was your daughter, but you would pay for her education and you were enrolling her in some fancy school.'

Daniel shook his head. 'That never happened.'

Cooper tensed up. 'Are you calling me a liar?' he said. 'I'll show you the fucking letter.'

Daniel raised a hand protectively. 'I believe you. But that letter wasn't from me.'

'Then you should keep a better watch on your lawyers,' said Cooper. He folded his arms again.

'So what did you do?' said Daniel.

'Nothing. We figured that Pam had what she wanted, and if she wasn't happy then she'd come back to us. And when she didn't call, we thought she was cutting off ties.'

'What's the name of the school?'

'The True Signs Academy,' said Cooper.

'The letter's up there somewhere,' Marjorie said, pointing to a cardboard box sitting on top of the cupboard. 'Do you want me to find it for you?'

'Please,' said Daniel.

She climbed up on to the bed and pulled at the dusty box. She wasn't tall and the box was heavy, but she managed to slide it far enough out for Cooper to catch it. He hauled it on to the bed and opened it for Daniel.

Inside was a collection of Pamela's old things – dresses and jeans, old toys and school notebooks. Cooper found the letter and handed it to Daniel. It had the Lapton family lawyers' letterhead and was signed by one of the senior partners. Daniel skimmed it and felt his anger growing again. Cooper hadn't told him how infuriatingly passive and impersonal the letter was. There was no indication that it had come from a human being.

Marjorie Scarsdale poked through the box and pulled out an old, grey plastic videotape.

'You might want this too,' she said.

Daniel looked up. 'What is it?'

'Pam's fifth birthday. If you're interested.'

Daniel took it and turned it over in his hands. It had a handwritten label: *PAM B-DAY*.

'Look after it,' said Marjorie. 'It's our only copy.'

Daniel felt as if he wasn't in the room any more. Everything was breaking apart, drifting in different directions. He clutched the tape tightly and hoped that it could bring things back together. It was a fragment of the life he'd missed. Maybe if he watched it everything would start to make sense.

He didn't even know what his daughter looked like. He was finally going to see her face.

Chapter Sixteen

Lindi lay on her side in bed and read the story on her phone: 'TOP COP MURDER SUSPECT FREED'. It didn't even mention her name. All it said was that the police didn't have strong enough evidence to hold Boysen, and that Aries Rising and the Aries Advocacy Fund had worked together to organize a legal counsel and make sure his rights were respected. He was still considered a witness in the case and was under orders not to leave the city.

The bedroom door swung open and Megan stuck her head in. She had her work bag slung over her shoulder.

'I'm out,' she said, and pointed at the coffee mug on Lindi's bedside table. 'That's for you, sleepyhead. And the dishwasher's ready to go when you're done.'

'Thanks,' said Lindi. 'Love ya.'

Megan blew her a kiss as she headed for the front door.

They'd had another night on the town, followed by drunken sex. It had been a long time coming. They'd known each other for years, but until now they'd both been in other relationships. Megan was still kind of seeing someone else, off and on. Now it was the morning after, Lindi was having mixed feelings. Things were going to get complicated.

She sat up in bed and sipped her coffee while scrolling through the article again. She thought about it, then closed the browser and opened a basic astrology app on her phone. She formulated the question in her mind.

'Who killed Chief Peter Williams?' she asked aloud, and hit the button 'Make Chart Now'.

A horary chart appeared on her phone's screen showing the planets, constellations, houses and aspects. She studied it while biting her lower lip, then flicked through the app screens to check specific times and dates of upcoming astrological events.

After half an hour she closed the app and went to her computer in the living room. She did a Web search, which sent her down a rabbit hole of conspiracy theories. It didn't take her too long to find what she was looking for. Burton was going to want to see this. She saved it on a thumb drive, had a shower, put on her favourite owl-patterned dress and glasses, tied back her hair and went down to her car.

She put the radio on as she drove to the police station. The DJ was interviewing an Aries heavy metal vocalist, who talked about the banality of the music scene. 'When I sing about violence, I'm just telling the truth of the world I grew up in. The people who want to shut me up are trying to invalidate my experience. They're perpetrating the same oppression that's been going on since the end of the Aries state. Solomon Mahout may be a criminal to the people who own this station, and to their sponsors, but to most of this city he's a hero. He's the only one giving us a voice.'

At the entrance to the station, a security guard stopped her. She waved a metal-detecting wand around Lindi's body, sketching a careless picture of her in the air.

'Who you seeing?' said the guard, with the lifeless attitude of someone who earned their wage by getting in
other people's way.

'Detective Jerome Burton. Homicide. Third floor.'

The guard went to a phone on the edge of the front
desk and dialled a three-digit number. She spoke into the
handset while keeping an eye on Lindi. Lindi couldn't
hear the conversation, but after a short while the guard
held the handset to her chest and beckoned Lindi over.

'He wants to know what you're here for,' she said.

'What?' said Lindi. 'Can I talk to him?'

The guard rolled her eyes and held out the handset.
Lindi took it.

'Hi? Burton?'

'What is it, Lindi?' said Burton. He sounded tired.

'Listen, I've looked into the case more and I made a
new chart . . .'

'Thanks, but I told you, I don't need any assistance
right now. I'm doing this step by step. You saw the papers?
I've had reporters hounding me all morning.'

Lindi pressed a fist against a pillar next to the desk. The
guard was staring at her, trying to hurry her up. Lindi
turned away from her.

'I've got something to show you,' she said.

'A chart?'

'No, some evidence for the Williams case. Do you
know about Bram Coine?'

'Who?' said Burton.

Lindi smiled to herself. She was ahead of Burton.

'If you don't know, then you should definitely see this.'

'OK. I'll show you up. Hold tight.'

After five minutes, Burton arrived in an elevator. He signed Lindi in and the guard finally gave her a visitor's badge.

'Look, I'm sorry,' said Lindi as they rode up in the elevator together. 'I read Boysen's chart as well as I could in the circumstances. I didn't mean to waste your time.'

'No, it's OK,' said Burton. 'I put you in a bad position. I was looking for a way to connect the murder to Aries Rising. You were just giving me the result I wanted to hear.'

Lindi felt her cheeks flush. 'My readings are objective, Burton.'

He led her back to his office and closed the frosted-glass door.

'You said you have something to show me?' he said.

'Right,' she said. 'Can I use your computer?'

'Sure.'

She sat down at the desk and plugged in her thumb drive. As the anti-virus scanned it, she swivelled around on the chair to face Burton.

'OK. Boysen's birth chart was obviously a washout, and a horoscope of the time of the murder has conflicting interpretations. So this morning I did what I should have done in the beginning, which is to do a horary reading. It's an ancient predictive technique, very tricky but powerful. The emphasis is on essential dignities —'

'I'm sorry,' said Burton, cutting her off. 'I thought you said it wasn't astrological evidence.'

'It isn't,' she said. 'I'm just explaining how I ended up finding what I found.'

'And proving that you know your business.'

'That too,' she said. 'OK. Quick summary. Horary astrology works because, when you ask a question, the sky at that exact moment holds the answer.'

Burton frowned. 'Really?'

'Trust me. The chart I made was hard to read, but the tenth-house activity basically implied that Williams was killed for political reasons. And so I did an online search for Williams on a bunch of political forums and, well, have a look at this.'

She opened a video file. It looked like webcam footage and showed a young man in his early twenties sitting in an unlit room, looking directly into the camera. His face was illuminated light blue by an unseen computer screen. He had messy brown hair and glasses, and one earring half-way up his right ear.

'What's up, Internet!' he said cheerfully. 'It's three thirty on a Wednesday morning. It's that time of night when you wake up from your troubled sleep feeling that the world is collapsing, and, you know what, you're never completely wrong. Have a look.'

The video cut to news footage, which looked like it was filmed by pointing a cell phone camera at a TV screen. Solomon Mahout was making a speech in front of an Aries Rising crowd on the steps of the town hall.

'We can't respect the law. The law was written by those in power to maintain their power. It's a machine designed to crush us. Fight back! Don't stop until the law speaks for you! Shout! Scream! Get their attention!'

Back in the bedroom, the young man looked thoughtful.

'OK, that's scary stuff,' he said. 'And we know from history what happens when large groups of Aries get together under charismatic leaders. But let's just look at the meat of what Solomon Mahout is saying.'

Next up was a graph that looked like a screen-grab from a spreadsheet program.

'What's the most violent sign? Aries, right? After all, look at the statistics. Despite being a minority in the population, Aries make up the vast majority of the prison population.'

The video cut back to the young man's earnest face.

'But what if there's more to this than meets the eye? For one thing, most Aries are living in poverty, and that plays a significant role in how many of them turn to crime. But there's also the astonishing fact that people who live in predominantly Aries areas are over nine times more likely to be stopped and searched by the police, even though people randomly searched outside those areas were twice as likely to be carrying drugs or concealed weapons. Why? Well, maybe it has something to do with these fine fellas.'

The screen now showed a stock photo of a policeman pointing out a location on a map held by a pretty female tourist. They were standing against a neutral background and smiling. There was a faint copyright watermark across the whole image.

'The San Celeste Police Department,' said the young man's voice. 'They patrol our streets and keep us safe. So why am I laying the blame for our malfunctioning society at their feet?'

The image dissolved to a picture of chaos. The air was grey with smoke. A row of parked cars was on fire and blurred men and women were running past in both directions. In the foreground, a woman was lying in the street. Her forehead was cut open and bleeding, painting the whole side of her face red. A policeman had her in a chokehold, while another lunged towards the camera with an outstretched hand, trying to grab it.

'Twenty-five years ago, the Cardinal Fire riots devastated the city for two solid weeks. They began after calls to repair a deteriorating housing project were ignored.'

A new picture came up, this time of a group of policemen in black SWAT gear. They were posing proudly with a large manual battering ram.

'After the riots were suppressed, the police force formed the notorious Ram Squad, the special unit set up to control the Aries population so that the situation would never arise again. Arrests of citizens living in north San Celeste, commonly known as Ariesville, went up by over 400 per cent and stop-and-search became the new norm.'

The video cut back to the young man in his room.

'The fact that in this day and age the police are profiling and targeting a particular sign is inexcusable, but that's not the worst of it. The Ram Squad regularly perform strip searches and demand identity documents. They can take our privacy and dignity, and yet they're completely opaque. Information about their activities, their funding and even their basic operating principles are considered state secrets and are not obtainable through the Freedom of Information Act. This has to stop, starting now.'

A text box faded in under his face and began crawling up the screen. It was a list of names with blurred-out phone numbers and addresses next to them. Chief Peter

Williams's name was at the top of the list, and Vince Hare's was second. Either the young man thought this was all a game, or he had an actual death wish.

'Here's a list of every member of the Ram Squad and their superiors in the SCPD. Now we can have some kind of transparency. You can ask them yourself what they're up to, and how they justify it to themselves, and you can tell them what you think about this obvious violation of our rights.'

He waved a finger up and down the superimposed list.

'You've got to be kidding me,' said Burton, and leaned in closer. 'Why are all the numbers blurred?'

'This isn't the original video,' said Lindi. 'It was taken down on Saturday afternoon, after the news of the murder broke. But before it went down, someone from a right-wing website copied it and blurred out the numbers. They posted it on their own site, on an article saying it's proof that Williams was assassinated by the left wing.'

'Have a lot of people seen this video?' said Burton.

'Maybe,' said Lindi. 'It said 301 views when I looked this morning, but that could mean anything. If a video gets a lot of views quickly, the view counter reads 301 until after a moderator has checked it.'

Burton pulled the thumb drive out of the laptop without ejecting it and carried it to the door.

'Where are you going?' said Lindi.

Burton turned. 'Where do you think? I'm going to get that little bastard arrested.'

Chapter Seventeen

That night, the hotel staff at the Lapton Celestia brought up a video cassette player for Daniel and plugged it into the widescreen TV in his penthouse suite. He closed the glass double doors to the balcony to quieten the sound of the sea crashing into the rocks below and sat down on the white leather sofa to watch the Scarsdales' video.

The screen filled with static. At first, Daniel worried that his staff hadn't plugged in the player correctly or that the tape was damaged. But the static broke apart slowly, clearing like mist to reveal a young girl.

She had a round face and pink cheeks. Daniel saw the resemblance to Penny immediately, but her hair was brown and her eyes were like looking into a mirror.

She was in an unfamiliar house, somewhere bigger than the Scarsdales' cramped home, and was bouncing up and down on the spot. The camera swung around to show the extended Scarsdale family sitting on sofas and comfy chairs around her and watching happily. Daniel spotted a younger, thinner Cooper, with long hair. And there was Penny, older than Daniel remembered, coming in carrying a cake with five candles. Young Pamela saw it and her jaw dropped. She looked around the room, wide-eyed.

'I get a cake?' she said.

In another time, everyone in the room laughed. Daniel closed his eyes, trying to block out the pain.

The screen went to static again and came back, zooming in and out, trying to find focus. It settled on Pamela's face again, this time in a kitchen. The cake was in front of her with five lit candles. Pamela was sitting in Penny's lap and the family was singing off-screen. Pamela's attention was entirely taken up by the cake.

The song ended and the family clapped. Penny Scarsdale nudged Pamela forward, and she leaned in and blew, making an ineffective raspberry with her mouth. Penny steered her gently until she had extinguished all five candles. When the last one was out, everybody cheered.

'Did you make a wish?' said Penny. She was in her mid-twenties now. Her face was a little fuller and her cheeks were a little lower than Daniel remembered. But she was still beautiful and she still smiled easily. He tried to hold back, but his eyes welled with tears.

Pamela looked around the room, suddenly shy. She was the most beautiful, perfect thing that Daniel had ever seen. She whispered into her mother's ear and Penny laughed.

'She wished for more cake!' she said, and Pamela curled up to defend herself from the eruption of laughter.

Daniel turned off the video and blinked at the blank screen.

He had seen scenes like this before. Nothing was new. A cute kid. A loving family. Nothing out of the ordinary. Except that it was his daughter. And he had missed seventeen years of her life.

Chapter Eighteen

'What did I do?' said the young man from the video. 'Tell me what I did that was illegal.'

Bram Coine was a sociology student at Westcroft University. He was also, it turned out, a paranoid anti-capitalist with 176 regular viewers on his Internet video channel. And he was sweating. Burton and Lindi watched through the window into the interview room as Kolacny did the grilling.

'You can't, can you?' said Bram Coine. 'Because I did nothing illegal and nothing wrong.'

'I don't believe that, and I don't think you do either,' said Kolacny, leaning forward in his chair and putting his elbows on the desk, getting into Bram's space. 'You know why I don't think you believe it? Because you deleted that video after you found out that the Chief of Police was murdered. Which makes me think that you know damn well that what you did got him killed.'

'It's not like that at all,' said Bram. 'I took it down because I knew that someone out there would make that mental connection, and they totally did. But guess what? Williams's address and phone number were already on the Internet. It took me, like, less than fifteen minutes to dig them up. And the same goes for all the Ram Squad numbers. There's nothing illegal or immoral about posting information if it's already freely available, right? Can I get my asthma pump, please?'

Kolacny had a notepad on the table in front of him. He picked up a pen and tapped it on his teeth thoughtfully.

'You posted his address online, in a video telling people that he's been targeting Aries. The same Aries who have been threatening violence for years. You're not going to take responsibility for that? That's got to be some kind of incitement to violence.'

'Please!' said Bram, sounding frustrated. 'Just look at the video! All I said was, talk to these guys and tell them that picking on people of one sign isn't OK. I'm not a violent person. Do I look like a violent person?'

'No, you look like a hacker,' said Kolacny. 'You look like a kid who sits alone in his room and messes with people through a computer screen, because you think you're smarter than them and you think they'll never catch you. But guess what? We did.'

'Show me the law I've broken.'

Burton leaned closer to Lindi and spoke quietly. 'Little dickhead. How does he think he's going to get away with this?'

Lindi was standing next to him. She ran a finger along the frame of the glass and said, 'Hmm.'

'What does "hmm" mean?' said Burton. 'What are you thinking?'

'Can I use your computer again?'

They went back through to Burton's room. After a few minutes at his computer, Lindi showed him a website that was just a page of names, numbers and addresses. Peter Williams was right near the bottom.

'He isn't a hacker,' she said. 'He was telling the truth. All those names and addresses were already online.'

Burton leaned over her shoulder.

'What? How? How's that possible?'

'Marketing websites. If something's immoral but not illegal, it's business.'

'Well, we can still get him for something else. Harassing police officers. Interfering with an ongoing investigation.'

'Why?' said Lindi, swivelling in the chair. 'Bram isn't a suspect. He never was. I was just showing you a possible avenue of investigation. If his video was the trigger that sent some psycho after Williams, then maybe Williams got a letter or email or phone call from the killer before he was actually murdered.'

Burton shook his head. 'No. We checked all of those. No unusual texts, phone calls or letters, and nothing out of the ordinary on his personal email. His work email is covered by the State Secrets Act.'

'Well, then, maybe there's something in there that will help your investigation,' said Lindi. 'Or maybe Chief Williams was up to something shady and whatever it was got him killed.'

Burton looked at her disbelievingly. 'Whose side are you on?' he said.

She pointed at herself. 'I'm an Aquarius hipster liberal, remember? I've got my own views. Now, why don't you go and talk to your Ram Squad friends and ask them if they've been up to anything you ought to know about? Because I'll bet there's been some overreach that someone just responded to with murder.'

Chapter Nineteen

'Burton! Hey, Burton!'

The voice came from behind him. Burton was walking through the Homicide Department with a cup of coffee for Lindi and a tea for himself. He turned to see Captain Mendez strutting angrily towards him.

'What the hell is this?' said Mendez, holding up a printed page. It was Burton's most recent report. 'You're letting Coine go!'

'He's not a suspect,' said Burton.

'The hell he isn't!' said Mendez. He looked like he wanted to spit. 'Do you know how pissed off the Ram Squad is? They wanted to go to his cell and beat the shit out of him, and I only kept them away by promising we'd deal with him properly. And now you're letting him go? They're going to lose their shit!'

Mendez stood too close to Burton and stuck his chest out, like he was squaring up for a fight.

'Sorry, Captain,' said Burton. 'I don't like the kid either, but the newspapers are watching how we deal with him. Half the city is calling him a free speech champion.'

'Fuck what they think, he's a traitor! And fuck your rulebook shit! The rulebook is the shield we hide behind while we do what we do to get the job done. You don't work for the rulebook, you work for the police, and when you forget that we all go to shit. Remember what happened when you fucked around with the Cronin case! Bram Coine stays with us. I want him sent down for harassment, at least.'

'It's too late, sir,' said Burton. 'The Deputy Chief ordered his release. The Mayor wants us focusing on finding Williams's killer.'

Mendez glared up at Burton, then turned away in disgust.

'You need to get your priorities right, Burton. Remember who you work for.'

Bram Coine was released later that afternoon. News crews gathered outside the front of the station to catch the moment. He came to the main gate, where he was hugged by his father, a middle-aged man with greying hair and a jacket with patches on the elbows. The cameras flashed greedily, capturing Coine's embarrassment. Lindi and Burton watched through the revolving doors as the father and son tried to walk away but were blocked by the lenses and microphones of half a dozen news stations.

'Please,' said Bram's father. 'Please just leave us alone.'

He stretched out a hand, trying vainly to block the camera flashes. The attention seemed to be pushing him towards a mental breakdown. Burton could relate.

'They're all really watching this case, aren't they?' said Lindi.

'Yep,' said Burton.

She looked at his sour face and gave him a sympathetic half-smile.

'Don't worry. You'll do fine in the spotlight. You're a square-jawed hero cop. You were born for it.'

Outside, the cameras kept flashing, and it didn't look like they would ever stop.

Chapter Twenty

'Here's a list of every member of the Ram Squad and their superiors in the SCPD,' said Bram Coine on the video. 'Now we can have some kind of transparency.'

The censored red numbers scrolled up the screen in front of Bram's face with the added blurriness of a low-resolution Internet video blown up to HD. The image froze and shrank down until it was a window next to the television presenter, Harvey Hammond, who looked directly into camera and let the moment hang.

'Wow,' he said. 'I mean, wow. I've seen some left-wing pinheadedness, but this has got to win some kind of prize. Even if that video was taken down the second it was posted, I'd still call it treachery against the people of San Celeste. But the fact is, that video was posted two weeks before our police chief, a hero of the city and someone I was proud to consider a friend, was brutally murdered.'

The screen cut to footage of Bram and his father exiting the arch at the front of the Central Police Station. Reporters and cameramen closed in on them. Bram's father stood in the way and hunched his shoulder up protectively, but he couldn't block his son's tired, upset face.

'Here's the maker of that video, Bram Coine, leaving police custody earlier today. Why was he leaving custody, you ask? Well, according to the police, nothing he did was technically – technically! – against the law.'

Hammond came back on-screen. He leaned forward and looked into the camera sincerely.

'And that got me thinking. Because if that's not against the law, then there's something really, really wrong. And it's not just that one law that's broken, but all the laws that young Mr Coine thinks he's so vigorously defending. The equality laws.'

Another cut, this time to footage of the Cardinal Fire riots from twenty-five years before. A young man in a red shirt was throwing a brick through the window of a music store. Amps and guitars were visible through the shattering glass.

'These laws are based on some pie-in-the-sky idea that you should treat people of different signs the same way. And you can't. Because, guess what, they're not the same. People of different signs behave differently. Signs like Leo and Gemini are more outgoing. Signs like Aquarius and Sagittarius, you'd better believe they don't watch my show. And signs like Aries are more prone to violence. And I sure as hell don't sleep comfortably at night at the thought that the police might have to ignore that and let their prime suspects go free, just because some pinheads think that the Aries are getting treated unfairly.'

Graphs and charts created by the graphics team filled the screen. They were 3D-rendered, metallic and smooth.

'Well, let's look at the statistics. Who makes up most of the population in the prison system? Aries. Who has the highest rate of unemployment? Aries. And let's not forget what happened last century, in the countries that allowed the Aries parties to establish dominance. The Aries Nations.'

A montage of black-and-white shots: soldiers marching and saluting, barbed wire, death camps.

Hammond returned to the screen.

'So maybe the police are right and this Bram Coine child isn't to blame. The law is to blame and what the boy did was within the law. So, to be absolutely fair to the boy, here's his home address, his phone number and his email.'

The information scrolled along the bottom of the screen, just above the constant news ticker. Hammond smiled wryly.

'Get in touch with Mr Coine and tell him your thoughts about what he did to our brave officers and our former Chief of Police. *Hammond Tonite* will be right back after the break.'

Chapter Twenty-One

Hammond sat back in the soft leather seat and let the stress from the shoot melt away. The ice clinked as he took a sip of Scotch. There was a glass of it ready for him at the end of every show, prepared out of sight and handed to him to drink as he was chauffeured to his home in the hills overlooking San Celeste. He gazed out of the window as they drove away from the city centre. He could see the riverside apartments for Gemini yuppies, with their wide windows and unused balconies, and the spire of San Celeste Cathedral lit up by multicoloured spotlights in front of the logo-topped buildings of the central business district. It really was a beautiful city at night. The graffiti and the beggars were gone, leaving only the lights of commerce and prosperity.

Hammond had been doing his show every weekday evening for the last thirteen years and still, each time, his nerves were grated by some intern messing around in his field of view, or by his producer Jonathan rearranging the segments at the last minute, or by some interview subject umming and ahhing like they'd never spoken the goddam English language before. He let the anger fuel his performance, not that the liberals and creeping anti-signists didn't annoy him enough already. The minor irritations of hosting the show gave him the extra boost of fury he needed to grab the audience's attention.

He hadn't needed any of that tonight, though. Police Chief Williams had been a good man and seeing the investigation of his murder hamstrung over technicalities was infuriating. In Hammond's opinion, anyone and everyone who interfered with the investigation or slowed it down was, in their own way, a traitor who was contributing to the crime.

He put the whisky glass into the cup-holder and took out his phone. His team at the station handled the social media and managed his account, but he always liked to see what all the good viewers thought of the latest episode.

'@HammondTonite nailed that stupid Virgo! #SuckItLibtards.'

'Great ep of @HammondTonite. Spot on. Most criminals are Aries, fact.'

'Hahahaha hope that little twit on @HammondTonite gets his house burned down!'

And there was the usual impotent rage from the other side, of course.

'@HammondTonite Blowhard Bastard.'

'@HammondTonite yr phone numbr is next, asshole.'

'@HammondTonite FUCK YOU.'

'Can't believe the bullshit @HammondTonite spouts. Aries criminality & poverty due to diminished opportunities & constant oppression.'

The good thing was, every time he saw something he wanted to argue with, he could be sure that one of his loyal fans would step in to do it for him. He never had to sink down into the pit of endless mud-slinging. He clicked on the last message and there was already a reply.

'Yeah? You know why Aries have diminished opportunities? COZ THEY KEEP ROBBING PPL. #Thanks
AndGoodnite.'

The brakes locked. Rubber screamed on the asphalt
and Hammond tumbled forward out of his seat. His legs
twisted under him as he slumped into the rear footwell
and his shoulder slammed into the back of the driver's
seat. The force held him in place while the world swung
around outside the car, then the screech and the movement ended in an abrupt jolt. Hammond fell back into the
soft black leather.

He reached up and touched his face. His lip was
bleeding.

'Dammit, Donny!'

His driver looked back at him through the gap between
the seats. He was a young Libra with hair parted in the
centre.

'You all right, Mr Hammond?'

'No, of course I'm not fucking all right, you little
asshole!'

An orange light was flickering in front of the car. Harvey craned past Donny to see.

'What the fuck's going on out there?'

'Fire, Mr Hammond. Someone poured gas across the
road.'

They had turned off the highway on to Enterprise
Road, which was on the way back to Hammond's home in
the southern suburbs. It was a long, straight, mostly unlit
road that wound past the national parkland. On the left
was a hillside going up, covered in trees and thick bushes.
On the right was a row of semi-industrial businesses and

wholesalers. Enterprise Road generally made a good, quiet short cut. Not tonight.

'Who the fuck would –'

Donny's window exploded inwards in a shower of glass cubes. A man outside the car tossed aside a hammer. He was wearing black, with a peaked sports cap and a scarf wrapped around his lower face. His eyes were blue and cold. Before Donny could react, he stuck the barrel of a gun in through the window and pushed it against his temple.

'Get out. Now.'

Donny raised one hand in surrender and reached for the door handle with the other. He slid out of the car sideways, keeping his face towards the attacker, not making any sudden moves.

As slowly as possible, Hammond pulled himself forward. He reached down into the footwell for his dropped phone and flipped it over. The lock screen had a 'slide for emergency services' button. He ran a fingertip over it and it clicked.

Donny stepped clear of the car with his palms towards the attacker.

'You're going to run now,' said the man. His voice was a drawl. 'You're going to run down this road as far as you can and you don't stop. Understand me?'

Donny nodded.

'Now say "thank you" and run.'

'Thank you,' said Donny. He looked through the rear window at Hammond apologetically, then ran back down the road the way they'd come, away from the car and the flames.

It was past midnight. There were no houses around. No passers-by. No witnesses.

'What do you want from me?' Hammond called out, trying to sound commanding.

In answer, the man in black swung the barrel of his gun at Harvey and fired.

Hammond's window shattered on to him like hailstones. He felt the impact of the bullet in his chest a split second before he felt the pain. He fell across the back seat, reached to the other rear door and scrabbled at the lock. There was another explosion behind him and a bullet thudded into the leather. The door mechanism clunked open and Hammond tumbled out of the car.

He scrambled forward on all fours, trying to get to his feet. A memory flashed into his head, something he'd heard from Williams – before movies, people didn't drop to the ground when they got shot, the way they do nowadays. Cinema told people what ought to happen and they just followed the script, like sheep. Hammond wasn't a sheep. But the pain was an anchor weighing him down. He wasn't going to fall. He was better than that.

The world tilted and Hammond felt an impact against the side of his head. His face grated against the asphalt. His arms were giving out on him. Dizzily, he pushed himself up on to his elbows and looked back over his shoulder. Behind him, lit by the flames, the figure in black was watching. Hammond expected him to raise the gun. Instead, he turned away from the road and walked back towards the trees on the hillside.

Hammond felt a burst of hope. The killer underestimated him. He was leaving him for dead. But Hammond wasn't dead yet. He was going to live.

A hollow metal clunk came from between the trees. The man came back into the light carrying a can of gas. He pulled off the lid and began pouring it out next to the car, swishing it in a long curve.

Hammond pulled himself back on to his hands and knees. His mouth was making involuntary bleating sounds. He couldn't help it. He felt a warmth spreading on his trousers. His bladder had given up. His left arm wouldn't move any more. He tucked it in under his chest and kept crawling forward with his right arm.

Up ahead was the other side of the road. There was a sidewalk, a patch of dry dirt and then a chain-link fence around the parking lot of a timber yard. The gate was padlocked and there was no sign of a way through. He'd have to go around.

The man in black's boots crunched closer and black-jeaned legs came into view next to Hammond's head.

'Fuu . . . Fuuu . . .' said Hammond.

'Shh,' said the man in black.

Hammond felt a boot kick him in the side. It wasn't hard, just enough to knock him back down on to the asphalt. His legs flailed weakly.

He felt warm liquid sloshing on to him, starting at his face and moving down his body. The sting of the gasoline trickling into his wound shocked him back to his senses.

'Guuuuh!'

'Shh,' said the man again.

Hammond tried to pull himself up, but the man in black pushed him back down firmly with a gloved hand and leaned in close. Hammond felt the man's breath on the side of his face.

'Embrace your element,' he said quietly.

Then the sound of a lighter. It was the last thing in Hammond's life that wasn't pain.

Chapter Twenty-Two

Burton had seen the Channel 23 studio on television many, many times. His father used to watch Hammond's show in the evenings, and it was always playing in the police station rec room. In all that time, Burton had never thought of it as a real place. He knew that it was recorded somewhere, but as a casual viewer he had never bothered to imagine the reality of lights, cables, make-up artists, stress and sweat.

'So you have no idea, then?' he said, following Hammond's producer across the sound stage.

The producer, Jonathan Frank, was overweight and unhealthy-looking, but he moved fast. His head whipped around as he checked a dozen things simultaneously, all invisible to Burton. He pushed past a kid carrying a roll of cables and a man and a woman arguing over a clipboard. Up ahead, some men cleared a path through the crowd with a large camera that rolled silently and smoothly over the black polished floor. Through the gap, Burton saw Harvey Hammond's legendary desk, smaller and less impressive than it appeared on-screen.

'No,' said the producer, not looking back at Burton. 'Half the population of the country wanted to kill Hammond. Thirty-five million unhinged atheists and anti-signists.'

Burton looked at the tense crew around him. He didn't

know if it was like this every night, or if they were react-ing to Hammond's death. There was no mourning period for the *Tonite* crew.

They hadn't even seen the body. Burton had. The heat of the flames had partially melted the asphalt and Ham-mond's charred bones had been glued in place by the time he arrived on the scene. There were tyre tracks on the verge that matched the skid marks left outside Chief Wil-liams's house, most likely made by the same car that had taken Rachel Wells. And next to the body was a large Leo sign, marked out in scorched asphalt.

The channel already had a replacement lined up for Hammond, a young radio personality called Dick Aubrey, who was shriller and less tolerant than Hammond had ever been. He was in the dressing room, being prepped for an emotional show. From what Burton had seen, the plan was for Aubrey to spend the first five minutes weep-ing for the loss of his predecessor and the rest of the TV hour turning the tragedy into fury at the uncontrolled lower signs and the over-lenient policies of the president, who like all Sagittarians was a left-leaning social activist.

'So nothing specific?' said Burton. 'No threats that seemed out of the ordinary?'

'Look, Detective,' said Jonathan Frank, turning to Burton wearily. He had enough rings under his eyes to make his face look like a melting candle. 'We've all been affected by this. Everyone at Channel 23 has been won-dering who could have done it, and if we're next. Trust me, if anyone here had a good suspicion of who killed Harvey Hammond, we would have come to you. Can someone please replace those goddam rear lights?'

A gaffer in a Channel 23 T-shirt ran behind the stage and began unplugging cables.

'OK,' said Burton. 'If anyone thinks of anything else . . .'

'Yeah, yeah, we'll call you. Where's Aubrey? He's meant to be at his place. Clear the set! Dry run in five!'

'This way, sir,' said a man behind Burton. He had an earpiece and was sweating from the lights. He pointed Burton towards the soundproof exit doors of the studio.

Burton left the set along with a group of people from the lower rungs of the production – the interns and runners. The big door slammed shut after them, sealing off the studio.

He walked back along the corridors in the direction of the parking lot, thinking of who to try next. He had already spoken with Hammond's weeping wife and stone-faced adult son, and to the people from Hammond's production office – all his assistants, his secretary and the line manager. Everyone said the same thing. Hammond had a temper and he enjoyed provoking people on-screen, but he was a man of his convictions. Beyond the controversy he stirred up on his show, he had a moral code and no real enemies in his personal life. He believed in the rule of law. He used to run an educational charity. He believed it was his job to help fix the world. He was, they all said, one of the good guys.

Two men were coming down the corridor towards Burton, arguing with each other. The one in the lead was in his mid-twenties, wearing a black band T-shirt and carrying a box of printouts. The man behind him was older, in his forties. He was wearing an expensive-looking suit, but he had a slouched posture and he stammered anxiously.

'Please, Steve,' he said. 'I'm still . . . still on contract for the next five months.'

'Sorry, Jules,' said the younger man. 'Your contract was with *Hammond Tonite*, not Channel 23. *Hammond Tonite*'s over. It's a whole new show. You're going to have to renegotiate.'

The man in the suit tried to get ahead and block the younger man's path.

'But Harvey said I was valuable! I'm useful for the show!'

The younger man pushed past him. 'I don't know what to tell you. Take it up with Jonathan. Now get back to your desk, the rehearsal's starting.'

He continued down the corridor past Burton. The older man's mouth opened and closed in fury.

'Well, fuck you, Steve!' he shouted.

Steve didn't give any sign that he'd heard the outburst and walked off calmly. The man in the suit stormed after him, then closed his eyes and started berating himself.

'Fuck,' he said. 'Fuck!'

'Excuse me,' said Burton, walking past the man, trying not to get involved in whatever was happening. He took a few more steps down the corridor before the man called out to him.

'Hey! You're Burton, aren't you? You're Detective Burton!'

'That's me,' said Burton, still walking.

'Wait. I need to talk to you.'

Burton stopped and turned. The man scurried up to him, licking his upper lip anxiously.

'Has anyone spoken to you about the school?'

'No,' said Burton. 'What school?'

'The True Signs Academy. My brother's school. The one he set up for me.'

'Who's your brother?'

The man stared at Burton. 'Who do you think? Harvey Hammond! I'm Jules Hammond. You haven't heard about me?'

'I'm sorry,' said Burton. 'No one told me Hammond had a brother.'

For a moment it looked as if Jules would shout again. Instead, his shoulders slumped.

'Of course they wouldn't,' he said. 'Obviously.'

'What's this about a school?'

Jules Hammond looked up and down the corridor. No one was there, but he still dropped his voice to a whisper.

'I can't tell you about it now. Meet me after the show, at my house. I'll give you the address . . . hold on.'

He took a fountain pen out of his top pocket and wrote a street address on the back of one of his business cards.

'What time does the show end?' said Burton.

'Hmm? Oh, I get off at one a.m.'

'Can't we meet tomorrow?'

'No!' Jules snapped, as if the request was dumbfounding. 'No! It has to be tonight! I'm a busy man. And tomorrow could be too late for you.'

'For me?'

'See you tonight, Detective.'

Jules Hammond stormed back down the corridor to his office. When he was gone, Burton took out his phone and called Lindi Childs.

'Hey,' he said. 'Are you busy this evening? I might need your help with something.'

Burton didn't want to make her life harder, but Lindi had signed up for this case. She didn't realize what she was getting into.

'Sure,' she said. 'No plans. I was just going to watch a series.'

'Are you only into predictive astrology?' he said. 'How good are you with clinical conditions?'

'Hmm,' said Lindi. She sounded doubtful. 'I studied astropathology for my first couple of years. There was a practical component. I spent some time with the Astrological Care Unit.'

He looked down the corridor, to make sure Jules Hammond was out of earshot.

'Great. Do you think you could handle a Neo-Cap?' he said.

'That's tricky,' said Lindi. 'It depends. Probably.'

'Now here's the real question,' he said. 'How do you feel about working at one thirty?'

Chapter Twenty-Three

Daniel called the True Signs Academy repeatedly, but the number was permanently engaged. After the fifth call, he decided he had no choice but to go there in person. It was a half-hour drive in his rented car, parallel to the river, out past the billboards and malls and the suburbs that were spreading out into what had once been farmland. As he drove, he had a fantasy that he would get to the school and see his daughter in the playground. She would be halfway through a game with her friends, but she would look up and recognize him immediately. He would spread his arms and tell her that he was sorry. She would run to him and he would take her away from that place for good.

Or maybe it wouldn't be easy. Maybe he would come face to face with some stern authority figure, some sceptical principal or bureaucrat who would tell him that he couldn't take her. He almost hoped it could be that way, so he could face them down in righteous fury. He would prove himself as a father. He would fight for her, and win.

He turned off the highway on to the road leading to the school. As soon as he saw it, all his fantasies faded.

He parked outside the gates, walked up to the chain-link fence and held on to it for support. The school looked like it had once been a military base. There were long buildings with roofs of curved corrugated iron, and cracked asphalt between them. The flagpoles on either side of the entrance were bare and their ropes clinked against them in the wind. The strip of grass between the buildings and the fence was yellow and dry.

The gates were bolted. There were no cars parked outside. Some of the windows were broken and there was nothing visible through them but darkness. Leaves had blown through the gaps in the fence and were piled up at the side of the building, waist-high in places.

The school was abandoned. No one had been there for many, many months.

There would be no picture-perfect reunion with Pamela. The path had ended and now Daniel was helpless. She wasn't there and he had no idea where to look next.

Chapter Twenty-Four

When Burton was sixteen years old he discovered that one of his school friends, a boy called Colin, was a pathological liar. Colin had been smart and charming, and his lies had built up so slowly that no one had questioned them. He read a lot and always had something interesting to say. He claimed that his father worked in special effects and that his older brother was a war reporter. He told his friends that he could get them all cheap tickets to see the Fists of Heaven concert because his uncle was their manager, and it didn't seem unlikely because Colin's family were all so great. He brought a small bundle of tickets to school and swapped them for whatever people would give. Some of his friends paid a few dollars, others gave him their lunch or let him borrow their homework. Burton gave Colin his skateboard, which he wasn't really using any more.

On the evening of the concert Burton's father dropped him off in the parking lot, where he met up with all his other friends. They waited in line, shouting, joking and showing off to the passing girls. When they got to the front of the line the ticket collector stopped them.

'What are these?' he said, pointing at their tickets.

'You really know your job, don't you?' said Burton sarcastically, thinking he was being clever.

'These aren't real tickets,' said the collector. 'That's what the tickets look like.'

He pointed to a bundle on the counter next to him. All his tickets were made of thin card and had a silver strip. They were covered in fine green lines like a banknote, to make them hard to copy. The tickets Colin had given them were paper, black and white, and printed on just one side.

'These are real,' Burton insisted. 'They must be special. They're from the Fists of Heaven's manager. He'll tell you. Call him!'

'They're fake,' said the collector. 'Next.'

He pushed Burton aside with the back of his arm and turned his attention to the next people in the line.

'Hey!' said Burton. 'We're not done!'

Burton stood his ground until a security guard came and led him and his friends away. They stood in the parking lot, swearing about the stupid ticket collector and the security guard and deciding what to do next. Colin had promised that he'd be coming and Burton was sure that once he was there he'd be able to sort out the whole situation.

So they waited. The minutes crept into hours. The music started playing and the crowd inside the stadium roared. Burton and his friends got more and more frustrated. One of them tried to sneak in a side entrance and was caught by security. He got an elbow in the cheek as they dragged him away and ended up with a black eye. Eventually Burton admitted defeat and went to find a payphone to call his father.

But still, even as the friends waited for rescue, none of them wanted to admit what had just happened. It was a misunderstanding. The tickets were real, but probably just a kind that the ticket collector hadn't seen before because they came straight from the manager. Or there was some mix-up backstage. Colin's uncle would sort it out. Colin was a Taurus, like them, and everyone knew that Tauruses were loyal. Admitting that Colin was a liar would mean admitting that they had been profoundly wrong, and not just about him.

That Monday, Colin wasn't at school. He was back on Wednesday, saying that he had been kidnapped. He spun a detailed story about being ambushed on Friday and put on a train but outwitting his captors just before the border. Of course, in reality, Colin had run away from home. His parents were embarrassed. The other parents, and then the school, stepped in. There were closed-door meetings. Colin was suspended and sent for astrological evaluation. He never came back to Burton's school.

When Burton couldn't deny that Colin was a liar any longer, it broke something inside him. He lost his sense of trust and his faith in close friendships. He approached both strangers and friends with far more caution. He wasn't a pack animal any more.

But the situation with Colin also had another, long-lasting, paradoxical effect. Burton stopped believing that anyone else would trust him. He never felt comfortable unless he could prove himself. He didn't brag and he didn't lie. He never wanted to be doubted. He didn't fabricate evidence or fake his testimony in court, even when it was the only way to secure a conviction. And he definitely didn't cheat on Kate.

'I know how it sounds,' he said to her.

He was sitting at the computer table in the living room.

Kate was standing at the doorway with her belly bulging from the front of her dressing gown. She was wearing a white T-shirt, stretched tight enough for Burton to see her belly button poking out.

'A clandestine meeting that includes a new female co-worker, at a mysterious house in the middle of the night?' she said. 'How does that sound?'

Burton rubbed his forehead.

'It's not like that. We're dealing with a loon. I need her help.'

'I'm teasing,' she said. She came behind him and put her hands on his shoulders, letting her weight rest on him. 'When will you be back?'

'As soon as I can. Two thirty? Three?'

'OK. Try not to wake me when you come in.'

She went through to the bedroom and he heard the wooden frame squeak as she got into bed. After a while, the bedside light clicked off.

He worked at the computer until twelve thirty, reading articles about Hammond and Williams. When it was time he headed out, being careful not to slam the front door.

He drove to Shoredell, a niceish district just east of the city centre. All the houses were old, mostly three storeys high. At first glance it looked like any other upper-middle-class area, with its fancy cars parked on the side of the street. But there were hints that this wasn't a classic Sagittarius or Aquarius neighbourhood. None of the buildings were being renovated with wider windows. There were no edgy yet artistic murals, or theatres, or posters advertising gallery openings. This was a place where rich people came to live alone.

There was also hardly any parking. Burton found a space a block away from Jules Hammond's apartment and walked the rest of the way on foot. The lights were on in the third-floor windows and Burton could see the movement of someone pacing inside. He sighed inwardly and went to the entrance.

Apartment six on the third floor had a navy-blue door. Burton knocked and Jules opened it. Immediately, Burton was hit by the overpowering smell of cat litter.

'Come in,' said Jules.

The inside of the apartment was dim. There were elegant ceiling-mounted light rails, but most of the bulbs in them had blown and not been replaced. The room was mainly bare. One wall was covered in a large framed black-and-white print of a seascape and opposite it was a long white couch covered in cat scratches. The only other object in the room was an uncleaned litter tray in the corner. It was a curiously expensive kind of squalor. Scratchy jazz music was playing from somewhere else in the apartment.

Lindi had arrived ahead of Burton and was standing by the window with her arms folded.

'Hi!' she said, rather too brightly. She was wearing a chunky jacket and her reading glasses. 'I have to be up at seven. Just so you know.'

Jules closed the door behind Burton.

'I've just met my unexpected guest,' he said, looking at Lindi. His tone was reprimanding.

'Lindi Childs is a consultant on the case,' said Burton. 'I thought it would be useful if she was present.'

Jules clucked disapprovingly. 'Very well.'

He sat down on the sofa, without offering either of the others a seat. An old white cat came in from one of the apartment's inner doors, stretched and jumped up on to his lap.

'I know why there was that Taurus sign next to Williams,' he said. 'And I'll bet there was a Leo sign burned on the road next to my brother's body, am I right?'

Burton and Lindi looked at each other.

'None of that information was made available to the public.'

Burton was suddenly aware that he could be in the same room as the killer. It would make sense if the murders were committed by a crazed Neo-Cap, and Jules fitted the profile. Burton had informed dispatch of this meeting, so the other cops would know where to look if he and Lindi went missing. It wasn't an immediate comfort, though.

Jules nodded. 'I work for a news channel, Detective. We found out about the Taurus sign on the first day. And I'm pretty sure I know what it means.'

'Something to do with a school?' said Burton.

Jules's leg started jiggling. The cat jumped off him and went to rub against Burton, who was allergic. He ignored it.

'You've heard about my brother's educational charity? Achievers Unlimited?'

Burton nodded. 'It's to help disadvantaged children, isn't it?'

'No,' said Jules. 'No!' he said again, louder. 'It was for me!'

'Why?' said Lindi.

Jules looked over at her, irritated.

'Because I'm a fucking Neo-Cap, obviously!' he said. 'I was born a Capricorn to Leo parents. A big family embarrassment! All the bad qualities of a Capricorn, with none of the lineage. And, of course, everyone accused them of being social climbers.'

'So they sent you to special schools.'

'That's right. And when my brother became famous, he used his influence to set up the charity to fund the kinds of schools I was going to, for children born under different signs from their parents. As their major source of income, he could tell them to keep my existence quiet. Had either of you heard of me?'

They looked at each other again.

'No,' Jules nodded. 'Exactly.'

'OK, sorry,' said Lindi, 'but what does that have to do with the Taurus and Leo symbols?'

Jules's agitation increased. He got to his feet and started pacing.

'There was one school my brother helped set up. It was the big one, run by Harvey's university friend Werner Kruger.'

'The astrologer?' said Lindi.

Burton saw her eyes lighting up. He raised an eyebrow at her.

'Sorry,' she said. 'I did my thesis on his theory of resonance in the essential dignities. I've read pretty much everything he's done . . .'

'He had ideas,' said Jules, wincing slightly. 'A big part of his education programme was getting the students to behave more like their own signs so they'd fit better into society. He tried all sorts of things to get us to connect with what he called our cosmic essence. But I don't think he was only there to educate us.'

'What was he doing?' Burton asked.

Jules Hammond looked out of the window. The moon had just begun to rise over the central city.

'He was experimenting,' he said.

Chapter Twenty-Five

A year after he met the Scarsdales, Daniel was still watching videos. It was all he ever did any more. He sat on his couch in his father's mansion and watched tape after tape from morning until evening. It had taken a court order to make the Achievers Unlimited charity hand them over, and even then only after his lawyers had butted heads with a very reluctant judge.

Daniel watched the tapes in fast forward, searching for the familiar face. It was endless footage from surveillance cameras in corridors, classes and interview rooms. Somewhere, at some point in time, there must have been incident sheets that could guide Daniel to specific moments, but if they ever existed they were shredded long before he got a chance to see them.

The videos were piled up in the delivery crate. He watched them all, stacking the worthless ones on the hardwood coffee table and keeping any that showed his daughter on the floor next to him.

The first tape he watched was her enrolment interview. She was fourteen and her face had lost most of its childish roundness since the birthday tape. Her jaw was narrow and she reminded Daniel of his own mother. Her cheeks were pink. The camera pointed straight at her, and the wall behind her was a light institutional green.

'Could you say your name and sign, please,' said a man's voice from off-screen.

'Why?' said Pamela, glaring at the unseen interviewer. Her shoulders were bunched up near her ears, making her look like a trapped animal.

'This is just for the record.'

'I don't want to be here,' she said. 'I told you! I want my real dad!'

'Well, you are here, so it's best to make the most of it,' said the voice calmly.

'This is a mistake. I need to talk to my grandma.'

'Of course you do, and you will be allowed to once you're ready. But first you need to work with us. Do you want to work with us?'

Pamela didn't answer. She looked down and Daniel could see she was gritting her teeth.

'OK,' said the voice after a while. 'Let's try again. Once we're done here you can go through to the cafeteria. I'm sure you're hungry by now. What's your name and sign?'

'Pamela Scarsdale. Pisces,' she said defiantly.

'Good,' said the voice. It had a sing-song lilt, as if it was praising a dog for doing a trick. 'And tell me what being a Pisces means to you.'

'What?' said Pamela, disbelieving. 'It doesn't mean anything. It's just, like, the people I grew up with and whatever. Look, this is fucked up. I was trying to find my dad. It was a mistake, OK? Can I just go? I'll leave him alone. Just please. I want to get out of here!'

'Pamela, stay calm. Donald Lapton has placed you in our care. Do you know who Donald Lapton is?'

Pamela paused and then nodded.

'He says that he will acknowledge that you are his granddaughter, just like you wanted, and you can meet your real father, but he wants to take responsibility for your education first. Isn't that good?'

Pamela looked around helplessly.

'I . . . I dunno. What's going on?'

'He wants what's best for you and he wants to make sure that you get the education most suitable for your sign. That's why he sent you to us. Once you're educated, you can take your part in your new family and in society as a whole. Isn't that what you want?'

Pamela looked very doubtful.

'Maybe. I don't know!'

'All right, then,' said the voice. 'So let's work together. What does being Pisces mean to you?'

'We're, like, the normal people,' said Pamela. 'We're not uptight or weird or anything, like Aries or Capricorns. Just normal.'

The next five videos in Daniel's stack had only brief flashes of Pamela. He caught her walking down hallways in her new school uniform. There were long stretches of her sitting in class while teachers mumbled on about plate tectonics and the passive voice. The next big moment came on another interview tape. Again, the camera was pointed at Pamela's face. It was date-stamped a few months later, and her hair was brushed straight back and tied in a ponytail. She was wearing a white blouse with a tie and a dark green school blazer with a Pisces badge pinned to her breast pocket. There was a glass bowl next to her, half-full of water. Ice cubes were floating on its surface.

'So, Pamela,' said the voice off-screen. It was a woman this time. 'Imagine you're on a bus. You've been walking and your feet are sore. Another girl gets on board. She's your age and she's walking with a limp. There are no other free seats on the bus. What do you do?'

Pamela scratched her nose.

'Mind my own business, I guess. Someone else will get up for her.'

'No, you wouldn't,' said the voice. It sounded impatient.

'Yeah, well, you asked,' said Pamela. She had a half-smile, as if she thought the interviewer was joking.

'No,' said the interviewer. 'You are Pisces, so you are empathetic. Her pain outweighs yours. You would stand.'

'But she could be faking it,' said Pamela. 'And I know my own feet. If no one stands after a bit I'll get up, or I'll scootch over and let her sit next to me. But I'm not going to leap to my feet for a stranger.'

'It would be easier for you and everyone around you if you did,' said the voice sharply. 'What's our motto?'

'True Signs in Harmony,' Pamela said, rolling her eyes.

'That's right,' said the voice. 'True Signs in Harmony. There will never be peace in society until we stop fighting against our true natures. So. When the limping girl comes on to the bus, what do you do?'

'I get up and give her my seat.'

Pamela was clearly bored and was playing along to get it over with.

'That's good,' said the voice. 'Now. Take the bowl of water.'

Pamela dragged the bowl in front of her. The water sloshed, but didn't spill over the rim.

'Put your hands into the bowl.'

Pamela hesitated, but obeyed. She winced.

'Ow.'

'We've found that this works best with iced water,' said the voice. 'The discomfort makes the lesson more memorable. Now close your eyes and picture the Pisces symbol.'

Pamela closed her eyes tight.

'Are you picturing it clearly?'

Pamela nodded. From her expression, the cold wasn't getting any more bearable.

'Move your hands through the water in the shape of the Pisces symbol.'

Pamela splashed the water.

'Gently!' said the voice.

Pamela slowed down, moving her hands in two arcs through the water, joining in the centre and parting, again and again. The tension gradually left her face. Daniel guessed that her hands were becoming numb.

'Feel yourself flowing through the water,' said the voice. It had become slow and soothing, almost hypnotic. 'You are Pisces. Water is your element. You are water. You flow through the world and it flows through you. Embrace your element.'

Pamela kept moving her hands. Arcing in, touching, parting. Arcing in, touching, parting.

'Are you embracing your element?' said the voice.

'Yes.'

'Good. Now picture yourself on the bus again. You're surrounded by people. The doors hiss open. There's the girl. She's your age. She's limping. What do you?'

'I stand up.'

'Are you picturing yourself standing up and moving aside for her? Are you doing it?'

'Yes,' said Pamela.

Daniel couldn't tell if she was still just playing along or if she was serious.

'Doesn't it feel better than fighting your true nature?'

'Yes.'

'Good. Now imagine someone pushes in front of you in a line. What do you do?'

The next few tapes in Daniel's pile were just more corridor and classroom footage. Months of it. Daniel fast-forwarded through most of them, catching brief moments here and there. Pamela seemed to have a few friends, all with the same Pisces symbol on their blazers. They walked together between classes and seemed to be having minor feuds with girls of other signs.

He watched a video of Pamela's art class. Rows of Pisces students were lined up with easels in front of them. All they were allowed to draw was the Pisces symbol, again and again and again.

'This is calligraphy as the expression of the soul,' said the art teacher. 'Don't worry if you get bored. If you do an action enough times you wear away all thought, until what's left is pure motion, pure essence.'

Many of her other classes were equally single-minded and strange. In one of them, she was alone in a small room with plastic sheeting on the ground. She had a bowl of water crooked under her left arm.

'All right, Pamela,' said her instructor. 'Dunk your right hand into the water and then let your arm hang down. Let the water drip from your fingers and swing your arm gently so it makes a Pisces sign on the ground.'

'What's this for?'

'It's for biomotive alignment,' said the instructor. 'Think of it like a special dance class.'

Pamela dipped her hand in the water and flicked her fingers at the ground.

'No,' said the instructor. 'Gently. Flow like the water.'

Pamela dipped her hand again and flopped it over the ground. The water dripped into the rough shape of a Pisces symbol.

The instructor nodded happily. 'Very good. Now keep going until there's no more water. And keep that gentle flowing motion. Embrace your element.'

The strange and pointless lessons went on for months. Then, one lunch break, Pamela got attacked.

It was caught on the black-and-white camera in the cafeteria, which had poor sound and a low frame rate. Pamela had collected a tray of food and was walking between the rows of tables, which were separated by sign. As she passed one of the Cancer tables, an overweight blonde girl threw a glass of juice at her back.

'Embrace your element!'

Pamela dropped her tray. Her glass shattered and her plate rolled away across the cafeteria floor. Students from the other signs turned to look and the other Cancer girls laughed.

Daniel was proud of Pamela's reaction. She grabbed the girl who attacked her by the arm, but didn't fight.

'Apologize!' she said firmly.

The Cancer girl seemed taken by surprise.

'Apologize now!'

Pamela was firm and kept her eyes locked on the girl's face. She was enraged but in control of herself. The tittering died down.

'You bitches started it!' said the Cancer girl. 'I heard what you said!'

The cafeteria door swung open. Standing in the doorway was a tall, thin man. He wore glasses and his hair and suit were dark.

'No fighting!' he bellowed. 'What's going on here?'

'She threw juice at me!' said Pamela.

The man strode up to the girls and pushed them apart.

'True Signs in Harmony!' he said. 'Christina, what are the characteristics of Cancer?'

Christina, the Cancer girl, hung her head.

'Sorry, Dr Kruger.'

'I asked you a question.'

Christina struggled to find her voice.

'Cancers are . . . nurturing. Cancers are adaptable. Cancers are dependable.'

'And is this nurturing behaviour?'

'No, Dr Kruger,' said Christina, on the point of tears.

Kruger turned his furious gaze on Pamela.

'And you. What were you doing with your hands on Christina? That is not how Pisces interact with Cancers!'

Daniel saw Christina take the opportunity to back away.

'Pisces do not engage in personal conflict,' said Kruger. 'Never. Is that understood?'

'But how do I defend myself, sir?'

'You don't!' said Kruger. 'That's what the other signs are for. Where were the Leos?'

He looked around the room. A table of Leos looked sheepish.

'Their instinct is to defend you. If you don't back down, you're not letting them step up. By fighting back, you're not only betraying your own true nature, you're denying them the opportunity to find themselves! Now you and Christina can both go to the Water Room.'

'Dr Kruger —' said Pamela.

'Now!'

The two girls left the cafeteria, Christina with her head hanging in shame and Pamela with her shoulders hunched in anger. Kruger looked around the room at all the staring faces.

'That's that,' he said. 'Back to your food.'

He stayed in the centre of the room until everyone was eating again. When he was sure that calm was restored, he came to the corner of the room and looked directly into the camera.

'Did you see?' he said to the unseen watchers. 'Very interesting dynamics in the expression of elemental energy. Recreate that in the four quadrants and note the results. Very interesting indeed.'

Next video.

It was another interview. There was one with Christina before it, but Daniel fast-forwarded. He wanted to see his daughter.

The camera was pointing at her face again. It looked like she hadn't slept. Her eyes wandered around the interview room distractedly.

'Pamela! Please focus.' It was Kruger's voice.

'Hmm? Sorry,' she said, slurring.

'Are you ready for your test?'

'I guess.' Pamela blinked slowly. 'Why did you keep me in that room?'

'We isolate you for your own good, Pamela,' said Kruger. 'Being alone with yourself gives you the opportunity to find your true nature. Did you enjoy the Water Room?'

'It's horrible. I just wanted someone to talk to.'

'The longer you're apart from people, the more you realize you need them and the more willing you'll be to fall in to your proper place.'

Kruger's voice was infuriatingly calm and reasonable.

'Now, are you ready for your next test?' he asked again.

Pamela looked at Kruger off-screen. Her eyes were bleary. After a moment, she nodded.

'Good. So, someone in your class gets full marks in a test, but you find out they were cheating. What do you do?'

And then more footage from the corridors. There were months of it. And another fight. Daniel couldn't make this one out – the corridor cameras had no audio and only took one frame a second. Pamela was walking down the corridor one way and a group of Capricorn girls was walking the other. One of them said something as they passed and Pamela said something back. The girls stopped and turned. There was an exchange. And then, suddenly, Pamela was on top of one of the girls. This time she wasn't holding back. She brought her fist back and punched, again and again. The girl dropped to the ground. Pamela kicked. The other Capricorns piled in, pushing her backwards into the wall. A teacher came down the corridor. Pamela was led away and the Capricorns kept walking.

Pamela's next appearance in the corridors was two

weeks later. She was wearing an apron and was down on her knees, scrubbing the floor.

That went on for a month.

After her punishment was over, Daniel saw Pamela back in her uniform, but things had changed. Her friends weren't walking with her between classes any more and Daniel had a hard time spotting her in the footage. She walked with her head down, not making eye contact with anyone she passed.

Finally there was another interview and Daniel got to see and hear his daughter again. This one was different, though. The camera was placed side-on, showing Pamela at a table and two adults sitting opposite her. One was Dr Kruger, the other was a woman with grey permed hair and glasses.

Pamela looked much thinner. Her uniform hung loose on her body. There were rings under her eyes and her jaw looked more pronounced.

'Don't worry about this, Pamela,' said Kruger. 'You're not in trouble. We're just having these meetings with all the students who have been in their element rooms on a regular basis. It's just to see how you've been doing.'

Pamela stared down at the table's surface and said nothing.

'We've been watching your behaviour and you've been doing wonderfully,' said the woman.

'Thank you.' Her eyes stayed down.

'We're concerned that you haven't been eating,' said Kruger, tapping his pen on the table.

'Thank you for your concern,' she said politely, and Daniel, watching, gripped the leather arm of the sofa in fury.

'I'm going to ask you to finish everything on your plate from now on, all right?'

'All right.'

'And even if it's hard, I'd really appreciate it if you ate every last bite. We'll be checking.'

'Yes, Dr Kruger,' said Pamela.

'How are you finding your lessons? Are you keeping up?'

'Yes, Dr Kruger.'

'Good. Thank you. You can go now. Send the next one in.'

Pamela got quietly to her feet and walked out of the room. The woman with the perm leaned in closer to Kruger.

'What do you think?' she said.

'I think she's made great progress,' said Kruger. 'No displays of aggression or egocentrism in months.'

'But her health?'

'I'll have the nurse take a look at her,' said Kruger. 'It's probably just a bug. Mentally, she's doing superbly. A textbook Pisces. It's probably not worth even looking at the rest of the Pisces, to be honest. They're in touch with their emotions. Problems will be easy to spot now that they're properly aligned. We should be looking more closely at the Geminis.'

And then there was only one unwatched tape in the crate. Daniel knew what was on it. For the last nine months, he had known how the story would end. It wouldn't be a surprise. But he had to see it for himself.

It was corridor footage again. Black and white, and one frame a second.

His daughter walked to her dormitory, alone. She went in and the door swung shut behind her.

Then a cut to black for three seconds. There was a new time stamp when the corridor reappeared. It was one hour later.

A group of Pisces students were also walking to the dormitory. They were talking to each other and laughing. They pushed open the door and went inside.

For twenty seconds, the corridor was empty. Daniel balled his fists and held them to his face.

One of the girls ran out of the dormitory, the slow frame rate making her movement jerky. There was no sound on the tape, but Daniel could see she was screaming. She ran away down the corridor.

The other two girls ran out behind her.

The first girl ran back, leading a supervisor.

Cut to black. A new time stamp. Forty minutes later.

A team of paramedics stormed down the corridor and into the dormitory, carrying crates of medical gear and a stretcher between them.

Five agonizing minutes. Daniel didn't fast-forward. He didn't want to move.

The paramedics came back out of the dormitory, much slower, carrying a body bag on the stretcher.

Cut to black. End of tape.

Chapter Twenty-Six

'Three girls died,' said Jules. 'One after the other. The school closed for good a few weeks later and I went back to a specialist care facility. That was ten years ago.'

'How did the girls die?' said Burton.

'Suicide. There was an investigation and everyone involved was cleared. They said it was one of those things where one kid does something and the others just copy it.'

Lindi pushed her glasses up her nose. 'Why isn't this better known?' she said.

'Oh, it was in the papers, but it was news one day and then it wasn't. I suppose Kruger was well respected and above reproach, and no one wanted to exploit the tragedy. And, of course, a lot of people who gave money to the Achievers Unlimited charity were wealthy. They didn't want their names associated with a public disaster, so the school was quietly closed and the police investigation was conducted sensitively. Nothing really came out of it. The whole thing just evaporated.'

'OK,' said Burton. 'So why all this secrecy? Why are we meeting after midnight?'

'Channel 23 doesn't like me saying anything negative about my brother or his actions, or anything which might tar the channel's name,' said Jules. 'And I had to tell you tonight so that you'd have a head start. You'll need it after what Aubrey's trying to pull on you, am I right? I'm on your side. Fellow black sheep. Or black ram . . . ? You know, after everything, Harvey was still my brother, and he was burned to death – oh, my God, he was burned to death . . .'

Jules's babbling petered out and he stared at the wall, lost in thought. Burton was thankful. He only understood about half of what Jules was saying.

'Would you be willing to testify about this in court?' he said.

Jules snapped back to reality. 'Oh, no, please,' he said. 'Not unless it's absolutely necessary.'

That was all right, thought Burton. Jules wouldn't do well on the stand. His mental health issues were obvious.

'OK,' said Burton. 'So, then, thank you for everything. It's greatly appreciated.'

He walked to Jules a little unsteadily and offered him his hand. Shit, he was exhausted. He didn't know how he was going to handle staying up all night to look after a child. He guessed he'd have to adapt.

'You're more than welcome,' said Jules, shaking Burton's hand vigorously. 'I'm almost surprised that you came, considering. I hope this makes us even.'

Burton pulled his hand away.

'Even? For what?'

Jules's smile dropped from his face.

'You know. For my part in tonight's show. I'm a researcher, after all.'

Lindi looked from one of them to the other.

'Mr Hammond?' she said. 'What was on the show?'

'Neither of you saw it?' he said, and shook his head. 'Oh dear. If you'd seen it, you'd know why no one was allowed to talk to you.'

'What was on the show?' said Burton, getting angry.

'Aubrey wanted to start with a bang,' said Jules. He picked up a plastic pouch of cat food from the window-sill, tore off the corner and squeezed the meat until it slopped out into a bowl by the litter tray.

'He went on the attack,' he said. 'He got personal. Really personal.'

Chapter Twenty-Seven

Burton got back home half an hour later. He opened the front door quietly and turned on the lamp on the living-room desk, leaving most of the room in darkness. He found the remote on the couch and switched on the TV, quickly turning down the volume until it was barely audible.

It didn't take long to find the *Aubrey Tonite* episode on the DVR and load it up. He half-watched, half-skimmed the episode. It was a big thing for Aubrey to be taking over the show. Hammond had been an institution, so Aubrey had to put his own stamp on it. He had to out-Hammond Hammond. The episode started with a eulogy, with #HammondForever appearing in the bottom-right corner, then for the next forty-five minutes Aubrey tore into everyone he thought was responsible for the murder. That included Bram Coine, Solomon Mahout, the Aries Rising movement, the liberals, the president, the SCPD and Detective Jerome Burton.

'Solomon Mahout and his idiot followers in Aries Rising are bad enough, but at least we expect them to try to tear down society. They're loud and proud about it. What blows my mind is how much the police are dragging their feet. The police, who are meant to be on the side of law-abiding citizens. You'd think they'd pull the finger out of their orifices to get justice for one of their own, their own beloved Chief, but I guess that when you get down to it, they're just government employees like all the rest. Bureaucrats, am I right? Or maybe there's something more sinister going on.'

An unflattering photograph of Burton came up on-screen showing him getting out of his car in front of the station. He hadn't even known the photograph was being taken.

'This is Detective Jerome Burton of the SCPD's Homicide Department. He's been handling the murder investigations of Williams and Hammond since day one. He's a Taurus, he's married, he's a hard worker with a good record. So why's he taking so much time with this case?'

There was the sound of movement behind Burton. He looked around to see Kate coming out from the bedroom, eyes half-closed, with a fluffy blanket over her shoulders.

'Jerry?' she said. 'What is it?'

On-screen, the camera cut back to Aubrey at his desk. He looked uncomfortable on camera, but was covering it with bombast.

'It could be a tough case, but maybe it's because his Taurus bona fides aren't what they seem. Our researchers at *Aubrey Tonite* have been looking into Detective Burton for a while, probably a little harder than he's been looking into the murder investigations, and what they found is pretty shocking. Burton was born in Liberty Hospital in north San Celeste. Now you may recognize that name. It's where the notorious Dr Suarez practised his trade.'

A new picture came up, this time a black-and-white photograph of a man in a polo-neck sweater being led towards a police van in handcuffs.

'Suarez, as many of you will remember, was arrested

thirty years ago for faking hundreds of birth certificates, so that children would appear to have been born in the same sign as their parents.'

It cut back to Aubrey, on a tighter zoom this time.

'Now, to be fair, it's not certain that he performed this service for Detective Burton's parents, but let's look at the facts.'

A scan of some hospital records came up on-screen. They zoomed in slowly as names and dates were highlighted by graphics.

'Burton's mother went into labour several days prematurely. She was admitted to hospital on 17 April, which is in Aries. Yet Burton is recorded as having been born on the 21st, four days later . . . in Taurus, like his parents. And the signature on the birth certificate? Dr Theo Suarez.'

Aubrey came back on the screen, looking directly into the camera.

'It's possible that Burton's delivery took four days. However, I don't know about you folks, but when I hear that the investigation of the murders of two of the most staunch defenders against the Aries menace is being conducted by someone who may well be an Aries impostor, all I can say is, God help us. We'll be back with final thoughts after these messages. Don't go anywhere.'

'Bullshit,' said Burton. 'That's complete bullshit.'

His hands trembled. Kate took the remote from him and turned off the television halfway through a commercial for buying gold online.

'I know,' she said. 'I know my Jerry.'

They held each other silently in the half-darkened room.

Chapter Twenty-Eight

The Plow Tavern was on a grimy side street three blocks away from San Celeste Central Police Station. It had once been a mechanic's garage, but had been bought up and converted by an ex-cop a few decades before. The Plow was the venue of choice for police officers who wanted to unwind while steering clear of civilians or meaningful conversation. The bar was wood-panelled, covered in bottles and knick-knacks. There was a pool table and a row of comfortable booths at the back. Classic rock played from midday onwards, loud enough to keep the customers drinking but not so loud as to drive them away. Even so, there was something about the place that still felt like a garage. It had no real ceiling, just strip lighting hanging down from the metal frame under a corrugated-aluminum roof. It was impossible to hear anything inside when it rained. There was a concrete column in the middle of the room that was scratched by the marks of a dozen careless drivers. The regulars told the owner that they liked the place that way. They said it felt real.

Daniel Lapton's chauffeur pulled up outside and turned on the hazards.

'Wait for me here,' said Daniel.

The chauffeur nodded, keeping his head forward. He was new and someone must have given him instructions not to be chatty. Daniel took a deep breath, checked the tape recorder in his pocket and got out of the car.

There was no sign to advertise the tavern, just the neon word 'OPEN' and a pair of rusty brackets above it that had once held up a real antique plow. The last of the daylight had drained from the clouds over the city and the wind was blowing in from the north. Daniel appreciated the burst of warmth as he came in through the tavern's sprung front entrance.

A few heads turned as he entered. As far as Daniel could tell there was no maliciousness in anyone's eyes, he was just a moving object in the drunk patrons' field of view. He spotted Detective Peter Williams, who was sitting at a table of bulky cops with black shirts and crew cuts. Williams saw Daniel coming and grabbed one of the men on the upper arm.

'Hold up,' he said. 'I've got some business.'

'Sure you do,' said the man, and mimed sucking a cock. The others laughed.

'Hilarious,' said Williams, deadpan. 'See you in a second.'

He picked up a half-finished beer from the table and beckoned for Daniel to follow him to one of the booths at the back of the bar.

'Hey, buddy!' shouted one of the blackshirts. 'Don't forget to tickle Williams's balls!'

Another peal of laughter. Williams gave them the finger.

'Who're they?' said Daniel, as they sat down in the overstuffed leather seats.

'The Ram Squad,' said Williams. 'They're the new

SWAT team that's just been assigned to Ariesville. Bringing it under control, at last.'

'They look like assholes.'

'Well, they have to go into a war zone every day,' said Williams. 'So I cut them some slack. What can I do for you?'

Daniel could see Williams was holding his head too steady, pretending to be sober. He was definitely too drunk to notice Daniel put his hand in his pocket to turn on the tape recorder. Daniel had arranged this meeting with him under the pretence of being one of the donors for the now-closed True Signs Academy, which, it turns out, wasn't completely untrue. His family had made significant donations to Harvey Hammond's educational charity. Williams thought that Daniel was there to grill him and make sure that the scandal wouldn't be coming back to haunt them.

'I wanted to know as much as possible about what happened at True Signs,' said Daniel.

Williams blinked slowly. 'It's all in my report.'

'I wanted to hear it from you and see if there's anything you missed.'

Williams took a gulp of his beer and wiped his moustache with the back of his forearm.

'I want to assure you, from my point of view, the school did nothing wrong,' he said. 'Yes, it looks bad. But True Signs did everything right. They weren't ignoring those kids' needs. All three girls who died were unbalanced! The school did everything they could to help them. They were all already getting ongoing counselling with some of the best astrologers in the country. And after the first suicide, they immediately started counselling sessions for everyone else, particularly the ones that the teachers and administrators thought were vulnerable.'

'Why didn't they close the place down after the first suicide?' said Daniel.

It had been a girl called Emma Pescowski. Virgo. Addicted to painkillers.

'They did as much as they could. And they couldn't exactly send the rest of the kids home, could they? Where would they go?'

He finished his beer and burped discreetly. He didn't seem to notice Daniel's white-knuckled hand on the edge of the table.

'What about the abuse?' said Daniel.

'What abuse?'

'Solitary confinement. Sleep deprivation.'

'The judge ruled that nothing they did there crossed the line.'

'Based on your evidence!'

Daniel realized he was being too loud. The blackshirts glanced over to the booth. Williams raised a hand to show them everything was all right, then leaned in closer to Daniel.

'I didn't see any abuse,' he said. 'I'll tell you what I saw. I saw a school dealing with some of the most difficult students in the country and trying out new ideas to unbreak this city. It was necessary. And you know what, it was brave, especially with all these politically correct Aquarians and Sagittarians calling everything signist.'

Williams must have realized that Daniel wasn't coming here to pat him on the back. He rolled his empty glass from hand to hand and looked down into it sourly. 'It was a good school,' he said, almost to himself.

'Would you send your kids to a place like that?' said Daniel.

Williams sneered. 'I'll never need to. Any kid I have will be a pure Taurus. I'm not one of these idiots who doesn't know how to use contraception or a calendar. You want the truth? It doesn't matter what anyone thinks about that place. It did what it needed to do.'

'And what was that?'

'It kept a bunch of glue-sniffing cuckoos off the street.'

Daniel's fist flew up from the edge of the table into Williams's face. He did it before he could control himself. Williams looked shocked, but his reactions were quick. He flung himself across the table and grabbed Daniel's wrists.

'You'll have to come at me much harder than that,' he said, baring his teeth.

Daniel struggled, but Williams held on tight.

'Let go!'

A sharp blow glanced off the side of Daniel's head and his vision sparked. One of the black-shirted cops had thrown a bottle and the rest were pushing away from their table and coming his way.

'Fucking rich boy!' yelled the biggest one, who had a piggy face and a flat-topped crew cut. He grabbed Daniel by his lapels and hauled him out of the booth. Self-preservation told Daniel to curl up and protect himself. He was weak, outnumbered and inexperienced. Instead, rage and adrenalin took control of his limbs.

He surprised himself by punching Flat-top hard under

the chin. His head snapped backwards and he let go of Daniel to grab his mouth, which was suddenly red with blood. Daniel fell to the ground and his head cracked on the wooden dividing screen between two of the booths. Instantly, the blackshirts' boots were kicking him in the neck, ribs and sides of his leg. As he reached down to the tape recorder, his face was exposed for a kick to the cheek-bone. He heard the bone crunch and felt an explosion of agony.

'That's enough,' said Williams. 'He's a Capricorn.'

'I don't give a fuck,' said one of the blackshirts.

More kicks, aimed just under the ribs. Daniel finally gave in and curled up, twisting himself to block the constant blows. A boot came down on his arm, pinning it to the ground, and another got him in the belly. He croaked for breath. The rock music was still playing. A man wailing about his lost love, to the sound of squealing guitars.

There was the clunk of the tavern door opening and a familiar-sounding voice shouted, 'Gentlemen!'

The kicking stopped.

'Who the fuck are you?' said one of the blackshirts.

'I'm here to collect my client.'

Daniel looked up at the figure in the doorway through a bruised, swollen eye. It was Hamlin. He was in a light-coloured suit and looked like he had just stepped out of the UrSec boardroom. Behind him were two of his men. Hamlin's hands were down and spread, showing he was unarmed but unintimidated. Daniel had no idea what he was doing there.

'I'm afraid your client just assaulted two police officers,' said Williams, folding his arms.

'And resisted arrest,' said Flat-top. He nudged Daniel's bruised, curled-up body with the tip of his boot.

'That's unfortunate,' said Hamlin mildly. 'Still, I'm glad you managed to get the situation under control.'

He looked around the room as if he was coming to a decision.

'Who did he assault?'

'Me,' said Detective Williams.

'Did he do much damage?'

Williams touched his face where Daniel had punched him. He shook his head.

'No.'

'And will you be pressing charges?'

Williams shook his head again.

'I will,' said Flat-top.

'I'm sure Mr Lapton will regret his behaviour soon, if he doesn't already,' said Hamlin. 'I'm sure he'll compensate you both very generously for any harm he caused, and time he wasted, and any damage to your clothes or property. In fact, I guarantee it.'

Flat-top sneered, but Daniel could see that he was considering it. He looked to Williams, who nodded.

'Do it, Vince.'

'Fine,' said Flat-top. 'Take the Cappy fuck. Not worth going back on duty for anyway.'

Hamlin's men came to Daniel. One of them knelt down at his side.

'Sir, can you move your toes?'

It took a while for Daniel to understand what was expected of him. He flexed both his feet. No spinal damage. The man looked at the other one and nodded. They lifted him up under his armpits and carefully escorted him to the door.

Outside, a polished black car was parked behind Daniel's. One of Hamlin's men opened a door for him and the other lowered him into the back seat.

'Wait, put me in my car.'

'It's all right, sir,' said the second man, lifting Daniel's legs off the kerb and into the footwell. 'Your car will be fine. We're taking you to the hospital.'

His voice was calm but firm, as if he was talking to a child who didn't understand why he couldn't have more pudding. They closed the door and Daniel rested the side of his head against the cold glass of the window, looking out through his almost-swollen-shut eye.

Up ahead, Hamlin was talking to the chauffeur. He put a slip of paper into the man's top pocket and patted him on the shoulder. The chauffeur nodded gratefully and got back into Daniel's car. Hamlin returned to the black car and sat down next to Daniel. His men got in the front and the car pulled out into the street.

After a few minutes, Daniel said, 'You were spying on me.'

Hamlin was typing on his phone. He put it down.

'Excuse me?'

'I didn't ask you to be there,' said Daniel. 'I didn't tell anyone where I was going. You were following me.'

'We've been hired by your family trust to keep you safe. It's part of being a Lapton. You refused a bodyguard, so we chose the next-best course of action.'

'By having me followed,' said Daniel flatly.

'Non-invasive information gathering,' said Hamlin.

'Now, what exactly were you doing, picking a fight with the Ram Squad?'

'He covered up the death of my daughter. The school killed her. He wrote the report. He covered it up.'

'And you attacked him physically. In a room full of cops.'

'I don't have to explain myself to you.'

Daniel looked out of the window angrily. After a few more minutes, he said, 'You can run surveillance on people? Gather evidence?'

'Within limits, yes,' said Hamlin.

'I want you to look into Detective Peter Williams. Find out who bought him off. I want the people who ran that school brought to justice. Real justice.'

Hamlin frowned.

'I'm sorry, Mr Lapton,' he said. 'That's simply not possible.'

Daniel looked across at Hamlin, whose expression was unreadable. He tried the hard sell.

'If it's a question of legality, you've met my lawyers. And you'd be compensated well for your risk.'

'Mr Lapton, it's not a question of legality. Or money.'

'Then what is it?'

Hamlin didn't answer. The answer came to Daniel slowly. Nausea sloshed through him.

'Other clients,' he said.

'I'm not at liberty to say,' said Hamlin. And for a split second, Daniel thought he saw the scorn beneath Hamlin's mask. He answered the question himself.

'Rich families. The school's donors. They want to bury this, so they hired you. And they got you to spy on me.'

Hamlin didn't respond.

Daniel pulled up on the door lock.

'I want to get out of this car. Now.'

'Mr Lapton, please don't be dramatic. We're here to look after you.'

'You're spying on me. For them.'

'No, Mr Lapton. That would be a conflict of interest. We're protecting you.'

Daniel gritted his teeth.

'Stop this car or I'm throwing myself out of it.'

Hamlin hesitated for a moment.

'Edward, pull over.'

They were halfway across Newton Bridge. The car came to a stop on the yellow-striped concrete on the roadside and Daniel got out.

He limped along the sidewalk at the side of the bridge, holding his aching ribs. There were a few hundred yards to go and then he could turn on to the paved footpath along the riverbank, away from the road. A voice inside him told him how pointless this was and how petulant he must seem. He didn't have a plan about what to do next, except to get away from these people.

The black car crawled alongside him and the rear window hummed down. Hamlin was typing on his phone. Without looking up, he said, 'Your chauffeur will be here shortly and Dr Ramsey is waiting for you in the hospital's north wing.'

'I'm not going to the fucking hospital.'

'You're injured, Mr Lapton. Please don't make things worse for yourself just to spite me.'

Daniel was in agony. His face and side were throbbing.

His cheekbone and his ribs were probably cracked. But he would go to hospital tomorrow, on his own terms. He needed to get out of this poisoned cocoon.

'Fuck off. You're fired.'

'We're employed by the trust, Mr Lapton.'

'I'll make sure they fire you.'

Hamlin sighed.

'That's regrettable. Until then, we will have to continue to protect you, as much as you will let us.'

The black car pulled off and drove away over the bridge. Soon, Daniel knew, his chauffeur would pick him up, and his brief experiment with self-determination would be ended. Or he could walk away down the riverside path until . . . what? He got tired? Hungry? Mugged?

He reached into his pocket and pulled out the tape recorder.

The plastic casing was cracked. The tape wasn't turning.

Daniel felt the weight of shame. What was he doing, trying to pull himself free from his swaddling? What was he without the people he hired to protect him, to do his will, to make him more money?

He was nothing. Nothing at all.

Chapter Twenty-Nine

'Have you seen this, Jerry?' said Burton's father, holding out his phone.

Burton took it and looked at the screen. It was a list of names and phone numbers, like an address book.

'What is it?' he said, handing it back.

'It's a chat group for the Neighbourhood Watch,' said Burton's father proudly.

He was skinnier than when Burton had last visited him and he needed a haircut. His white hair was starting to grow wild.

'It's genius,' Burton's father went on, smiling wide with enthusiasm. 'Everyone looks out for each other. And if we see a dodgy character walking down the street, everyone knows immediately. We keep an eye on those types. We've even got little codes. "Peanut Butter" means a PB. Pisces Beggar.'

The kettle whistled. Burton's father took it from the hot plate and made a cup of tea for Burton and a mug of instant coffee for himself. The milk was in a plastic container in the mini-fridge. He poured for both of them and handed the tea to Burton, who was sitting at the tiny kitchen table.

His father lived alone in a small house in Southglade. He'd moved into it shortly after he retired from the police force, and had committed himself to the Neighbourhood

Watch with manic energy. Every time Burton visited him, he had new stories about foiled break-ins and dodgy characters on the corner.

'And if the ladies are out for a walk, or if they visit their friends or something and they stay too late, and it's night when they walk home, they can just post a message on here and we can look out our curtains and . . .'

'Dad,' said Burton firmly.

Burton's father stopped talking. He sat down at the kitchen table opposite Burton.

'Sorry,' he said. 'Blah blah blah, eh?' He smiled apologetically.

'Did you see the Aubrey show last night?' said Burton.

Burton's father looked down into his coffee.

'No,' he said. 'But Dennis called me up this morning and told me about it. Disgusting. I used to like that guy, but now he's just shouting all the time. He shouldn't have brought that stuff up. Everyone on the phone group says so. They all support you.'

'Did you do it? Am I really a –'

Burton's father looked him in the eyes, cutting him off.

'What are you doing, Jerry?' he said. 'Don't go looking into the past. What good's it going to do you?'

'Dad . . .' said Burton. He ran a hand down his face.

'Listen,' said Burton's father. 'You're a Burton and Burtons are Taurus. If you were born a little early, we fixed it. You're still a Burton. You're 100 per cent Burton.'

'So all the times anyone told me what job I'd be good at and who I should marry . . . that was based on a false chart. And my school and my friends . . .'

'They were all yours,' said Burton's father practically.

'And it turned out all right, didn't it? Don't let it mess with your head. You got the life you were meant to have. You were born in Aries, but that doesn't make you Aries. You're Taurus, through and through, just like your old man. Now have some of these oatmeal cookies. Brenda down the road makes them for the whole Neighbourhood Watch. She's such a sweetheart.'

Chapter Thirty

'NEUTRAL INFLUENCE COLONY. Visitors, please call Dr W. Kruger, 314 159 2653. TRESPASSERS WILL BE PROSECUTED TO THE FULL EXTENT OF THE LAW.'

Lindi lifted the gate and pulled it open over the cattle grid. Burton drove in and waited as she closed the gate. The mesh fence on either side was six feet tall and topped with barbed wire.

'You see that sign?' she said as she got back in.

'Yeah,' said Burton. 'They're not too fond of uninvited guests.'

'No, I meant the Neutral Influence part. You know about Neutral Influence?'

'Never heard of it.'

'It was a theory that was big a couple of years ago. They were trying to block out the influence of society to see how it would alter people's behaviour. Fringe astrology.'

Burton put the car into gear and pulled off down the dirt road. They were two and a half hours' drive out of the city and up in the hills. It had been a long journey. Burton appreciated the fact that during the whole trip Lindi hadn't asked him once about the *Aubrey Tonite* piece on him, although she must have been dying to. Instead, they'd listened to Lindi's alternative music, which sounded a lot like the mainstream music that Burton had grown up on. It had gone from pop to outdated to retro-chic without Burton even noticing.

They got to the top of the hill and the road turned towards the farm buildings. As Burton drove between them the dirt road became concrete. To the left was a row of newly painted single-storey cottages roofed with corrugated metal. On the right were older, rougher-looking farm buildings. An old cartwheel was stuck to the front of the largest one, in a way that Burton thought was self-consciously folksy.

A man came out of the main building door, shielding his eyes from the daylight. Burton recognized him from photographs he'd found online as Dr Werner Kruger, although he was several years older than he had been in the True Signs Academy informational brochures. If he was a cult leader, he didn't look like it. His hair was white and neatly trimmed, and his sleeves were rolled up past the elbow.

'Lindi Childs?' he said, smiling, with the faintest hint of a German accent.

Lindi came around the side of car and shook his hand.

'Thank you for seeing us like this, Doctor,' she said. 'I did my dissertation expanding on your theory of the essential dignities. The concept was so elegant.'

'Ah, my advanced horary research,' he said, with a wide smile. 'I was so obsessed with the ephemera. I've come a long way since then. Some interesting new discoveries.'

'That's wonderful!'

Lindi was beaming. Burton looked at her quizzically. She met his eyes, but couldn't suppress her smile. Fan-girl, he thought.

Kruger offered Burton a hand. 'And you are?'

'Detective Burton, SCPD. Thank you for agreeing to see us.'

'Yes, good,' said Kruger. 'Whatever I can do to help. Did you come straight from San Celeste? It's quite a drive. Would you like water? Something to eat?'

'Water, please,' said Burton.

Kruger led them into the main building. The walls were thick, which made the room inside surprisingly cool and pleasant. It was furnished in a way that reminded Burton of a retirement home. There were sofas and comfy chairs, all from different sets, arranged around the walls and facing inwards. Several of them were covered in crocheted blankets. A map of the world was up on one wall and there was a bookshelf with some magazines on it opposite. A beaded curtain covered a door deeper into the building.

A middle-aged woman was sitting in the corner, writing in a notebook. She looked up as they came in and her pen hovered over the page uncertainly.

'Ah, sorry, Carol,' said Kruger, and turned to Burton and Lindi. 'Carol is just writing in her journal. I've asked her to keep extensive notes on her thoughts and feelings. Her honesty has been extremely helpful in my research. I'm grateful, very grateful.'

Carol started picking up her papers. 'I'll finish up in my room later,' she said, speaking in a clipped Capricorn accent. 'Do you need anything?'

'Yes please. Water for the guests,' said Kruger.

'No problem.'

Carol left the room, hugging her journal to her chest

protectively. When she was gone, Kruger gestured to the comfy chairs.

'Such a shame,' he said, as he sat down opposite Burton and Lindi. 'Carol was born to Capricorn parents. They forged a birth certificate for her to make her seem Capricorn too, but she was Libra. She only found out about it in her forties. It's been a struggle, but nowadays she's registering as a Libra by almost every behavioural metric. I'm so proud of her. But, I'm sorry, you have questions for me.'

'Yes,' said Burton. 'I apologize for bothering you in person. You're a hard man to get hold of.'

'Ha! Yes. It's true,' said Kruger. 'I've become something of a recluse these days.'

'Have you heard what happened to Harvey Hammond?'

'Ah,' said Kruger. His slight smile melted away. 'Yes. It's terrible. I knew Hammond very well. We were at university together. His brother Jules was born a Capricorn although his family was Leo . . .'

'We've met him,' said Burton. 'Actually, he's the one who suggested we should speak to you.'

Kruger nodded sadly. 'Poor Jules. A classic Neo-Capricorn. Back when I treated him, astrological therapy was relatively ineffective. There was very little that I could do for misaligned individuals at the time. I would love the chance to work with him again.'

'What do you mean by misaligned?' said Burton.

'A cuckoo,' said Lindi.

'I'm not too happy with that word,' said Kruger. 'It carries a lot of negative weight. We must treat such individuals with sympathy.'

He looked at Burton seriously and Burton became

self-conscious. Kruger may well have seen Aubrey's hatchet job. Burton wondered whether he was being inspected for Aries behaviour.

'Anyway,' said Kruger. 'I was young and overambitious, and I believed I had all the answers already, and Harvey trusted me. He convinced a large number of wealthy people to give us money for a school to fix these misaligned individuals.'

Carol came back into the room with a tray and handed out glasses of water.

'Thanks,' said Burton. It felt weird to be served by someone with a Capricorn accent. He didn't know if he should talk up or down to her.

'So what happened at the True Signs Academy?' said Lindi. 'We heard there were suicides.'

Kruger looked pained. 'You must understand,' he said. 'Most of the students were deeply disturbed. These were children whose parents faked their birth certificates to make it seem like they were born into a higher sign, or whose parents were so poor that they simply didn't care. Life was a disaster for them. No one knew how to treat them. They hadn't learned the necessary code of behaviour to fit into their proper sign.'

'And you were trying to fix them?' said Lindi encouragingly.

'Yes,' said Kruger. 'And because they were in such distress, I wanted to do it as quickly as possible, for their own good. I assumed that rigid streaming and an immersive environment were the best way to make children fit in. I had a lot of success and I learned a great deal. In the grand scheme of things, I believe that I did more good than harm, and the court agreed, but . . . yes. There were fights, eating disorders and suicides, of course, most tragically.'

For a moment Kruger looked sad, and old.

'Did you know the girls who died well?'

'As much as I knew any of the students. All three were different ages. A Virgo, a Sagittarius and a Pisces, in the space of a few days. The school closed immediately. There was an investigation, like I said. Still. It was tragic.'

Burton frowned.

'So is it possible that Hammond was killed by a former student of the school? Or maybe one of the family members of the dead girls, seeking revenge?'

'Good question,' said Kruger. 'And it's not an easy one to answer. My first thought is that if that were the case, why haven't they come for me? After all, I was more responsible than Hammond. My second thought is that it's very hard to keep track of previous students. Most of our files were confiscated during the investigation and many of the students were from rich families who wanted to keep their shame a secret. The rest were charity cases from the streets. After the school closed, who knows what happened to them? I can only name one or two students from memory. You've heard of Solomon Mahout?'

Burton's head snapped up.

'What?'

'Mahout was one of your students?' said Lindi.

'That's right,' said Kruger. 'His parents were Sagittarius, I believe. It was quite a shock to see his face on television. He's a very disturbing influence.' Kruger pursed his lips sourly. 'A great failure.'

'So what happened between you and Hammond after the academy closed?' said Burton.

'Oh, he was not happy with me. Not happy at all. Bringing his charity into disrepute like that, and I didn't even fix his little brother. He was a very angry man. He called me a kook.'

'So, bad blood?'

Kruger waved a hand in the air, as if dispelling the thought.

'Only a little. Hammond had it in for me for a while after that. He publicly attacked everything I did.'

'How did you feel about that?' said Burton.

'Ah,' said Kruger, smiling impishly. 'You're wondering maybe if our feud was bad enough for me to resort to murder? No, no, no. Public opinion doesn't bother me. And science is science! In the end, he came to respect what I am doing here now. I think it speaks for itself.'

'What exactly are you doing here?' said Burton.

Lindi nodded. She was obviously dying to know.

'Would you like to see?' said Kruger. He got to his feet. 'Come! I'll show you around.'

He led them out of the farmhouse and back into the sunshine, on to the concrete road between the buildings. The air was warm, but not oppressive like San Celeste. The bushes were startlingly green. Burton caught himself wondering when he'd last enjoyed being outside. It had been a long while.

'How many people live in your commune?' he said.

'We prefer "community",' said Kruger. 'There's forty-eight of us. Only about a quarter were ever misaligned, although I like to believe that I have successfully cured them. The rest are perfectly healthy individuals. They're all grad students or former grad students, or simply people who wanted to join us and went through the necessary evaluation. I give them a place to live and they help me with my research. I'm finally able to complete the work I was doing at True Signs, and to push it further. Have a look.'

He pointed ahead. They were approaching a long corrugated-aluminum roof held up by wooden poles. There was a row of trestle tables underneath and some men and women in shorts and T-shirts were going through boxes of loose oranges, examining them and packing them into crates.

Kruger called out, 'Greg! Tanya!'

A man and a woman in the sorting group looked up at them. The man lifted one side of his headphones. He was in his mid-twenties, with wild red hair and a tight white T-shirt. The girl was a little shorter than him, with straight brown hair. She was wearing a 'Westcroft U' T-shirt. They both looked young, fit and energetic. Kruger waved them closer, and Greg and Tanya pushed between the trestle tables.

'Hi!' Greg said loudly, taking off his headphones. He shook Lindi's hand vigorously. 'I'm Greg.'

Tanya, behind him, looked at Lindi and Greg together. 'It's the gathering of the Afros,' she said, teasing good-naturedly. She shook Burton's hand. 'Tanya. And you guys? New recruits?'

Kruger shook his head.

'No, Detective Burton and Lindi Childs are just visiting. They're investigating a murder.'

'Oh, man!' said Greg. 'I'm sorry. Is there anything I can do?'

'What happened?' said Tanya, wide-eyed.

'Don't worry,' said Kruger. 'It's nothing to do with us. I'm just showing them around. Making them feel welcome here.'

Greg nodded. 'Great, OK. Cool.'

Burton looked at the two of them. Their pupils were dilated. They were high.

'Listen, I don't want to be rude, but we've got a shit-ton of oranges to sort over there,' said Tanya. 'If you need help with anything, come right to us, OK?'

'Yeah,' said Greg. 'Anything at all. It was great meeting you both! Good luck!'

They went back to the tables. Greg slid his headphones back on and bobbed his head unselfconsciously to the music.

'Charming, aren't they?' said Kruger. 'They've been a great help. Endlessly positive.'

'What was that all about?' said Burton.

Kruger looked at him with a small smile.

'What are their signs, would you say?'

'Leo and Gemini, I'd guess,' said Burton.

'Definitely,' said Lindi.

'Exactly!' said Kruger, as if Lindi and Burton were smart students who just needed the final push. 'And they're more than just that. Greg's sun, moon and ascendant are all in Leo, and they're both descended from more than five generations of their sign. They are both unusually pure astrological specimens.'

'All right,' said Burton, not quite following.

'Don't you see?' said Kruger. 'We have forty-eight people here, four of each sign, and they're all perfectly aligned. We can see what an ideal Taurus–Aries interaction should be like, or Cancer–Aquarius or Gemini–Capricorn. This is an astrological laboratory.'

'Like that reality show,' said Burton. 'Twelve people in a house, one from each sign, how do they react . . .'

Kruger looked a little disgusted.

'No, no, no. That's entertainment. This is science. And there is a huge difference between the current way the signs behave in our society and their true celestial natures.'

Lindi looked around at the compound.

'Oh, my God,' she said. Her eyes were wide.

'What?' said Burton.

'Ah,' said Kruger. 'You're getting it.'

'This isn't just a laboratory,' she said. 'It's a microcosm.'

Kruger smiled broadly. 'Exactly,' he said. 'What we have here is a tiny scale model of society, with all twelve signs perfectly balanced. But again, it's more than that. A founding principle of our science is that the world is a mechanism that follows rules as elegant and immutable as the orbits of the planets. Our own foolish urge to escape our true natures has broken the mechanism and led to great suffering. Society is a broken machine. But here, I'm creating the template to put it back together.'

He spread his hands majestically.

'This is more than a laboratory,' he said. 'It's Utopia.'

Chapter Thirty-One

Kruger showed them around the rest of the compound as he answered some of Lindi's questions, and deflected others. He was happy to talk about the interactions of pure or near-pure signs, but he wasn't forthcoming about his techniques for curing the misaligned.

'I'm afraid I'm sworn to secrecy,' he said. 'It's one of the conditions of my funding.'

'And who's funding you?' said Burton.

'That's also a secret,' Kruger said. He smiled apologetically.

A howl rang out from a long barn halfway down the hillside.

'What was that?' said Burton, immediately alert.

'Ah, that's just our little side project,' said Kruger calmly. 'We needed activities to keep the community occupied as the dynamics between them developed. We're lucky to have the orange grove for that, but to keep things interesting we also have the coyotes.'

'You have literal coyotes here?' said Lindi. 'Why?'

'Come and see. I'd say we're bound to get a paper out of this too.'

He led them down the stone-paved path and opened the wooden door for them. The inside of the barn was divided up by wire fencing into six-by-nine-foot cages. It was a battery farm. Each cage held either an individual coyote or a mother with pups. A woman was going from cage to cage, doling out dog food and making notes on a clipboard. Now that Burton knew how the commune worked, he could see that she was obviously Virgo.

'We're replicating a domestication study from Russia,' Kruger said. 'They were using foxes, but foxes don't do so well in this climate. They found that it didn't take many generations to change a wild animal into a non-assertive, domesticated creature.'

He pointed into one of the cages. A mother was suckling a litter of pups. She looked up at him submissively with her tail down.

'You'll notice that after only three or four generations of selective breeding, we're already seeing a change in morphology. Her juvenile physical characteristics are more prominent than in a wild coyote. It's probable that the hormones that make coyotes aggressive also alter their final shape. Perhaps there's something in phrenology after all. Of course, we still have to do something about the howl.'

The coyotes yipped and whined as the food approached their cages.

'But what's the point of this?' said Burton.

'What's the point of anything?' said Kruger. 'To learn and grow. And I suppose dog breeders would be overjoyed to have an entirely new domesticated breed. Once the project is completed, these animals will be in great demand.'

'How are you doing this?' said Lindi. 'Are you just breeding the most docile ones and spaying the aggressive ones?'

'That would be expensive,' said Kruger. 'No, if they have aggressive traits, there's no point in keeping them alive. They're coyotes.'

Lindi looked into the next cage. The young male inside snarled at her.

'Down,' Kruger said to it absently.

He led them back out of the shed. Lindi seemed a little more subdued and thoughtful.

'This has all been very interesting,' said Burton. 'Can we get back to Hammond's murder?'

'Of course,' said Kruger. 'Actually, I have something for you. Come.'

He led them back up the hill and to the door of one of the new white buildings. They waited for him as he went inside.

'Maybe he'll bring out a signed T-shirt for you,' said Burton. '"To my number one fan."'

'Shut up,' said Lindi. Her cheeks were red.

Kruger came back with a black folder and handed it to Burton.

'What's this?'

'It's everything I have relating to the True Signs Academy,' said Kruger. 'Mainly the student records. I ask you not to get your hopes up, though. Most of the wealthy parents put their children into the academy under assumed names, and all the addresses and contact information are ten years out of date, but I hope it's useful.'

'Can we take this as evidence?' said Burton.

'Of course. Whatever I can do to help.'

He led Lindi and Burton back to their car. As they were getting in, Burton remembered something important.

'Oh,' he said. 'Sorry, Dr Kruger, this is a long shot, but did you know Chief Peter Williams too?'

'I did!' said Kruger. 'It's a terrible loss. I met him when I was a postgrad, teaching forensic astrology part-time at the Police Academy. Actually, I was the one who introduced Williams to Hammond.'

Lindi and Burton glanced at each other. Burton looked back at Kruger, and chose his words carefully.

'Dr Kruger, do you know if Williams was, in any way, involved in the investigation into the True Signs Academy?'

'Of course,' said Kruger, sounding surprised. 'I assumed you already knew. He was the one who led it.'

Chapter Thirty-Two

For the first time in his life, Daniel felt utterly impotent. He couldn't make himself forget the daughter he never knew. Her absence was seared into him. She was everything that could have been right with the world. His obsession led him to Maria Natalia Estevez. She was the legal guardian at a large group foster home located in a converted block of flats north of the city centre, right on the edge of Ariesville. For more than twenty years Maria had been running the place, with a bare minimum of support from the San Celeste Uplift charity. She was the guardian of fifteen minors, but with the recent cutbacks in child services the building had become an unofficial catch-all for many more homeless children, serving as emergency shelter, soup kitchen and halfway house for recovering underage addicts. And Maria was responsible for them all.

'Reckon you'll be back on your feet in two weeks?' she said to a teenage girl on a foam mattress.

The girl had stringy hair that was prematurely grey and terrifyingly thin arms. She pushed herself up on to her elbows and took a plate of food from Maria – a burger patty between two pieces of pre-sliced bread, glued together with ketchup, and a side of greasy potato chips.

'I'll try,' she said weakly.

'Good,' said Maria.

She was in her late forties and was a head shorter than Daniel – stocky but not fat, with a wide face that moved easily between sympathy and anger. She wore jeans and a purple T-shirt that was clearly chosen for easy washability over fashion. Her black hair was tied up in a ponytail that was secured by a red elastic band.

'I phoned the school and they said they'll take you back if you're strong enough. You can go back into Mrs McKenna's class. You got on with Mrs McKenna last time, didn't you, Kelly?'

'Yeah,' said Kelly. Her eyes drifted, unfocused. 'She was OK.'

'Good. Finish up your burger.'

Outside the room, some girls were chasing each other down the corridor, shouting happily. Maria stood over Kelly with her arms folded. Kelly took a bite of her meal and immediately started coughing.

'I need to go to the bathroom.'

'OK.'

Maria bent down and lifted Kelly up under her arm-pits, while calling out through the open door, 'Elaine? Elaine!'

The shouting in the corridor stopped and a gap-toothed girl poked her head in the room.

'What?'

'Don't say "what?". Come on. Help me here,' said Maria. Her voice struck a balance between impatience and affection.

Elaine came around to the other side of Kelly and helped Maria pull her upright.

'Take her to the bathroom.'

'O-K,' Elaine said in a sing-song voice. She supported Kelly's weight as they walked together out of the room.

After a few seconds Kelly's cough started again, echoing down the hallway. Maria looked back to Daniel, who had been watching quietly from the corner of the room.

'Flu,' she said. 'Compounded with malnutrition and heroin withdrawal. And maybe more. I haven't had her tested yet.'

'Fuck,' said Daniel. 'Shouldn't she be in hospital?'

'Sure,' said Maria. 'In a perfect world. But . . . look where we are.'

She gestured around at the room. The walls were freshly painted, although there was some discoloration and bubbling from damp up by the ceiling. Pictures were taped up everywhere, mostly of celebrities cut out from magazines. An old wooden chest of drawers sat in the corner under a cracked window. There were three foam mattresses on the floor, with mismatching blankets and pillows. Daniel couldn't imagine what it was like to grow up there.

'You said she'll be better in two weeks, though.'

Maria shook her head.

'I doubt it. But if I stopped pushing, she'd know I'd given up on her. When I start acting nice around the kids they know something's wrong. Come.'

She walked out of the small room brusquely. Daniel followed her into the dark corridor.

'So, Mr Lapton, have you had enough of this place yet?'

She looked into the next room, quickly checking it was clean and the beds were made, before continuing down the corridor. A small boy was in the way, kneeling on the ground and drawing on some scrap paper. Maria and Daniel pushed past him.

'Marco, do that in your room.'

'Can't,' said the boy. 'Joey's in there.'

'Well, then, do it downstairs.'

Daniel looked over his shoulder as the kid sighed and packed up his art project.

'They're pretty obedient,' he said to Maria.

'Not always,' she said. 'Sometimes I have to scream like a drill sergeant, but there's too many of them to handle any other way. I get the bigger kids to look after the smaller ones, otherwise it would be impossible. It mostly works out, but it's not easy. Now, what is it you wanted to see me for? Were you checking us out before offering a donation?'

'That's right,' he said. 'An annual contribution. With a condition, though.'

'Conditions, huh?' said Maria. She didn't disguise her scepticism.

'I'm specifically looking for kids who went to the True Signs Academy. A lot of them went missing. I heard that some of them have come through here and I need to talk with them.'

'Oh yeah?' said Maria. 'Why are you so interested in True Signs?'

'I need to find out more about that place. And, really, I want them to testify. I'm trying to put together a class-action lawsuit against the people behind True Signs. There are strong grounds for a civil case . . .'

Maria stopped in the middle of the corridor and scratched her cheek. It looked like she was judging him, hard.

'No, I don't think that's a good idea at all.'

She shook her head and continued on her rounds.

'You haven't heard what I'm offering,' he said, following behind her. 'I've seen the records you send in to the Uplift charity. Most of your money's going on rent. I can cover that. It'll more than double your current income.'

'That's great, and believe me we need it. But every time I've taken money on "conditions" it's caused major problems for me and the kids. If you give me "conditions" suddenly I'm working for you, when I'm meant to be working for more than fifteen young, troubled people. I can't afford to let any other "conditions" become my business. So if you want to give a donation, then I'll thank my lucky stars. If you want to ask the kids about their lives, fine. But you're not bribing anyone. If you've got an axe to grind, grind it somewhere else.'

'I'm not grinding an axe,' said Daniel. 'I'm trying to help.'

Maria didn't look back at him.

'Great,' she said. 'Come and help. Help me cook and clean and check the homework and keep the kids entertained and break up fights, or just give a donation and let me get on with it. But you're wasting your time and your money if you think that the True Signs Academy was the worst thing that ever happened to these kids. It was bad, but for every kid who went there it was just a shitty situation in a lifetime of shitty situations. You want to really help out? Spend some time and find out what the kids genuinely need before you go on a crusade. But a lawsuit isn't going to fix these kids' lives. You can't sue the stars.'

Chapter Thirty-Three

Daniel almost never came back to the San Celeste Uplift home. He would probably have left the city for good if, at that moment, he hadn't been mugged.

It was his own stupid mistake. His car was parked a block and a half away from the home. He had driven past it, thinking it was just another block of rundown flats, and went in through the gates of a clinic instead. He realized his mistake in the parking lot and checked the map in his car, then decided to park and walk. Capricorn society had warned him against this. Capricorns that broke down in Aries areas were fodder for a thousand dinner party horror stories, echoed and amplified within the tiny community. Daniel recognized the paranoia for what it was and ignored it.

But paranoia doesn't always lie.

'Hey!' came a voice from behind him. 'Mountain goat!'

He saw them coming out of the corner of his eye. They were kids. Seventeen, maybe eighteen years old, in tracksuits. He kept walking, head down, pretending to be lost in his own thoughts.

'Big man!' the kid at the front of the group called again. His red-and-white jacket hung off his shoulders.

'He can't hear us,' said one of the others, a fat kid with a peaked cap over a do-rag. 'He's up on his mountain. We're too far beneath him.'

The rest of the pack started bleating and closed in around him. He was ambushed.

He turned to face as many of them as he could, trying to keep his movements calm while his heart raced. 'What do you want?' he said loudly, hoping to attract the attention of any passers-by, but there were no other pedestrians in sight, and if anyone was watching from out of a grimy window then they weren't making it known.

'Quiet, big man,' said the kid in red and white. Despite being the smallest in the group, he looked like their leader. He was blond-haired and blue-eyed, and there was something familiar about his sunken cheeks. 'We just want to know if you have any spare change.'

Daniel reached into his trouser pocket and took out a handful of coins.

'No, man,' said the kid, stepping right in front of Daniel. The others closed in around him. 'Look at all of us. You can't just give enough for me. That wouldn't be fair on my brothers, would it? Are you trying to insult us? Gotta share, that's what they teach us. Sharing is good.'

The others snickered. The kid reached into Daniel's jacket pocket and brazenly pulled out his wallet.

'That's more like it.'

Daniel felt other hands on him, patting him down. Someone started pulling his car keys from his trouser pocket.

'Hey!' said Daniel, grabbing at the other kid's hand.

He knew it wasn't smart, but he was too angry to make things easy for anyone, including himself. If they wanted to rob him, they were going to have to fight him. It didn't matter who won. He squeezed the hand holding his keys as hard as he could.

'Ow, fuck,' said the boy holding the keys, pulling his crushed hand away. The keys fell to the ground.

The boy in the red-and-white jacket was suddenly up in Daniel's face. 'What're you doing to my boy?' he said.

All his fake charm was instantly gone. He gut-punched Daniel with a sharp blow under the ribs. Daniel was expecting an attack and his muscles were tense, but he still doubled over, and that was bad. He had raised dogs as a child and knew what happened when their prey showed weakness.

A car hooted, frantically and repeatedly. A taxi cab was rolling down the road towards them with the driver leaning out of the open window. He was wearing a baseball cap with an eagle on it and his cheeks were red with anger.

'You little bastards! Fuck off, all of you!'

The kid in the red jacket pulled a lazy finger at him.

The cab driver pulled a small black handgun out of his glove box. He pointed it at the group. They scattered immediately, except for the kid in the red jacket.

'Much obliged,' the kid said sarcastically, waving Daniel's wallet under his nose.

Before Daniel could grab it, the kid turned and ran. The cab driver tried to reverse down the street to catch him, but the kid was too fast. He escaped through a gap in a barbed-wire-topped fence.

'Hey, buddy,' the cab driver called to Daniel. 'You all right? Did they get anything?'

'Just my wallet,' said Daniel. He went over to the cab driver's window. 'Thanks for scaring them off. I owe you.'

'Any time. These fucking kids, man. Why do we even

let the Aries breed when we know what their kids will turn into? I'm gonna get them, next time I see them.'

He waggled his gun, showing it off. Daniel could see that he'd never had proper weapons training.

'Don't worry,' said Daniel. 'That kid's going to get what's coming to him.'

Because, if Daniel was remembering right, he'd seen the kid's face before, in the background of a grainy black-and-white security tape from the True Signs Academy. Which meant he probably had the kid's interview footage and a clear picture of his face. Clear enough to show to the cops.

Chapter Thirty-Four

At three a.m., Burton's front window shattered.

He sat up in bed, not sure if the noise had been part of a dream. Feet were running away down the street outside.

'What was that?' said Kate, sitting up next to him.

He touched her shoulder protectively and slid out of the bedclothes. There was a towel hanging on a hook on the bedroom door. He wrapped it around his naked waist and ran through to the living room. The light of the street lamp outside the window reflected off the broken glass on the dark floor.

He ran to the window and leaned out. A couple of men, too far away to recognize, looked back at him as they got into a car. Tyres screeched as they pulled off without turning on their lights. Burton couldn't see the licence plate.

He turned on the floor lamp. Kate came into the room behind him wearing a T-shirt. It had once been oversized, and it still hung loosely off her shoulders, but with the pregnancy it was stretched tight around her middle. 'You're bleeding,' she said.

Burton looked down at his feet. A shard of glass had caught him on the heel.

'Fuck,' he said, and pulled it out. Blood dribbled from the wound.

Kate sniffed the air. 'And what's that smell?'

They found out at the front door. Someone had shoved shit through their letter box. It had splattered on the black-and-white tiles.

Kate covered her mouth and heaved. 'Oh, God. I'm going to be sick.'

'I'll sort it out,' said Burton.

By the time he'd bandaged his foot, put on clothes and shoes, and wiped up most of the mess by the front door with paper towels, Kate was finishing a long phone call to her brother.

'No, it's not . . . It'll be fine. OK. OK, Hugo. Just now. OK. Thanks.'

She hung up.

'Hugo's coming round,' she said.

'What?' said Burton, looking back over his shoulder at her. He threw the wadded-up paper he was holding into a black bin bag at his side. 'Why? I've got this.'

'He says I can stay with him and Shelley until this is over.'

'Now hold on,' said Burton. 'We shouldn't panic. I'm going to mop this with disinfectant and tape up the window . . .'

'Jerry,' said Kate. She had one hand over her belly.

Burton felt his life slipping out of his hands. He looked at her face, both sad and firm. It wasn't about him. It wasn't even about her. She was going and he was staying. That was the way it had to be.

Chapter Thirty-Five

Burton was halfway through taping a rectangle of cardboard over the broken window when a white hatchback pulled up outside. He unlocked the front door and Kate's brother, Hugo, strode in past him. Hugo was a health-and-safety monitor on big construction sites. He had started out as a bricklayer and still had the build for it.

'Katie?' he said. 'Katie?'

Kate came out of the bedroom carrying her overnight bag. She stood up on her tiptoes and hugged Hugo.

'Thanks for coming,' she said.

'I told you, anything you need, we're here to help,' said Hugo. 'Shit. This is terrible.'

He made eye contact with Burton. They'd never got on, but up until now they had both tried their best.

'I'm ready to go when you are,' said Kate.

'No problem. Any idea who did this?'

'Jerry says it's probably the Cancers. It's probably the same ones who were mad at him for arresting that guy who killed the senator.'

Burton watched them from the other end of the corridor. He could see the family resemblance. They both had the same strong features and a look of pragmatic determination that he knew well from his arguments with Kate. It meant that a decision had been made. And it had, of course. This was best for Kate and for the child.

Hugo didn't say anything else to Burton. He carried Kate's bag out and put it in the trunk.

Burton kissed Kate goodbye. 'I'll call you tomorrow morning,' he said, touching the side of her face.

'Sure. Thanks.'

She got into the pickup, which drove away down the dark street. When it was gone he turned back to the doorway. The slogan 'GO BACK TO ARIESVILLE' was spray-painted in red across his white front wall. He stared at it, waiting for his frustration and rage to subside.

Chapter Thirty-Six

'Fuck you, you Cappy fuck,' said the young man, pulling at his handcuffs. They were chained to a metal loop on the table in the police interview room. He leaned forward and strained at the chain, trying to look intimidating.

'No,' said Daniel calmly. His hands flat down on the table. 'I know you're the big man out on the street and you'd beat me in a fair fight. But the world isn't fair and this isn't the street. If you want my respect you'll have to be smarter than that.'

'And why would I want your respect?' the kid sneered, doubling down on his bravado.

'Good question,' said Daniel. 'Who do you think I am?'

'I think you're a cop. Or the others wouldn't leave you in a room alone with me.'

Smart, but not experienced.

'No,' said Daniel. 'Guess again.'

'Then you're a fucking social worker, or some kind of special agent, or . . .'

'No.'

The kid looked Daniel up and down.

'Whatever it is, you're fucking smug,' he said. 'You got me arrested and now you're here to gloat about it. You're showing off how powerful you are.'

'That's it,' said Daniel. 'That's who I am. I'm someone powerful enough to have you arrested whenever I want.

I'm someone the police will allow into a room with you, just because I asked.'

'This is how you get your rocks off,' said the kid. 'You're a pervert.'

He was trying to get a reaction. Daniel knew exactly how the game worked.

'Normally I'd be quite happy to never see your face again. But you've got lucky. I need you for something.'

The kid leaned back in his metal chair and looked around at the walls. He had disengaged.

'Are you listening to me?'

'No,' said the kid. 'Cos you're playing games.'

'I'm here because I want to make a deal with you.'

'A deal?' said the kid. 'You can't lock me up and say you want to make a deal. You got a gun to my head. That's not a deal, that's a jacking. You're saying "do what I want or else". Well, fuck you.'

'David Cray,' said Daniel slowly, 'the reason you are here is because – I want to make this very clear – you robbed me. I would rather not be here.'

'Great,' said Cray. 'Neither would I. Let's hit the road.'

He held up his wrists.

'Nice try. Tell me something about the True Signs Academy.'

'Like what?'

'There were special rooms that the teachers used to put the kids into. What happened in those rooms?'

Cray's jaw clamped shut.

'You don't want to tell me?' said Daniel.

'No.'

'OK. Here's my offer. If you won't talk, tell me who

will. Tell me the names of ten of your classmates from True Signs Academy right now and I'll drop the charges. If you want to make a deal with me after that, you can decide for yourself. I need someone to help me find more kids from that school. Call me, or don't.'

He took out a business card and slid it across to Cray.

'What do you pay?' said Cray.

Daniel smiled. After a lifetime of guarded business deals, Cray was refreshingly direct.

'Let's say ... five dollars an hour. And more once you've paid off what you stole from my wallet,' said Daniel.

Cray sneered in doubt.

'Come on!' said Daniel. 'What have you got to lose?'

'Reputation and pride.'

'I'm not taking either. And if you work for me I guarantee you'll get both back in spades. But right now, all I want is ten names. Ten simple names. You think you can still remember?'

Cray nodded.

'Good,' said Daniel. He took out his notepad. 'Tell me.'

Chapter Thirty-Seven

Lindi rang the doorbell of the Coine residence. After a few moments Bram Coine's father opened the door a crack.

'Detective,' he said.

'No, sorry,' she said, and attempted a charming smile. 'I'm just a consultant working with the police. May I speak with your son, please? Is he around?'

'Do you have a warrant?' said Bram's father, adjusting his glasses nervously.

Lindi kept her smile.

'No,' she said. 'Like I said, I'm not a cop. Your son asked to see me about something.'

Bram's father hesitated, clearly doubtful. He wasn't making eye contact with her. Lindi remembered hearing that there was a high prevalence of autism in the Virgo community. Maybe the population was selecting for it, like Kruger's coyotes.

'I promise I'll leave immediately if he doesn't want to see me,' she said.

'Promise?'

'I promise.'

He opened the door for her. Inside, the walls were white and bare, and the floor was shiny. Everything smelled faintly of disinfectant. He led Lindi down the corridor, past bookshelves that looked like they were made from old server racks. The only decoration she saw on the wall was a framed advertisement for an ancient gaming console.

A quiet thumping came from the back of the house, which got louder as they approached. Bram's father opened a door and noise flooded out.

'Bram,' he said, 'someone to see you.'

Bram was lying on his bed, playing with his phone. Speakers in the corners of the room were pumping out complex, bass-filled music. Lindi recognized the posters on the wall opposite the desk from Bram's video: one for a math-rock band proud of its complicated time signatures ('Harder than metal!') and one for a flow chart asking, 'Which science fiction movie universe are you in?' It was all very, very Young Virgo.

He looked up at them.

'Oh, hi,' he said, sitting upright. 'You're the astrologer.'

'Lindi Childs,' she said, offering him her hand. 'Nice to finally meet you properly.'

'Is it?' said Bram. But he shook it.

'I got your email,' said Lindi.

'Yeah,' said Bram. 'To be honest, I was really wanting to talk to Burton, but you'll do.'

That was the thing about Virgos. Lindi tried to get on with them because they were smart and interesting and independent, but they were often so socially blunt that talking to them was like boxing.

'Burton's got a lot on his mind right now,' she said.

And, truthfully, when Bram emailed them saying that he had information regarding the murders, Burton didn't believe it. Lindi was only there out of guilt, since she was the one who'd called attention to him in the first place.

193

'Yeah,' said Bram. 'I saw that Aubrey piece on Burton. Even if it's a lie, people are going to be looking at him weird. And I should know.'

'Excuse me,' said Bram's father from behind Lindi. He had been so quiet that she hadn't realized he was still there. 'Bram? Do you want her to stay?'

'Yeah, Dad, it's OK.'

'OK. Good.' Bram's father hovered in the doorway. Lindi could see that he didn't know how to deal with her. 'Do you need anything? Coffee? Tea?' he said.

'No thanks,' said Lindi, with an embarrassed smile.

'Oh, OK.' He closed the door behind him. A strange, quiet man.

'So,' said Lindi, 'what have you discovered?'

Bram got off the bed and went to the swivel chair by his empty desk. With nowhere else to sit, Lindi perched on the corner of the bed.

'The first thing I discovered was that every right-winger in the country hates me.'

'Has it been bad?' she asked.

'On the first day I got, like, five thousand death threats,' said Bram, matter-of-factly. 'They all thought I killed Harvey Hammond *and* Chief Williams. I bet I would have been arrested for Hammond's murder if the police weren't already watching me. And the police confiscated my computer, and my dad's too, under civil forfeiture. He's flipping out about it. He's got, like, three years of work on it and they're not giving it back.'

'Fuck,' said Lindi in sympathy.

'Yeah,' said Bram. 'So I really want my name cleared quickly, but the cops hate my guts and the newspapers are useless. I give them interviews, but they keep on taking small things I say and blowing them up into the wrong story. Like, I mentioned that I'm a regular on the social change message boards, and they wrote about it like I'm part of some online conspiracy. Actually, the message boards have been more helpful than anyone else. They're normally just a bunch of politics geeks trying to one-up each other, but after I was arrested they've been pretty great at rallying around me. A bunch of them are amateur-sleuthing the case and trying to clear my name, which is pretty rad of them. You wanna see?'

Lindi nodded. 'Sure.'

'Can I borrow your laptop? I'd use my computer, but . . .' He pointed to the empty space on his desk.

Lindi put a protective arm around her laptop bag. She had strong reservations about giving it to someone recently accused of hacking, even if she knew it wasn't true.

'Please,' he said. 'It's worth it.'

Reluctantly, she took it out of the case and handed it to him. He spent a minute setting up the Wi-Fi, then opened the Web browser and typed in an address. Lindi looked over his shoulder as he typed rapidly. This was second nature to Bram.

'My laptop isn't going to end up on some government watch list, is it?' said Lindi.

Bram frowned thoughtfully. 'If it isn't already I'll be very surprised.'

The message boards came up on the screen, with the title 'ACTIVENATION'. Bram clicked on the post '<<MARB>> arrested: the facts'.

'"Marb"?' said Lindi.

'My name backwards,' said Bram, faintly embarrassed. 'Here. Maybe you'll find this useful.'

A page of comments came up.

RomanRoulette: Guys! There's lots of info in lots of different threads about <<MARB>>'s arrest. It's getting messy. Let's put everything we know in one place.

<<MARB>>'s Original Video
<<MARB>>'s Video (redacted version)
<<MARB>>'s Video (transcript)
Chief Williams's Murder Report on Channel 23
Chief Williams's Murder Investigation: Detective Jerome Burton (various links)
Chief William's Murder Investigation: Detective Lloyd Kolacny (various links)
Chief Williams's Murder Investigation: Astrologer Lindiwe Childs (various links)
Ram Squad Members (various links)
Ram Squad History and Complaints (various links)
Williams and Hammond – Shared History (various links, need to split into sections)
<<MARB>>'s Arrest on Channel 23
Hammond Tonite's Segment on <<MARB>>
Aubrey Tonite's Segment on Detective Burton
Carapace Website Article about <<MARB>>

KungFuJez: Thanks, Roman! Hope Marb's OK. Fuck, this is weird.

DeepFryer: Yeah, thanks. I'm scared Hammond's death was a false flag operation or something. Let's see what we can dig up. Post all new links you find in this thread.

Lindi pointed at her own name on the screen. 'Your friends are investigating me?' she said. 'What did they find?'

'Nothing much,' said Bram. 'Just your Wiki article and a couple of papers you wrote, and all your social media stuff. There was some speculation about whether you were a pawn for the Ram Squad.'

'I'm not,' she said firmly.

'I believe you. I've seen the flame wars you've been in. You're quite a social justice warrior, even if you do specialize in a fundamentally unjustifiable discipline.'

'Thanks,' said Lindi, feeling uncomfortable.

Bram clicked at the bottom of the page, skipping over twelve pages of conversation. His arrest was clearly big news in the politics nerd community.

'Here are the most recent comments,' he said. 'This is all from the last hour or so.'

RomanRoulette: New links, guys! Rachel Wells (Chief Williams's maid) Social Media (various links)

Kart33: Finally! I've been saying we should be following up on the missing maid.

DeepFryer: Why didn't you get these links yourself, then?

Kart33: Busy.

Octagon: Phew! Those links are rough. A bunch of trolls are spamming her accounts saying she's faking it and she's one of the murderers. People are total dicks.

Kart33: She could be a murderer, though.

Octagon: Yeah, but don't say that to her grieving family's faces!

Bram must have seen Lindi's face while she read this,

because he said, 'They're sweet when you get to know them,' and typed in a new comment.

<<MARB>>: Hey all. Got Lindi Childs here at my house. Just showing her what you dweebs are up to.

After a few seconds a bunch of new comments came up.

DeepFryer: She the one working for the cops? Don't trust her.
Kart33: Is she hawt? Asking for a friend.

'Are all your friends fourteen-year-old boys?' said Lindi, folding her arms.

Bram grinned. 'They're being ironic.'

'Hm,' said Lindi. From her experience, the distance between irony and sexism was pretty thin.

'We should play back. Can I take a photo?' said Bram.

Before she replied, he held up his phone and turned on the front camera.

'Smile.'

Bram took a picture with himself in the foreground and Lindi on the corner of his bed behind him looking unimpressed. He tapped at his phone and after a few seconds it appeared on the forum with a gentle popping sound. After a few more seconds the replies started coming in.

Octagon: Yeah. Hawt.
Kart33: Shame you're blocking the view, <<MARB>>. More like a total eclipse of the hawt.

'OK,' said Lindi. She got to her feet. 'Well, I'm meant to be at the station, so –'

'No, wait, I'm sorry,' said Bram, finally realizing his mistake. 'I told you. They're just messing. They're good guys.'

'Did you just want to show me that list of links?' said Lindi. 'Or did you have anything special you wanted to tell me?'

'Yes, yes, hold on,' said Bram. 'The good thing about sharing this online is that hundreds of people can work on a problem simultaneously. That's why we can find things that the cops miss. We're like a massively parallel processor. We looked into Williams's and Hammond's pasts, looking for a connection, and we found a man called –'

'Dr Werner Kruger,' said Lindi, finishing his sentence. 'Yes. We met him.'

'Oh,' said Bram, deflated. 'And? Any luck with that?'

'I'm not allowed to discuss an ongoing investigation.'

She left Bram Coine's house ten minutes later and walked to her car, hugely relieved. Bram had been arrogant and had nothing useful to add to the investigation. She didn't have to feel guilty about getting him arrested any longer.

Chapter Thirty-Eight

For three weeks after young Cray was released from police custody, Daniel heard nothing. Then, one morning, he was woken up by a phone call.

'You still offering that job?' said Cray.

Daniel drove to the outskirts of Ariesville and met him in the parking lot of a fast-food restaurant. He was leaning against a chain-link fence, next to the line of cars that were waiting for the drive-thru.

Daniel pulled his car up next to him and rolled down his window. The first thing he noticed was Cray's black eye.

'Who did that to you?'

'Doesn't matter,' said Cray. 'It's no big deal.'

Cray was still puffed up like a cornered cat, but he wasn't quite so aggressive this time. Daniel guessed that something had happened to make young Cray understand that he couldn't take on the world alone. He was curious to know what it was, but Cray clearly wasn't interested in talking about it.

'Why'd you choose this place?' he said, pointing at the thrumming cars and the plastic menu signs. 'Is this so that there's people around if I try to mug you again?'

'Exactly right,' said Daniel. Why lie?

'I could do it anyway. I don't give a fuck. I just don't want to.'

'That's quite a way to talk to your new boss. Do you have those addresses?'

'Yeah, I found about thirty kids, from all different classes,' said Cray.

Impressive.

'How'd you get them?'

'I asked around. Some of them I know, and they know other kids. I've got contacts.'

He fished a scrap of paper out of his pocket and held it up for Daniel to see. Names and addresses were scrawled on both sides.

'You got the money?' said Cray.

'Sure. Five bucks for every accurate address. After I've checked.'

Cray blew air out of his mouth in disgust.

'Pfft. You think I'd make them up?' he said.

'Wouldn't you? Get off your high horse, mugger.'

Cray tried to hand Daniel the messy page, but he waved it away.

'Keep that for now. I'd like you to drive with me, if you've got the time.'

He unlocked the doors. Cray looked suspicious.

'Where are you going?'

'To talk to all the families on your list.'

'What if I don't want to get in?' said Cray.

'What are you scared of? Those addresses are legitimate, right?'

'Sure they're "legitimate",' said Cray, overemphasizing the word to make fun of it. 'I just don't wanna get in your car. Everyone's gonna think you're taking me away so I can suck you off.'

'Don't be stupid,' said Daniel. 'You know the people on your list and you know where they live. And your handwriting's terrible. I'll pay you ten dollars an hour to be my tour guide.'

Cray went around to the passenger-side door and swung it open.

'Fifteen an hour,' he said, leaning in. 'And only if you call me your bodyguard.'

'Deal,' said Daniel. 'What's the first address?'

Cray got in and looked at his page, running his finger down it, moving his lips as he deciphered his own handwriting. It was a mess.

'If you work for me longer than today, you're going to need to learn how to use a spreadsheet,' said Daniel.

'I'm not going to be your fucking secretary.'

'You're not getting anywhere in life without a basic education.'

'Whatever,' said Cray. 'There's ways to make money that don't need that shit.'

'Drug dealers use spreadsheets,' said Daniel. 'And if you write a note to rob a bank, you're going to need better handwriting.'

They drove through Ariesville, visiting the names from Cray's list, crossing them off one by one. Every family they visited was in a different situation, but nearly all of them were – from Daniel's point of view – dire. These were families that had sent off their children to an unknown boarding school mostly because they had heard it was free. Some had wanted a chance for their children to have an education that they couldn't afford. Some hadn't had the time to look after their own kids. And some had been told that this was the only way to get their difficult children 'fixed'.

As easy as it would have been for Cray to give Daniel a list of fake names and addresses, it looked like he had done the job properly. Not that it helped Daniel much. It was a weekday and a lot of the parents were working, leaving their children at home untended. In a few cases that Daniel felt played into the worst stereotypes about the Aries, one or the other parent was home and already drunk.

And then there were the really bad cases. In a concrete apartment block, a family of four was living in a tiny room off the side of a stairwell. Their door was broken and blocked ineffectively by some planks. After the father refused to speak to them, Daniel and Cray walked back through the cold corridors of the building. The other apartment residents met them with hard stares or jeered at them from across the courtyard. Daniel was increasingly glad that he had a bodyguard.

'Shit,' said Cray as they walked to the car. 'That place was brutal.'

'I thought you said you knew these people.'

'I knew where they lived,' said Cray. 'And I knew it was rough. I didn't know it was like that.'

'What about you?' said Daniel. 'What's your home like?'

'It's shit. But not like that,' said Cray.

By the end of the day, there weren't many families who were willing to open their doors to a strange Capricorn and an Aries kid. And the very few who did – six families in total – greeted Daniel's offer to fund a class-action lawsuit with bewilderment or suspicion. In the last house that Daniel tried, the child's guardian, a white-haired woman who looked like she was in her eighties, showed Daniel a lawyer's letter.

'I wanted to sue, believe me,' she said. 'But I signed an indemnity form. There's nothing I can do.'

At the end of the day, she was one of only three people who even seemed to understand what Daniel was trying to do. None of them agreed to sign up for his lawsuit.

Back in the car, he buried his head in his hands. 'Shit.'

'Why're you trying to get them all to sign that?' said Cray from the passenger seat. 'What difference is it going to make?'

'I just want to help them.'

'Yeah?' said Cray. 'You could go back and give them all cash.'

Daniel turned to Cray. 'Enough,' he said firmly.

'I don't get you,' said Cray. 'That school was shit. Every day I was there I wanted to burn it to the ground with those teachers inside. But worse shit's happened since then, and I've got more bad shit coming, and it's the same for every other kid who went there. So if you want to help them, why's it got to be about that school?'

'Because that's all I care about!' said Daniel loudly.

Cray looked at Daniel, calculating.

'Why do you care? Unless you're the dad of one of those three girls or something.'

Daniel strongly regretted his decision to spend time with Cray. He had only done it to prove a point to himself – that Cray was salvageable, and if he could save Cray he could save the rest of them. If he did that he would know that he could have saved his daughter if he'd had the chance.

'Oh, shit,' said Cray. 'I'm right. That's what this is about. Why'd you send your own daughter to a place like that?'

Daniel felt a moment of fury, but he let it subside. A fight with Cray would end badly for both of them.

'I didn't,' he said.

Cray looked at Daniel's face.

'Emma Pescowski,' he said. 'Trudy Norris. Pam Scarsdale.'

Daniel gripped the steering wheel hard.

'It's Pam,' said Cray. 'You look like her too. But you're a Cappy and she was a Pike.'

'Get out of the car,' he said.

Cray snorted. He got out of the car and closed the door behind him without a word. But he couldn't control his expression, which said that Daniel was a fool and that he'd got the better of him.

Chapter Thirty-Nine

Mendez leaned forward in his chair and gave Burton a long, cold stare. He pushed the newspaper across the desk and pointed at a paragraph in the article.

'Read it,' he said.

Even though the opening is more than two weeks away, the new police station is already causing tensions in the precinct. The Aries Rising leader Solomon Mahout is a particularly vocal critic. 'The Aries population of San Celeste lives in a state of constant fear. We know that any time we are out on the street we can be legally assaulted by state-sponsored thugs. And when we are in our homes, the doors can be kicked in without cause. This new police station isn't being built to keep our neighbourhood safe. There's no community outreach planned. There isn't even a public entrance for people to come in and report crimes. This building is a Ram Squad stronghold. It's a military base, and we are the occupied territory.'

Burton looked up from the article.

'OK, sir,' he said. 'What's this got to do with me?'

'You need me to spell it out for you now? What happened to the great Super Detective? We've got more and more protesters outside the new station every day. We've doubled the patrols in the area. We're about to start a curfew. We're doing everything we can to stop new Cardinal

Fire riots and you're asking for a patrol car to sit outside your house all day and all night to protect your precious ass, in case the big bad men come back? Who the fuck do you think you are?'

'Yes, sir,' said Burton, controlling his temper. 'I'm sorry for asking.'

'Yeah, well,' said Mendez. 'Be smarter. Now, what's the progress on the case?'

'Hammond's brother suggested that the murders are connected to a string of suicides from about ten years ago. I'm looking into an earlier investigation that Williams conducted and I'm waiting for some files out of storage. If there's strong evidence of a connection, I'll let you know. It was at Mahout's old school.'

Mendez's eyes snapped open. 'What?' he said. 'There's a connection to Mahout and you didn't fucking tell me?'

'He was one of hundreds of students. There's no evidence that he's involved yet. But if I get a chance to go through the old investigation –'

'What the hell are you talking about, Burton? Of course Mahout is involved! He's Solomon fucking Mahout! Who else could get two of the most influential people in the city killed? Who else has the rabid followers? You stupid fucking –'

Mendez didn't finish the slur, but he kept glaring at Burton.

'I want a report on my desk in fifteen minutes,' he said. 'And Mahout's name better be in it.'

Chapter Forty

That afternoon, Lindi worked from her apartment. Burton was preoccupied with the case and his home situation and was barely talking to her, so she dropped her work on the murder investigations and went back to the airport security procedures to restructure them for clarity. Every half an hour or so, a new text message came in from Bram Coine's phone number. She ignored them all.

> Hey, Lindi. I'm sorry about that, I was being dumb. Chat?

> Like I said, everyone was just playing around. It was just fun. No one was objectifying you. They're all enlightened & cool.

> They're being helpful. You should check out the board.

> Lindi, check out the board now!

She finally cracked. She picked up the phone and replied angrily.

> Bram, I don't care about the site. I'm trying to work. Please stop messaging me.

He replied almost instantly.

You'll care about this one. JUST LOOK.

She sighed out loud with the kind of exasperation you can only get away with in an empty apartment. Her laptop was buried under a pile of papers. She pulled it out and struggled to remember the name of Bram's message board. ACTIVENATION. So stupid. She found it in her Web history.

There were a few dozen new messages. Most of the text was in excitable all-caps, interspersed with images of police vehicles and riot cops and billowing tear gas. Every few seconds a new post appeared at the bottom of the screen, jolting the old news up.

'What the hell?' Lindi said aloud.

She scrolled back up and tried to figure out what was happening. The first picture was of police vehicles parked outside an unmarked brick building.

DurESSS: Police outside the Aries Rising headquarters in Ariesville. 3 Ram Squad & 6 patrol cars too. Looks like a raid.
Kart33: What? When did this happen?
DurESSS: RIGHT NOW.
AKT: HOLY SHIT THEY'RE ARRESTING SOLOMON MAHOUT! LIVE STREAM!!!!

Lindi clicked the link and a new window opened. After a few seconds of spinning buffer-wheel it cut to video with the washed-out look of cell phone footage, blocky from compression. The camera was pointing straight down at a tiled sidewalk that jumped around jerkily.

Lindi turned up the volume on her laptop until she could hear the choppy sound. It was mostly heavy breathing with screaming and sirens in the background.

'Oh, shit, look at this,' came a girl's voice.

The camera tilted up to a street corner, where a black police vehicle rolled past slowly. The whole thing was armour-plated, with grating over slit-like windows. A hatch opened on the roof and a cop climbed out up to the waist. He was wearing a helmet with a gas mask and thick armour plating, like an astronaut painted black. He pointed at the camera and shouted something unintelligible.

'What?' the unseen girl shouted back.

The cop didn't answer, but lifted something out of the hatch. It looked like an assault rifle. Lindi couldn't be sure, because the image blurred almost immediately. The speakers crackled.

For a terrified moment, Lindi thought that the girl holding the phone camera had been shot, but something blurred back and forth across the screen. It took a moment for her to figure out that the phone was being held upside down. She was seeing the girl's leg as she ran for her life.

Lindi leaned in closer to the image, trying to decipher the blurring movement. The camera swung towards a brick wall and edged around it cautiously to reveal a scene of chaos. There was a double-storey building on a commercial street with smoke pouring out of the upstairs and downstairs windows. Police vehicles were parked nearby and more men in body armour were running into the building. Lindi recognized it from the earlier picture as the Aries Rising HQ.

The camera panned around to show a group of bystanders. A pair of cops ran towards them and the crowd scattered. One of the cops aimed a thick-barrelled weapon at them and fired. A projectile landed among them and thick grey smoke billowed out.

'Shit!' said the girl with the camera.

The image bounced around and found the front of the building again. Some men and women wearing mainly red were being shoved out of the entrance ahead of the cops. The captives were choking from tear gas and their hands were bound. When they were far enough from the building they were forced down on to their knees and watched over by an armed cop while the others went back into the building. Lindi squinted at the screen. The phone camera had no zoom and the live stream was badly compressed, but one of the kneeling figures looked like Solomon Mahout. His shirt was torn and bloody and his face was bruised.

The camera shook and swung around again. More red-shirted figures were coming down the road towards the police vehicles. There was a roar of voices, although Lindi couldn't work out whether it was coming from the police or the approaching crowd. Some of the people at the front drew back their arms and threw rocks at the police. Cops with riot shields and raised truncheons ran from the vehicles towards the attackers. The camera swung back again and the image became an abstract streak of blocky light and dark, and froze. The buffer-wheel spun for a few seconds and a small text bubble popped up: 'STREAM DISCONNECTED'.

'No!' said Lindi, swiping at the track pad.

She closed the window and clicked back to the message board. The complaints were already flooding in with a stream of quiet pops.

DurESSS: My stream cut out.
Octagon: Mine too.
Kart33: Hey, where'd the stream go?
RomanRoulette: WTF? Is AKT all right? Anyone got her details?
Funkt: Trying to call other peeps on the scene. Hold tight!

Lindi spotted Bram joining in the conversation.

<<MARB>>: Anyone else got a feed going?

There was a pause that seemed to last for ever, then a new message popped up.

Funkt: Can't get msgs or streams from anyone in the area. Tried calling but all phones engaged. Worried.

And then:

Funkt: HOLY SHIT POLICE ARE BLOCKING CELL PHONES!
RomanRoulette: All carriers?
Funkt: Y.

Lindi took out her phone and checked the signal. She had four bars, but she wasn't in Ariesville.

She pressed on Burton's number. After five rings, he answered. His voice was testy.

'Hello, Lindi.'

'Burton, what the hell is going on in Ariesville? Are you there?'

'No, I'm in my office.'

'Why are you arresting Solomon Mahout?'

'I'm not,' said Burton. 'I had to hand in a report on our meeting with Kruger. I said that Mahout went to the school. I can't stop Mendez from doing what he wants with that information.'

'And you didn't want to investigate any deeper? What did you think was going to happen?'

'Don't start that, Lindi,' said Burton. 'I don't like it any more than you do, but what am I going to do? It's my job. And sorry if I can't exactly be as much of a stickler as I'd like. I don't know if you've realized, but I'm suddenly under a lot of fucking scrutiny.'

Chapter Forty-One

Daniel couldn't leave San Celeste. He knew himself too well. If he went back to his family home, then it wouldn't be long before he was back to his old depressed lifestyle. He had given up on his battle against the True Signs Academy, but that left him with nothing to do and nothing to believe in. The only thought that managed to prick through his thick shell of self-absorption was Maria's foster home in Ariesville. With some misgivings, he went back to offer his services.

'I'm glad you're here,' she said. 'Take these.'

She handed him a stack of clean sheets from the linen cupboard.

'Follow me.'

He carried them for her as she went on her morning clean-up rounds and helped her change the bedding in all the children's rooms. After that, he cleaned the kitchen and took the garbage to the dumpster in the fenced-off parking lot outside.

'How are you doing so far?' said Maria at the end of the morning.

'Fine,' he said.

He didn't want to play into the Capricorn stereotype by complaining. Part of him had been thinking that his time could be better spent hiring someone to help Maria do her chores. But it felt good to be involved at a basic level and get his hands dirty.

'Great,' she said. 'Come back tomorrow morning at eight.'

And just like that, his life had purpose.

It wasn't easy, though. He was used to a world without unpleasant encounters or upsetting incidents, and Maria's home had both on a regular basis. The kids fought, got sick, shouted, ran away and got hurt, but Daniel did his best to keep it all under control. He swept floors and chopped vegetables. He learned all the children's names, even though it meant embarrassing himself by having to ask more than once. He listened to complaints and arbitrated disputes. In that, at least, he had an advantage. The Capricorn accent was ingrained in popular culture as the voice of authority and even though the kids sometimes had a hard time understanding him they mostly obeyed his requests.

After a few weeks he was starting to feel like a valuable member of the home. He worked through the finances with Maria and donated some money of his own. In exchange, Maria gave him his own 'office' on the top floor, which was really just an empty supply room that he could go to whenever the noise and activity got too much. He appreciated it.

He was still himself, though. He was a rich man in Ariesville and, whenever he was outside the gates, he was an easy target. And not just him. The school was three blocks away and the kids had to walk that distance every morning and evening.

One day, Daniel called Cray's number to see if he was available. Cray gave him a hard time for 'acting like an asshole' the last time they had met, but he said he wasn't busy. They negotiated a new deal and Cray came to work as a security guard and assistant at the home.

Maria wasn't happy about it. 'He scares the kids,' she said.

'Why?' said Daniel. 'What's he doing?'

'Nothing. But they've all heard about him. He's got a reputation around here. He could end up being a bad influence. And I've got teenaged girls here.'

'I'll tell him that if he even looks at any of them, we'll cut off his testicles. OK?'

'Hmf,' said Maria, unconvinced.

'I just feel like I owe him a favour. And he's smart. He's better than you think he is.'

Fortunately, Cray kept to himself and the kids stayed away from him, until one day, when he came into the home carrying a bleeding girl.

It was mid-afternoon. Maria was out, leaving Daniel in charge for a few hours while she did the bulk shopping. He was in the fenced-off parking lot, playing a compact version of soccer and trying to explain to the kids why they should pick up their litter – which, growing up in Ariesville, was a laughable idea to them – when Cray came in through the main gate carrying Ella, one of the twelve-year-olds, in his arms. There was a cut across her forehead and her eye was swollen shut. She was moaning with a raw voice, like she had screamed as much as a child could. Another one of the really young girls, Brandy, followed behind Cray. She looked terrified to the point of tears and tried to hide from Daniel behind Cray's legs.

'What happened? Who did this?' said Daniel.

'Some of the kids snuck out of school after lunch,' said Cray. 'I found them on Weyland Street.'

The street had a row of old buildings that had recently been demolished. Despite the 'DANGER – NO TRESPASSING' signs, they had become an unofficial playground for the kids of Ariesville.

'The bigger kids were throwing bricks. One of them hit her,' said Brandy, and started crying.

Daniel took the girl out of Cray's arms.

'Look after all the children until Maria gets back,' he said.

He put young Ella into the car and took her to the nearest hospital, Deacon Avenue General.

The place was a shock. The only hospitals he had experienced personally were clean and private, with highly paid professionals who listened patiently and spoke with quiet authority. Deacon Avenue was overcrowded, loud and terrifying. The waiting room was filled with bleeding, coughing and dying people. A handful of impossibly young doctors ran from room to room, screaming instructions at each other, while exhausted-looking nurses waited passively until they received people's medical aid information. The floor was covered with filth. Daniel could only stand it for half an hour, then he put Ella back into the car again and took her to South SC General.

When Maria arrived two hours later, she found him in the waiting room reading a magazine.

'How is she?'

'Fine,' he said. 'But it was close. They told me her ocular orbit was fractured. If she hadn't been treated properly she could have been blinded permanently. I'm sorry for leaving the kids with Cray. There was no one else around.'

'It's fine. They're all watching TV. He's a little asshole, but at least he listens to me when it counts.'

'Yes,' said Daniel. 'And the other kids listen to him.'

'Huh,' said Maria.

She was tense. Daniel looked up at her.

'What is it?'

'I can't pay for her treatment at this place.' She waved her hand at the polished floor and abstract art on the walls. 'I can't afford it.'

'I know. I've already sorted it out.'

'Oh,' she said, relieved. 'Thank you.'

She sat down next to him and looked at him sidelong. He closed the magazine.

'Is something wrong?' he asked.

'I'm wondering if you think I suckered you.'

Daniel frowned. 'What do you mean?'

She took a deep breath. 'I used to work for a garment import business,' she said. 'My boss was a Capricorn and I never understood her until I realized that she was seeing every social interaction as a transaction. She never wanted to give more than she was getting, emotionally or financially. So I know what she would be thinking in your situation. She'd be thinking that the reason I asked you to donate your time was that it would get you in too deep. Once you knew these kids, you'd realize that a few hundred dollars a month isn't enough to cover all the clothes and shoes and school fees and broken bones. It's not enough to keep them alive.'

'But that wasn't your plan,' said Daniel.

'No. Maybe. I didn't think ahead like that. But . . . what if I did?' said Maria. 'Those kids are mine to look after and I can only do so much by myself. Before you started coming to the home, we were on the point of starving. Literally starving. No, I wasn't planning to milk you dry. But who else has the money?'

Daniel rubbed his temples.

Maria sighed. 'Right now, the home is a disaster. I'm doing what I can, but it's barely better than the places the kids came from. I need to make it work properly. I need new ideas. I thought I'd try to go to some corporations and see if they'd sponsor the place, but no one wants to touch it. It's in a slum and everything is always chaotic. They don't want to be associated with a mess, no matter what good intentions I have or how impossible it is to fix the situation any other way. They want something simple to understand. What's their word? Quantifiable. A man at one of the corporations told me straight out, "If you had a murder or rape at your home, our image would be tarnished."' She shook her head. 'But, with you around . . . you know these businesspeople. You can talk their language, right? Can you think of . . . I don't know, a charity gala event or something? Some way to fix things? Because right now I've got more kids than I can handle. Every day I have to turn away more and I need new ideas, because I'm out. I'm all out.'

Chapter Forty-Two

Burton pushed his way into Bram Coine's room ahead of Bram's father. Lindi was sitting on the bed surrounded by printed astrology charts. Bram swivelled around from his desk, where he had been typing on Lindi's laptop. A speaker system in the corner was pumping out the kind of thudding music that Burton had never, in his life, been young enough to enjoy.

'What the hell, Lindi?'

'Now hold on, Detective –' said Bram's father from the hallway behind him. He was within his rights to stop Burton from entering his house, but he hadn't stood up for them, and Burton was too angry to be stopped by politeness.

Burton raised a finger. 'It's all right, Mr Coine. I'm just here to collect my colleague. Lindi, can I talk with you outside, please? Pack up your things.'

'What's your problem?' said Lindi.

Bram's father put a hand on Burton's upper arm and tried to steer him out of the room. 'Please, Detective –'

'I am leaving,' said Burton, pulling himself away. 'I'll wait outside your house. Thank you for your time. Lindi?'

She glared back at him. It seemed that she was going to refuse, but there was no way she could without looking petulant.

'Fine,' she said.

Bram's father escorted Burton outside and he leaned against his car in the street. There was nothing to alleviate the boredom of waiting for Lindi except to play out in his mind the argument he was about to have with her.

Five minutes later she still wasn't out and Burton started to think she was annoying him deliberately. He was going to ring the bell again when the door opened and she came out with her laptop bag under one arm and a folder full of papers under the other. She looked flustered.

'What the fuck, Burton?' she said. 'There was no reason to flip out. We were working.'

'Working?' said Burton. 'You're legally prohibited from sharing any information about the investigation with outsiders. Especially with someone who was a suspect less than a week ago. And especially if it's Bram fucking Coine!'

'I didn't share anything with him. I know he pissed off the cops, but that doesn't mean he isn't useful. He's in this online group and they're looking into the case –'

'Oh, great,' said Burton. 'Internet vigilantes.'

'Listen for a second, Burton. You're being childish.'

Burton was close to exploding. 'Childish?' he said. 'I just found you sitting on a bed with superhero sheets –'

'Can we have one argument at a time please?' she said. 'Bram says his friends were looking into exactly how Hammond raised the funding for Kruger's school and it's really strange. Some of it came from private donors, but a lot of the money was actually from local government as part of the Civil Response Act. You've heard about the Civil Response Act?'

'Sure,' said Burton.

The CRA was some controversial legislation pushed

through after the Cardinal Fire riots twenty-five years ago. It gave local government and law enforcement agencies special powers to deal with rioters and terrorist organizations, ostensibly on a temporary basis. Civil rights groups used to complain about it, saying that the new laws were overreaching and lacked transparency, but the outrage slowly burned out. The CRA became just another fact of life, as unalterable as the orbit of the planets.

'So why would a school get funds that were meant to be used for stopping riots?' said Lindi. 'It sounds like maybe Hammond was working with someone in City Hall to misappropriate funds. And maybe whoever that money was earmarked for got angry?'

'Are you saying the Ram Squad killed them?'

'I'm not saying anything. I'm just pointing out the irregularities.'

Burton pinched the bridge of his nose.

'OK, listen,' he said. 'I don't know why the school got CRA money. Maybe City Hall was trying something new. Maybe they thought that educating kids would be a better long-term solution than arresting them. Who knows? The only thing I know for sure is that I'm not going to spend the next five years writing Freedom of Information requests that will never be honoured. I have to find this killer now. So I won't tell Mendez that you've been talking to Coine, but I need you to stop antagonizing our allies. Let's go back to the office and piece together the evidence against Mahout. Either I need a watertight case against him or I need to prove him innocent and get him out of the station before someone else does it by force.'

Chapter Forty-Three

Daniel waited at the hospital until ten p.m., when young Ella was finally discharged. She had bandages across half of her face and was very subdued on the car ride back to Ariesville. Maria welcomed them with a great deal of relief. While she put Ella to bed, Daniel went upstairs to his small private office to get his briefcase.

The light in the room was already on and Cray was sitting at his desk. He got to his feet when he saw Daniel at the door.

'Relax,' said Daniel. 'It's fine. You can use this place too. I'm just here to get some things.'

Cray lowered himself back into the chair.

'Thanks,' he said. 'The kids are all in bed. Margie and Ellen are still fighting, so I put them in separate rooms.'

'Good. Well done,' said Daniel. He saw a bottle of whiskey and two glasses on his desk. 'Hey, where'd you get that?'

'I bought it,' said Cray. The glass in front of him was half-full. He poured a finger-width into the other.

'You're too young to drink,' said Daniel.

'Says who?' said Cray dismissively. 'The law?'

He screwed the cap back on to the bottle and pushed the glass across the table. Daniel wanted to set a good example, but it had been a heavy day and, honestly, he didn't really care. As far as he was concerned, Cray was old enough to make his own bad decisions. He sipped the whiskey and winced.

'That's terrible,' he said.

'You buy the next bottle, then.'

'Not a chance.'

Cray reached under the desk and lifted up a fast-food bag.

'I've got a chicken burger too, if you want it,' he said.

Daniel hadn't eaten since lunch. He reached out and Cray handed the bag over. It was still warm. Daniel would normally barely consider this food, but he ate the burger fast and polished off the half-cooled chips. He wiped his mouth with a paper napkin while Cray poured them both another whiskey.

'Thanks,' said Daniel.

They sat in silence for a while, sipping their drinks, then Daniel said, 'I've got a question. If it was up to you, how would you fix these kids' lives?'

Cray narrowed his eyes at Daniel.

'Where the fuck did that come from?'

'Maria asked me for ideas on how to get more money, but I don't know if that's the solution. It seems like you could pump money into this place and the kids would still have the same life to look forward to when they left. They'd still have the same trouble finding jobs, or getting loans, or finding a safe place to live. I don't have the answers for her. But she asked for a fresh perspective. Maybe you have one.'

Cray finished his drink and put the glass down on the table. He tilted it at an angle, resting it on the edge of its base, and put a finger on the upper rim. He flicked it and watched the glass spin.

'I'll tell you what I think,' he said. 'I think this place is a lifeboat. You need lifeboats, but you can't get far in one.

Problem is, all the other boats round here are sinking. At least these kids have Maria to look out for them. Everyone else in Ariesville is fending for themselves, one way or the other. You can't fix these kids' lives until you fix Ariesville.'

'How?'

Cray grunted and shrugged. 'I don't know. Politics or something.' He kept staring into the glass.

Daniel tried another tack. 'When you were growing up, what were the biggest problems?'

'Ha,' said Cray flatly. 'Dead Libra mom. Drunk Aries dad. Asshole brother. A million assholes in the streets outside.'

'I didn't know you had a brother.'

'He died. He was in the army for, like, three days and got his back broken in a hazing ritual. He moped around for a couple of months in a wheelchair before he died in hospital. Pneumonia.'

'Shit,' said Daniel. 'Sorry.'

Cray gave Daniel a look like he didn't know what he was talking about. Daniel didn't push it.

'And your dad?'

'Also an asshole.'

'Did he beat you?'

'Nah,' said Cray, and wiped his nose with his sleeve. 'A bit when we were younger, but we learned to fight back. And he was normally so shit-faced that we could take him down. He doesn't try that on me any more. He's just pathetic now.'

'What did he do?'

'He was a tiler. He was doing OK until the landlord broke his fingers. He gave up mostly after that.'

'What?' said Daniel, shocked.

'You gotta pay the rent on time,' said Cray. 'Everyone

in Ariesville knows that. People go to those payday loan companies with crazy interest rather than getting on the wrong side of Hernandez.'

'Who?' said Daniel.

Cray raised his eyebrows. 'Hernandez! How come you never heard of Miguel Hernandez?' he said. 'I thought you were a big shot.'

Over the next hour he explained it all to Daniel. Most of the property in Ariesville was owned by only three or four family businesses. They fixed prices, which was why the cost of rent in Ariesville was higher than in the rest of the city despite the terrible conditions. The poorest people in the city were trapped there because no one in any other area would rent to them, and because there was no limit to the number of people that the landlords would allow them to pack in. Whole extended families were living in single-room apartments.

'Hernandez is the biggest one,' said Cray. 'He owns most of this area, just north of the river. I can't believe you haven't heard of him. If he wasn't an Aries, everyone in the city would know his name.'

'That's straight-up exploitation,' said Daniel.

'Huh,' said Cray into his whiskey glass.

'And no one's tried to stop him?'

'How? The only people richer than him in Ariesville are the dealers and they don't care. They're in it with him. The rest of the city couldn't give a fuck.'

'And his men broke your father's fingers?'

'Not just my father. Ask anyone. The landlords make sure everyone knows what happens when you don't pay your rent.'

Chapter Forty-Four

Lindi sat in Burton's office and did her astrological investigation while he typed up his detailed progress report on the other side of the L-shaped desk. They had hardly spoken since they had arrived at the station. He was still mad about her talking to Bram, and she was still angry at him for flipping out and for not taking Bram's investigation seriously.

There was a tap on the open office door and Detective Rico leaned in.

'Here are Hammond's and Mahout's unabridged birth certificates,' he said, holding out an envelope for Burton.

Lindi turned on her chair. 'I'll take them,' she said.

Rico looked to Burton, checking that it was OK. Unabridged certificates allowed Lindi or any other astrologer to make accurate birth charts, which naturally made them highly confidential documents. Companies could fire employees for having inauspicious charts. Insurance companies could use them as a basis to raise their clients' premiums.

Burton nodded and Rico handed Lindi the envelope.

'Thanks,' she said, and turned back to her desk to open it.

She could feel both men's eyes on her. Burton had probably told Rico about her and Bram. She focused on typing up the information into her astrology software, creating two new birth charts and running synastry comparisons. After a while, she muttered under her breath.

'Weird.'

'What?' said Burton over his shoulder.

She showed him one of the charts.

'Look. It's a weird coincidence.'

'What is?'

'This is Harvey Hammond's chart compared to Chief Williams's. You see? Their suns are almost exactly ninety degrees to each other. Eighty-nine point eight degrees.'

'OK,' said Burton, a little impatiently. 'Just let me know if you find anything connecting either of them to Mahout.'

He turned back to his keyboard and kept on typing. Lindi looked at the chart and tapped her fingers on the desk, thinking about it.

After a few minutes, Burton sighed from behind her.

'It doesn't mean anything,' he said. 'Forget it.'

'Sorry,' said Lindi. Her eyes darted over her screen. 'But I really think that it does.'

'Can you please just look at Mahout's chart and see if there are any coincidences there that you can use to tie him to either Hammond or Williams? It doesn't matter that Hammond and Williams are connected.'

'Why not?' said Lindi, turning her chair to face him.

'Because we already knew that. They were friends. We don't need to prove it to a jury. But we do need to prove that Mahout's involved, right now, convincingly enough to stop a riot.'

Lindi folded her arms.

'What would it take for me to prove to you that this was important?' she said.

Burton thought about it. 'Three things,' he said finally, and counted them off on his fingers. 'One, is it such a weird coincidence that it needs a special explanation? I once had a case where two victims and a killer all had the same middle name. It didn't need investigating, because unlikely things just happen sometimes. It's a roll of the dice. Two, is there any possible underlying explanation for the coincidence? And three, can we use it to predict our killer?'

'OK,' said Lindi, and mimicked his finger-counting. 'Well, one, yes, I think that it's an odd enough coincidence that it's worth looking into. Two, we've got hundreds of years of astrological theory to give us the underlying explanation. And three, we can only find out if it'll help the case if we look a little deeper. But I think that it's a hell of an interesting pattern.'

'Why?' said Burton. 'What's so great about it?'

'Because we don't know Kruger's exact birth date, but he's an Aquarius like me, so we know that he was born in January or February, which means that his sun is ninety degrees from Williams and 180 degrees from Hammond. Hang on.'

She took a piece of paper from Burton's desk and drew six lines on it, all crossing each other at a centre point, making twelve evenly spaced segments. With practised ease she drew the astrological symbols into each of the segments: Aries, Taurus, Gemini, Cancer, Leo, Virgo, Libra, Scorpio, Sagittarius, Capricorn, Aquarius, Pisces.

'This is the heavens,' she said.

'Yeah,' said Burton. 'I know.'

She ignored his tone.

'Now, Astrology 101. Each of these signs gets their qualities from two things: their element . . .'

She started with Aries and went clockwise around the symbols, writing in 'FIRE', 'EARTH', 'AIR', 'WATER', 'FIRE', 'EARTH', 'AIR', 'WATER' . . .

'And the quality of that element.'

She went around the circle, writing in 'CARDINAL', 'FIXED', 'MUTABLE', 'CARDINAL', 'FIXED', 'MUTABLE' . . .

'So you're Taurus, which is fixed earth. That means you get the qualities of the earth element, so you're down to earth, trustworthy, reliable, loyal. And Pisces are mutable water, which means they're wishy-washy and they go with the flow. What I'm saying is, our elements are a fundamental part of who we are. Are you following all of this?'

'Mostly,' said Burton.

'OK. So Williams was born when the sun was in Taurus . . .'

She wrote 'WILLIAMS' over 'EARTH'.

'And Hammond was born when the sun was in Leo.'

She wrote 'HAMMOND' over 'FIRE'.

'You see?' she said.

'Holy shit,' said Burton.

'Exactly,' said Lindi. 'Two people killed in the element of their sign. It's so basic that it's barely astrology. And look at this.'

She drew a dotted line from 'HAMMOND' through the centre of the chart to Aquarius. She wrote 'KRU-GER' over 'AIR'.

'And if I'm right about this, there should be one more point in the square . . .'

She drew a dotted line from 'WILLIAMS' to Scorpio, but didn't write a name.

'This,' she said, 'is what we call a grand crux. It's normally considered highly inauspicious, because a square aspect means that energies are being blocked, although I've heard that some people deliberately seek it out. The Branch Morinians believe that square aspects are actually superimposed harmonics that . . .'

She saw Burton's face and dialled back.

'Sorry,' she said. 'It all boils down to the fact that this is astrologically significant.'

'But what's it telling us that we didn't already know?' said Burton. 'Williams, Hammond and Kruger all knew each other. Isn't this just proof of that, written in the stars?'

'Yeah, but look at this,' said Lindi. She pointed at the element names. 'Death by earth. Death by fire. Kruger's going to die by air, and a fourth person, we don't know who, is going to be killed by water.'

Burton looked at the diagram. His eyes darted from one element to the other.

'Shit,' he said quietly.

'Yeah. How's that for a prediction?'

Chapter Forty-Five

The next morning, Daniel didn't go to Maria's foster home. Instead, he made some phone calls and visited his lawyers' offices. The day after that, he called up Cray.

'How much do you know about Miguel Hernandez?' he asked.

'As much as anyone round here knows,' said Cray. 'Why?'

'Would you recognize his rent collectors? The violent ones?'

'Sure! Some of them. There's Gill, Hank, Cesar . . .'

'Great. Meet me outside the home in one hour.'

When Daniel arrived, Cray was leaning against the front gate. He came over to Daniel's car and got in the passenger side.

'What's all this spy business?' he said. 'What are you doing? Are you taking on Hernandez somehow?'

'I'll show you. Seat belt.'

Cray rolled his eyes, but buckled up.

They left Ariesville on Western Boulevard, driving through the industrial area and out the other side. The buildings thinned out and rolling green lawns became visible behind high security fences.

Daniel turned through a gate marked 'Stone River Business Park'. He showed an ID card to a security guard, who raised a barrier and waved them in. They parked in an underground lot and walked up through a second security gate and into a brick-paved courtyard. Doors led into the offices of various businesses: NRV Sports, Axonic Consulting, Dynamic Human Logistics.

Daniel led Cray to an unmarked door at the far end of the courtyard, behind a small circular fountain that some skinny Virgo and Sagittarius types were sitting around, chatting and throwing pieces of pastry to the seagulls. He took out a key and unlocked the door, setting off the high-pitched whine of a security system. Cray winced. Daniel tapped a code into a keypad next to the door and the noise cut out with three beeps. He turned on the strip lighting and showed Cray inside.

The walls of the office were bare. There was no furniture besides a stack of desks and six bubble-wrapped swivel chairs to the side of the entrance. The carpet was blue-grey, marked with circular dimples from where table legs had once rested. In one corner there was a small empty kitchenette area and at the back was an open door going through to a private office. Cardboard boxes and computer monitors were lined up against the rear wall.

'What the hell's this?' said Cray as he walked in. He looked around, genuinely confused.

'This,' said Daniel, 'is how we're going to take down Miguel Hernandez. I'm registering a new company, Regrowth Properties. What do you think?'

Cray snorted. 'You're going to take out Hernandez from this dinky little office?'

'Why not? For what I'm planning I don't need a big staff. At least, not yet. This place has everything we need to run a legitimate business and the overheads are low.'

'I don't get you,' said Cray. 'You understand that if you come after Hernandez, his guys will straight-up kill you, right? When you said you were taking me to see something, I thought you'd bought, like, a gun and a bulletproof vest.'

'What, really?' said Daniel.

'Or, like, night-vision goggles and, I don't know, a taser or something. So you could take out Hernandez's guys in a dark alleyway and no one would see, and then put handcuffs on them and leave them for the cops.'

Daniel couldn't stop himself from laughing. 'Like a superhero?' he said.

Cray's cheeks reddened. 'I don't know! It's as crazy as whatever it is you're planning!'

Daniel felt a little bad. Cray was normally sharp and he had been forced to grow up so fast that Daniel sometimes forgot how young he still was. There was a lot he didn't know.

'Listen, Cray,' he said. 'Hernandez might be a gangster, but he's playing at being a businessman, and he's failing. That means we can take him out honestly and there's nothing he can do about it. There's a whole system in place to take out people like him. If what you say is true and he's openly using violence to get the money owed to him, it shouldn't be hard to prove. And that gives us leverage. We can force him into selling his properties at a reasonable price, and that's the first step in cleaning up Ariesville.'

'He'll fight back. If he finds out what you're planning, he won't think twice about burning this place down.'

'He won't find out,' said Daniel. 'Don't worry. I'm

low-key and I have a major advantage. I know who he is, so I can easily keep track of what he's up to. And remember, he has no idea who I am. So if he wants to threaten me, he has to find out what I'm up to first and then find me in person. And with what I'm planning to do, I can take him down from anywhere in the world. This office could be in Helsinki and I'd still get him.'

'You'll wish it was if he finds out,' said Cray.

Daniel shrugged. 'He can do what he likes to this place. It's rented.'

Chapter Forty-Six

Detective Kolacny stuck his fingers through the aluminum blinds in the Homicide Department and pulled them apart. He looked down at the protesters in the street below.

'There's a lot more of them,' he said.

Burton came to join him. Some of the crowd were in red shirts, but a lot of them looked like standard San Celeste citizens, which was scary. They'd arrested Solomon Mahout too early and now Aries Rising was winning the war of words. Someone had mass-printed signs saying 'FREE MAHOUT'.

'Joke's on them,' said Rico. 'We don't even have Mahout here.'

'Really? Where is he?'

'The Ram Squad took him away last night. I think they've got him at their new station in Ariesville.'

'I thought that wasn't open yet,' said Burton.

'Oh, it's open. They haven't got the Mayor there with the big novelty scissors and the ribbon, but it's a fully functional station. They've been in there for weeks.'

The roar of the crowd outside turned into a regular chant.

'Aries Rights! Aries Rights!'

'Fuck this,' said Rico. 'They've got no right to protest for that son of a bitch. My house was broken into by Aries thugs. My sister got assaulted on the train. Where's our protest march?'

'Burton!' came a voice from the doors at the far end of the department. Mendez was strutting towards them. 'Thanks for the report on Mahout. You did your best, but some solid evidence would go a long way towards shutting up those people outside.'

'Yes, sir,' said Burton. 'Did you get my report on that star pattern Lindi Childs found?'

'I did.'

'And did you see the note I attached to it? Because the only prominent Scorpio that Williams and Hammond knew was the Mayor, and if he's a target of the killer –'

Mendez raised a hand.

'No, Burton. Just look outside. We already know that the Mayor needs protection and Special Investigation Services is looking after him. He'll be fine. I sent the SIS a warning, and Kruger too, but Lindi Childs's theory is sketchy as hell. The Mayor is under a lot of pressure as it is. He might have to declare martial law. Don't interfere with him until we get something solid. Now, where do we stand on Mahout?'

Chapter Forty-Seven

That evening, on his way home, Burton received a call from an unknown number. He put it on speaker.

'Hello?'

'Good evening, Detective. This is Bruce Redfield.'

The voice was calm and assured. It took Burton a few seconds to place the name.

'Mr Mayor,' he said, surprised.

'That's right. Captain Mendez says that you found something interesting in my birth chart.'

'Not me, sir. The astrologer I'm working with, Lindi Childs.'

'Ah, yes,' said the Mayor, and paused. 'And have either of you told anyone else?'

'No, sir. Not that I'm aware of.'

'All right, Detective. If you're free tomorrow afternoon, I'd very much like to speak to you both, privately. Come around to my house at five. I'll let the guard know.'

'Sir,' said Burton, 'is something wrong?'

'No, no, not at all,' said the Mayor. 'It's just that . . . I have been warned that the particular thing that she found in my chart could be misunderstood. I want to get you both here so I can explain it to you in person, so you'll understand why I prefer if it doesn't become public knowledge. And, obviously, the meeting shouldn't be public knowledge either. I appreciate your discretion.'

'Yes, sir. Five o'clock.'

'Thank you, Burton. And I was very sorry to see that Aubrey piece. Hammond would have never stooped to that level of baseless accusation. You're the furthest person from an Aries I've met.'

Burton knew that the Mayor was just being a politician, but he still felt grateful. He had needed to hear that, from anyone.

'Thank you, sir,' he said. 'That means a lot to me.'

Chapter Forty-Eight

In less than a month Daniel's new venture was up and running, with a staff of fifteen that included receptionists, payroll, project management and a sizeable legal department. Cray was Daniel's first employee and his official assistant. To his credit, Cray dropped a lot of his normal swagger around the office. He threw himself into the work, which was whatever Daniel needed him to do – generally basic office-related tasks like entering data, looking up publicly accessible records and getting comparative prices. He stayed late at night to get work done, and was tenacious and focused. He went the extra mile, doing more research, making suggestions and, most importantly, asking questions. He was learning quickly.

Daniel had to remind himself not to trust Cray too far, though. Cray had gained some respect for Daniel, probably because Daniel showed the same respect back, but he had hard limits. If Daniel talked about the True Signs Academy, Cray would clam up or deflect sarcastically. Everyone else at the office was wary of him, and Daniel kept him away from any tasks that required talking on the phone. Cray could be ruthless and it was possible, however unlikely, that he was ingratiating himself with Daniel only long enough to get himself into a position of trust. Once he had access to the company account, it was entirely possible that he would clean it out and disappear.

After all, this was the same boy who had once punched Daniel in the gut for his wallet.

But suspicion was exhausting. Over the next few months, Daniel gave Cray plenty of opportunities to screw him over, sometimes deliberately, sometimes by accident. Cray didn't take any of them. He never complained and he never took so much as a stapler. Even though Daniel had laughed when Cray suggested he was becoming a superhero, Daniel liked the idea that they were a kind of dynamic duo. Cray had good instincts and an abrasive charisma. Daniel had wealth and influence. Together they could change the city. And the first thing they needed to do was to get Miguel Hernandez arrested.

It was a simple enough plan. Daniel had discussed it at length with their small legal department. Hernandez was clearly getting around various laws and city statutes by bribing the inspectors. Having him arrested would put him on the back foot and make it harder to run his business in the way he was accustomed to. It would put the spotlight on him, forcing him to play by the rules, and as soon as he did that Daniel had him by the balls.

The only person who wasn't on board with the plan was Maria.

'This is bullshit, Daniel.'

Daniel and Cray still spent most of their weekends working at the home. Cray was in the recreation room, making sure the games didn't get out of hand, while Daniel and Maria were getting supper ready in the kitchen. At Daniel's insistence they were preparing vegetables to go along with the deep-fried chicken, even though he knew that most of the kids would leave them at the side of their plate. He chopped tomatoes while Maria berated him.

'Why are you doing this?' she said. 'If Hernandez finds out what you're planning, who do you think he's going to come after? Not you, at your fancy hotel, with your security.'

'He's not going to find out about me,' said Daniel. 'And I'm going after him so I can fix things around here. If Ariesville stays the way it is, you'll have generation after generation of kids to look after. This is in their own best interests.'

'Don't give me that, you asshole!' said Maria, dunking chipped potatoes into the boiling oil. 'Don't pretend to be coming in here as a saviour! This is about your own business interests!'

'That's not fair,' said Daniel. 'You want Hernandez running Ariesville? No? OK. Then someone else has to own his land. At least I'm not going to exploit these people.'

'No, you're just going to take their money to let them live on your land.'

Daniel put down his knife. 'You can't seriously be blaming me for the concept of property ownership,' he said. 'What do you want me to do? Give the land away to the tenants?'

'No, but you can stop lying to yourself and everyone else about what you're doing. And please don't make my kids the pawns in your property game.'

'I'm not going to turn into Hernandez, Maria.'

'Oh, yeah?' she said. 'And how are you going to handle it when your tenants can't pay you? Or when they break the law and jam whole families into small apartments because they can't afford to do anything else?'

'I'm going to give them a fair chance and a reasonable rent.'

Maria gave him side-eyes.

'Sure,' she said. 'And after that and they still don't pay, you're going to kick them out because you can't afford to make a loss, right? So they'll end up on the street, and their kids will end up here, and that's just the way that life works. Don't get excited about how much of a hero you are.'

Beyond Maria's scepticism, getting Hernandez arrested turned out to be more of a challenge than Daniel expected. While there was no doubt that Hernandez was criminally exploitative, none of the tenants Daniel approached agreed to testify against him, even after he promised them safety and security. He needed a new source of evidence. As the weeks went by and his costs started mounting, he began to consider desperate measures. He purchased surveillance equipment – microphones, micro cameras and GPS trackers – and got his lawyers to lay out the exact limits of the legality and admissibility of any recordings he might make.

Capturing audio or video inside Hernandez's properties was out of the question, so it would have to be in public. Fortunately, Hernandez's collectors weren't shy. At the beginning of the new month Daniel and Cray followed them from a safe distance as they went on their collection run through Ariesville. Before the first hour was up, the men had already kicked in a door and dragged a screaming lady out on to the street by the hair. Daniel filmed it with a telephoto lens from his car, and Cray walked past and caught the audio on a microphone strapped to his wrist. It was getting close to the superhero action of Cray's imagination, except that, after it was over, the poor woman was still sobbing in the street and Hernandez's men had taken everything from the wallet in her handbag. Daniel was shocked at how open the men were about what they did. Then again, no one ever called the cops in Ariesville.

'This isn't enough,' said one of Daniel's lawyers after reviewing the recordings back at the office. 'Hernandez could just say he doesn't condone this behaviour and fire his men. Now, if they'd mentioned his name, it might be easier to make this stick . . .'

Daniel thought about it. 'If those guys were arrested, do you think they'd turn on Hernandez?'

Cray shook his head. 'Not a chance,' he said. 'He'd murder them.'

Daniel stayed late that evening, putting together investment proposals to secure the funding to buy out Hernandez's properties, assuming he could ever get Hernandez to sell. Cray stayed on too, educating himself on property owner responsibilities and going through government records on one of the office computers.

After a few hours, he looked across at Daniel.

'Hernandez has got some apartment buildings due for inspection. Fire safety, structural integrity, stuff like that.'

'I know,' said Daniel. 'I wanted to get him arrested before they happened, so the inspectors would be less likely to accept bribes. Then he'd be on the ropes.'

'Yeah,' said Cray. 'But maybe you're doing it the wrong way around.'

'What do you mean?'

'We can't lean on the tenants and we can't lean on Hernandez's men, but how about a nice city inspector who's just taken a bribe? They don't know Hernandez that well, so they're more scared of jail.'

Daniel stared at him. 'Cray,' he said, 'you genius.'

They didn't even have to use any of the surveillance equipment. All it took was an anonymous complaint to the department of housing and, two days later, an inspector was sent out to investigate three of Hernandez's buildings ahead of schedule. She gave them all a pass, as expected. Cray went in afterwards and surreptitiously took some photos on his cell phone showing the building damage, disconnected fire escapes, overcrowded rooms, broken elevators, crumbling concrete and rusted rebar, all next to a newspaper showing the current date. Daniel emailed them anonymously to the inspector's superior at the department. The inspector was quietly let go, but Daniel pulled some strings and spoke to an acquaintance at City Hall. The supervisor was called in for a disciplinary hearing and the inspector was arrested.

Daniel even got to see a transcript of her tearful confession. She admitted that Hernandez offered her money and threatened her family if she didn't take it. And she thought, It's only Ariesville . . .

An arrest warrant was issued for Miguel Hernandez, and because he lived in Ariesville it was the Ram Squad that picked him up. There was a risk that Hernandez was bribing cops too, which is why Daniel had been so cautious in the first place, but this was one time that the hardboiled signism of the Taurus cops was to Daniel's advantage. None of them were on Hernandez's payroll. He had no traction with any of them. Some of his drug-dealer friends may have had the leverage to help him out, but none of them stuck their necks out for him. He was going down and his legal fees were about to go up. And Daniel was about to step in as his financial saviour.

The evening he found out that Hernandez had been arrested, Daniel held a celebration at the home. He ordered three cakes – one chocolate, one strawberry sponge and one vanilla with marzipan icing – and he brought streamers and party hats for the kids. He scattered multicoloured sweets on the long table.

'Why're you getting the kids to celebrate your business deal?' said Maria.

'There's no business deal yet,' said Daniel. 'That's coming next, if we can pull it off. This is just about taking a bad man down a notch and that's worth celebrating, right?'

'Who's it a party for?' asked one of the girls, Zoë. She had freckles and long frizzy hair in bunches.

'It was my birthday three days ago,' said a boy called Max, looking hopeful.

'It's Max's party?' said Zoë, and folded her arms. 'How come Max gets a big party when I didn't get anything?'

'It's not a party for Max,' said Maria firmly.

'Ha! You hear that?' said one of the bigger boys. He grabbed Max by the shoulder and pulled him away from the table. 'None for you!'

He laughed at his joke, but Maria raised a stern finger in warning.

'Brad! Knock it off! It's Mr Lapton's party.'

The children all turned to look at Daniel suspiciously.

'Mr Lapton? Is it your birthday?'

'No,' he said.

'Then why are you throwing yourself a party?' said Brad. 'Is that something Capricorns do?'

Maria raised an eyebrow at Daniel, trying not to grin too smugly.

Daniel looked around at all the expectant faces. He couldn't tell them. If Hernandez found out about Daniel's part in his arrest, then any possible deal would be out of the question and his company would be sunk.

'No,' said Daniel. 'It's a celebration for all of you.'

They looked doubtful.

'I wanted to give you something,' he said. 'To pay you back. You've all given me something worth fighting for. Thank you. All of you.'

It wasn't the whole truth, but it was part of it and he meant it sincerely. The answer seemed good enough for the kids, who cheered themselves unselfconsciously and pounced on the sweets and soda. Even Maria's scepticism seemed to abate temporarily. Daniel hit play on the home's busted CD player system with only one working speaker. Combined with the natural energy of the kids, it was more than enough to get a lively party started.

Daniel was cutting up and serving the cakes when his phone buzzed. He pulled it out and checked the screen.

It was Cray. Daniel had assumed that he wasn't coming. Cray was eighteen and he didn't have to hang out with a bunch of young kids if he didn't want to. It wasn't strange that he wasn't there. It was strange that he was even calling about it.

Daniel answered. 'Hello?'

The line rustled and clunked. It sounded like Cray was out in the street. In the background were distant shouts and car engines.

'Hernandez knows,' said Cray. There was panic in his voice.

'What?'

'His guys kicked in my door. He kicked my dad into the street and threw out all our stuff. My dad said they were looking for me. He knows. I don't know how, but he knows.'

Daniel looked around the room, at the brightly coloured sweets and the happy, oblivious faces of the kids. The front gate was locked and the doors were bolted, but he suddenly felt vulnerable.

The light outside was wrong. He hadn't noticed before because of all the activity in the room, but there was a gentle flickering coming in from behind the room's old red curtains.

'Shit!' said Daniel.

He pulled them back. The window didn't look out directly on to the parking lot, but he could see the orange and yellow glow reflecting off the peeling white paint of the home's side wall.

The kids slowly started realizing that something was wrong and their happy chatter turned to shouts of panic. Daniel dropped his phone on the table and ran to the kitchen. He shoved his way past Maria, who was bringing in more soda.

'Hey!' she said. 'What's happening?'

'Fire!'

In the corner of the kitchen cabinet, next to the six-plate gas stove, was an old extinguisher. Daniel hoped it would still work – it was covered in a thin layer of dust and he knew that fire extinguishers had expiry dates. He pulled the deadbolt on the back door that led out on to the parking lot. It shrieked on its hinges.

His car was on fire. The flames engulfed it, spreading across its roof and pooling on the asphalt around it. It was gasoline. Someone had set fire to his car. The gate of the home hung down at an angle, still chained shut. The lower hinge had been crowbarred off and the whole gate was twisted, making a space to enter underneath.

Daniel ran towards the flames, with one arm raised to protect his face from the scorching heat. He choked on the fumes of burning gasoline and tyre rubber. His fingers fumbled at the top of the extinguisher and found the plastic safety tag that held the pin in place. A man ran up beside him and pulled the extinguisher from his hands. For a moment Daniel thought it was someone who knew how to use it coming to the rescue, but instead the man swung it up into his face and smashed it across his jaw like a baseball bat.

Tendons snapped. He felt his jaw dislocating. The pain was like nothing he had ever experienced. His legs gave out from under him. He stumbled and fell sideways down to the gravel.

The man standing over him was wearing a brown leather biker's jacket and a black balaclava. He threw the extinguisher down on Daniel, spiking it like a football player. Daniel couldn't move in time to protect himself and it hit him in the chest. His ribs cracked. The man reached down, grabbed Daniel by the hair and pulled him around until he was facing the kitchen entrance. Two more men in balaclavas were walking into the home carrying jerrycans. Screams broke out inside. The man above Daniel kept his grip on Daniel's scalp, making sure that he couldn't look away.

'Watch, you bastard! Watch what happens when you fuck with Hernandez!'

Chapter Forty-Nine

Burton came to Lindi's flat to pick her up at four thirty. She seemed to be in a much better mood than the last time he had seen her.

'Hey,' he said, as they drove along the freeway down to the southern suburbs. 'I'm sorry I got angry about you visiting Bram. I was just trying to hold things together. But you're an adult. You can violate your own contract if you want to.'

'No,' she said. 'It's OK. To be honest, it was getting a little too familiar in that room.'

'You mean the boy-smell?' said Burton.

It had reminded him of his own room in his late teens and early twenties, when he thought that the shame of his natural scent could be masked by a thick application of cologne.

'No,' said Lindi. 'That wasn't so bad. But I think he has a bit of a crush on me.'

Burton glanced over at her. She was suppressing a grin.

'He hit on you?'

'Not exactly. but he's very eager to please, and I think he's showing off a bit. It's sweet, really.'

'He knows about . . . you, right?'

'What,' said Lindi, 'that I'm a big ol' lesbian?'

Burton looked back to the road, feeling his ears burn.

'Not yet,' she said. 'But it's going to be an awkward conversation.'

The Mayor's house was far out of town, right on the transition line where high-walled estates turned into farmland, and the smell of fertilizer hung faintly in the air. The property was ringed by a thorny hedge that hid a concrete wall. At the front gate, they were stopped by a Special Investigation Services cop.

'Hi,' said Burton. 'Burton and Childs to see Mayor Redfield.'

The cop nodded. 'Get out of the car, please, sir and ma'am.'

'What? Why?'

'Extra precautions.'

The cop was slightly overweight, with a moustache. He had his own booth just outside the Mayor's wrought-iron front gate. Burton could see a crime novel lying on his small desk, in front of a bank of eight security monitors.

Burton and Lindi got out. The guard walked around the vehicle, checking all sides, then used a mirror on a stick to look at the underside. He looked under the seats, in the glove box, in the trunk and under the hood.

'You do this to every car that comes through?' said Burton.

'Yes, sir,' said the SIS cop gruffly. 'I'm going to need to pat you down too before I let you in.'

Burton was starting to get annoyed.

'I'm going to be late for the Mayor.'

'Don't worry, sir. He knows these inspections take about fifteen minutes or so. He'll have factored it into his time.'

'Well, I didn't.'

He turned around and let the cop thoroughly pat him down. It made him feel like a criminal.

When it came to Lindi's turn, she folded her arms.

'I thought it was only legal to pat down someone of the same sex.'

'That's if you're being arrested, ma'am,' said the cop. 'This is entirely voluntary.'

'Well, you're not patting me down,' she said firmly.

The cop frowned at her as if he couldn't understand why she would object. He sucked on his moustache thoughtfully.

'I can't let you in without a pat-down, ma'am. You're going to have to wait outside the gate.'

'Oh, come on!' said Lindi.

The cop folded his arms, mirroring her.

'Sorry, ma'am. It's the rules.'

'This is stupid,' said Lindi. 'It's discrimination.'

She looked to Burton for solidarity.

'I'll go in and talk to the Mayor. He'll understand. He wants to see you. He'll make an exception.'

'Fine,' said Lindi.

The SIS cop raised an eyebrow sceptically, but he opened the gate for Burton and pointed him up the driveway.

'Go straight up.'

'Thanks.'

Burton drove up the long brick driveway, past green lawns and hissing sprinklers. On one side was a small bamboo forest and on the other a rectangular carp pond. He parked outside the front of the two-storey mansion. The door was standing slightly open, which was unexpected after the strict security at the gate.

Burton went to it and looked through the gap. Inside was a sunlit foyer with a brown-carpeted staircase. There was no doorbell, only an old brass knocker in the middle of the door. He tapped it, but there was no response.

After a minute he knocked louder and called in, 'Mr Mayor? It's Detective Burton for you.'

He listened. There was a distant rumble and a hiss that could have been the sprinklers.

'Mayor Redfield!' he called. 'This is Detective Burton! Your door's standing open!'

Burton pushed the door fully open. The foyer was two storeys high, with a staircase on either side that joined together at a landing above. A chandelier was hanging down from the ceiling and there were three large paintings on the walls, one ahead and one at the foot of either staircase, forming a wrap-around hunting scene. The elegant riders were on the left, the dogs were in the middle and the bleeding boar was on the right. It was a slightly off-key approximation of old-money classiness.

The drumming was coming from upstairs. Now that Burton was inside, it was clearly the sound of running water.

Who invites people around and then runs a bath?

He took a few cautious steps into the house. A drip fell from the landing above, followed by a thin lukewarm stream. It splashed in a puddle at his feet.

Burton looked up the stairs. He ought to go back for the gate cop.

'Mayor Redfield!' he called again.

The water pouring off the balcony was turning into a torrent.

254

'Shit,' he said, and ran up the stairs.

The dark red carpet on the landing was soaked through. The noise of running water was coming from the right-hand corridor off the balcony. Burton ran down it with every footstep squelching. He felt warm water leaking into the sides of his polished shoes.

The second door on the right was half-open. Burton could see white tiles and the air was steaming. The water thundered like war drums. The bathroom inside was much bigger than it needed to be. There was a toilet in one corner and a towel cupboard in the other. An antique Victorian bathtub with bronze legs was positioned half-way along the wall, under a wide frosted-glass window. The bathtub's shower attachment was a flexible metal tube with a showerhead at the end.

Mayor Bruce Redfield was lying on his back in the middle of the room. His eyes were open, staring unblinking at the ceiling. The water on the tiled floor around him was pink with diluted blood. Someone had taken the head off the shower attachment. The pipe was shoved down Bruce Redfield's throat, into his lungs. Water poured out of his open mouth and nose.

Burton pulled the pipe out and checked the Mayor's pulse. Nothing. He tried compressing his chest, rhythmically pushing his own weight down under the sternum. Bones clicked and more water spilled out of the Mayor's mouth.

Burton had to clear the man's lungs. He needed to do mouth-to-mouth. As he put his hands on the sides of the Mayor's head to steady it, something moved under his fingertips. He turned the Mayor's head to the side.

The back of the skull was dented inwards. Bone fragments stuck out between the matted hair. The Mayor had been bludgeoned from behind. All the water was just for show.

Burton turned off the tap. Without the sound of running water, the house was eerily silent. The only noise was the distant splash of water streaming off the balcony and into the foyer, and a quiet scratching from somewhere behind Burton.

Next to the sink was a shelf holding soaps, skin creams and shaving equipment. There was a small blue cardboard gift box on it, with a bow on the lid. The scratching sound was coming from inside. Burton went to it, pulled the bow off and lifted the lid.

A large, black scorpion struck forward with its tail, narrowly missing Burton's hand. He jumped back.

Through the frosted window, he could make out the shape of someone running. He threw open the window and saw a man in a peaked cap sprinting away across the lawn below. He had a black scarf covering the lower half of his face.

'Stop!' Burton shouted.

The man looked back at Burton over his shoulder, but he didn't slow down.

Chapter Fifty

Lindi waited by the gate, standing with her back to the wall to keep out of the afternoon sunlight. The cop was back in his booth, reading his book. She wanted to text Burton and tell him to forget it. This wasn't worth it. She could get a taxi home.

A silver convertible came slowly down the road, driven by a woman with platinum-blonde hair tied up under a gold and purple scarf. She was in her mid- to late forties. She pulled up next to Lindi and looked at her through dark glasses.

'Who are you?' she said, with a West Coast Scorpio accent.

'I'm Lindi Childs. Who are you?'

'Veronica Redfield. Why are you outside my house?'

The woman was wearing a short white dress and earrings. If it wasn't still daytime, she would have looked like she was on her way to an elegant soirée. Lindi didn't like her tone.

'The Mayor invited me here. But your guard wanted to grope me.'

The Mayor's wife took off her sunglasses and squinted at Lindi. She turned around in her seat and called to the guardhouse.

'Ian!'

The Special Investigation Services cop came out again.

'Yes, ma'am?'

'Who is this?'

'It's one of your husband's guests. She's here for a five o'clock meeting. She wouldn't submit to the pat-down.'

Burton's voice shouted in the distance. 'Stop! . . . Freeze! Police!'

The cop's jaw tensed. Lindi saw his hand automatically reach for his holster. He pressed the button inside his booth to make the gate slide open.

'Ladies, I think you should stay here.'

'Fuck that,' said the Mayor's wife, pulling off in the convertible and heading up the driveway.

Chapter Fifty-One

'Freeze!' Burton shouted out the window. 'Police!'

The man below ran across the lawn towards the line of trees at the rear of the property. Burton turned and ran out into the hallway. The killer had a huge head start. Burton would have to go out of the front entrance and all the way around the house. And shit, he still didn't have a gun.

He ran on to the first-floor balcony and down into the foyer. As he came out of the door a silver convertible pulled up outside the front of the building. The driver, a woman in a white dress, saw Burton and screamed.

Burton looked down at himself. His white shirt was stained with the Mayor's blood.

He didn't have time for this. The killer was getting away. He kept running, towards the side of the house. The cop from the front gate ran up the driveway, closely followed by Lindi. When the cop saw Burton he pulled out his gun.

'Freeze!'

Burton stopped at the side of the house, just by the corner.

'Where's the Mayor?' shouted the gate cop.

'Upstairs, in the bathroom, but –'

The cop ran towards the entrance. 'Stay where you are! Don't move!'

'I'm a police detective!'

The cop wasn't listening. He ran up the steps and inside. The Mayor's wife ran in after him. Burton looked at the edge of the building. Fuck it, he thought. He ran around the corner towards the rear lawn, and Lindi followed him.

As they got to the back of the house, the Mayor's wife screamed again above them.

'Oh, God. Bruce. Bruce! He isn't breathing!'

Burton ran to the trees and bushes right at the back of the property, where the killer had disappeared. He found the rear wall. A concrete panel had been removed from it, halfway along its length, right underneath one of the security cameras.

Burton ran to the gap and bent over to look through. On the other side was a dirt road running parallel to the wall and, behind it, a field of corn. A black car was driving off into the distance. It was too far for Burton to read the plate.

'I told you to freeze!'

Burton pulled his head back through the gap and looked around. The SIS cop was standing on the lawn, pointing his gun at them. He was sweating. Lindi raised her palms.

'On the ground! Both of you! Face down!'

'Are you serious?' said Burton. 'He's getting away! It's a black car, I couldn't get the make —'

'I said get down!' He tilted his gun to Lindi. 'You too, ma'am. Now!'

This was stupid. Burton looked at the gap, then raised his palms and got down on to his knees.

'Properly! Lie down! Wrists back!'

Burton obeyed. 'This is crazy,' he said. 'The killer just escaped through this hole. I told you, I'm a cop! Look in my wallet!'

The handcuffs clicked into place around his wrists.

'I will,' said the SIS cop, 'but you're not going anywhere.'

He cable-tied Lindi's hands together and called for back-up over his radio.

The Mayor's wife stumbled across the grass to them, looking shell-shocked.

'Keep your distance please, ma'am,' said the cop.

'You killed him,' she said quietly, looking down at Burton. 'You piece of Aries shit. You killed my husband.'

So she knew who he was. Everyone knew who he was.

Chapter Fifty-Two

If life had been a movie, Daniel would have lost consciousness and woken up in a clean white hospital room.
That wasn't the way things happened. He watched the
men coming back out of the kitchen door and throwing
the lighter behind them. He saw the flames and heard the
panic inside. He felt the agony as the man holding him up
finally threw him down, face-first, his broken jaw hitting
the gravel, then pinned him to the ground as he went
through his pockets. He felt the man stand on his knee,
breaking it, and shove a knife into his back, in between
the muscles binding his ribs. He saw the man running off
with the others, under the broken fence and into the
night. But still, Daniel stayed conscious. He felt every
second of the pain.

He was awake every minute of the long wait before
the fire engines arrived and he heard every scream from
the home. Some of the kids made it out – they must have
unbolted the main exit. He saw their feet all around. He
tried to count them, but he couldn't remember how many
there should be. One way or the other, there weren't
enough. He tried to get to his feet and help the ones still
in the building, but every time he moved it felt as if axes
were being driven through his whole body.

The home was a column of flame four storeys high
when the fire engines came. The ambulance arrived half

an hour after that. The medics couldn't find Daniel's wallet and he couldn't speak, so they took him to San Celeste General Hospital, where there was another hour's wait for the emergency room. Eventually, a bored-looking nurse handed him a piece of paper and a pen to write down his insurance details. Within minutes he was upgraded to a private room and was being prepped by skilled and attentive surgeons. An anaesthetist gave him an injection on the back of his hand and the world finally went away.

After that, consciousness came and went, washing him with a wave of pain before withdrawing again. He was somewhere blue. He had a distant memory from childhood, when he had fallen into a pool before he had learned to swim. He remembered the calm certainty that he would never breathe again. Maybe he was still there. Through half-closed eyes, all he could see was a light blue wall.

'You're awake again,' said a voice. A face swam into view. 'Recognize me this time?'

Daniel wanted to talk, but his mouth wouldn't open.

'Crr?'

'Shh,' said Cray. 'Careful. They wired your jaw shut. Here.'

Cray handed Daniel a notepad and a pen. Daniel was on his side, which wasn't the best position to be writing in, but the pain from his face and his back warned him that it would be a bad idea to move. Woozily, he scrawled the word 'Kids'.

Cray read and understood.

'Most of them got out,' he said.

He let it hang in the air. Daniel guessed that Cray had

been told not to upset him. He looked at Cray pleadingly. Finally, Cray gave in.

'Kelly was still upstairs and . . . you know how she was.'

Daniel closed his eyes tight. When he was feeling strong enough, he wrote 'Maria'.

'She went back in for Kelly.'

He couldn't help himself. Tears ran down his face. His chest heaved as pain tore through his ribcage. He swore through his wired-up jaw.

'Fck . . . Fck . . . Sht . . . Sht.'

'The police asked who did it. I didn't tell them. I wanted to check with you first.'

Daniel tried to shake his head, but the pain was too great. He wrote the word *NO* and held it up. As scared and angry as he was, and even in his woozy state, he knew that striking out at Hernandez wasn't an option any more. The kids were in danger. Shit, he didn't even know who was looking after them. Another, even more pressing thought swam into his mind.

How did he find out?

'Don't know,' said Cray, as if it was wasn't important. 'People talk.'

Daniel thought hard before writing the next line. He knew it would anger Cray. But Cray hadn't been there, and Cray was the last one to come and see him. He scrawled on the page, *Was it you?*

He kept his finger on the 'call nurse' button.

'What?' said Cray, first startled, then angry. 'No. No! How fucking dare you! After what I've done for you!'

Who else knew?

'Hernandez isn't a fucking idiot!' said Cray. 'He pays

attention to what's happening around him. Maybe he was paying off someone else in the housing department. You were all over that place.'

Daniel turned his face away, which seemed to infuriate Cray even more.

'I didn't tell him! Why would I tell him? You still don't trust me? I thought you fucking respected me.'

A youngish nurse in a cap and green scrubs looked in the room.

'What's the matter here?'

'Nothing,' Cray snapped. 'Me and my boss were just catching up.'

'Mr Lapton needs his rest,' said the nurse, quite firmly.

'It's OK,' said Cray bitterly. 'I'll shut up when he hears what I'm saying.'

'Please, sir. Come back tomorrow.'

The nurse took him gently by the elbow. Cray shook her off, but he walked to the door.

'You want me to prove I didn't tell him?' he said to Daniel. 'You want me to show you? I'll fucking show you.'

Chapter Fifty-Three

Cray waited and watched the entrance of The Knife. It wasn't a classy nightclub, but it was the place to be on a Friday night in Ariesville: a three-storey bar, with the second and third floors connected by a rickety metal staircase bolted to the outside of the building that doubled as a balcony, where dozens of people stood and smoked and pushed past each other and stared out at the view. Cray didn't want to be noticed. He sat in a doorway opposite, head down, hood up, hugging his knees, pretending to be drunk.

Patience paid off. At about eleven, when the music inside was at its loudest, Hernandez's sleek black limousine came to a stop outside the entrance. The bouncer jogged forward to move the traffic cone that reserved a private parking space and the limo pulled in. Hernandez and two of his men got out and entered The Knife.

Cray had figured he would come. Hernandez was out on bail and needed to show that he wasn't concerned. He needed to prove to everyone that he was in control.

Now the real wait began. Cray got to his feet, stretched his legs, had a piss in an alley and went to get the gun. He'd stashed it under a dumpster around the corner, in case anyone noticed him loitering. He'd stolen it a few years back when he had broken into one of the beach-front flats up north with his friend Elroy. Every so often they would take Elroy's brother's busted-up car and drive out to the woods to shoot bottles. Elroy normally kept the gun, but he'd just got a job as the night security guard at a gas station and was being high-and-mighty about going straight. He was happy to let Cray take it permanently.

Cray hooked the gun into the elastic of his sweatpants. The weight pulled them down on one side. He zipped up his jacket so its waist acted like a belt, holding the gun in place and disguising its bulk, and went back to the street outside The Knife. He got a cigarette from some drunk girls who were on their way out and smoked it with them, chatting and flirting casually, then went back to his doorway, lowered his head again and waited.

After about half an hour, he saw Hernandez and his men pushing their way down the outside steps that led from the third floor of the club to the second. Shit, he thought. He was hoping they'd take more time. The longer they were in the club, the drunker they'd be.

He walked over to the front wall and stood casually a dozen feet from the entrance. Hernandez came out with a girl in a tight dress and a fur collar on his arm, and his men behind him. Cray started walking.

He thought about Daniel, the kids and Maria. He thought that if he was killed, Daniel would hear about it and know he wasn't a snitch. He didn't care if he died. It was easier when you didn't care.

It was like lying. It was so easy if you just slipped it into whatever else you were doing, not thinking too hard and not calling attention to it.

Here he was, walking closer to Hernandez and his men, on a course that would take him straight past them.

His body language was relaxed. He didn't look at them. His hood was up, but that wasn't weird. It was a cold night.

Here he was, reaching to his side, feeling for the gun's safety catch and clicking it off.

Here he was, turning his head away, glancing at one of the posters on the wall, an old beer ad that had been graffitied almost out of existence.

Here he was, close enough to hear Hernandez giving orders to his men.

'You get in the back,' he said to one of them. 'Eddie's driving.'

'Why do I have to drive?' said the one called Eddie, hurt.

'Because you heard me say so.'

Here he was, pushing the gun into Hernandez's back. Firing. Sprinting.

The woman screamed behind him. Hernandez's men acted faster than he expected. Their first shot exploded behind him almost instantly.

He rounded the corner, which bought him a few extra seconds, and ran flat-out down the street. He knew that if he got a lead of a few hundred feet on the men then the chances that they'd hit him with a handgun were slim. They were trying to fire while running, which made them highly inaccurate. He was younger than them, and faster, and he had his escape planned. He just had to make it to the bridge.

He kept on sprinting through the laughably named Central Improvement District, over Delaney Street, which ran parallel to the river, and up to the fence to the right of the highway bridge. Halfway along he found the hole he'd made earlier and ducked through it. The slope down to the riverbank was steep and the bottom was far enough away to be in the shadow of the street lights. Cray slid into darkness.

There was a muddy path worn along the riverbank, going both ways. The left was blocked by the bridge. The right led towards the industrial area, which would be the obvious place for a running man to go.

Cray turned left.

There was the glow up ahead. A dozen tents surrounded a small campfire that stank of burning plastic. Some homeless people had made use of the natural protection of the area – river on one side, fence on the other, concrete wall of bridge behind – to establish a makeshift camp where they could set up their nylon homes. Some of them were asleep, but Cray saw a few faces in the firelight. There was a dreadlocked girl in an oversized jacket and a one-legged old man with a white beard and a wrinkled face. A German shepherd on a leash barked at Cray as he ran past.

The tent dwellers watched him curiously, but didn't try to stop him as he ran to the sheer concrete wall that formed the side of the highway bridge. It stretched out into the water a few dozen feet. There was no way around it without swimming, which would be dangerously slow. Luckily, Cray didn't plan to do anything of the sort.

About eight feet up there was a gap, one and a half feet high, between the concrete of the base and the bridge itself. The two were held apart by the dumpy stubs of columns, but there was enough of a gap between them to crawl through, if you didn't mind getting seagull shit on your clothes. Cray had done it dozens of times when he was a kid and knew he'd be able to get through it fast. On the other side of the bridge was another fence, but it was much shorter. Once he got around it, it would be a quick run back to the relative safety of the Ariesville alleys, and his pursuers would have no idea where the fuck he'd disappeared to.

He jumped and grabbed on to the edge of the gap. His feet scrabbled on the concrete as he pulled himself in. He expected to see a little light coming through from the other side, but it was completely dark under the bridge. As he crawled forward, one of his fingers snared on warm fabric.

Any sounds in the crawlspace were drowned out by his own heavy breathing. He held his breath for a moment and listened. Through the pounding of the blood in his ears he heard a quiet cough and rustling nylon.

Shit.

There must have been ten or more people wrapped in sleeping bags blocking his way. It was a maze of bodies. He tried to crawl between them, feeling his way in the dark.

He hadn't thought this through. It hadn't occurred to him that anyone would use this crack at night, but of course they would. It was shelter.

There was a click and a spark of light in front of him. A man a little older than him with a straggly blond beard was holding up a cigarette lighter and looking at Cray sleepily. He was wrapped in a green-and-blue sleeping bag.

'Who the fuck are you?' the man whispered harshly. 'This is our place!'

He was trying not to wake the others. Even so, faces were turning and eyes were opening all around Cray.

'Shh!' hissed Cray. He pulled the gun out of his pants and pointed it at the guy's head.

'What the fuck?' said the guy. He probably would have been louder, but he was choked with surprise.

'I said "shh!"'

The terror must have shown on Cray's face, because the guy did shut up. Cray rolled over on to his back and looked at the opening. He could hear running feet.

'Which way'd he go?' someone shouted.

It was one of Hernandez's men. A tent dweller replied indistinctly, but Cray didn't doubt that he'd been ratted out. He spread his legs a little and aimed the gun between his feet. He'd probably only get one shot.

A pair of hands appeared at the bottom of the opening, silhouetted against the fractional light of the night sky. A head came up, checking out the gap. It was a stupid mistake, and one that Cray had relied on.

He fired.

In the enclosed space, the gunshot slammed into his ears like nails. Around him, sleeping or half-asleep, the vagrants all started screaming in shock and pain.

The silhouetted head had a chunk missing. It dropped out of view.

The bodies all around Cray started moving. Sleeping bags writhed like fat maggots. The homeless people would be fools if they weren't armed and Cray was sure it was a matter of seconds before the knives came out. He couldn't stay. Even without the threat around him, he had given away his position. There was no way ahead and no time to threaten these people to get them out of his way. And he wasn't going back – his other pursuer was almost definitely waiting for him. There was only one thing to do.

He tucked in his arms and rolled sideways between the round columns towards the water's edge.

It was a shorter distance than he had thought. The concrete disappeared from under him unexpectedly and he tumbled down to the water. For a moment he thought it wouldn't be deep enough and he'd land on rocks or river junk. Then he hit the water, knocking the air out of him.

He quickly pulled himself upright. The water came to above his waist. The splash had been loud – if Hernandez's man didn't know where he was before, he knew now. Cray had to move. He gritted his teeth and pushed himself through the stinking river towards the other side of the bridge.

He waded up on to the riverbank, shivering. There were no fires on this side. The wind was blowing from the east, so it was colder and more exposed. There was some trash left over from an abandoned homeless camp – mainly a broken refrigerator that had been opened face-up and used as a fireplace, and a big piece of white plastic sheeting blown against the concrete. He looked up at the glow of the street lights on Delaney Street. He didn't know for sure where the other pursuer was. If he went up now there was a chance he'd be cut off. The light down by the riverbank was low and it was as good as any place he'd found to make a stand. He lay down against the concrete of the bridge and wrapped the plastic sheet around himself like one of the homeless people. In the dark, he hoped that he looked like the rest of the garbage scattered around.

He waited and watched. He expected to hear the splashing of the second man coming around the bridge through the water and he kept his gun aimed at the riverbank. Instead, a shadow moved above him. Someone was coming along the fence by the road.

Shit.

They must have figured out his plan early. While Cray shot the first guy, the second must have been going back up to the road, ready to catch him in an ambush. If he had seen Cray wrapping himself in the plastic sheet, it was already over.

But the guy was moving slowly, uncertainly. He went all the way around the fence and climbed down to the water's edge. In the dark, Cray could see his silhouette coming closer. He had his gun in both hands, pointing down at the ground in a way that looked professional to Cray, like a soldier or a cop.

He knew the plastic he was hiding under would break up his shape and make him hard to spot. But it would also rustle if he moved too fast. Slowly, carefully, he raised his gun beneath the sheet and pointed it at the approaching man. His head was above the plastic but his arms and gun were under it, so he couldn't aim with any accuracy. He would have to wait until the last possible moment.

The man was about fifteen feet away, at the water's edge. He stopped, listening, facing the corner of the bridge that Cray had just come around. It was an ambush. He didn't realize that Cray had got there first.

Cray pulled the trigger.

Nothing happened. There was no shot. He was gripped by cold panic. Would the gun fire if it was wet? He felt along the barrel and his fingers touched the safety catch. It was on. It must have caught on something since he'd fired it on the bridge.

He pushed the catch and it clicked.

The man spun around and finally saw Cray.

'Shit!' he said, raising his gun.

Cray fired. The bullet hit the man's shoulder, knocking him back. He stumbled, screaming, and dropped the gun.

He fell to his knees and reached around in the dark for his weapon. 'Oh, shit. Oh, shit. Oh, shit . . .'

Cray fired two more times. The second shot got the man in the throat. He hit the ground and lay still, making a gentle bubbling sound.

Cray scrambled to his feet and threw off the plastic. He tossed the gun out into the river as hard as he could. It clattered off one of the bridge's concrete columns and splashed into the water. Then he ran.

He wished that he'd taken the plastic sheeting with him. He was still soaking wet and shaking with the cold and adrenalin. He didn't have his father's house to stay at tonight or Maria's home. The only other place he could think of to hide and sleep was in the rubble of the demolished buildings that the kids used as a playground. He knew a hiding hole – part of an old basement that still had concrete stairs – which would be a safe enough place to spend the rest of the night. And the next morning he could go back to the hospital and tell Daniel that the danger was over.

He'd done it.

Chapter Fifty-Four

A police car arrived, then another, then an ambulance and the CS van. Burton and Lindi waited outside the mansion, their hands cuffed, under the watchful eye of the SIS cop, while paramedics, detectives and forensic investigators entered the building, exited, and entered again.

'How did the killer get past the cameras?' Lindi asked.

Burton thought about it. 'They must have known that the cop out front wasn't watching the monitors whenever he was screening visitors.'

The killer, whoever he was, had planned it meticulously. He had waited for the detective investigating the murders to visit too. That took a special kind of arrogance.

The evening crept on and the sun went down behind the bamboo forest. An hour after sunset Captain Mendez arrived in person. He went into the Mayor's mansion for twenty minutes, then came out and went to talk to the Mayor's wife, who was in the back of the ambulance being treated for shock. When he was done, he finally came to speak to Lindi and Burton.

'She's accusing you of murder, Burton.'

'And what do you think, sir?' said Burton.

'What do I think?' said Mendez. 'I think fuck you, Burton. I gave you clear instructions. I told you to stay away from the Mayor and to finish investigating Mahout. And what did you do? You get found at the Mayor's murder scene, covered in blood.'

'The Mayor asked for a private meeting,' said Burton.

'Yeah? And why didn't you tell me first?' said Mendez.

Burton didn't answer. The simple truth was, he didn't need to and he didn't want to.

'Yeah,' said Mendez, reading his face. 'I see how it is.'

'Hang on,' said Lindi. 'We told you this was going to happen. The chart I made –'

'Counts for exactly jack shit,' said Mendez, cutting her off, 'because that information came from you and you've just been caught at the crime scene. It doesn't take a genius to predict a crime that you're going to commit yourself.'

'No! Hold on. A chart's a chart. Show it to any astrologer –'

'Give it a rest, Childs,' said Mendez. 'I don't know why I even let you get involved, you goddam charlatan.'

He turned away from them and walked back towards the entrance.

'So what do we do, then, sir?' Burton called after him. 'Are we arrested? Do we just stand here for the rest of the night?'

'You can get fucked,' Mendez shouted over his shoulder. 'Rico and Kolacny will take over the case in the morning.'

'Kolacny? You've got to be kidding me!'

Kolacny had only just completed detective training. He was a good kid, but he had no experience.

'You don't get a say in who I choose!' said Mendez, pointing a finger at Burton. 'In my infinite kindness and generosity I'm letting you go free, rather than making you spend the night in a cell like you deserve. So go home, get some sleep and then wake the fuck up. And stop expecting everyone to keep treating you like a hero cop. You found the senator's killer. Get over yourself. No one cares.'

Chapter Fifty-Five

Cray came back to Daniel's room the next morning and told him everything. He'd had hardly any sleep and was still freezing cold and pumped full of adrenalin. He spoke quietly so that none of the hospital staff would over-hear, but his eyes were wide and his voice shook with excitement.

Daniel listened intently, without moving anything but his eyes. His jaw was still wired and bandaged, so Cray couldn't see his expression, but at the end of it he reached over, picked up his pad and pen from the bedside table and wrote one word: *Leave.*

Cray stared at it, first in disbelief, then anger.

'You sick Cappy asshole,' he hissed. 'I killed the guys who did this to you. You want to get rid of me? Fuck you!'

Daniel's hand scrawled over the page: *You don't get it. We're both in danger now. For your own safety, stay away.*

'My own safety? You think I care about that?'

Take the money in my wallet, then go. NOW!

Cray took the wallet from the bedside table. He pulled out a wad of twenties and dropped it on the floor.

'I warned you,' he said to Daniel. 'You thought you could deal with Hernandez like a businessman, but I fucking told you.'

He left the room before the nurses had the chance to throw him out.

That night, he slept at a Topp Hotel in the city centre. Topp Hotels were the same across the country – cheap, with tiny rooms that all had an identical mass-produced shower-sink combo made from moulded plastic. It cost less than twenty dollars for the night. The room was clean and the shower was warm, and Cray got to pocket most of Daniel's money for when he needed it.

The next morning he had a complimentary breakfast. It was self-service, so he piled up his plate with bacon and eggs and waffles and picked at them, thinking about his next move. He didn't have any plans, other than getting back to Ariesville and finding a new place to stay, far away from his dad. He'd need some way to make money, and robbing people was harder without his gang. Most of his friends had already been picked off by the police.

He wasn't done with Daniel yet, though. The whole morning he kept turning it over in his mind. Daniel wanted to keep him at arm's length now that he was in the shit, but Cray could take Daniel down easily. If Daniel was going to drop him, then there was no reason to feel any loyalty, no matter what they'd done for each other. He could say he was going to the cops. He didn't have to do it. He could say he would bargain with them and tell them the murders were Daniel's idea. And, yes, Daniel had his lawyers, but Cray bet it would still ruin Daniel's reputation. He had more to lose than Cray, after all.

After breakfast he took a bus back to the hospital. He was crossing the street to the entrance when a car pulled up in front of him and the window rolled down. The driver was a serious-looking woman in a dark grey suit, with a black bob cut and sunglasses.

'David Cray!'

Cray was going to run, until he recognized her as one of Daniel's lawyers.

'Don't go inside,' she said. 'Meet me in the park in half an hour. The benches by the lower gate.'

The car pulled off and merged with the traffic. Cray stared after it, then at the revolving doors at the hospital entrance. There was no reason why he couldn't ignore her and go to confront Daniel on his own terms. Meeting with the lawyer could be some kind of trap. He considered it, then put his hands in his pockets and walked to Fellowship Park.

It was five minutes away from the hospital – a green patch about three blocks square, cut in half diagonally by a palm-tree-lined jogging path. The north end had an old playground with broken swings and a rusting slide, and the south end had a picnic lawn where the Leo and Sagittarius students from the university came in hot weather to throw around their Frisbees and hang around shirtless.

Cray sat in the shade of some trees on the opposite side of the lawn from the park's south entrance and waited. Right on time, the lawyer came in and sat on an empty bench. Cray looked at everyone else in the park, but couldn't see anyone who was obviously the lawyer's back-up. She checked her phone, probably looking at the time, and her leg jiggled impatiently. After ten minutes he felt confident that she really was alone and approached her out of the shadows.

'What's with all the spy business?' he said.

She looked up at him through her dark glasses. He couldn't see her expression, but her lips were pressed tight.

'I've been trying to call you,' she said. 'Lapton gave me your number.'

'I threw away my phone.'

She nodded. 'That's what I figured. And I guessed you'd end up coming back to the hospital. I'd been waiting since visiting hours started.'

He came and sat next to her. She slid away, keeping space between them.

'What's all this about?' he said.

'I don't know. And I saw what happened to Hernandez on the news, so I'm not going to ask. Here.'

She handed him a thin envelope. Cray turned it over in his hands. It had the number *1* written on it in Daniel's neat handwriting.

'He said open it now.'

Cray tore it open. There was a single handwritten page inside.

Dear Cray

Sorry that I was rude yesterday. This was not the way I expected our friendship to end. And I'm sorry to say that our friendship has most definitely ended.

What you did was far beyond what I thought you were capable of. At first I didn't think it was justifiable, but the more I think about it, the less certain I am. Considering the circumstances, it might have been the only honest way to respond.

As well intentioned as it may have been, though, it brings a world of trouble down on both of us. Right now, I'm making myself complicit in your action by not reporting it and by doing everything in my power to keep us both safe. I'm giving up any attempt to get the properties, as it would make our connection to H. obvious, and I am closing down the office and having all the documents shredded. I am also keeping an eye on the relevant authorities, to the best of my ability, and doing what I can to steer them clear of either of us.

Unfortunately, it means that we cannot see or be in contact with each other, for the safety of both of us. Considering my business dealings and your actions, either of us is equally likely to come under suspicion, and neither of us should have to pay for the other one.

I hope that you understand that I am trying to act fairly to you and am not taking you or your actions for granted. I have to thank you for our time together and for everything you have done for me. It was a horrifying act in a horrifying time, but it was more satisfying than the justice of any court.

Jessica has another envelope for you. I hope it is satisfactory.

Sincerely,
D. L.

'You done?' said Jessica, reaching for the page. He gave it back to her and she tore it up into pieces.

'What are you going to do with it?' he asked.

'He told me to burn it when I get home.'

'Aren't you curious what it says?'

She looked at him for a second, then shook her head. She put the torn pieces into her jacket's inner pocket and took out a second envelope, this one with the number 2. Cray took it. From its shape and weight, he didn't doubt that it contained money.

'He said don't open it here.'

'Thanks.'

'All right,' she said. She stood up quickly and walked off towards the park gate.

'Jessica!' he called.

She spun around.

'Tell him he's still a fucking Cappy.'

She hesitated, then nodded and turned to walk away quickly. Cray smiled. She wasn't going to tell him. And she was going to burn that torn-up note.

Because otherwise, Cray would be coming for her.

Chapter Fifty-Six

Burton sat in the office that now belonged to Kolacny and Rico, with a cardboard box on his knees. His framed newspaper clipping lay at the bottom. It was his only personal possession in the room. Kolacny looked into a mug and rolled it between his hands.

'So, do you have everything you need?' said Burton.

Kolacny came back to life. 'Sure, sure. Thanks. I'm looking forward to it. I just need the last of the files and I'm ready to go.'

'What do you mean?' said Burton. 'I gave you everything you need.'

'Almost. I went through the checklist and it looks like you booked the Ram Squad audit out of storage, right?'

'Right,' said Burton. 'But that file never came up.'

'The computer system says it did.'

Burton scratched his stubbled chin. He'd missed his alarm that morning and had only made it to work on time at the expense of his morning bath and shave.

'What did you want those financial records for anyway?' said Kolacny.

'I wanted to find out why Kruger was getting city funds. It might have something to do with the murders. Since most of the CRA money goes through the Ram Squad, I thought there might be some mention of Kruger in their records.'

'Well, the printout says you got them.'

'Huh,' said Burton. 'We could go down and check.'

The records office was in a sub-basement, with metal racks stretching between the columns that supported the building. They were mostly filled with cream-coloured cardboard boxes containing printed files. The spaces between the racks were filled with boxes that had nowhere else to go and the stacks rose up to ceiling height. The boxes at ground level were crumpling under the weight and going dark from mildew. The whole room had become largely pointless since the automated systems upstairs were set up, and a decade ago everyone had expected that it would be cleared out and turned into something more useful, such as evidence storage. But like all traditions, bureaucracies don't disappear just because they have no point. The room was still filling up, only now it was referred to as 'hard-copy back-up'. Not many people took out the actual boxes any more, except for the occasional over-thorough detective like Burton.

Walters, one of the record keepers, was standing in the small, well-lit corner of the room by the entrance. Around him were three tall shelves (records of the records), a desk with a computer, a wall-heater and a large printer that Walters used to print out more documents, which he stacked into another cream-coloured box. He was a pale, sickly-looking man. Either living underground was killing him or it was the only thing keeping him alive. He flinched as Burton walked in, followed by Kolacny.

'Whoa,' he said. 'Sorry. Wasn't expecting anyone.'

'Hey, Rob,' said Kolacny. 'Burton says he asked for some files on the Ram Squad, but he didn't get them.'

'Huh,' said Walters. 'Weird.'

He showed them through the dark stacks. There was no light beyond the small patch by the door, but Walters led them confidently to the other side of the room, where he found a light switch on one of the concrete columns. A bare power-saving bulb flickered on.

'JR97, JR97,' Walters muttered to himself, looking at the stacks of boxes around him. 'Ha.'

He went to one of the shorter stacks and counted off the numbers written on the side in black marker pen.

'JR95, JR96 . . . and then JR100. See? Three boxes missing from the pile.'

'So, who has them?' said Burton.

'I don't know. No one requested them before you. You're the only name on the computer. If anyone else was here, I'd be telling them you had them.'

Burton caught Kolacny looking at him thoughtfully.

'Could anyone have checked them out without going through the computer?' Burton asked.

Walters shook his head.

'I mean . . . it's possible,' he said. 'But it would have had to have happened before my time. These days it's just me.'

Chapter Fifty-Seven

'Something's going on here,' Burton said quietly as they walked down the corridor back to the elevator.

He knew there was corruption in the department. Nothing major, but once in a while, if an officer found themselves in trouble, everyone would close ranks. After all, they were on the same side. Every day they put their lives at risk. If they couldn't count on each other, who could they count on? But Burton could sense bigger, darker things hiding behind the averted glances and little lies that wallpapered the San Celeste Police Department.

'You should tell Mendez,' he said. 'If someone's covering something up, he needs to know.'

Kolacny was doubtful. 'Covering up what?'

'I'm not sure, but we know that Kruger's connected to Williams and Hammond, and it looks like he's tied to the Ram Squad somehow. Williams supported the Ram Squad for years, and you know those guys. Every day they're beating someone down or firing bullets through closed doors. In all that time, you don't think Williams helped them out after they crossed the line? They didn't ask him to, maybe, change the location of a body or the time of a death? Or maybe ignore some inconvenient bullets at a crime scene?'

'Burton!' said Kolacny.

Burton realized he was saying too much. Kolacny

looked around the Homicide room, but no one was listening.

'Me and Rico are handling this case now,' he said. 'You can stop being paranoid. Yeah, it's weird that those boxes went missing, but I'll chase it up. This isn't your case.'

Burton examined Kolacny's face, but the young cop's expression was innocent. Even so, Burton couldn't help himself.

'I didn't take those files. You believe me, right?'

'Yeah,' said Kolacny, and smiled. 'Sure, man. I believe you.'

Chapter Fifty-Eight

After work, Burton went to visit Kate, who was still staying at Hugo's house on the other side of town. Burton's sister-in-law, Shelley, greeted him awkwardly at the door. She smiled and gave him a probing look, as if she was trying to spot the Aries lurking beneath his familiar surface.

Kate was sitting at the dinner table with Hugo and Shelley's two-year-old son, Benjy, on her knees. He was swirling red paint across a page with his small, pudgy hands.

'Well done!' said Kate. 'What are you making?'

'Fire,' said Benjy earnestly.

Kate looked up and saw Burton.

'Jerry!'

They kissed. Shelley swept in around them and scooped Benjy up off Kate's lap.

'Let's get your hands clean, shall we?'

She held Benjy under the armpits to keep his paint-covered paws away from her clothes or furniture, and carried him out the room.

'Not done yet!' he wailed.

'You can finish painting after supper.'

Burton pulled out a chair and sat down next to his wife.

'That was cute,' he said.

Kate smiled. 'Yeah,' she said. 'He's really sweet. Totally mad about dragons right now. Were you like that as a kid?'

'It was airplanes for me,' said Burton. 'Until Grandpa told me that Tauruses should be into trains and earth-movers and things.'

Kate raised her eyebrows.

'It was a different time,' said Burton. 'How have things been?'

'Fine,' she said, and held out a hand to him. He supported her as she hauled herself to her feet.

'Oof,' she said. 'I keep on feeling like I'm going to fall forward.'

She went through to the kitchen and Burton followed.

'Shelley bought me this herbal tea which is meant to be good if you're pregnant. Want a cup?'

Burton shook his head. 'No thanks.'

'Yeah,' she said. 'It tastes kinda weird.'

She filled the kettle with water and put it on the stove.

'I heard you had some trouble last night.' She said it casually, but Burton had known her long enough to see it weighing on her.

'Yeah,' he said. 'Who told you?'

'Charlie and Sarah.' The neighbours from across the street. 'Was it bad?'

'No,' he said. 'Not really.' Another couple of rocks thrown from a moving car. One of them had gone high and cracked the gutter.

'Listen, Jerry . . . are you sure you want to stay there? Until this is over. I just want to know you're safe.'

Burton took a deep breath and let it go in a sigh.

'I can't leave,' he said. 'I have to look after our house. We're going to need it soon, aren't we? She's got to have somewhere to come home to.'

He put his hands on either side of Kate's bulging belly.

'Is she still moving?' he asked.

'Too much now,' said Kate. 'She was kicking like crazy a few minutes ago. She got me square in the bladder.'

'Great,' said Burton.

Kate raised an unimpressed eyebrow at him.

'You know what I mean.'

Kate wasn't going to be deflected.

'Please, just move out of there for a bit,' she said. 'Find someone to stay with. You need to be around people. I'm worried for you.'

'Do you think Hugo and Shelley would let me stay here with you, then?' he asked.

Kate looked pained. 'Jerry . . .'

'No?' said Burton. 'OK, then.'

'Don't take it like that. They're just thinking about Benjy. You don't want any of those lunatics following you here, do you?'

'Of course not.'

Shelley came into the kitchen, holding a now-clean Benjy in the crook of her arm.

'Hugo's going to be home in half an hour,' she said. 'I'm sorry, I didn't get enough supper for four.'

'It's all right,' said Burton. 'I have to head out anyway. I still need to buy paint for the front wall.'

He kissed Kate on the lips.

'Be safe,' she said.

'I will,' said Burton. 'I'm off the case now. It's over. Everyone will forget about me soon enough.'

Chapter Fifty-Nine

Burton got a call from Bram Coine as he walked back towards his car. He ignored it. He got another as he was opening the door. He leaned his elbow on the roof of the car and answered it.

'What is it?'

'Detective Burton?' said Bram. 'Listen, I don't know if you've been on social media lately, but you're being crucified.'

'I only use email,' said Burton.

'What? How's that even possible?'

Burton didn't have the energy for this.

'Just tell me what's happening, please, sir.'

Bram hesitated. Burton was pretty sure he didn't like being called 'sir'.

'The Cancers are going crazy online. Some channel interviewed the Mayor's wife and got her saying that she thinks that you killed him and the other cops are covering for you. Now there's a bunch of blogs saying you're a sleeper agent for Aries Rising and that you murdered Williams, Hammond and Redfield.'

'So? Who cares what lunatics say?' said Burton.

'Everyone! All the serious journalists are writing articles about it, because it's easier for them to talk about what's happening on social media than it is to leave their desks. They know it's bullshit, but they're writing articles, like, "Can you believe what people are saying about this cop?" and it's just making it worse. You're on trial here!'

'So what do you want me to do about it, Mr Coine?' said Burton. He felt exhausted at the world.

'Defend yourself!' said Bram. 'Make a stand! Come back to my place. We can do an AMA, or an interview, or –'

'No,' said Burton. 'Forget it. Absolutely not.'

'But this is your reputation! The narrative of your life is being taken over by a bunch of assholes!'

'I'm a cop, Bram. If I do any kind of interview, it has to go through the Communications Department.'

'Are you serious? Last thing I heard, the other cops were crucifying you too. You're being used as a scapegoat, Detective. Get the word out! Expose the corruption!'

The missing boxes were weighing on Burton's mind, but this was too much.

'What the hell are you suggesting? You want me to go on the Internet and badmouth other cops? How do you think that's going to play out for either of us, Bram?'

'This is your opportunity to defend yourself!' said Bram earnestly. 'I'm trying to help you here!'

'No!' shouted Burton. The pressure and anger and paranoia of the last few days exploded out of him. 'Listen to me! If it wasn't for you and Lindi, I wouldn't be losing my job! I wouldn't be getting attacked every night by lunatics! I wouldn't be being torn apart on television! I wouldn't even know I was a goddam Aries! I don't have to listen to another one of these calls, or listen to any more crackpot theories by every paranoid schizophrenic with a keyboard!'

Bram was silent. 'Man, sorry,' he said finally.

Burton knew he was being harsh, but he was too tired to care.

'I don't need your help, Mr Coine. It's not my case any more anyway. I'm out. Just leave me to pick up my life.'

Chapter Sixty

Bram hung up on Burton and put his phone back in his jeans pocket. His cheeks were flushed with anger and embarrassment. He had spent the last two days running damage control for Burton online, because Lindi had said he was a good guy and because Bram had felt sorry for him. What an asshole. He should have left him to burn in the fire of popular opinion.

The university was a little over a mile away from Bram's house. Because the weather was cool, he had decided to skip the bus and walk back home through Palmolive Court. It was a wide, concrete-paved square in the centre of the city – someone's idea of a futuristic capitalist paradise. The buildings all around were tall, bland and covered in glass. Uniformed security guards stood at the entrances of the different companies, mostly banking institutes and insurance firms. Buried below Bram's feet were three levels of parking for luxury cars. The centre of the square was taken up by a gigantic abstract sculpture that was incapable of sparking joy or imagination in anyone.

The only activity was happening outside a franchise café at the corner of the square, where a homeless man was sitting on a blocky concrete bench and throwing crusts of bread to a flock of miserable-looking pigeons. A security guard in an orange vest approached the man, who saw him coming and started packing up all the belongings scattered around him – a water bottle, a rain-coat and a bundle of plastic bags.

Bram knew without asking that the homeless man was Aries or Pisces. Maybe, at a stretch, a Taurus or Cancer with mental health issues and no family support. Not for the first time, he wondered what the world would be like if the social divides were made properly visible. What if everyone was colour-coded, so you could see their cultural group at a glance – red for Aries, white for Capricorn, blue for Virgo. He imagined a map of the city with everyone marked down as little dots. They could all move freely and yet they stayed in clumps of their own colour, from their own choice and from financial and social pressures. A big red patch in Aries-ville, a white band in the outer suburbs and a swirl of colours where Aquarius, Virgo and Sagittarius mingled and mixed but never truly gave up their identities.

How would society change if people could see the divisions more clearly? Would things be better or worse? At the moment, recognizing someone's sign was a subtle game – judging their clothing by cost and style, listening to their word choices and patterns of speech, gauging their interests and political views. Judging signs was such a common and vital skill that it was automatic for most people. Only Virgos and little children had difficulty with it. It wasn't something taught in schools, everyone just understood it. Even when some eccentrics – Sagittarians in particular – tried to break out of their mould, they would still give enough of their background away to get caught in the web of judgement. Very few people had dif-ficulty judging signs, but it still required watching, listening and thinking.

How much worse would the world be if everyone was colour-coded? If people thought they could tell someone's essence at a glance? If discrimination became purely thoughtless? Although maybe people would be a bit less fucked up about it. Maybe people wouldn't spend so much time making sure they acted, sounded and thought the same as their neighbours because they were terrified of being mistaken for the wrong sign. Maybe they'd realize how arbitrary it truly was.

He walked through a gap between two of the towering buildings and into an alley that served as life support for the capitalist Utopia behind him. The air conditioning roared and the ground stank of garbage leaking out from hidden bins. It was as if the grime from the square was only displaced the bare minimum distance, giving it a protective coating of awfulness.

The alley led on to a smaller side road that Bram knew only really came alive after dark. There was a sex shop, an abandoned record store, a couple of gay bars and Club K Plus, a windowless Korean nightclub with a handwritten sign on the door that offered *KARAOKE DRINKS FUN*. Bram wondered if there were equivalent Western bars in Korea.

A white sedan cruised past him slowly. The driver was a middle-aged man in mirrored sunglasses, leaning his elbow on the open driver's side window. He looked at Bram, unsmiling, and continued down the road. It was unnerving. Bram walked faster.

He had almost convinced himself that it was nothing – just a random creep – when a big black van came past with its tinted, bulletproof-glass windows rolled up. Bram recognized the vehicle from a dozen online news reports. It was the Ram Squad. Cold terror washed over him.

The vehicle crawled along next to him, matching his speed. After a minute it accelerated and drove off ahead. Bram felt his fear curdling into anger. This was intimidation, plain and simple.

'Fuck you!' he called after it.

The van slammed on its brakes and Bram stopped walking. For a moment he wanted to run, but instead he squared his shoulders. They were messing with him now. Laughing at him. This was bullshit.

The driver's door of the van opened and a Ram Squad cop unfolded out of the vehicle. He had the typical SWAT gear – body armour, black helmet, eye-protection goggles, shotgun.

'You have something to say, boy?' shouted the cop. 'Spit it out!'

'You're harassing me!' Bram shouted back. 'It's intimidation! Back off!'

He took his phone out of his pocket. He needed to record this.

'Hey!' shouted the cop. 'Hands where I can see them!'

Bram raised his hands, still holding his phone. He kept the screen away from the cop. Without looking he flicked his thumb up, quick-starting the camera.

'Drop the phone now!' said the cop, striding forward.

'What?' said Bram. He thumbed the screen, hoping he was hitting 'record'.

The Ram Squad cop strode up to him and slapped the phone out of his hand. It clattered to the ground and Bram heard the screen crack.

'Fuck!' said Bram. 'I can sue you for that!'

'Shut up!'

The cop kicked the phone away. It skidded off the sidewalk and into the middle of the road. He grabbed Bram by the front of the shirt and tugged.

'You're coming with us. You need to learn some manners.'

Bram stumbled forward and caught the cop's body armour for support. The cop slapped his hands away.

'Assaulting an officer!' he shouted to anyone listening. He elbowed Bram in the face and pulled him by the arm towards his van.

Bram looked around for help. He could see only two other people in the street – a woman a block away, wearing headphones and walking in the other direction, and a middle-aged man poking his head out of the door of the tattoo parlour. He was raising his phone too. The cop saw.

'Don't you dare!' shouted the cop.

The man hesitated, then lowered it.

Bram's feet skidded on the sidewalk as the cop pulled him bodily towards the back of the vehicle. The rear doors opened, revealing another two SWAT-geared cops inside.

'You drive, Ken,' shouted the cop hauling Bram.

'Help!' Bram shouted desperately.

The cop pulled his head back and snapped it forward, head-butting him in the face. Bram fell to the metal floor of the back of the van. The cop clambered in after him and dragged him deeper into the vehicle as another cop pushed past him, going out. The doors slammed shut.

After a moment the engine started and the cold floor rumbled under Bram's face.

The only light inside the van came from a pair of grilled slit-windows by the roof, fogged up with grime. Under them were two long benches, one on either side of the vehicle. One of the cops was leaning in the corner, helmet off, arms folded. The floor was damp and as the van accelerated some antiseptic-smelling water trickled across it towards the back, between the grid of almond-shaped bumps covering the floor. It washed the side of Bram's face.

Bram turned away from it on to his back, and the cop pinned him down with a hand to the throat. Bram tried to push him away.

'Hands at your sides,' said the cop.

Bram tried to sit up, but the cop put his palm against Bram's forehead and shoved his head down hard into the metal floor.

'I said hands down!' He leaned in close. Bram could smell cigarette smoke on his breath. 'Assaulting a police officer and resisting arrest, Mr Coine. What a pleasure to meet you in person.'

Bram was choking. His breath rasped as he tried to cough.

'What was that?' said the cop, tilting his ear to Bram. 'Did I hear a "sorry"?'

He took a nightstick and jabbed it in under Bram's ribs, hard, then he took his arm off Bram's throat. Bram curled up into a ball on his side and croaked, winded. Tears came to his eyes.

'Look! The little boy's crying.'

'Easy, Captain,' said the other cop, who sounded bored.

'Fuck off,' said the Captain. 'Everyone knows he's got it in for us. No one's going to believe him except the assholes who already think we're the devil.' He pushed Bram's head back down into the ground. 'I've got a family, you little fucking dipshit. I don't need Aries assholes calling me and threatening my kids. I don't need them knowing where I live. I said hands down!'

He lifted his nightstick and cracked it down across Bram's forearms. Bram screamed.

'Fuck, Captain,' said the other cop, leaning forward, suddenly concerned.

Through the pain, Bram felt a strange clicking in his left forearm. One of his bones was broken.

The Captain saw. A strange grin spread across his face. He grabbed Bram's wrist and twisted. Bram screamed again, so hard that he started retching.

'Apologize!' the Captain shouted into Bram's face.

Bram couldn't speak. His arm felt white hot. His lips moved, but couldn't make any coherent noise.

'Not good enough!'

The Captain twisted again. This time, Bram couldn't even scream.

'Say "Sorry, Captain." Say it! I can't hear you! Say "Sorry, Captain" and this will all stop. Say it!'

'Sorry!' Bram barely articulated the word before screaming again.

'Sorry what?' said the Captain, and punched Bram just below the eye.

'Sorry, Captain.' Bram coughed the words out.

'Captain!' said the other cop. 'Please!'

'For fuck's sake, stop being such a pussy! You're getting on my nerves!' the Captain shouted. He pulled Bram up into a sitting position by the hair. 'Hey,' he said. Bram's eyes rolled. 'Hey!' the Captain said again, slapping Bram across the face. 'Who did this to you? When people ask who did this to you, what are you going to say?'

Bram shook his head, unable to speak.

'Hey!' the Captain shouted, and slapped him again. 'You're going to say Aries muggers did this to you. You hear me? Aries muggers. Say it!'

A simple thought cut through Bram's mind. These cops were fucked. It wasn't just his word against theirs – the more they hurt him, the more there was physical evidence of violence. And he had a name too. There was only one Ram Squad captain.

'I said "Say it"!' said Vincent Hare. 'Unless you want us coming around and picking you up again! We're like a taxi, Mr Coine! You want another one of these little trips? We'll pick you up day or night! Who did this to you? Say it!'

Bram leaned forward. It was difficult to answer through his swelling jaw.

'Fuuuck . . . oouu . . .'

'Wrong answer,' said Vince, and pushed Bram back down, hard.

The back of Bram's head caught the sharp edge of the metal bench. He lay on his back, trying to suck in air. His breath rasped. He reached for his bag, trying to get his inhaler, which would at least give him the ability to talk.

'Uh-uh,' said Hare, kicking Bram's bag away, and clambered on top of him.

Bram felt a weight across his neck. Hare was kneeling on his throat. Bram's hands and feet began to crawl with pins and needles, and the van suddenly seemed far away.

'I only want to hear one thing out of you. "Aries muggers did this to me." Are you ready? Say it.'

Vince released the pressure and the world came back to Bram, like he was waking up. He was momentarily surprised to find himself still in the van. He wanted to speak, but could only croak. His lungs were closed.

'Nope,' said Hare, and slammed his knee back on to Bram's throat.

The pain faded away again, into a tingling calm. One time, long ago, his friends had got their hands on a canister of nitrous oxide and Bram had experienced a sensation where all thought was nothing but mental geometry against a background of velvet. He slipped away to that place and the pain in his lungs and his body stopped being such a pressing concern. It would all work out. He just had to be patient. Justice was coming for them all.

Chapter Sixty-One

Ten years after the assault, Daniel still walked with a cane. His jaw had needed reconstructive surgery. The best doctors in the country had worked on him, but afterwards Daniel found his new face disconcerting. The skin on his chin was shiny and stretched. He had wanted to grow a beard to cover it up, but the hair grew unevenly and in the end he was forced to shave and live with a face that was ever so slightly *off*.

That, coupled with his ongoing regimen of painkillers, made his normal social anxiety much worse. He knew that he would never make any new friends. He wasn't going to bump into a potential wife or an exciting new business partner. He would scare off superficial people with his looks and everyone else with his attitude. In some ways it was a relief. It gave him an excuse to hole up in his family home and sink back into his previous squalor, knowing that it was inevitable. He had food and drugs delivered twice a week, and occasional visits from his physio and speech therapists. Other than that, he had nothing to do with his life, except obsess over his loss.

In the isolation he found his mind wandering back to Maria's home, or further back to the search for his daughter, and latching on to moments – something someone had said or an expression on a face. He would get lost analysing it, trying to find its significance. He found himself replaying Cray's final words to him in the hospital, and Maria's warning, and his fight with Detective Williams at the police pub, and he tried to work out what was really meant, and what he should have said, and how things could have played out differently. And then he would look around at what he was doing, and realize that twenty minutes had passed and he was still standing in front of his open fridge, or lying in his bath, or staring at the same page of a book. The painkillers, he realized, were messing with his mind, but he couldn't live without them. It wasn't just the physical pain. They were the only reason he was able to get up and walk around. Without them, it took all day to summon the energy simply to get out of bed. He knew he had no excuse. He had one of the most privileged lives of anyone in the country, but that just made his depression worse. He could have done anything, but he had done nothing, and he never would do anything, because of who he was. The world was a worse place for having him in it.

He steered into the skid. Every evening he sat in his office, going through the old documents from Maria's home and his old property company, and old news reports about Hernandez and Williams and the True Signs Academy. He read and reread them, cataloguing all the ways he had failed. And he decided to kill himself.

Cyanide seemed to be the most straightforward, least reversible way. There was very little chance of failure. He found someone at a pest control company who was selling cyanide salts for an exorbitant sum and bought 500 milligrams. More than twice a fatal dose.

It appeared one morning in his mailbox – just some

colourless crystals in the bottom of a sealed test tube. He took it into his house and put it in the middle of the table. It wasn't time yet. He went about his day, and then his week, knowing that he was ready and prepared. Sometimes he stared at the test tube, seconds away from pulling out the stopper. Sometimes he thought of throwing it away.

It could have gone on like that for months, but one Wednesday he woke up late. He was already taking more than the recommended dose of his painkillers and on this particular morning he swallowed an extra three gel capsules before running a bath. As he was getting out he became dizzy and stumbled over the edge of the tub, cracking his head on the rim of the toilet.

He was disorientated. Blood poured down from a gash in his head. In a daze he held a towel to it, but it didn't seem to stop the bleeding. He found some bandages in the bathroom cabinet and stared at them, trying to understand how they worked.

He went back through to his bedroom and pulled on some clothes. There was blood everywhere. Where was it all coming from? His head hurt. He brought his fingers up to it and they came away warm and red. Oh, yes, he had fallen.

He should call for help. He didn't want to meet new people, but he didn't know what else to do. He dialled 911 and a man on the other end of the line asked a lot of confusing questions. Daniel tried to answer them as well as he could, but when he couldn't he got angry, shouted and then started crying.

He thought the man on the other end of the line

wouldn't like him any more, but the man spoke sooth-ingly and asked the same confusing questions again, and Daniel remembered his address and told the man, and then sat in the corner of the room next to the phone and waited.

The doorbell rang after a while and Daniel went to answer it. Some men dressed in orange wanted him to go with them. He didn't want to leave his house because it wasn't safe, but they were very nice and he didn't like to be rude, so he got in the back of their ambulance and they took him away from his home.

He was in the hospital for two weeks. The first few days were agony. The painkillers wore off and no one would give him any more. Even after the concussion receded and his mental faculties returned, the specialists treated him both cautiously and patronizingly, like a child who had found his father's handgun. The lead neurologist gave him a battery of tests and asked him to complete a long questionnaire about his daily life. Daniel answered honestly.

'How long are you going to keep me?' he asked after completing it.

'You're free to go home whenever you'd like,' said the neurologist.

He was a stocky man. Daniel appreciated the way he handled his patients, which was straightforward but not dispassionate.

'It sounds to me like you have depression, obsession, addiction and probably PTSD, and drugs aren't going to help you. Honestly, I strongly recommend talking to a psy-chologist or an astrotherapist. Kelly Milton works in your area. She has an excellent track record with helping people reorientate themselves after trauma and addiction.'

And so, every Friday after lunch, Daniel drove himself to Kelly Milton's private practice in a converted cottage in her backyard for a two-hour therapy session.

Every session started the same way. For the first hour Kelly, a silver-haired Virgo in her sixties, would listen quietly and non-judgementally from behind her desk while Daniel sat back in a comfortable leather chair and talked about whatever he felt needed talking about. In the second half of the session Kelly would use her computer to make a chart of the current position of the planets and compare it to Daniel's birth chart. She would talk to him about how the energies from the planets were currently being amplified or dampened within him, and how it resulted in his current feelings and concerns. She explained it to him in great detail, to give him an in-depth understanding of the astrological forces underpinning his life and his connectedness with the cosmos. Over time, he began to understand the way she saw the world – not as cause and effect, but as the manifestation of a gigantic machine made of pure energy, with cogs the size of the planets' orbits, in which every piece moved with perfect regularity and perfect predictability. In her eyes, every-thing that happened on planet Earth was a reflection of the movements of the cosmos. Everything that happened was both significant and inevitable.

'Astrology reveals the true nature of the world,' she said. 'Nothing in our lives or our society makes sense until you draw aside the veil of physical appearances and see the cosmic world beneath.'

Daniel could understand why the idea was seductive. For one thing, it meant that he was absolved from guilt. It meant that the privilege he was born into was his destiny and that there were no imbalances to be addressed. The alignment of the cosmos at the time of his birth gave him particular qualities that other people lacked, and those qualities were what brought him his wealth and power, not his father's money or the education it had afforded him, or the thousands of small opportunities he was given by a society that assumed that male Capricorns were the default humans and everyone else was somehow *less*. Kelly encouraged him to find inner peace and to accept himself and the world as they were.

He despised her.

Still, he needed the sessions. He knew that it was self-indulgent and playing into his cycle of self-obsession, but he needed to verbalize his issues to a stranger. Putting his problems into words gave them structure and made them easier to manage.

Then one day, after he had talked about Pamela and the True Signs Academy for what seemed like the thousandth time, Kelly said, 'That school is really weighing on you.'

It was a massive understatement. 'Yes.'

'Would you like to book an extra session for a horary reading? We could ask the heavens for insight. What do you want to know?'

Daniel thought about it.

'I want to know what those astrologers and teachers were doing to those kids in those private rooms. I want to know . . . I want to know what they did to my daughter.'

'We don't need a horary for that. Just ask them.'

Burton twisted in his chair and looked at Kelly. 'What do you mean?'

'I've got contact details for most good astrologers around the country. There are quite a few in San Celeste. I'll bet that some were working at that school back then, given how much counselling was needed. I'm sure I could arrange a meeting. Would that put your mind at rest?'

'Yes,' said Daniel, with a spark of excitement that he hadn't felt in years. 'It definitely would.'

Chapter Sixty-Two

Daniel flew from his home on the East Coast back down to San Celeste. It hadn't changed much over ten years. Some businesses had moved, there were more cell phone towers and the highways that had been under construction were finally complete. But the city was still too hot, the streets were still dirty and he could still feel the tension in the air.

The astrologer Kelly put him in contact with was called Cynthia Marsh. She had been in her late sixties when she taught at the True Signs Academy and had partially retired since then. She was now doing readings by appointment out of her living room.

Daniel texted her to make an appointment and came to visit her in the early evening. He recognized her immediately. She was the woman with a perm whom he had seen teaching classes and interviewing his daughter. Her house was a modest bungalow in a quiet district, with a well-maintained flower garden and an elderly dog sleeping on the porch. The interior was decorated with antique furniture and art deco wallpaper. A grey parrot watched them beadily from a wooden stand in the corner of the room.

'We really thought we were helping them,' said Cynthia Marsh over a cup of tea. 'Werner was an astrology genius. He was convinced that he could fix them all and he

convinced the rest of us too. I suppose that was his pri-
mary trait, as a person. He was convincing.'

'Tell me about the rooms,' said Daniel.

'What rooms?'

'I saw the tapes. Kruger put children in special
rooms. He called them the Water Room or the Fire Room
or the Earth Room. I never saw any footage from inside
them and no one talks about what happens in them. Can
you tell me?'

Cynthia stirred a second sugar cube into her tea and
leaned back in her chair.

'No,' she said. 'I can't. Not exactly. It was Werner's little
secret. I was curious about it, of course. I asked the children, but all they could tell me was nonsense. Some of
them said that those rooms were doors into worlds that
were pure fire or pure earth. Some told me that Werner
was a magician who changed them into those things. I
don't know what was happening to those children. Maybe
they were hallucinating. It was a very strange time. Insanity was in the air, disguised as progress.'

Daniel's heart sank. Another dead end.

'Are you still in contact with Kruger?' he asked. Maybe
he could get the truth from the man himself.

'No,' said Cynthia. 'Even before True Signs closed, we
weren't getting on. He was becoming obsessed with eso-
teric astrological ideas. He started to completely ignore
the children. All he could talk about was creating a grand
crux.'

'What's that?'

'Hmm,' said Cynthia. 'It's a little hard to explain, but
basically . . . Kruger believed there was a way to take four

people, all of different signs, and make it so they would share the same . . . cosmic essence.'

'Why would you do that?' said Daniel.

'I'm not sure,' said Cynthia. 'Maybe to prove that it could be done. Or maybe he knew that when four people with very different spheres of influence work with a common purpose, they can achieve a lot more than any of them could on their own.'

Daniel stared at her. She avoided his eyes and swirled the leaves at the bottom of her cup.

'He did it, didn't he?'

'I think he did, yes,' said Cynthia, looking down at the leaves.

'What's the problem?'

For a moment it looked like she wasn't going to tell him. She opened her mouth and closed it again.

'I was scared when Kelly told me you were going to call me, Mr Lapton,' she said. 'Scared, but glad too, because I can finally get this off my chest.'

He leaned forward.

'Get what off?'

She blinked slowly.

'He wanted to do magic,' she said. 'He would dress it up in scientific terms, but that was what he wanted. Magic comes from rituals, and rituals are weak without sacrifice. Rituals can be ignored, or laughed off, or forgotten. But once you make a sacrifice, once blood is spilled, the ritual can't be laughed off, because someone died for it.'

Daniel's hand started shaking involuntarily. He tried to control it.

'Who –' he said, and stopped himself. He couldn't ask the question.

'I don't know if that's what Kruger did,' said Cynthia. There were tears in her eyes. 'I hope it isn't what he did. But he had children there, children no one would miss –'

She stopped.

'What's happening? Everything's spinning. I'm sorry, I'm going to be sick.'

She got up and stumbled forward, tripping over the table between them. The tea tray clattered. In the corner, the parrot squawked in alarm.

She lay on the dusty Persian carpet, looking up at Daniel. He couldn't meet her eye. He was still weeping.

'Please help,' she croaked. 'Help me.'

She reached out an arm towards him, but couldn't hold it up. She breathed shallowly for another minute, eyes rolling back in her head.

Daniel waited until her breathing stopped and took her phone out of her handbag. He deleted his messages to her, wiped it down with his handkerchief and put it back.

He left the building, pulling the door so the latch clicked shut behind him. The elderly dog on the porch looked up at him for a moment, then went back to sleep with a long sigh.

A week later, he got a phone call.

'Hi, Daniel, it's Kelly. How are things?'

'Good,' said Daniel. 'What can I do for you?'

'I'm sorry to say this, but you remember Cynthia Marsh, the astrologer in San Celeste? I gave you her phone number. I just found out today, she died.'

'Oh, no,' said Daniel. 'That's terrible.'

'Yes. They found her dead in her living room. They think it was a heart attack. Did you manage to speak with her?'

'No,' said Daniel. 'I never had the chance. I suppose I never will. Was she old?'

'She was in her seventies,' said Kelly. 'And she had a great run. She'll be dearly missed.'

Daniel didn't do any more sessions with Kelly Milton. He paid her invoices, quietly cancelled his upcoming appointments and dealt with his problems his own way.

Chapter Sixty-Three

Lindi felt like she was having a panic attack. She tried to slow down her breathing.

'Bram Coine's dead,' she said into the phone.

On the other end of the line, Burton said, 'What? How?'

'They found him in a ditch on Emperor Street, Burton. In Ariesville. What was he doing in Ariesville? Oh, my God, his poor father . . .'

'Lindi, please, you're talking too fast. Are you sure he's dead?'

'Yes, Burton! It was on the news. I can't believe it. I . . .'

'Do you need to talk? Would you like to come over? My house is a mess right now, but –'

'Yes please,' said Lindi.

Megan wasn't answering her calls. Lindi was pretty sure that Megan's other on-again-off-again relationship was back on.

'OK. Come round any time. I'm outside, painting my front wall.'

She arrived at Burton's house half an hour later. True to his word, Burton was outside and there was a long strip of fresh paint next to the front door, slightly lighter than the rest of the wall. He brought the paint cans in with him and put them down by the door.

'Would you like a drink?'

'Red wine?'

'I've got some for cooking. It's probably OK.'

'I'll give it a shot,' she said, wincing a little. 'Thanks.'

They sat together in the living room. Lindi drank the wine and Burton sipped whiskey.

'He was a good kid,' said Burton eventually. 'A pain in the ass, but his heart was right.'

'He was defending you online,' said Lindi.

'I know. It was doing my reputation a world of good.'

Lindi half-laughed, but stopped herself. They sat in silence.

'I need to show you something,' she said after a while.

'Sure.'

'Can I use your computer?'

She pointed to the old machine on Burton's work desk in the living room. He nodded. When it had finished booting up she opened the message board that Bram Coine was always on. The comments were filled with shock and anger. Halfway down there was a post from someone called AKT.

I knew Bram well. We were in the same classes in first year. I'm Aries and he was Virgo, but that didn't make a difference to our friendship because Bram didn't see signs. Or couldn't. When he saw me, he saw me.

He may have been socially difficult, but he cared about people hugely, and it hurt and frustrated him when he saw injustice. We were working together right up until the end. Some of the things Bram did may have been illegal, but they were never unnecessary. I don't know if his death was a random crime or if it was related to what we've been doing. I do know that, before he died, he managed to get his hands on some information that the local government was refusing to release through Freedom of Information requests. We debated releasing it, because it would mean that Bram would risk jail. But it's too late to worry about that.

I'm sending this out now. It might get me into trouble too, but I have to do it for Bram.

At the bottom of the post was a link to a file. Lindi opened it and showed it to Burton. It took a while for him to work his way through the legalese.

'This can't be real,' he said.

'I think it is.'

It was a list of projects being run by the local government under the Civil Response Act. There weren't any real details, but funding and legal confidentiality had been secured for projects called:

Macro-Social Intervention
Chemical Astrotherapy
Enhanced Interrogation
Advanced Rehabilitation

The second half of the document was an extensive threat against any unauthorized person caught in possession of materials relating to these projects. As far as Burton could understand it, the CRA was allowing detention and interrogation without trial.

'What's "Chemical Astrotherapy"?' said Burton.

'I have no idea. But whatever it is, Bram was in way over his head. And so are we.'

They kept on drinking in silence.

Chapter Sixty-Four

Daniel didn't really accept the premise of astrology. The more he'd seen of the world, the more sure he was that the character traits it put on people were self-fulfilling prophecies. He knew that made him an anti-signist, which would have made him a social pariah if he wasn't one already. But just because he thought something was laughable, it didn't mean there weren't people out there who treated it with deadly seriousness. Which meant he had to treat it seriously too.

He went to the astrology section of the library and found as many books as he could that made any reference to the grand crux. He read them diligently, like a general studying the enemy.

It was everything he despised in society and himself, in its most condensed form. It wasn't just inequality, it was flying in the face of both compassion and reason. Kruger was using fictional astrology to make his own microconspiracy, for his own purposes. And Daniel knew, in a fury that overrode all doubt, exactly who Kruger had suckered into joining his little cabal.

The first one was the cop who had botched the investigation into the True Signs Academy, Detective Williams. Daniel had felt it during their encounter. Williams had behaved like a man who was just playing at being a Taurus to fit in with the cops around him. And the sign ninety degrees from him was Leo. It was easy enough to figure out who that was: the blowhard Hammond, who fronted the charity that funded True Signs. There would be a Scorpio too. The Mayor of San Celeste.

Through his rage, Daniel knew it was true. It couldn't be anyone else. The four of them thought they were some magical square, untouchable by the world, and his daughter was the victim of their certainty.

And Daniel, who had lacked certainty his whole life, knew what he had to do.

He couldn't do it alone, though.

Finding Cray was easy. Daniel already had a lawyer keeping track of his movements, to make sure that he never said or did anything that might cause trouble for Daniel.

Cray was surprised and wary to get a phone call out of the blue, but agreed to let Daniel come and visit. He was still living in Ariesville, in an apartment that had once belonged to Hernandez but now belonged to his cousin. When Daniel had seen him last he was a child, but he was in his late twenties now and his body had bulked out. He held himself like someone in charge.

'Come in,' he said proudly, and introduced Daniel to his new wife and son.

'Here's Ella,' he said.

'Ella!'

The last time Daniel had seen her, she was a twelve-year-old girl with a bandage over her eye. Now she was a twenty-two-year-old mother. She hugged Daniel with one arm, while keeping her baby crooked in the other.

'And here's young Danny.'

Daniel met his eyes. 'Danny?'

Cray showed him through to the tiny kitchen. As he poured drinks, Daniel looked around at the artwork pinned up on the walls. They were chalk drawings of Ariesville street scenes, with an impressionist flourish.

'Did you draw these?'

'No, they're all Ella.'

'They're very good,' said Daniel.

Ella smiled proudly.

Cray filled three glasses, but before they could drink young Danny started squalling.

'Fuck, Ella. Sort that out, will you?' said Cray.

Ella rolled her eyes. 'I'll take him out. He's quieter after I've taken him for a walk.'

She carried him out of the tiny apartment. His cries echoed down the hall outside.

'So, said Daniel, 'what have you been up to since I saw you?'

Cray shrugged. 'I was in the Midwest. Had a pretty good job as a bouncer for a while. Then I came back here and I met up with Ella again and, well, she was older and I was older . . .'

'Congratulations,' said Daniel.

They clinked glasses and sipped. Cray's choice of whiskey was as bad as ever.

'So,' said Daniel, 'I should tell you, this isn't just a social visit.'

'I guessed.'

'There's a job I need to do. It's a big one.'

Cray nodded. 'Office work? Or . . . the other kind?'

'The other.'

Cray gave him a long, hard look. 'I can't,' he said. 'I won't. I have the boy now and I have Ella. I'm getting in with a team that fixes elevators. It's unskilled labour, but it pays great. We could be out of here in a few months. Get a place in the south. You need me to break the law?'

Daniel nodded.

'Then I can't. I've moved on, Daniel. I've found my place.'

Daniel smiled, finished his drink, said his goodbyes and left Ariesville. His mind processed the news. It wasn't acceptable. Daniel had his plan, but he needed Cray to make it work.

Cray may have moved on, but Daniel could always bring him back.

Ella was a talented artist. Daniel knew several academies on the East Coast that were desperate to add diversity by recruiting students from impoverished backgrounds. A bursary would be easy enough to manage. And Cray's elevator repair company, well, the big corporations hiring them could always decide to hire someone else.

He knew it was unfair. He knew it would cause Cray pain. But it had to be done. It was in service of the only thing that mattered – bringing justice to a broken world.

Chapter Sixty-Five

'I wonder if they recognized him,' said Detective Rico.

'Who?' said Vince Hare, the Captain of the Ram Squad.

He was sitting opposite Rico and Kolacny, leaning back in one of their office chairs.

'The Aries,' said Rico. 'You would have thought they'd show some loyalty to such a vocal supporter, sir.'

Hare sniffed and shrugged.

'I guess it's not in their nature,' he said. 'Or maybe they never heard of him. Maybe they don't waste their lives tapping away at computer screens, like some signs do.'

Rico looked down at the initial report on his desk. Bram Coine's body had been found just before dawn in a ditch for a new sewage pipe in Ariesville. Lividity showed that he had died some time the previous afternoon and probably been dumped at around midnight. A ticket seller at the train station had discovered him on her way to work.

'You find a lot of bodies like this in Ariesville, don't you, sir?' said Rico.

'Yeah,' said Hare calmly. 'Mostly dealers and gang leaders. It's lucky they kill each other, isn't it? They're normally hard to prosecute, and even when we manage to lock them up they end up back on the streets in a couple of years with twice as many contacts from their time in prison. It's good that someone always seems to take care of them.'

Rico tapped his pen on his desk. This was infuriating. Not just because of the nature of what he was expected to ignore, but because the expectation was right. No one in Personal Crimes could challenge the Ram Squad. That's why Hare had agreed to be interviewed. The Homicide Department meant nothing to him.

'So, Mr Coine was just an unhappy accident,' said Rico. 'Walking through the wrong neighbourhood at the wrong time.'

'Exactly.' Hare shook his head. 'It's like, no matter how many times we warn people, they don't listen.'

If he tried, Rico could probably find enough evidence to rein them in. He was sure that, over all their years, the Ram Squad had left enough of a stink to make themselves easily traceable. But going after them would tear the station in half. A lot of good cops would go down with them too. And it would take a long time, during which the Ram Squad could find many ways to ruin him.

And, of course, the truth was that the Ram Squad did a job that no one else could do, even if they wanted to.

Hare stretched his arms. 'Are we done here?' he said. 'Because there are reports of looting in Ellen Street. Got to crack down.'

'One more thing,' said Kolacny from the seat next to Rico. 'You have Solomon Mahout at the new station, but this department still needs to interview him. Can we –'

'Don't worry about Mahout. We've got our own interview system. Anything we find, we'll share. Am I good to go?'

'Sure,' said Detective Rico. 'Thanks for seeing us.'

'Anything for my fellow police officers,' said Hare sarcastically. He got to his feet.

'You had a good relationship with Chief Williams, didn't you?' said Rico.

'Me personally?' said Hare. 'A little. He respected the Ram Squad. He cleared the way for us. Made it easy for us to do our job. He was a good cop.' He smiled at Rico. 'And you're doing pretty well yourself, boys.'

Chapter Sixty-Six

Six months after the last time he saw Daniel Lapton, Cray got his best shirt out of one of the balled-up plastic bags at the back of his locker in the homeless shelter. He took it to the corner laundromat, along with his only good pair of pants, and spent an hour waiting for them to wash and dry. When the shirt came out it was still badly wrinkled, but the laundromat didn't have an iron and Cray had never used one anyway. He gave up on the shirt and shoved it back into the plastic bag. He went back to the shelter to get his cleanest T-shirt, which he put on under his brother's old army jacket.

He went to the corner coffee shop to meet the old man. In the ten years since they'd first met, Daniel had changed a lot. His skin hung looser on his body and his shoulders were hunched protectively. He sat at a dark corner table, under a black-and-white picture of an old roastery. There was a walking stick next to his seat and his leg jiggled in agitation. But when he saw Cray he smiled and beckoned him closer.

'My God, look at you,' said Daniel, as Cray sat opposite him. 'Are you all right? What happened?'

Cray grunted and raised a finger, beckoning a waitress from the far end of the shop. She was handing out menus to some other customers, but she nodded at him in acknowledgement.

'How are things with Ella?' said Daniel.

'Not good,' said Cray.

'Oh?'

'She got offered a place at a school on the other side of the country. All paid for. She wanted to go and I told her no. I've got things happening here. But she wouldn't listen. And I said some things.'

'Oh?' said Daniel. 'What things?'

Cray tensed. He'd forgotten how persistent Daniel could be. Anyone else would have got a punch in the face for talking to him in this way, but Daniel was like a child. Wealth and ignorance meant he'd never learned when to keep his mouth shut.

'Things she doesn't want to forgive me for,' said Cray flatly. 'She took Danny with her to the East Coast.'

'And what about your job? Is that still OK?'

If Daniel noticed Cray's growing anger, it wasn't slowing him down. Cray wanted to reach across the table and crush the old man's scarred throat.

'It didn't work out,' he said. 'All the work dried up a couple of months ago.'

'Well, then,' said Daniel, 'it's lucky I'm here.'

The waitress came to the table with a smile. She had a short checked dress and an apron, blonde hair tied back in a ponytail and bangs. The owner was probably making her wear that dress to play out some fantasy.

'Can I take your order?'

'Coffee,' said Cray.

'And are you still OK?' she said to Daniel. He nodded.

When she'd gone, Daniel leaned in closer. 'I've got something to ask you,' he said. 'It's private. Can we go somewhere? I'd rather we weren't disturbed every five minutes.'

'No,' said Cray. 'Here's fine. Whatever you've got to say, this is the place to say it. No one's close enough to hear us and if we don't act strange the waitress won't remember our faces. You're not going to act strange, are you?'

He kept his gaze steady on Daniel. The old man opened and closed his mouth. It looked like he wasn't used to being challenged, or maybe his mind had just been worn away over the last ten years. Cray needed work, but he wasn't going to get tangled up with Daniel again until he was sure of him.

Daniel sighed sharply. 'I wanted to know if I can still trust you,' he said.

Cray didn't raise his voice and he didn't blink. 'I killed three people for you.' He wanted to say, *so fuck you.*

'I know,' said Daniel.

'So what do you need me to do now?'

'I want you to do it again. Four this time.'

The waitress arrived with Cray's coffee.

'Milk?' she asked.

Cray nodded, keeping his eyes on Daniel. She poured it for him and left some sugar sachets on the table between them.

When she was gone, Cray said, 'Who and why?'

'How much do you know about astrology?' said Daniel.

He started talking about cruxes and squares and other academic bullshit. Cray half-listened but mostly watched. He could see that Daniel was wrapped up in his own inner world, spouting words that Cray had never been taught. He wasn't even looking in Cray's direction. It was a bad sign. Cray was getting ready to walk out when Daniel got to the important bit.

'Kruger was the principal of True Signs. Hammond was the one who funded and whitewashed it. Williams and Redfield covered things up when it all went wrong. They're toying with people's lives, and for what? To protect themselves and their bullshit idea of how they think the world works.'

Cray was done playing subservient.

'So?' he said. 'So are you. So am I. Everyone does that. And you should talk! The Capricorns are worse than anyone.'

Daniel gritted his teeth. Cray noticed something odd about his jaw. It looked like it had set differently after it was broken. It made Daniel seem like a different person, although Cray had never really known him anyway.

'Fine,' said Daniel tensely. 'Forget the justification. They murdered my daughter before I met her, for stupid, selfish reasons. I wasted my life thinking about right and wrong, but I've got enough money and power to destroy them and I've got nothing else I want to live for.'

This was more like it. Cray finished his coffee and pushed the cup aside.

'Revenge,' he said.

'Yes. A chance to get back at the people who hurt both of us.'

'The last time I did that, you threw me aside and ignored me for ten years.'

Cray didn't know why he was messing with Daniel now. Maybe just to see how he would react.

'I don't remember it like that,' Daniel said.

'Yeah? How good's your memory?' said Cray. 'What's the last thing I said to you back then?'

'You said that I was wrong to deal with Hernandez like a businessman,' said Daniel. 'You were right about a lot of things back then. And right now I need your help. This job matters more to me than my own life.'

'Does it matter more than 80,000 dollars?'

Daniel stopped moving. His eyes darted over Cray's face. 'What?' he said.

'I used to do things for loyalty,' said Cray. 'I hadn't met many real Capricorns in person, so when you came into my life you were like a king or something. I thought if I did what you wanted and was loyal to you, you'd take care of me and I wouldn't have to worry about all the normal shitty stuff. Then I killed those guys and you dropped me, and I had to look after myself. Sure, I can kill those guys, but I'm not going to do it for fun. If you want me to do it for you, I want you to make it worth my while.'

'And I want you to make it worth mine,' said Daniel.

'Eighty grand,' said Cray. 'Twenty for each of them. And we do it right. We take our time, we plan it and we disappear. Is that a deal?'

'Call it an even hundred,' said Daniel, and offered a hand across the table.

Cray looked at it. There was still a lot to consider. How serious was Daniel? If it came to it, would he sell Cray out? The promise of money was a good start, but it wasn't as good as knowing what was going on in Daniel's head. If that was possible between an Aries and a Cappy.

He took Daniel's hand and shook it.

'Deal.'

Chapter Sixty-Seven

'This is insane, Captain!'

Burton knew the consequences of fighting a superior, but this had been going on for too long and Burton was too angry to rein himself in.

'I saw the killer with my own eyes,' he said. 'I was there seconds after the Mayor was murdered. If you want to take me off the case, fine. You're the captain. But Rico and Kolacny are throwing out entire avenues of investigation. What the hell are they doing with this case? They're far too inexperienced for something like this!'

'Yes, they are,' said Captain Mendez. He was standing at the desk in his office, leaning over some reports, the way Burton had found him when he'd burst in. 'And look where experience got you on the case.'

He was too calm. He must have been expecting this. Burton stared him in the eye.

'You told them to scrap my work, didn't you?'

Mendez glared back. 'I told them to do the investigation properly. To follow the most likely suspects, like Mahout.'

'Fuck you!' said Burton, slamming his hands down on the front edge of Mendez's desk. 'You think I don't know what's happening? I start asking questions about the Mayor and the Ram Squad and suddenly my files go missing and I get taken off the case. One of my witnesses gets killed and dumped in Ariesville. This isn't even a cover-up! It's blatant corruption. When the press finds out –'

'And who's going to listen to you?' Mendez shouted. 'Huh? Who do you think's going to listen to a cuckoo? You're not some hero whistle-blower. You trampled all over this case, you failed to find evidence, you lost vital files –'

'Those files were stolen by the goddam Ram Squad!' said Burton.

'Shut up and get out!' Mendez shouted back. 'I'm done saving your ass.'

'Saving me?' said Burton. He could feel his face heating up. 'You've been fucking with me since the beginning!'

'Full suspension, Burton. Get the fuck out of my building.'

Mendez shoved Burton in the chest and he stumbled backward, catching the door frame to keep himself upright. Some of the other Homicide detectives were standing outside the room. They'd been drawn in by the sound of the fight and were watching Burton coldly, not getting involved but making their presence known. If Burton fought back, he knew which side they'd be on. He raised his palms in defeat and locked eyes with Mendez.

'Yes, sir,' he said.

He backed away from the Captain's office. The cops stood aside and let him past without a word.

Chapter Sixty-Eight

Daniel took his time planning the murders. He used an assumed name to rent two cars and get a short-term lease on a house near Conway Heights – a single-storey building with a wood finish and a gravel driveway. It was a perfect discreet headquarters for the operation. A few days later, he took Cray to the bank and showed him a safe deposit box under Cray's name that contained 100,000 dollars. He showed Cray the money, then locked the box and gave the key to a lawyer, on the understanding that it would be given to Cray after the job was completed. Daniel organized a fake ID for Cray, a convincing cover story and a bus ticket to an undisclosed city up north. Whether or not Daniel was arrested, Cray would be able to disappear.

The next step was research. They needed to get close to their victims. Their history with Hernandez gave them some experience of how to pull off surveillance. Daniel spared no expense buying equipment anonymously and having it shipped to his rented house. They put a GPS tracker on the cars of Williams and his immediate neighbours, which allowed Daniel to learn everybody's basic schedule. They managed to get microphones into his house through the ventilation bricks in the outer walls. They bugged his landline, although Williams barely used it. More successfully, by anonymously paying off the right people at Williams's cell phone company, Daniel was able to track Williams's phone calls and messages, and by paying off a bored employee at the security company he was able to get the schematics and layout of Williams's home security system.

The other three targets were slightly harder. Hammond was a public figure and was more paranoid, which meant that his house was more secure. Kruger was living on a compound outside town, under constant surveillance. His trips into San Celeste were hard to predict and he used different vehicles each time. It was almost as if he knew that someone was out to get him. And the Mayor was the trickiest of them all. He was under constant police protection so Daniel had to approach him with extra caution, fully aware that the security team had probably already anticipated most of the angles of attack that he could think of.

It took months, but in the end they had it all planned out, like any good Capricorn enterprise. They were ready. They sat together one night at the dining-room table in the rented house, with a bottle of whiskey between them for old times' sake.

'Saturday morning is best,' said Cray. 'Williams has the day off and most of his neighbours will be out. I can be in and out of there in a minute.'

Daniel shook his head. 'I want to do this one myself.'

Cray looked sceptical, but Daniel stayed firm.

'I've spent my life paying other people to do the important things for me,' he said. 'This is my revenge. I'm not going to deny myself this.'

Chapter Sixty-Nine

On Saturday morning, Daniel and Cray parked around the corner from Williams's house. Daniel stood a little way down the street out of sight from the front door, while Cray rang the doorbell.

After a few seconds the door opened. Daniel heard Cray use the opening that they'd planned.

'Chief Williams? I'm sorry to disturb you at home, but I have something to tell you and I can't do it at the station. It's about Aries Rising. Can I come in?'

'What about Aries Rising?'

Daniel could see Cray shift his weight from foot to foot. They had hoped that Williams would take the bait within the first few sentences. If he didn't, Cray would need to improvise.

'I've been a member for about five years, but they kicked me out after I argued with Solomon Mahout. I know things, though. Like, you've got some Aries sympathizers working in Homicide and Narcotics. Sorry, man, I don't think I should say this in the street.'

There was a pause. Daniel couldn't see Williams, but he guessed he was sizing Cray up.

'OK,' he said. 'Wait here. I'm calling a friend in the Ram Squad.'

'No, man. I came here to speak to you personally. You

can't trust anyone else.' Cray stepped forward, but Williams was blocking his way.

'Stay there!'

So much for that. Daniel limped forward and saw Cray jamming his boot in the door. Williams was quick. He kicked Cray's foot out of the way and slammed the door in his face.

Daniel knew that the alarm system in the house had two panic buttons, one in the bedroom and one in the living room. If Williams got to either of them, then Daniel and Cray were in trouble. Cray slammed his shoulder into the door. It boomed, but didn't break. On his second try, it smashed open.

Daniel saw movement inside the house. Williams was running to the right, towards his bedroom. Cray pulled out his knife as he chased after him.

'The box!' shouted Daniel. 'Get the box!'

Cray turned left at the end of the hallway, heading for the security box. Daniel was sure he'd hear the piercing wail of the security system any moment, but there was silence. Cray must have cut the cable before Williams could press the panic button.

Daniel limped in the front door. Cray came out of the security system's alcove, nodded at Daniel and stalked towards the bedroom with his knife. They rounded the corner. Williams was standing in the bedroom doorway, holding a golf club defensively.

'Get the fuck out of my house you Aries pieces of shit.'

This was going to be easier than Daniel had thought. He pulled out the gun from the shoulder holster under his jacket and pointed it at Williams.

'Drop it,' he said firmly.

Williams hesitated. He looked at the knife and the gun, and sized up both men.

'Now!' said Cray.

Williams dropped the club and showed them his palms. He kept his shoulders hunched and his knees bent, ready to move if he needed to.

'You've got the tape?' said Daniel.

Cray nodded. He stuck his knife into the sheath on his belt and took out a roll of silver duct tape, pulling out a two-foot length.

As Cray got closer, Williams attacked. He was surprisingly fast for an old man, curling his fingers and punching up with his lower palm. He was trying to break Cray's nose, but Cray dodged left. Williams got him on the cheek.

He darted for Daniel's gun, but Cray barrelled into him sideways. Williams rebounded off the corridor wall and fell to the ground. Cray pinned him down.

'That's enough,' said Daniel, pointing the gun at Williams's head. 'Stop struggling. We're going to tape you up, then we're going to take some of your things and we're going to leave. If you make this easy for us, we'll be out of your house in ten minutes and you can get on with your life. OK? Now stay still.'

Cray covered Williams's mouth with the tape and bound his wrists and legs.

'OK,' he said to Daniel when it was done. 'Where do you want to do this?'

'I was thinking out back,' said Daniel. 'He's getting some ditches dug for his pool drainage pipes. We should make him embrace his element.'

Williams looked from one of them to the other, eyes widening, realizing that they'd lied to him.

'Huh,' said Cray, a grin growing his face. 'This is serious serial killer shit.'

Williams flailed forward, trying to worm away from them. It was a pointless gesture. Cray grabbed him by the hair to keep him still and looked up at Daniel.

'It's risky outside. Are you sure you want to do it there?'

Daniel stared down at Williams.

'Yes,' he said. 'I want to get people's attention with this. I want to horrify them. I want to expose Werner Kruger's underbelly. If I'm going to do it, I'm going to do it right.'

Cray took Williams under the armpits and Daniel grabbed his legs. They dragged him through the house and down the three white-tiled steps into the living room. He writhed in their arms.

'Cut it out,' said Cray.

He dropped Williams on the ground and gave him a kick, but that didn't stop him from moving. Why would it? Williams knew what was coming for him.

Cray unlocked and opened the sliding glass doors into the backyard. He went outside to check that the coast was clear, then came back in.

'How do you want to do this?' he asked Daniel. 'You wanna tell him why you're killing him?'

'I should, shouldn't I?' said Daniel.

'Whatever you want to do, keep it quick.'

Daniel leaned in close to Williams.

'This is for my daughter,' he said. 'This is for everything you've done with Redfield and Kruger and Hammond.

This is for twisting people to fit your little reality. This is for thinking you're above the law. I guess I think that too. Forget all that. This is because I want to kill you.'

Williams shook his head. Tears started running down his face. It looked like he wanted to beg Daniel for his life, but things were too far along for that.

Cray took him under the armpits again and dragged him outside. He dropped him by the ditch next to the swimming pool. Daniel limped over to Williams's side and held his gun up to the Chief's head.

'What the fuck are you doing?' hissed Cray. 'That's going to make too much noise.'

'Well, what do you want me to do? Strangle him?'

Cray reached into the sheath at his hip and pulled out his knife. He gave it to Daniel, handle first.

'Do it,' said Cray, taking a step back.

Daniel pointed the blade towards the writhing Williams. 'Do it!'

This was it. Daniel lunged forward and pushed the knife blade into the side of Williams's belly. He did it too slowly, and felt the knife tearing and popping through skin and muscle. Williams screamed into the tape. His eyes rolled back and his whole body spasmed. Hot blood poured out around Daniel's hand. This was worse than he had imagined, but he steadied himself.

You want this.

Using both his hands and all his weight, he pulled sideways on the knife, tearing Williams's belly open. Williams screamed into the tape again and his nostrils bubbled. He'd thrown up and was choking. His intestines bulged out of the cut. It smelled unspeakable.

'You're making a fucking mess,' said Cray. 'Just cut his throat!'

'Hello? Jiffyclean Maid Service!'

The voice came from inside the house. Cray and David both turned towards it.

'Was there someone in the house with him?' Cray whispered.

'I don't know.'

'Fuck.'

Daniel quietly limped back into the house. Behind him, Cray kicked Williams's body into the ditch.

'Hello?'

It was a girl's voice, coming from the front door. She had a Pisces accent. The intercom buzzed. Daniel walked quietly through the house, until he was just around the corner from the door. It was still ajar and light was shining in through it. A moving shadow told him that someone was just outside, standing at the doorway.

After a moment she started talking to someone quietly. He couldn't make out her words. He thought she might have company, but her intonation told him that she was talking on the phone.

The shadow moved as she walked away. Daniel crept closer and looked out through the gap in the open door. There she was, a young woman in a blue checked dress and an apron, with blonde hair in a ponytail, talking on the phone. She walked around the corner of the building and disappeared from Daniel's sight. He thought she might have gone for good, until he heard the sound of a side gate opening.

Shit.

'Hello? Mr Williams?' she called again.

Daniel hobbled through to the living room as fast as he could. Cray was back inside, looking out from between the cream-coloured curtains. Daniel joined him silently. After a moment the girl came along the path around the side of the house and into the backyard. She was slow and cautious, and was still talking on her phone. She looked around nervously.

Daniel stayed still. He knew that he would be hard to spot in the darkness of the house. Slowly, Cray reached and pulled up his black scarf to cover his lower face.

The girl walked towards the pool and stopped dead. She had seen Williams in the ditch. She dropped the plastic bag she was carrying and ran forward. She cradled her phone to the side of her head like it was comforting her. Her eyes were locked on Williams and Daniel could see that she was crying.

Daniel felt like shouting at her, *No, stop. He's a monster.*

'I'm getting the car,' he whispered to Cray.

Cray nodded, but kept his eyes on the girl.

Daniel limped back to the front door and out into the street. The car was on the corner. He got in and turned the ignition.

As the engine started, he saw the side gate to Williams's house swing open.

'Shit!'

The girl came out and slammed it shut behind her. Daniel pumped the accelerator and drove towards her, thinking of knocking her down. She ran into the street with her hands raised, and at the last moment he changed his mind and braked, coming to a stop in front of her. She ran around to his window.

'Help me!' she shouted. 'Let me in! Please!'

She thought he was there to rescue her. Cray came running up behind her from the side gate. Daniel disengaged the central locking and the girl threw herself into the back seat. She tried to slam the door behind her, but Cray grabbed it and held tight. The girl tried to kick him away.

'Drive!' she shouted to Daniel. 'Just drive!'

'Shhh,' said Daniel. He pointed the gun at her. 'Stay very still, please.'

Before they could tape her hands, sirens howled in the distance. Daniel pulled off and they drove back towards his rented house.

The murder had taken less than ten minutes. Other than the girl, no one had seen them.

Chapter Seventy

Burton was watching television, with a glass of whiskey on the side table next to him. He wasn't much of a drinker, but the whiskey – a Christmas gift from his brother-in-law – had been at the top of a kitchen cupboard for a while and tonight seemed as good a night as any to have a glass.

He was still himself, though. Half a bottle in, he was telling himself that getting drunk wouldn't solve anything and that nothing on television was worth getting distracted by. He wasn't someone who could drown their sorrows. There was nothing he could do physically to fix himself.

He had called Kate earlier that evening. She sounded fine, and she said that Hugo and Shelley were looking after her. They'd even gone shopping for a baby seat for the car. Burton had told her about his situation, because he never lied to her, but he did his best not to let fear creep into his voice. She took it all sympathetically and calmly, and said she hoped it all worked out.

Burton played the conversation back in his head. He didn't want her to worry, but no emotional reaction from her was just as bad. Consciously or unconsciously, he knew she was separating from his life.

He puzzled over the case. There was a conspiracy. He had been framed, more than once. The killer had known he was coming to the Mayor's house. He had timed it so that Burton would find the body. Obviously, the killer had already been watching the Mayor and knew the gate cop's routine. The killer had probably tapped the Mayor's phone too, so he knew when the Mayor was having visitors.

Or maybe the killer was bugging Burton. How else was he staying so far ahead?

Burton took another swig of whiskey and picked up his landline. He listened to it, hoping for some telltale clicking sound that would let him know he was being bugged. There was nothing, of course. He slammed the receiver back in its cradle and looked around the room. Where would the bugs be?

He felt under the table and looked in the vase holding dry bulrushes on the mantelpiece. He started pulling out furniture, checking behind the desk and the TV cabinet. He swept all the books off the bookshelf, accidentally knocking over another vase, which shattered. Outside the window, he saw the neighbours' lights come on. He kept searching through the house, looking for bugs. There had to be something.

After half an hour, he sat back down and thought about it. There were other ways the killer could have known about the meeting. Maybe it was someone in the dispatch office who tipped off the killer. He couldn't trust any of the other cops . . .

And then there was the thing that Lindi had found in the four charts. The grand crux. What did it mean?

Something was going on, either in the stars or in the shadows. Something connected Kruger, Williams, Hammond, Redfield and the Ram Squad. He couldn't ask

Lindi about it. It was past midnight. He went to his computer instead and looked up cruxes.

Immediately, he was bombarded by paranoia. Many of the websites he found had images of skulls and pentagrams inserted between capitalized text. Some insisted that cruxes were poisonous to society, while others suggested rituals to create them. It took Burton a little while to find a source that looked academic enough to have any credibility.

A grand crux is a theoretical structure in interpersonal astrology. In it, four entities with suns square to each other can become united into one single entity, sharing a singular essence. This is possible as the sun, the source of the self, is cancelled out by the square aspects, leaving all four entities under the influence of the union instead of the usual solar energy that gives them their definition. Grand cruxes do not occur spontaneously and they have not successfully been generated under research conditions. In recent years, their viability has become strongly doubted by the mainstream astrological community.

Burton stared at the text. *Singular essence?* What did that even mean?

A fist pounded on Burton's front door. 'Open up!'

Burton leapt to his feet.

'Open up now or we'll break down this door!' came another voice.

He stumbled through to the hallway. The attackers were back, but he was ready for them.

'Fuck off!' he yelled.

He ran to the kitchen and pulled open the top drawer. Next to the cutlery was a tray of kitchen knives. He picked up a red-handled chopping knife and weighed it in his hand.

A second later the door boomed. The attackers were trying to kick it in. Burton didn't know how many impacts it could survive.

He ran back and stood in his entrance hall, facing the door with his knife ready. He squared his shoulders and prepared himself.

'If you don't open this door, we'll be forced to break it down!'

'Yeah, that's right!' said Burton. 'Come and get me!'

He didn't care any more. If they broke into his home, then they deserved what was coming to them. He steadied his grip on the knife.

He expected the kicks to start again. Instead, there was silence, broken by the distant sound of a radio. Burton stayed frozen, wary of a trick. For a horrible moment he remembered the cardboard over the window in the living room. Maybe the door had been a decoy and the attackers were slipping in behind him. He crept back to look. Light was coming in from the window. Red. Blue. Red.

He went to unlock the front door and pushed it open cautiously. A pair of police cruisers were parked outside and two cops were standing on his path. Behind them was a black van.

'Drop the weapon! Drop the fucking weapon!'

Burton was so shocked that it took him a second to move. In that time, a third cop had got out of the passenger side of one of the vehicles and pointed his weapon at Burton too.

There had never been any attackers.

'I said drop it!'

Burton let the knife fall from his fingers and instinctively raised his hands.

'It's OK! I'm a –'

The closest cop rushed at him. He grabbed Burton by the shoulder and shoved him to the ground. Burton's knee hit one of the square concrete slabs that crossed the grass from the road to his front door.

'I'm a cop!' he screamed. 'I'm a goddam cop!'

'Shut up!' said the patrol cop, pushing Burton down and putting his knee on his neck as he cuffed his hands.

Chapter Seventy-One

Panic crawled through Rachel. Her arms and legs were tensing of their own accord. She was blindfolded and gagged in the back seat of a car, and there was nothing she could do but listen to her kidnappers talk.

'That was a fucking mess,' said the one next to her. 'From now on, I'm doing the killing.'

'I'm not paying anyone to kill for me,' said the driver, the old Capricorn whose face she'd seen.

'Well, that almost got us both caught. I do it from now on or you're on your own.'

'Fine.'

There was silence for a few minutes, then the one next to her said, 'What are you doing? Don't go back to the house. The girl saw your face. There's an old swamp up past North Beach. Lots of plants. They block the view and the noise. We won't get interrupted there.'

Rachel screamed into her duct tape gag and threw herself at the car door. She rammed her upper arm into it, trying to burst it open. *Do whatever you have to do, just get out of this.*

'Hey! Cut that out!' said the one next to her. 'We're going over seventy. If you fall out now the asphalt will rip your skin off.'

'I don't want to kill her,' said the Capricorn driver.

'Tough,' said the other one. He sounded like an Aries.

'The girl saw your face. And if they get you, they get me. That or I don't get paid. One way or the other . . .'

'They're not going to get me. After this I'm leaving San Celeste for ever.'

'What if she sees your face in the newspaper? What if the police call her as a witness?'

'I'm never in the newspaper. And even if she testifies, they'll never beat me in a court case. Trust me.'

'You just shoved a knife into someone's guts!' said the Aries. 'Why are you risking both of us to keep a stranger alive? Do you think you're some kind of hero? Are you out of your mind?'

'Yes, I am. I hired a mugger. Who does that?'

There was more silence, then the old man said, 'You're in no danger. You're disappearing after this anyway. After we kill the other three, you can go anywhere in the world. Even I won't be able to find you.'

'If you let her go, she'll head straight to the cops.'

'Then I'll keep her in the basement,' said the old man. 'When the job's done and you're safely out of town, I'll blindfold her again and drop her off on the side of the road. Then I'll disappear too.'

'That's a whole lot of trouble you're going to for her,' said the driver.

'Yeah,' said the old man. 'And I'm going to a lot of trouble to make sure you get out of this rich and happy. That's the deal. It's my problem, not yours.'

Rachel felt a fragment of hope, but she couldn't be sure. Maybe the men were sadists, pretending they would release her before changing their minds.

For a while there was no noise except the quiet thrum

of the engine. It got lower as they slowed down, and she felt the car taking a turn.

'It had better not be my problem,' said the Aries. 'Or I'll deal with it myself.' He leaned in closer to her. 'You tell anyone anything about us, I'll kill your whole family. Got that, honey? Yeah, you got that.'

Chapter Seventy-Two

Burton spent the night in an unfamiliar cell. It wasn't in San Celeste Central Police Station, where the suspects he caught were usually stowed in large holding pens. The cell he was in had a single bed and toilet, and the floor was white like a hospital's. It was one of a line of identical cells fronted by bars and walled off from each other. There was a small security camera on the corridor ceiling pointing directly at him.

At first Burton thought that they'd taken him to one of the richer precincts in the southern suburbs, but that didn't seem right. The building was far too silent for a working police station and it smelled of wet concrete and ammonia. After several hours without hearing another voice or seeing another inmate, he was certain that he was in the Ram Squad's new station in the heart of Ariesville.

He wanted to shout out and demand to know why he was there and how long they were keeping him, but he knew what cops did to inmates who behaved like that. Reluctantly, he lay down on the bed and tried to sleep. At least the mattress and the pillow were clean and unused.

He woke up to an echoing cough from a cell at the far end of the row. He wasn't sure if it was morning yet. There were no windows and the light from the neon bulbs in the corridor was bright and constant.

'Hello?' he called out. 'Anyone there?'

There was a moment's silence, then a voice called back, 'Prisoner or guard?'

'Prisoner,' said Burton.

'What's your sign?'

'That's a hard question.'

'You sound Taurus,' said the voice, and coughed again.

Whoever it was sounded very familiar. Burton recognized the gravelly confidence.

'Is that Solomon Mahout?'

'In the flesh,' said Mahout. 'And you?'

'Jerome Burton.'

'Already? The wheels of justice turn fast in San Celeste.'

'What do you mean, "already"?' said Burton.

'I've been watching you, Burton. They only just called you an Aries and you're already on the wrong side of the law. So either Channel 23 is right and all Aries are immoral, or I'm right and being Aries is illegal. What do you think?'

'I think you talk a lot, Mahout.'

Mahout chuckled.

'That's what they tell me. But we all like being heard, don't we.'

Mahout didn't say anything else for the next few minutes. Burton thought the conversation was over and lay back down on his bed. But Mahout finally spoke again.

'The wheels are always turning,' he said. 'The Chief of Police. The untouchable Mayor. The Ram Squad. You. Me. There are no good guys, Burton. The skies are too complicated. All you can hope is that the wheel doesn't crush you as it turns. Are people treating you differently now?'

'What do you think?'

'I think you need to make new friends.'

Burton didn't answer. The video camera in the corridor was still pointed at him. He had the paranoid thought that he wasn't talking to Mahout at all. Maybe it was an impersonator trying to see if he would renounce the police.

'I was hoping I'd get to talk to you,' said Mahout. 'You're in an interesting position. The star cop turned Aries. People don't listen to us, but they'd listen to you if you joined us.'

'Forget it.'

'Why? No one else will accept you for who you were.'

'That doesn't matter. I haven't changed. I'm still me,' said Burton.

Mahout's chuckle echoed down the corridor.

'What's so funny?' Burton called.

'Don't underestimate this place.'

A bolt clanked in the door on Burton's side of the corridor.

'Fuck,' said Mahout.

'What's wrong?'

'They're taking me back to the room.' Mahout was trying to control the fear in his voice.

'What room?'

A second bolt clanked and the door squealed open. Boots marched down the corridor.

'What are they doing here, Mahout?'

Three black-suited Ram Squad cops walked past Burton's cell towards Mahout. Their helmets were on and their faces were invisible behind the tinted glass.

Mahout spoke quickly. His time was running out.

'I can't explain. They've got an astrologer here. He made a Fire Room. He put me in it at the school and it's happening again . . .'

The boots stopped and one of the Ram Squad cops said, 'All right, Mahout, that's enough. Time for another session. Get the restraints.'

A cell door rattled open.

'Fight him, Burton. Don't believe –'

His voice became muffled. They were gagging him.

'Take him to Kruger,' said the cop.

The boots marched back towards Burton. There was the squeaking sound of a body being dragged.

The cops marched back past Burton's cell. One of them led the way, the other two pulled Mahout along by the arms. He was gagged and his wrists and ankles were restrained by straps. His feet were bare.

He made eye contact with Burton for a brief second and Burton saw his defiance. Then he was gone. The door shut and the bolts clanked back into place.

Chapter Seventy-Three

The kidnappers carried Rachel out of the car and up some steps. From the change in sound, she knew that she was indoors. The Aries put her down on something that felt like a sofa and left her there. It sounded like he and the old man were moving things around somewhere else in the house.

She was still terrified and her bladder was full. If they didn't untie her soon, she was going to have to wet the sofa. She could do it anyway, out of spite. She twisted herself upright and rubbed her head on the sofa back, trying to snag the tape and maybe pull it off. It didn't work.

What now? She could probably crawl away, but with the tape over her eyes she wasn't going to get very far. As much as she hated it, she was going to have to wait.

The Aries came back in and picked her up again. He carried her down some stairs into a much colder room, where he put her down on the concrete floor. She heard his feet walking away, back up the stairs. She thought she was alone until hands touched the back of her head and pulled the tape from her mouth. It stung her skin as it came off. She yelped.

'Shh,' said the old man.

She felt his hands again, this time pulling the tape off her eyes.

She was in a cellar with grey brick walls. The room was

almost completely empty. There was a bare workbench in one corner and a camping bed with a sleeping bag on it in the middle, next to a concrete column. In the far corner was a bucket with a toilet roll lying next it. The light came from an old-style iridescent bulb hanging from the ceiling, which looked like the underside of a wooden floor.

She finally got a good look at the old man, who was carefully rolling up the used tape. He wasn't actually that old, but he looked and moved like he was from a different time.

'Whenever I come down here,' he said, 'you must go over to that wall and you touch it.' He pointed at the wall opposite the door and the stairs. 'What do you do?'

'I touch it,' said Rachel. Her voice shook a little when she spoke, but she held herself together.

'Do it now.'

Rachel went over to the far wall and put her hand on it. She looked back at him.

'Good,' he said. 'What's your name?'

'Rachel.'

'All right, Rachel. I'm sorry about this. As you know, I'd rather not have kidnapped you, but considering the alternative . . .'

'Why did you kill that man?' she asked.

'The fewer questions you ask, the less concerned I'll be about letting you go. Do you understand me?'

He was polite, but she realized that that wasn't the same thing as kind. It was just a habit, a mask. She didn't know if she should nod, but she did anyway.

'Good,' said the man. 'I'm going to bring you food every morning and night. The morning meal will include snacks to tide you over until the evening. If there's anything reasonable you need, you can tell me and I'll bring it. Stay right there until I'm out of the door.'

He climbed up the stairs slowly. It looked like he had a limp.

Before he exited, she asked, 'How long are you going to keep me here?'

'I don't know yet,' said the man. 'It may be a few weeks. I advise you to get comfortable.'

When he was gone she finally cried, as quietly as she could.

A few hours later she heard his voice outside the door again. 'Rachel, touch the wall.'

She got off the camping bed and obeyed.

'Are you touching it?'

'Yes,' she called back.

She heard a lock sliding and the door opened. Through it, she caught a glimpse of a kitchen: the top of a large fridge and some white shelving. It all looked expensive.

The man came down the stairs with a plate of food. Roast chicken, mash and peas. Rachel hadn't eaten since breakfast. It looked good.

'Wait there,' he said, putting down the plate. 'Don't move.'

He went back up the stairs and through the door, locking it behind him. After a minute the door opened again and he came down carrying a stack of books.

'It's not a great selection,' he said. 'Sorry. The people I'm renting from don't have much of a taste in literature.'

'Where's your friend?' said Rachel.

The man raised an eyebrow at her, stern but lightly amused.

'What did I say about questions?' he said.

'Let me send a message to my mother,' she said. 'Let her know I'm all right.'

The man shook his head. 'Sorry. I can't do that.'

'Please!' Rachel begged. 'There's so many ways you could let her know without anyone finding you! She must be panicking. I bet she thinks I'm dead!'

The man's face hardened. 'I said no, Rachel. Don't ask again.'

He went back up the stairs slowly. At the top, he looked back at her.

'When the door's closed, you can go and get your food. Bon appétit.'

He went back through and the bolt clicked closed. Rachel ran to the plate and ate on the camping bed.

The next morning, the man called through the door and told her to put her hands on the wall. He came down the stairs carrying a plate of bacon and eggs and a fresh bucket.

'How was last night? Were any of the books readable?'

'I don't like reading,' said Rachel.

'Sorry. It's the best I can do.'

'Can I have a TV down here?'

'I'm afraid not. You might break the screen and use the glass as a weapon.'

She spent the rest of the day reading the books. They were all big and thick, and had their authors' names in large silver letters on the cover. Half were romances and the other half were crime and action stories. They were dumb, but there was nothing else to do.

The days passed. The man brought her a change of

clothes and some tampons when she asked for them. At first Rachel told herself, You're a Libra. Libras are good with people. Just obey and don't cause a fuss, and you'll get through this.

On the fifth day, she told herself, There's a reason Libras don't run the world.

She waited until a couple of hours after breakfast. She listened at the door and, when she couldn't hear any sound from the rest of the house, she started pounding on it. After a few minutes, when there was no response, she kicked it and started throwing her weight against it. It didn't budge.

She searched around for something to prise it open with and discovered that her camping bed could be disassembled. It was made from a canvas sheet and some interlocking steel bars that could be pulled apart and packed up like a tent. They were slightly curved to hold the canvas taut. She took one of them and tried to wedge it between the door and the frame, hoping to crowbar it open, but the gap was slightly too thin.

The only thing left to do was to try and make noise. She stood at the door and screamed for help as loudly and as long as she could.

After about ten minutes, as she was taking in breath, she heard footsteps coming closer. She felt a moment of hope, which was immediately crushed when the old man spoke. He sounded annoyed.

'Put your hand on the wall, Rachel.'

She stayed where she was, breathing heavily, body tense.

'Are you by the wall?' he said.

'Yes.'

'It doesn't sound like it.'

She backed down the stairs slowly and went to the far side of the room.

'I'm doing it,' she said finally.

The bolt rattled and the door opened. The old man stood at the top of the stairs, silhouetted by daylight.

'I think I should inform you that there are no other buildings within earshot,' he said testily. 'The only thing your screaming is doing is making your throat raw and wearing out my patience.'

'Good,' said Rachel, spitting the word out.

'My patience is what's keeping you alive, my dear.'

He examined the door.

'Have you been trying to break out?'

Rachel stayed silent.

'Of course you have. If you keep trying and my friend catches you . . . I'm sorry. I can only help you so much.'

'So your friend's back, then, is he?' said Rachel.

She hadn't heard anything from him for several days and was beginning to hope that he'd been arrested.

'He is,' said the old man.

Rachel didn't know if he was lying or not. She didn't want to believe him. But that evening, after he brought down supper, she listened at the cellar door and heard the two of them talking in the kitchen.

'Who's on the case?' said the Aries.

'Mainly a Homicide detective called Burton, as far as I can tell. You know him?'

'Nah.'

'I'm keeping an eye on him,' said the old man. 'We

should look into his past too. There might be some way to keep him distracted.'

'Like what?' said the Aries.

'I don't know. Suspicious activities. Who's his family? What's his background? I'll find something.'

'Yeah, you will. No one's clean, specially not cops.'

The days went by and the old man gave no sign that he was any closer to releasing her. From the beginning, Rachel had been thinking about those stories of kidnapped women who spent decades in a single room while the world went on without them and everyone who ever loved them thought they were dead.

One day, she couldn't take it any more. She made a break for it.

When the old man arrived at the door and told her to touch the wall, Rachel got herself ready. She called back from the far side of the room, then, as the door started to open, she charged.

The steps slowed her down but she got to the door before it was fully open. She pushed past the old man and was almost free when pain exploded across her back. Her arms and legs were paralysed, and she fell forward and slid on the tiled kitchen floor. She came to a stop, spasming in time to the bursts of pain through her body. The old man had a taser. Why hadn't she seen the taser?

'Oh, Rachel. Rachel, Rachel, Rachel,' said the old man, pulling the taser pins out of her back.

The pain stopped, but she still couldn't move.

'Come on,' he said, and lifted her up under the armpits.

He pulled her back into the cellar and left her at the top

of the stairs, closing the door behind him. She lay there, twitching in pain in the perfect dark.

That afternoon, the old man came in carrying a length of chain, a pair of handcuffs and a padlock. Rachel stood with her hand on the wall while he looped the chain around the column in the middle of the room and padlocked it closed. He hooked the handcuffs through the chain and beckoned Rachel closer.

'I'm sorry for this,' he said. 'We're so close to being done here. There's just one last person to take care of and it'll all be over. But I can't let you go free just yet.'

'No,' said Rachel.

She took out the metal bar from behind her back. It was the central curved bar from her camping bed, which she had spent the morning scraping on the rough concrete floor until it was about as sharp as a ballpoint pen. Before the old man could react Rachel rammed it up, with all her strength, into his armpit. He screamed.

Chapter Seventy-Four

After several hours Burton heard the door to the corridor clanking open again. The Ram Squad came past again with Mahout. The gag was gone and Mahout's hands and feet were unbound. His eyes were rolled back in his head.

Burton couldn't stop himself from calling out to the cops.

'What did you do to him? Hey! I'm talking to you!'

'Wait your turn,' one of the cops shouted back.

He heard them throwing Mahout back into his cell and slamming the barred door. After a few seconds there was the sound of Mahout vomiting on the floor.

'Just in time,' said a cop. Another one chuckled.

Burton felt the muscles in his back crawl. The boots clacked back down the corridor and the three cops came to a stop in front of his cell. The one at the front raised his visor, revealing the face of Vince Hare. He gave Burton a grin.

'Come on, Jerry,' he said. 'It's time for your doctor's appointment.'

'What are you doing, Hare? This is crazy.'

'No, Jerry. This is the only sane place in the city.'

Hare slid the cell door open and pulled Burton out. He didn't struggle the way Mahout had. He knew it wouldn't make any difference.

They led him out of the thick doors and up a flight of stairs to the floor above, walking closely on either side of him to keep him from running. At the end of a corridor was a pair of swing doors that led into another clean white area, with two rows of empty hospital beds lined up against the walls. The cops took him through a side door into what looked like an interview room. There was soundproof padding on the walls and a table with two opposing chairs, all clean and new. The only thing missing was a two-way mirror, or any cameras in the corners. The cops cuffed Burton's hands to a loop in the table and left him, closing the door behind them. He tugged at his restraints but the table was firmly bolted to the ground.

He knew that he should wait quietly, but his anger was growing. This was madness. He couldn't sit around waiting for these people to come to their senses.

'Hey!' he shouted. 'What am I doing here? What the fuck do you want from me? Hey!'

He pulled at his cuffs again, as hard as he could, until the metal bit into his flesh.

'Hey!' he screamed again. His throat began to feel raw.

The door opened and Dr Werner Kruger walked in. He was holding a sandwich in a triangular plastic container in one hand and a glass of water in the other. He acknowledged Burton with a brief wave of his fingers.

'Just a moment, Detective,' he said, sitting opposite him. 'It's been a busy morning. I haven't had a chance to eat yet. I hope you won't mind.'

He sat in the chair opposite and took a bite out of the sandwich, as if they were work colleagues on a break.

'Gas station food,' he said, pulling a face. 'Never great.'

'I'm entitled to a lawyer, Kruger,' said Burton. 'You know it.'

Kruger swallowed and wiped the crumbs from his mouth with the side of his hand.

'I'm sorry to say that, thanks to the Civil Response Act, you're not legally entitled to anything, Detective. Also, I'm not a policeman and you're not being questioned.'

Burton tugged at his cuffs again. It didn't matter that it hurt. The pain was the only thing making any sense.

'You can't do this. Let me go.'

'Don't worry, Detective, that's the plan. You've been flagged as a disruptive element in society, I'm afraid, but the good news is that I'm here to help you with some astrological therapy.'

He pushed the glass of water across to Burton. Burton hadn't had any since he was arrested. His cell had a toilet, but no basin.

'Can you drink with your restraints?'

Burton tried. He clasped the glass between his hands and tipped the water into his mouth. It was ice cool and faintly chemical.

'I'm sorry I couldn't tell you about my current work with the Ram Squad when we met before,' said Kruger. 'It would have saved you a lot of investigation time, I'm sure, but it's all a state secret under the CRA.'

Burton gulped the last of the water and pushed the glass away. It slid and stopped halfway across the table.

'Did you kill the others?' he said.

'Which others?' said Kruger, looking faintly puzzled.

'Williams,' said Burton. 'Hammond. Redfield.'

'Oh, no,' said Kruger. 'No, no, no. It was probably some paranoiac who discovered our grand crux online. I'm sure it's very disturbing to an unscientific mindset.

But I'm safe enough here in this little fortress and the Ram Squad are working hard with your former colleagues to track down the killer. It's not really important.'

He shrugged it off. Burton felt his hairs standing on end. Kruger was a psychopath. He was pleasant, charming and devoid of humanity.

'It's a conspiracy, isn't it?' he said.

'You make it sound so sinister, Detective!' said Kruger. 'Think of the crux as a little . . . gentlemen's club. Private, but hardly ominous. We were working together for a purpose greater than the interests of ourselves or our signs. We were already friends. I just created the crux to bind us, so that we could be certain of each other's trust. None of us could leave it without exposing all of us.'

'What was your greater purpose?'

'Peace, Detective Burton. The Ram Squad are very good at breaking down doors, but they upset people by their very nature. To maintain the peace we need to fix society. I told you before, it's a broken machine. It will only work when all the cogs are the correct shape. And I can fix the cogs.'

Burton felt himself sweating. The room was overheating. He expected Kruger to be sweating too, but the doctor seemed cool and relaxed. He smiled calmly at Burton.

'You're going to do something to me.'

'Yes,' said Kruger amiably.

'I saw what you did to Mahout. I'm not going into your mysterious room.'

Kruger smiled. His eyes gleamed.

'Oh, Detective! You're already here.'

The lights went out, leaving Burton in total darkness.

Chapter Seventy-Five

Rachel had seen self-defence videos online. She knew that stabbing someone in the armpit would stop an attack. The old man screamed and flailed, incapacitated by the pain.

She pulled the sharpened point of the metal bar out with a wet pop and brought the tip of it under his throat. She pushed it in so hard that it nearly pierced his skin again.

'Car keys!' she screamed in his face. 'Now!'

The old man's eyes rolled. She patted him down and pulled them out of his trouser pocket.

'You bitch!' he screamed.

She ran up the stairs away from him, slamming the cellar door behind her and sliding the bolt closed. She ran through the house, terrified with every turn that she was going to run into the Aries murderer. But there it was, the front door, with sunlight shining in through the stained-glass window.

She opened it and ran outside. There was a rolling front lawn going down a hill to an open gate. A black sedan was parked to the side of the house. There was a remote on the key chain in her hand. She pointed it at the car and pressed the button. The lights flashed and the doors unlocked.

She got in and turned the key in the ignition. Nothing happened.

She turned it again. Still nothing. She hit the steering wheel with her fists. She wanted to get out and run to the open gate, but before she did she steadied her nerves and tried again, this time pushing in the clutch before turning the key. The engine instantly roared to life. She was so relieved that tears welled in her eyes.

The gears grated as she put the car into reverse and pulled out of the gate and into the tree-lined street. By the look of it she was somewhere in the south of the city. If she kept on going west then she'd hit Beach Road, and from there it would be easy to find her way back into town.

As she drove, she realized that she should have taken the man's phone. She hadn't been thinking. He could call his friend to come and free him before the police arrived.

Worse. His friend could come after her or her mother. She pushed her foot down on the accelerator.

Chapter Seventy-Six

Lindi first tried calling Burton because she was bored. She was at the police station and had been told by Captain Mendez to continue the investigation, reading the birth charts for all the recently arrested Aries Rising activists in order to judge which ones were most likely to turn inform- ants. But as neither Rico nor Kolacny wanted anything to do with her, she had to stay out of their office. The time she'd spent with Burton had given her a reputation as a liberal Aries-lover. To the Homicide Department, she was career poison.

Burton wasn't answering her calls. His phone went to voicemail every time. He wasn't answering messages either and by lunch Lindi was starting to get worried. She decided to check on him and left a note for Rico saying she'd be working from home. She knew he wouldn't care.

When she got to Burton's house she knew for sure that something was wrong. His car was parked outside and the front door was open. She walked up to it.

'Hello? Burton?'

The paint cans were still stacked by the front door. One of them had a brush resting on the lid.

'Hello?' she called again, as she walked in through the empty house.

Everything was turned upside down. Tables had been pulled away from the walls and paintings were taken down. There was a chair by the boarded-over window and an empty bottle of whiskey lying on its side on the floor next to it.

It didn't look like Burton had been robbed, though. His television was still in the living room and the monitor for his computer was on his desk. Only the computer case was missing.

She went out of the front door and looked around. Across the road she saw movement in the neighbour's window. Someone was watching her from behind the curtains. She went over and rang the doorbell. After a few seconds, the door was opened by a man with white hair and reading glasses hanging around his neck.

'Sorry,' said Lindi. 'I'm working with Jerome Burton from across the road and he's gone missing. His door was open. Do you have any idea where he is?'

The old man nodded. He looked troubled.

'Yes. He was making a lot of noise last night and we'd had enough. We're looking after our grandkids and they deserve some quiet. So we called the police, but I thought they'd just tell him to keep it down. We didn't think they'd take him away.'

Lindi frowned in disbelief.

'You couldn't have just gone and spoken to him?'

'Well, I would have, but since we heard he was an Aries . . . I thought it would be safer.'

Asshole, thought Lindi.

'Thanks for your time,' she said.

She went back across the street and phoned Kolacny.

'Burton was arrested last night,' she said. 'Is he in the station?'

'Nope.'

'Could you check?'

'I don't need to,' said Kolacny impatiently. 'Trust me. We'd all know.'

'Then he's missing.'

'He could be anywhere,' said Kolacny. 'He's been acting crazy lately. Maybe he's with his wife? I'd heard they were separated, but maybe they're back together. Listen, I've got to go.'

He hung up on her.

Lindi slammed Burton's front door closed and pushed on it to make sure it was locked. She went back to the car and used her phone to log into the ACTIVENATION chat group.

LChildsSky: Detective Burton missing. Front door was left open (now closed). No sign of him. Apparently arrested, but not at police station. Possibly suicidal. I don't know who else to turn to. Please help me find him.

She included the links to her social media accounts and waited.

Almost immediately, the replies came in.

Kart33: Holy shit. For real?

AKT: Don't worry. We'll keep our eyes open.

There was nothing else she could do but go back to the station. On the way, she thought through the possibilities. She could try to get Burton's wife's number, although that would mean a difficult phone call. Or she could go down

371

and check out the holding cells herself. Of course, she could always make a horary chart.

She parked near the front of the station. A group of people were standing by the reception desk at the entrance, but the guards weren't letting anyone in.

'People with badges only,' said the bored-looking security guard.

'How are we meant to report a crime?' said a man in the crowd.

'The nearest precinct is Midtown. It's three blocks west. They'll handle reports.'

'No! Please!' shouted an older woman from the front of the mob. She had her arm protectively around a young blonde woman. 'We have to speak to a detective. He said I should talk to him, but he's not answering his calls! You have to let us in. It's an emergency!'

'We all have emergencies!' shouted the man.

The rest of the crowd called out in agreement.

'No one's getting in without a badge,' shouted the guard. 'Back up, all of you!'

Lindi pushed her way to the front, holding her visitor's badge above her head. The older woman and the young woman with her were still at the front, complaining.

'. . . going to die,' the young woman was saying. 'Please. He's in the Homicide Department!'

'I told you, back away,' said the guard.

The older woman started to cry and the young one put a hand on her arm to calm her down. Lindi was going to push past them when she saw the young woman's face.

It was Rachel Wells.

Chapter Seventy-Seven

Cray unbolted and opened the door and looked down into the dimly lit cellar. Daniel was leaning against the column and holding a hand to his armpit. His face was pale and blood was dripping from between his fingers, down the side of his white shirt and on to the floor.

'She stabbed me.'

'Bitch,' said Cray, walking down the stairs to him. 'I told her I'd kill her. I'll do it.'

'We've got to clear this place out,' said Daniel.

He grabbed Cray's shoulder for support. As they walked back up the stairs together, he sniffed.

'You've got booze on your breath.'

'So?' said Cray. 'I've been sitting in a car for five days. I've got to keep myself sane.'

He'd been staking out the new police station in Ariesville, watching the entrances. Kruger, who was working in the building, was coming and going with a police escort. Cray had been looking for an opportunity to strike but hadn't found it yet. It had been mindless work and he had bought a hip flask to keep him company.

He left Daniel at the top of the basement stairs and went to the first-aid kit stowed under the kitchen sink.

'What are you doing?' said Daniel.

'I'm going to patch you up.'

'There's no time. We have to clear the house.'

'You're still bleeding,' said Cray. 'You're leaking evidence.'

Daniel looked down at the red dots on the kitchen tiles.

'Shit,' he said. 'Give me a cloth. I'll be fine. We need to bleach this place down fast.'

Cray threw Daniel a dishcloth and he held it under his arm while they enacted their evacuation plan. Cray packed their bags and bundled their bedding into black bin bags, while Daniel mopped the floors and wiped bleach on the taps, door handles and anything else they had touched. He threw the mop into the back of the car, along with the bedding and the bags. After a final check of every room Cray locked the doors and drove them away from their temporary home, leaving nothing that could be traced back to them.

Cray looked over at Daniel as they drove. Daniel winced and adjusted the cloth under his arm.

'I'll take you to hospital,' said Cray.

'No, they'll be looking for someone with my injury. I'll be fine. I can bandage it up.'

'We need to find a place to lie low.'

'No,' said Daniel again. 'We're killing Kruger. Now.'

'Are you out of your mind?' said Cray.

'Nothing has changed.'

They pulled up at a red light. Cray punched the sides of the steering wheel in frustration.

'Everything's changed!' he said. 'Kruger's unreachable. There's no way he isn't expecting us. We've lost the house. The girl who saw your face and who we didn't kill, she's gone to the cops. It's fucked up.'

'All it means is we have to move faster.'

The car behind them started hooting. Cray looked up

and saw that the lights had turned green. He wanted to get out and shoot the driver of the car behind in the face. Instead, he put the pedal down and pulled off, making the tyres scream.

'There's a crowd outside that station,' he said. 'They're going to tear the doors off the place. We should wait. Let them kill Kruger for us.'

'No!' said Daniel, staring ahead, jaw set. 'If anyone else kills him, this whole thing is for nothing. I've already abandoned doing it personally. I'm not going to let some fucking mob steal his death!'

'I've killed three of them,' said Cray. 'I can't get the fourth. What do you want?'

'I want you to finish the deal!' shouted Daniel.

Cray slowed down and brought the car to a stop by the side of the road. The car behind hooted as it overtook him.

'Shout at me again,' he said to Daniel. 'Try it.'

'You want to give up now?' said Daniel. 'You want to lose 100,000 dollars? And you know what, it's a lot more than that. I was going to help you out with things you can't get with money. You want Ella back? You want your son? You're going to need influence. You're going to need lawyers. If you back out now you get nothing.'

Cray stared at Daniel in disbelief.

'You think I'm a child?' he said. 'You think you can play me like this?'

'Were you good at being a father?' said Daniel. 'Good at being a husband?'

Cray's lip curled. 'I could break your neck right now.'

'Right,' said Daniel. 'Because killing is what you're

good at. And who else is going to reward you for it? How else are you going to make 100,000 dollars today?'

'I've got one idea,' said Cray.

He could feel the weight of the gun in the holster under his jacket. It would be easy. He'd take Daniel somewhere quiet and bring a pair of gardening shears. First the toes, then the fingers. Daniel would tell him where to find the lawyer and how to get that key. And Cray could probably get a lot more out of him, if he tried.

But Daniel read his mind.

'I'm not stupid, Cray,' he said. 'You think I'm just trusting to your good nature? You think I'm not prepared for if you turn on me? I'm ready. If you try to force me to give you the money, I'll ruin you.'

Cray saw the conviction in his eyes. He wasn't lying.

'What did you do?' he said. 'You've got some thug ready to take me out? Or is your lawyer going to turn me in to the police?'

'The precautions I've taken don't matter,' said Daniel. 'Because you're going to kill Kruger. Today.'

Cray's anger turned to bitterness. He could murder Daniel in a heartbeat, but it didn't mean anything. Daniel held the power.

'I've been straight with you,' said Daniel firmly. 'Straighter than you're being with me. I'm giving you a clean deal. This city is going to burn. Are you going to get Ella and your kid with a handful of ashes? Or do you want to leave this place as one of the people with power? I want that for you. I want you to deserve it.'

'Fuck you,' said Cray. 'You want me to die for your little vendetta.'

'Vendetta?' said Daniel. 'Kruger tortured you! He murdered my daughter! This is justice! He has to die!'

'Shut up!'

Daniel narrowed his eyes at him. 'I know what it is. You're scared. You're scared of the Fire Room.'

Cray felt a jolt in his chest.

'Fuck you!' he said. 'Fuck! You! You don't know what it was like!'

His jaw tightened as he said it. Daniel knew his buttons after all. The sick, manipulative bastard. He looked up, expecting Daniel to look triumphant at being proved right, but Daniel was hanging his head. His voice was quiet.

'Yes,' he said. 'Get angry. Make Kruger pay. He stuck you in that room and you're still in it. You've been burning since you were a child. The only way out is through him. End this, Cray.'

Cray was ashamed. He was angry at Daniel for finding the only part of him that was still vulnerable.

'I'll do it,' he said. 'For me. Not for you.'

'Good,' said Daniel flatly. Hiding his smugness.

He's proud of himself, thought Cray. Getting me to do his dirty work and making me think it's my choice.

He would kill Kruger and take Daniel's money. And then, when the time was right, he would kill Daniel Lapton.

Chapter Seventy-Eight

The darkness turned into the static of an old television. Every point melted into a line and every line bloomed into a watching eye.

'You only ever experienced life from inside,' came Kruger's voice through the dark. It arrived in Burton's mind separated into syllables without meaning and truth devoid of words.

'What's happening?'

A million faces flashed in front of him, superimposing and blurring together. His father. Kate and Hugo and Shelley. His mother. A million images, like still photographs played one after the other. Each one a moment in his life.

'You are finally experiencing the world from the outside,' said Kruger. 'You believed you were a person. A little soul, contained in a husk. But you are not. The energy that controls you does not come from within. The husk is a puppet. You are the cosmos.'

The superimposed faces distorted to reveal the hidden forms beneath. Glowing archetypes. Gods and monsters. Burton pulled at his cuffed hands. He could not see them with his eyes, but he could feel their glow.

'Forget your losses and your disappointments. They were just the hard road you had to stumble down to get to this moment. The truth. Turn inside out. Become who you truly are.'

He blinked in the dark.

'The water was drugged,' he said. 'You poisoned me.'

'It's not a poison, Burton. It's unlocking the truth. Can you deny what you feel?'

Things were crawling at him in the darkness. Scorpions. Crabs. Larger animals, just out of touch, but getting closer. He could smell their sweat and feel their hot breath. The only escape was into the mystical light.

Chemical Astrotherapy.

'Feel the energies of the cosmos. Earth. Air. Water.'

Kruger paused after each word. Burton saw a sapling in soil, a hurricane tearing at palm trees during a dark-skied storm, a churning waterfall.

This is not real.

'But you are none of those things,' said Kruger. 'You are . . .'

Burton's body was overheating. When he looked at his hands the darkness cracked, revealing the lava beneath the world.

'. . . inferno.'

Hell opened up in front of Burton. Infinite pain and infinite loss. He froze in terror, moments from death.

'I want to talk to you about coyotes,' said Kruger. 'Remember my coyotes?'

Burton remembered the caged demons. Teeth and instinct.

'We are turning them into something better. There is hope for them. But most of the coyotes are vicious and untrainable. They are no good to anybody. So they must go, and what is left becomes the new truth. All progress is based on sacrifice.'

Kruger made it sound so reasonable. Burton could see the profound truth of it.

'They do not fit into the world we're making,' said Kruger. 'If they don't die, nothing will change.'

It wasn't death. It was taming.

No. It was madness. He was locked in a dark room with a mad doctor who was drugging him into insanity. Burton was gripped by fury. He snarled and pulled at his wrists.

'Yes, feel it in you,' said Kruger. 'Energy. Anger. You've been treated so badly. So much of you has been burned away. And what's left? The real you. You are not passive earth. You are fire!'

A distant supernova exploded in front of Burton. It was the first real light since the room blacked out and it hurt his eyes.

It was a flame. Kruger's face was illuminated in the darkness by a flip-lid cigarette lighter. It seemed tiny in comparison to the vast cosmos in Burton's mind.

'I'm going to hold this under your hands,' Kruger said. 'And you will feel no pain. Fire cannot burn fire.'

Burton watched the flame coming closer, until it was touching the fingertips of his right hand. Kruger was wrong. He felt the pain, but distantly. It didn't bother him. He watched the tip of his index finger blacken with smoke.

'Very good,' said Kruger.

Light shone in like a scythe through the dark, turning Kruger's white hair into a halo. The door of the room opened behind him and a Ram Squad cop came in with his visor up. Strips of light reflected off the sides of his black polished helmet. Kruger turned in his chair, suddenly angry. Burton was shocked to see the monster inside him.

'What are you doing? I'm in the middle of a session!'

'The riots are getting violent, Dr Kruger. We're not well defended here. Lots of the windows are still unbarred. Captain Hare says we might have to evacuate you in one of the vans.'

Kruger's mask of clinical detachment returned and he waved the cop away dismissively.

'There's no danger. I did a chart. They will not harm us.'

'Sorry, Doctor. He said to tell you that if you're going to do what he asked you to do, now's the time.'

Kruger looked at Burton and ran a hand down his face, tired but unbothered. 'Well, we might as well see if this therapy is taking hold.' He beckoned the cop into the room. 'Come. Unlock him. We'll continue this in the cells.'

The cop unlocked the chain connecting Burton's cuffed wrists to the table and grabbed him by the collar.

'Can you walk?'

Burton didn't answer. The cop hauled him upright and shoved him out of the door.

The white room outside was disorientating. Burton was aware of every scuff on the floor and every blemish on the newly painted walls. They seemed to be hanging over the pure, clean geometry of the architecture beneath.

He was pushed back through the doors and into the stairwell. Burton stopped on the top step. He couldn't go down. The distances kept shifting and he couldn't trust his legs.

'Move!' said the cop behind him.

Burton took a step and the vertigo overcame him.

'I said move!'

The cop shoved him forward and Burton stumbled down the steps.

On the next floor he was pushed back into the corridor. He hoped the cop and Kruger would leave him to recover, but they kept shoving him past his cell and towards the end of the corridor. Solomon Mahout was in his cell, lying on his side on the bed, one arm stretched forward. His face was grey and hollowed out. The cop shoved Burton in, and he turned to face Kruger as the door clanked shut.

'What are you doing?'

'This is on special orders from Captain Vince Hare,' said Kruger. 'Mahout is our biggest problem. Even the Ram Squad can't do whatever they'd like to him. He's a martyr-in-waiting. Fortunately, there are other ways to destroy someone. We need to burn him down. And you are the fire, Burton. There has to be a sacrifice.'

The word sounded strange. Burton repeated it in his head: *Sacrifice.*

'Officer,' said Kruger to the cop at his side, 'do you have the weapon?'

The cop removed something sharp-looking from his belt pouch. It took a moment for Burton to recognize it as a strip of metal, scraped sharp, with plastic wrapped around one end as a handle. The cop put it on the ground and kicked it into the cell. It slid to a stop at Burton's feet.

'We can't harm either of you,' said Kruger. 'Not visibly. All we can do is expose your true essence and let nature take its course. All these protesters have forgotten what an Aries truly is. This will make them remember.'

Burton looked at the shiv at his feet. Light reflected off the side of the blade. He felt laughter build up inside him. It was bitterly absurd. He giggled.

'Oh, man,' said the cop. 'He's too drugged up.'

Kruger stayed impassive in the face of Burton's laughter.

'This is your great plan?' said Burton. 'You think I'm going to kill him? You're insane. You can't just give someone LSD or PCP or . . . or whatever this is and think they'll kill for you. I . . . I'm drugged. I'm not brainwashed!'

'That's true,' said Kruger distractedly. He was looking over Burton's shoulder. 'But you've only had one session.'

With a crack, Burton's head jolted sideways. He'd been punched from behind. Pain bloomed from his right ear and across the back of his head. He stumbled forward and grabbed the bars, trying to stay upright.

'Mahout's had them all,' said Kruger.

Burton turned on the bars. Mahout was on his feet and had sweat dripping from his face. His eyes were wide and his pupils were pinpricks. His lips were pulled back in fear.

He dropped down on his haunches and reached for the shiv. Burton lashed out a foot. He connected with Mahout's shoulder and Mahout stumbled backwards, catching his balance in a crouch, ready to attack.

'This is their true nature,' Kruger said to the cop. 'The cogs bite into each other. Whoever wins, Mahout is destroyed. The Aries problem is solved by letting them embrace their truth.'

Chapter Seventy-Nine

There was no time left. The protesters demanding Solomon Mahout's release were getting louder and the cops guarding the front entrance were on edge. Everything was about to crack and Cray had to make his move now. He moved along with the crowd, staying near the fringes, searching for an opportunity.

He watched the Ram Squad cops. The two at the front of the station were holding their weapons with the barrels down, ready to bring them up at anyone who came too close. Hundreds of cell phones were held up in the air by the protesters, poised to capture any overreaction. Three more cops prowled around the outside of the crowd like wolves around a flock, letting everyone know they were surrounded. Those were the ones Cray was watching.

One young protester, a pimply kid with long hair under a sweatband, made the mistake of splitting off from the back of the crowd. He hurried towards an alleyway opposite the station, probably looking for a place to urinate. One of the patrolling cops saw and followed after him. The protesters didn't seem to notice. Cray waited until the young man and the cop had both disappeared into the alley, then went in after them.

The alley was an L-shaped gap between a two-storey brick building and a windowless parking garage. Cray could hear the cop's voice from around the corner.

'I said give it.'

'What? No!'

Cray edged around the corner, keeping his footfalls quiet. The cop had the young protester backed up against the brick wall.

'It's evidence,' he said. 'I want to know who's organizing the protests. Give it.'

'You can't take my phone!'

The cop held his nightstick up against the protester's throat.

'Heard of civil forfeiture?' he said.

He was wearing body armour and a helmet, and the screen over his face was up. Cray walked closer, until he was right behind him.

'Hey!' he shouted.

The cop dropped the kid and wheeled around, swinging his nightstick defensively. It was too late. Cray fired his taser into the cop's face.

One barb dug into his lip, the other just above his eye. The cop groaned and fell to the floor, spasming. Cray locked eyes with the young protester, who looked grateful but terrified.

'Shh,' he said, raising a finger to his lips. 'Run.'

The boy nodded and ran out of the alley. As soon as he was gone, Cray acted fast. He was already wearing black. All he needed was the belt, the helmet and the body armour. He stripped them off the cop to keep them clean, then quickly and efficiently sliced the paralysed cop's throat. The cop grunted and his eyes rolled. Blood bubbled out of his neck. Cray put on the gear, ignoring the dying man.

He walked out of the alley with the visor down. One of

the cops by the station entrance saw him and raised a hand in the air as if to say, I've got your back. Cray raised one back. The cop by the entrance nodded.

It was working. Cray walked around the outside of the crowd towards the front of the station. About halfway around, a chant started up.

'Ma-hout! Ma-hout!'

The crowd pushed closer to the station and spread out across its front. They were blocking Cray's way. The cops at the entrance raised their guns, but this time the crowd didn't back down.

'Drop!' a cop shouted into the face of one of the protesters. 'On your knees!'

The crowd kept coming. The protesters at the back were pushing forward and the ones at the front were being shoved into the cops, whether they liked it or not. A cop raised his gun and fired it above the crowd. Half the protesters scattered.

Cray was almost knocked off his feet as bodies surrounded him in a mindless stampede.

Shit.

One of the protesters took a swing at him with a length of metal pipe and it cracked off the side of Cray's helmet. Cray swung his nightstick into the man's side. The man stumbled. Cray swung again, into the man's face, and saw a bloody tooth skittering across the ground between the running feet.

He pushed the screaming man aside and kept walking towards the entrance. Hands grabbed his armour, slowing him down. He swung the nightstick again, knocking the protesters away, and ran up the steps.

'Get the riot shields!' shouted one of the cops at the door, pointing Cray inside. 'Get them now!'

The crowd surged forward like a wave, crashing into the cops, tugging the guns out of their hands and tearing off their helmets.

Cray got through the glass double doors. He slammed them behind him and found a bolt to lock. It wasn't going to hold, though. The bodies pushed forward and pounded against the frosted glass, silhouetted like zombies. The door rattled and shook under the pressure. One of the glass panes shattered.

Cray turned and ran into the building. Behind him, the doors burst open and red-shirted bodies spilled in.

Chapter Eighty

Gunfire came from outside the building like popping fireworks. The cop looked at Kruger.

'It's happening, Doctor. We have to go.'

'Shh,' said Kruger, his eyes on Burton and Mahout. 'I want to see this.'

Burton scrabbled for the shiv on the floor of the cell. Mahout threw himself on top of Burton and clawed at him. As they fell to the ground together, Burton grabbed the weapon. It would be so easy to hold it up and let Mahout throw himself on to it, but Burton controlled his fear. He slid the shiv out of the cell and beyond Mahout's reach. He pushed Mahout off and backed away to the corner, holding out his burnt fingers.

'Mahout, stop!' he shouted.

The cell swam around him.

Mahout froze like an animal. His eyes were manic and his teeth were bared.

'The wheels,' he said. 'The wheels.'

There was an echoing boom and the sound of smashing glass from the floor below. Voices roared outside and sirens reverberated in the building.

'That's enough, Doctor,' said the cop, grabbing Kruger by the arm. 'We're going to the vans. Now!'

Kruger tried to shake him off.

'Don't be paranoid. The rioters won't break in.'

'Those sirens mean they're already inside.'

'But these two –'

'Now, Doctor!' said the cop, holding firm.

Kruger looked at them, then nodded at the cop, who let go of him. Mahout was reaching through the bars, trying to grab the shiv at Kruger's feet. Kruger bent down to pick it up.

'One last thing,' he said.

In a swift motion he stuck the shiv into Mahout's jugular, as smoothly as if he were administering an injection.

Mahout's eyes bulged. He clawed at his throat, as Kruger followed the Ram Squad cop out of the cell corridor. The door clanked closed after them.

Blood dripped down Mahout's neck and bubbled in his mouth. He got a grip on the handle of the shiv and tugged.

'Mahout! No!' said Burton.

It was too late. The shiv had been plugging the wound. As Mahout pulled it out, the blood pumped out of his neck. Mahout fell to his knees, then to the floor.

Burton ran to his side and put his hand over the wound, trying to stop the blood flow. There was a thud from the far end of the corridor. Feet pounded closer and a dozen voices shouted over each other.

'They're all empty.'

'Over here!'

It was too much for Burton. He abandoned Mahout and grabbed the shiv off the ground, holding it up protectively as he backed away from the bars. Everything in his peripheral vision was crawling and he had to focus on his breathing to stop himself from panicking.

The invaders arrived outside his cell. At first Burton

thought they were covered in blood too and he pointed the shiv at them threateningly. But it was just red clothing. They seemed to move in slow motion, leaving trails in the air.

'What the fuck?'

'He's stabbed Mahout! He murdered him!'

'No!' said Burton. 'It wasn't me!'

They stared in the cell, horrified. They all looked impossibly young.

'It's Burton,' said a girl. The sides of her head were shaved down to smooth stubble and she was holding up her phone to record him. 'He's a cop.'

Burton turned his face away.

'No please, don't. Point that away.'

He didn't want anyone to see him like this.

'He killed Mahout!' said one of the boys.

'I didn't,' said Burton. 'I didn't. Kruger drugged us. He wanted me to kill him. But Kruger did it, I swear to you, I swear.'

The girl looked at Burton.

'My God, he's psychotic.'

Mahout coughed up more blood. He was still breathing.

'He's alive,' said the girl. 'We've got to get in there.'

'The crazy one has a knife,' said one of the boys.

The girl looked at Burton. 'We're coming into the cell,' she said firmly. 'I want you to put the knife down.'

'No,' said Burton. 'You think I killed Mahout. You'll kill me.' He was shivering and dripping sweat.

'That's not true,' said the girl. 'You've got to trust that I trust you. Now. Put down the knife.'

Burton hesitated, but he knew he couldn't fight them. He let the knife drop from his fingers.

The protesters found the door controls and the bars slid open. They came in and tried to lift Mahout. He struggled in their arms, but they held tight.

The girl came up to Burton's side.

'Detective,' she said gently, 'can you walk?'

'You broke into the station,' he said. He couldn't stop clenching his teeth.

'That's right,' said the girl, like he was a child. 'It's going to be OK now.'

'You don't understand the Ram Squad,' said Burton. 'They were holding back, but now they're justified. They're going to kill us. They're going to kill all of us.'

Chapter Eighty-One

Lindi waited with Rachel and her mother, Angela, in a nook just around the corner from the Homicide Department. There were four white plastic chairs next to an urn of instant coffee surrounded by dirty plastic cups, and laminated posters on the walls listed government employees' rights.

Lindi had managed to get them inside the station, but that didn't mean that Kolacny and Rico would see them. Neither of the detectives was in the office they shared, and everyone else Lindi tried to speak to was stressed out and in a hurry to be somewhere else. The police were getting ready for war.

As they waited, Rachel's mother grew more and more terrified and angry.

'Why can't they see her? What are we meant to do? After everything my daughter's been through, she has to put up with this too? There are killers after her! Don't they care?'

Lindi put a sympathetic hand on Angela's knee, trying not to let her get any more fired up. It wasn't helping Rachel, who was leaning backwards and forwards in her white plastic chair. Her mouth was closed tight and her eyes darted warily. She looked like she was seconds away from getting to her feet and running out of the building.

'I'm involved in the investigation,' said Lindi, taking a notebook and a pen out of her handbag. 'While we're waiting for the detectives, I need to know as much as I can about your kidnappers.'

Rachel looked doubtful. It was a transparent attempt to get her to calm down, but she was traumatized and after what she had been through she needed someone who would listen.

'There were two of them. An old, rich one and a young, scary one. The old one's Capricorn. He's really creepy. He thought he was being nice to me, but he talked about killing all these people. I never saw the young one's face, but he's an Aries. I know where their house is. I didn't get their names.'

Just saying it aloud seemed to take a weight off Rachel. She blinked away tears.

'And the old Capricorn? You saw his face?'

'Yes,' said Rachel. 'His hair was going grey and he walked with a limp. He always wore a suit. I could draw you a picture of him. He said they were killing four guys and there was only one left.'

'Yes, we figured that out,' said Lindi.

Kruger.

The elevators across the hall pinged. Lindi looked up to see Kolacny getting out and walking distractedly towards Homicide.

'Hey!' Lindi shouted, getting to her feet to chase after him. 'Kolacny!'

He spun around to face her. 'What?'

'Rachel Wells. The kidnapped girl.' She pointed back at Rachel.

'Holy shit,' said Kolacny, his irritation evaporating. 'Where the hell was she?'

393

'Kidnapped. She escaped.'

'Shit,' he said again.

He ran his fingers through his hair self-consciously, then went to the two women. They got to their feet as he approached and he shook their hands.

'Miss Wells,' he said to Rachel, putting on a reassuring voice, 'I'm Detective Kolacny. I'm very glad you came to us. I'm sorry if you haven't received our attention yet. You've probably heard, we're dealing with a large-scale disturbance, but you're my priority. Please, follow me.'

Lindi knew that Kolacny was putting on a mask of competence, but she was still glad to see him take control of the situation. Rachel and Angela looked thankful. He led them back through Homicide towards his office. When he got to the door he let Rachel and Angela through, but blocked Lindi.

'Just them,' he said. 'Not you.'

'What? Why not?'

He leaned in closer to her. The whites of his eyes were going pink. He looked exhausted.

'We saw what happened to Jerry, Miss Childs. I'm not saying you're to blame, I'm saying there's politics. So thanks for handling this,' he said, pointing into the room, 'but if I need you I'll ask for you. OK?'

The door swung shut after him.

Lindi grated her teeth and went back to the plastic chairs. *Shit*. Everything was happening without her. And everything was falling apart.

She sat back down and took out her phone again. She reopened the ACTIVENATION forum to see if anyone else had responded to her request for help. The new posts showed pictures of a crowd of people pouring into the Ariesville station.

Octagon: It's all kicking off.
Gilloteen: Gunshots!
RomanRoulette: Everyone stay unperforated, you hear?
AKT: WE'RE INSIDE! Searching for Mahout. Wish us luck.

There were blurred pictures from inside the new station, all posted by Bram's Aries friend AKT.

AKT: Found him.
DeepFryer: Pics plz.

A new picture popped up at the bottom of the thread. It was Mahout's face, sweating, looking sick. A hand was reaching into shot, holding a bunched-up T-shirt to his neck.

AKT: He's been stabbed!
DeepFryer: Shit!
AKT: Drugged too. Prob tortured. Getting him out. Found Detective Burton, also drugged.

Lindi's heart leapt. Her fingers raced across the keypad.

LChildsSky: Where is Burton?
AKT: We're bringing him outside. He needs to go to hospital. Come get him NOW, not much time. Don't know how long b4 they cut off phones again.

Lindi's fingers hovered over her phone's keypad. It was crazy, but she typed it anyway.

LChildsSky: On my way.

She looked back towards Kolacny and Rico's office. They wouldn't help her, and if she told them where she was going, they'd probably stop her. She ought to be stopping herself. But there was no one else to turn to, and if she didn't go, then no one else would come for Burton.

She ran to the elevators, past patrol cops who were strapping on their bulletproof vests.

Chapter Eighty-Two

What the fuck am I doing? Lindi asked herself as she sped towards Ariesville. The sun was setting, giving the city an amber glow. The streets started getting narrower and the oncoming traffic was getting heavier. Cars were flooding out of Ariesville. A lot of them were leaning on their hooters.

Up ahead, the intersection at Ninth Avenue and Trinity Street was blocked. Some cars had ignored the traffic lights and crawled into the intersection, creating a gridlock.

'Shit,' said Lindi.

She put her car into reverse but a car came in behind her, blocking her way. She put on her hazards and hooted.

'Move!' she shouted.

There were loud bangs behind her and billowing pink smoke rose up in the rear-view mirror. She leaned over her seat to look. A block away, someone had thrown a tear-gas canister. People were screaming and cars were driving forward to escape it, cramming into the road behind her. Sirens wailed and a convoy of black, military-looking vehicles with tinted windows drove out of the smoke. They skidded to a halt behind Lindi and a loud-speaker clicked on.

'Move your vehicles!' said a metallic voice. 'Clear the way!'

The instruction was drowned out by hooting and there was no way that anyone ahead of Lindi had heard it. It would have been impossible to obey anyway. The cars in front were locked in place and the tank-like vehicles were blocking the only way for the rest of the cars to escape.

'Oh, come on!' Lindi shouted, frustrated with herself and everyone else.

Some people ran towards her from ahead, sprinting through the rows of cars and out between the Ram Squad vehicles. One of them slammed his hand down on the hood of Lindi's car as he passed.

'Hey!' she shouted, though the man was already gone.

More were coming. At first it was just one or two runners, then more, until it was like a marathon. Most of them were dressed in red, but this wasn't a protest any more. There were no placards and no coordinated chants. The only things the people had were anger and fear.

A group of them slammed into the car ahead and started rocking it back and forth, like they were trying to tip it over with the driver still inside. The vehicle pulled away, its tyres screeching, and slammed into the side of one of the cars blocking the intersection.

'No, no, no,' said Lindi.

She tried to reverse up on to the sidewalk, but the car behind her was too close and their fenders collided. The car behind started honking.

Bodies flooded around her car, blocking the light from her windows. Fists slammed down on the hood, the doors and the roof. The drumming was deafening.

The window next to Lindi's head cracked, then shattered. Hands reached in and unlocked her door. The rioters dragged her out on to the street and she felt hands on her, pulling at her bag.

'Hey!'

They took it and ran, leaving her on the road. She pulled herself to her feet and chased after them.

'Fucking sons of . . .'

But they were already running off between the black vehicles. Before Lindi could get to them, the rear doors opened and Ram Squad cops started climbing out. One of them held out a palm.

'Freeze! Stay where you are!'

A cylindrical metal canister clattered on the ground next to her and tear gas started pouring out. The loudspeaker blared behind them.

'This gathering is illegal. Please clear the area. Under the CRA, all civilians in this area will be classified as rioters by the armed services, who will respond accordingly.'

Lindi turned and ran. She pushed her way through the blocked intersection and deeper into Ariesville.

She didn't have her car, her phone or even the ID that proved she was an Aquarius. She was in the middle of a riot. She hadn't been directly hit by the tear gas, but there was still enough of it in the air to make her eyes and lungs sting.

The cars thinned out up ahead, leaving a clearing by the new police station. She ran past more coughing and weeping rioters. A helicopter flew overhead, low enough to scatter the litter left by the protest. The police station was a concrete edifice looming above her. A crowd of people gathered at the front entrance, some pushing to get in, others to get out. Many of them looked scared. As

Lindi approached, a protective circle of Aries Rising members came out of the building carrying Solomon Mahout. His body was limp and blood dripped from under the T-shirt they were holding to his neck.

'Back away,' said a man at the front of the circle to the people gathering around. 'Make room.'

'Lindi Childs!'

A young woman with the sides of her head shaved and a light scattering of freckles was coming out of the station behind Mahout. She had her arm around Burton, who was splattered in blood and shivering.

'I'm glad to see you,' said the girl, coming closer.

'Have we met?' said Lindi.

'Not officially. I'm AKT on the forum. Sherry Reynard.' She helped Lindi take hold of Burton. 'Thanks for coming. We need to get him out of here. A lot of people are going to think he killed Mahout.'

'Shit,' said Lindi. 'I don't have my car or money. I was mugged.'

'You shouldn't be here,' Burton mumbled. 'Are you crazy? They're coming! Look!'

There was the screech of metal scraping on metal. The Ram Squad armoured vans were pushing their way through the cars, breaking windows and snapping off wing mirrors as they shoved all other vehicles aside.

The protesters outside the station turned and ran in the opposite direction, but more vehicles were coming up that street too. There were alleys between the buildings opposite, but too many people were trying to run through them. Some were getting trampled in the stampede.

Tear-gas canisters flew through the air, leaving thick

trails of smoke. People screamed. The circle carrying Mahout turned back towards the entrance.

'Inside!' said Sherry.

She led Lindi and Burton back into the building after Mahout. Lindi looked around. Everything about it was new and it still smelled of construction dust and fresh paint. The protesters laid Mahout out on the reception desk, while others brought chairs and leftover construction supplies to barricade the door.

Sherry went to look out through the broken glass. The black vehicles were coming to a stop. A loudspeaker clicked on outside.

'Members of the Aries Rising movement. By illegally seizing a government building, you have committed a felony. Come out of the building with your hands up or we will start firing.'

Sherry pushed the door open, just a crack, and shouted as loudly and clearly as she could, 'We'll negotiate!'

'I'll go out and talk to them,' said a man with close-cropped hair and an eyebrow ring. He was one of the people who had been carrying Mahout.

Sherry yelled, 'We're sending someone out to talk with you. All right?'

There was no response from the loudspeaker. The Aries boy took a deep breath and walked out through the station doors with his hands up, approaching the vehicles slowly. He was halfway across the courtyard when the first rubber bullets hit him. He clutched his face and screamed. More impacted all over his body. He dropped to the ground and tear-gas canisters fell around him.

Another flew at the front of the station and smashed

through the glass of the entrance. Thick smoke started to pour out of it. Burton and Lindi scattered with the rest of the protesters. Even without direct contact with the smoke, they all began to choke.

As Lindi pulled Burton along the corridor she looked back and saw Sherry taking off her cap, using it like an oven glove to pick up the canister and throw it back out through the door.

They went deeper into the station. In one room a row of desks had been piled up defensively across the entrance and a group of teenage protesters were huddled up against the back wall. They stared at Lindi and Burton with blank-faced terror.

'It's OK,' Lindi told them, and kept moving.

'They're going to die,' said Burton. 'Kruger. Kruger is here.'

'Really?' said Lindi. She wasn't sure how drugged Burton still was.

'I'm serious. He was going down to the garage. If the protesters have blocked the exit, then he's still in the building. He did this to me. He was trying to get Mahout to kill me. Or us to kill each other.'

'Calm down, Burton,' said Lindi.

'You're not listening! I'm telling you what happened!' said Burton. 'Kruger killed Mahout! He's insane!'

They passed rows of grey lockers. The sun had set and the light outside was getting dim. No one had turned on the corridor lights.

'What are we looking for?' said Burton.

'Somewhere safe.'

'Lindi,' said Burton flatly.

She ignored him.

'If we lock ourselves in a cell, we might have a better chance . . .'

'Lindi!'

He was pointing to the end of the dark corridor. She stared into the darkness, trying to see what he was seeing. She made out two figures in the shadows of the stairwell. From the halo of white hair, one of them was Kruger. The other was wearing body armour and a helmet, and was holding a gun to Kruger's back.

Chapter Eighty-Three

'Put the gun down please, sir,' Lindi called out, as calmly as she could.

The man jammed the gun harder into Kruger's back. 'You know who this is?' he called back to Lindi.

'Yes. I do.'

'He doesn't deserve to live,' he said. 'Walk!'

Kruger took a reluctant step up the flight of stairs. Burton and Lindi followed after them.

'Stop,' said the man in the body armour, tilting his head in their direction. 'Any closer and I'll finish this now.'

'You don't want to do this,' Lindi called up.

'You want me to leave the police to deal with him?' the man snorted, and jammed the barrel deeper into Kruger. 'I thought I told you to walk!'

'Where are we going?' Kruger asked.

'Up.'

The second, third and fourth floors of the building were also in darkness. The stairs continued to an access door to the roof. Lindi helped Burton up the stairs, keeping the killer and Kruger in sight.

'You killed the other three, didn't you?' Lindi called.

The killer stayed silent. He kept Kruger moving.

'Listen,' Kruger said to the killer. 'I'm sure you think you're stopping a conspiracy, but it's not like that. The crux was something I dreamed up at university. It was like a joke. It's not a real thing! It's a fiction!'

'I don't give a fuck about the crux,' said the killer. 'Open the door.'

Kruger fumbled at the door in the darkness of the stairwell.

'It's locked.'

The killer pointed his gun at the lock and fired twice. He kicked the door open and pulled Kruger on to the roof, with Lindi and Burton following at a safe distance. The killer had his visor raised and there was just enough light left in the twilight sky for Lindi to see his face. His eyes were a piercing blue.

Kruger saw it too.

'I remember you,' he said to the killer. 'You were at the academy.'

The killer still didn't speak. He pushed Kruger along the rooftop, towards the edge.

'Where are you taking me?'

'To embrace your element,' said the killer.

Kruger's voice shook. 'No. God, no . . . I'm just trying to fix things. All this, all that's happening, is because society is broken. I'm the one who can fix it! That's what I'm doing! If you kill me, this whole society will die!'

'Good.'

The killer put his hand against Kruger's back and pushed.

Chapter Eighty-Four

From the window of his police heavy vehicle, Vince Hare watched the body fall. It hit the edge of the steps outside the station entrance with a crack.

'Who the fuck was that?'

On the roof, a man in body armour was silhouetted against the sky. He looked down to make sure the body was dead, then walked back on to the roof.

'Was that one of us?' said Vince.

'No, sir,' said the sergeant next to him. 'We just found Polsen's body. Someone stole his armour.'

'They're making it look like we're murdering civilians.'

'What do we do, Captain?'

'Move in,' said Vince. 'Take down the door and clean that place out. Use all force necessary. Burn it to the ground if you have to. Go!'

Chapter Eighty-Five

In the low light, Kruger's blood ran black down the station steps. Cray watched for a few seconds and felt a calm coming over him. It was finally done, but it wasn't over yet. He turned back to the roof access door, which was being blocked by the cop and the astrologer. They had to go. He raised his gun and fired three shots.

The astrologer shoved the cop out of the way and backed off on the other side. She was deliberately letting him go. Cray could have taken care of them there and then, but he was going to need his bullets to get past the cops. He ran to the open door and down the stairs. He hoped they'd be smart enough to leave him alone, but after a few seconds he heard feet pounding down the steps behind him.

'Burton! Leave him!' came the astrologer's voice from the roof.

Cray turned and fired another bullet, but it hit the dark wall of the stairwell. There was the sound of crashing metal from downstairs. The Ram Squad was using a battering ram to break open the front entrance.

There had to be another way out. With the protesters gone, the garage exit should be clear. He just had to get down to it.

On the ground floor the corridor was filled with eye-stinging smoke. Boots stamped closer. Cray saw the gas-masked Ram Squad marching down the corridor and swinging their truncheons at the coughing, screaming protesters blocking their way. One of the cops pulled a pin out of another can of tear gas and threw it into an open door.

A cop at the front of the line saw Cray and pointed.

'Suspect armed!'

Cray instinctively raised his gun and fired again. The cop stumbled backwards with the impact, but stayed on his feet. He steadied himself and ran at Cray.

Cray kept firing until the clip was empty, then threw the gun to the side and ran up the stairs. A bullet in his back knocked the wind out of him, but his body armour saved his life. He stumbled up the stairs and got to the second-floor corridor. Doors were open on both sides. He ran into one of the dark rooms, where a wide, unbarred window led to the outside. It was only the second storey. It was worth the risk. He slid open the glass and looked down. There was a long drop, but it was better than what he had done to Kruger.

He lowered himself out of the window, just as the armoured cop got to the door of the room.

'Freeze!' shouted the cop, too late.

Cray let go and dropped to the ground.

Chapter Eighty-Six

The air in the station stabbed into Burton's eyes. There were screams and gunfire coming from downstairs. The drugs were finally wearing off, but his terror continued.

'Burton! Stop!' Lindi shouted from behind him. 'Where are you going?'

'There's got to be a fire escape.'

He ran down the stairs, with Lindi close behind. Some armed cops were coming up from the ground floor.

'Freeze!'

Lindi and Burton turned out of the stairwell and ran along the second-floor corridor. An armoured cop stepped out of a door ahead and threw a tear-gas canister at them. Burton managed to duck into a room to avoid it, but the smoke caught Lindi's face. She screamed.

'Come!' Burton said, pulling her into the open door.

'I can't see!' she said, choking. 'Oh, God, I can't see.'

'It's OK. We're going out the window.'

'It's the second floor!'

'You can do it.'

Burton opened the window and guided Lindi to it. She climbed over the windowsill.

'Lower yourself down,' he said. 'Hang down as far as your arms will let you and drop. It's about fifteen feet.'

He heard the armoured cops coming from both ends of the hallway.

'This is crazy, Burton! I'm blind!'

'You'll be fine, I promise. Go!'

She hung down from the window ledge, let go and fell. Her legs collapsed under her as she hit the ground, but her fall was safely broken.

Burton clambered out the window after her. He could hear the cops coming into the room behind him. He didn't have time to lower himself. All he could do was push himself away from the window and drop.

He hit the ground hard and felt the tendons rip in his ankle. He suppressed a scream.

'Burton?' said Lindi. 'Is that you?'

'I'm fine,' he said through clenched teeth. 'You?'

'I'm OK,' she said. Her eyes were puffy, but she'd managed to get the left one open slightly. 'I'll be fine. Which way?'

Burton pointed her to an alley opposite the station and started limping towards it. Lindi ran ahead of him, across the road and past the parked black vans.

His ankle was slowing him down considerably. He had only just cleared the corner of the station when he heard a familiar voice behind him.

'What have we here? Our hero's hanging out with his own kind.'

Burton turned. Captain Vince Hare was striding up to him. His face plate was up, but every other inch of his body was covered in armour. Two Ram Squad cops were following behind him.

'Vince,' said Burton, 'there's a serial killer. The one who killed Williams. He just murdered Kruger –'

'Shut your face.'

Vince cracked Burton across the jaw with his nightstick. Stars exploded across his vision and he fell to his knees.

'You've had this coming a long time, Burton,' said Vince, and kicked him in the gut.

Burton fell on his side. The other two cops laid into him with their nightsticks. He felt his ribs and fingers crack.

There was a burst of heat and the road next to them lit up with orange light. The side of one of the black vans was on fire.

'Shit, what was that?' said Vince.

'Molotov cocktail, sir.'

A huge throng of people in red shirts were charging down the road towards them, screaming like warriors. Those in the front were carrying rag-topped bottles.

'Defensive line!' Vince shouted. 'Form up! Now!'

'There's more coming from the north, Captain! They've pincered us!'

'Make a perimeter!'

Burton tried to crawl away, but Vince gave him another kick.

'Get the rioters. We'll pick this one up later.'

Chapter Eighty-Seven

Lindi ran through the alley towards the street lights up ahead.

On the other side was an encouraging sight. There was a police barrier with real cops, not Ram Squad goons, and behind it was an ambulance.

She turned to look for Burton. He had been right behind her.

'Burton?'

She walked back cautiously, past a line of dumpsters and overflowing bins. She was almost at the other entrance to the alley when an arm grabbed her by her collar.

'Not so fast.'

It dragged her back into the shadows and pushed her down to the ground. Standing over her was an armoured Ram Squad cop with his visor down. She put up her hands.

'I'm Aquarius!'

'I know what you are,' said a familiar voice. The killer.

He had a nightstick in one hand and took out a blade with the other. He lunged at Lindi, who rolled across the foul-smelling ground. The knife scraped on the concrete. He stabbed again, and Lindi felt steel between her ribs.

Outside the alley, Burton limped closer. He saw motion in the dark and heard Lindi's voice crying out in pain. Her attacker raised a nightstick, bringing it down on her, knocking her back to the ground.

'Stop!' he yelled.

The man looked up, then charged at him with the nightstick raised. Too late, Burton saw the knife in his other hand. He tried to grab the killer's arm but only partially blocked the blow. The point of the blade went through his shirt and into his shoulder.

The killer rammed the butt of his nightstick into Burton's solar plexus. Burton stumbled back but held on to the front of the body armour, pulling the killer over with him. They fell together against the dumpsters, which rolled sideways.

Burton dropped to the ground and the killer fell on top of him, pinning him down. He headbutted Burton so hard that the helmet visor cracked. Burton tried to tug himself free, but the helmet came down again, knocking his head back into the concrete. The jagged glass sliced across his face.

The killer tugged off the helmet and threw it aside. He picked up the knife from the ground next to him. Burton could only watch as it arced towards his neck.

There was a crunch. The killer froze, then fell forward on to Burton.

Lindi was standing over them, breathing heavily, holding a broken half-brick. She kicked the killer off Burton and brought the brick down on him again. And again. There was a wet cracking sound, followed by silence.

Lindi dropped down to the ground and lay next to Burton.

'You OK?'

He shook his head.

There were more sirens and screams beyond the alley. Red and blue lights glowed through the gas and smoke.

'Can you move?'

Burton shook his head again. His breathing was fast and shallow. He gritted his teeth, trying to contain his pain.

They huddled down together and waited for it all to end.

Chapter Eighty-Eight

Lindi woke shivering in the grey dawn light. The city was silent. Burton lay next to her. She could see his chest gently rising and falling.

She pushed herself up on to her elbows and gasped. The wound in her side started bleeding again. Outside the alley, on the other side of the street, the police station was in ruins. The windows were shattered and there were black streaks above them from where the smoke had poured out during the night.

People were coming down the road, followed by a slow-moving pickup truck. Lindi pushed herself back into the alley, but they saw her.

'We got casualties!' shouted a voice.

Three men ran over to her. One of them was wearing a yellow hi-vis vest. He looked official.

'Ma'am, are you injured?'

When Lindi nodded, another of the men took out a silver thermal blanket and wrapped it around her shivering body.

'What about your friend?'

The one in the reflective vest shone a pen torch into Burton's rolled-back eyes and looked up.

'We're going to need a body bag.'

In her half-awake state, Lindi felt a jolt of panic. She looked around and saw the killer's body.

'Who are you?' she asked the man who had given her the blanket.

'Reservists,' he said, with a Libra accent. 'You got any identification?'

'Stolen,' she whispered hoarsely, and coughed.

'No problem. We'll take care of you. The paramedics are coming. Everything's going to be fine.'

Chapter Eighty-Nine

Burton woke in a hospital bed. A green curtain hung from a rail on the roof, enclosing him like a tent.

Kate was sitting in a chair next to him, reading a book. 'Hey,' he croaked.

She looked up and smiled. 'You scared me,' she said quietly.

She put the book down and took his hand. He winced. Two of his fingers were bandaged and blisters had formed on his fingertips. There were plastic tubes coming out from under a bandage on his wrist.

'Sorry,' she said, relaxing her grip.

'You've lost weight,' he said woozily.

She laughed. It took a moment for him to realize.

'She's born?'

Kate nodded. 'Last week. She's back home already. My brother's looking after her.'

'And is she Taurus?'

Kate nodded. Burton felt tears welling and closed his eyes.

'I missed it. She's our child and I missed it . . .'

'It's all right,' said Kate soothingly. 'Get better now. She'll be happy to have a father.'

The next day, Lindi and Kolacny came to see him. Lindi showed him the stitches on her side.

'A scar from a serial killer. I'm going to get so laid.'

She said it jokingly, but he could see that she was still fragile. She told him that she had been offered a new job in Singapore, tracking potential criminals. While she said that she was still considering it, Burton could see that her mind was already made up. She'd had enough of San Celeste.

When she went back to her own ward, Kolacny stayed with Burton. He seemed embarrassed.

'You've got something to say?'

'Vince Hare died in the riots,' said Kolacny. 'A bullet caught him under the helmet. They say it was an accident. Friendly fire from one of the other cops. There's going to be an investigation. There's going to be a lot of investigations actually, after Mahout's death and the riots. Mendez has been suspended. So the good news is, you're back in.'

'Really?' said Burton.

Kolacny nodded. 'We're all pushing for officer's compensation for your injuries.'

'Thanks, Kolacny.'

'You're welcome. Anything you need.'

Which, Burton thought, was close enough to 'sorry'.

When Kolacny was gone, Burton unfolded a newspaper that Kate had left for him and looked through it. Rachel Wells was big news. She was young and beautiful, and she had escaped a horrifying situation through her own intelligence and bravery. The media were lapping her up and she was already something of a celebrity. The paper had an article about her selling the rights to her life story.

There was a puff piece near the back of the paper entitled 'Cruxes – What You Need to Know', which was largely just speculation about which other public figures and celebrities might be members of one of these sinister groups. The article was illustrated by a sketch Rachel had drawn of the old Capricorn man who had kidnapped her. It was captioned 'The Second Crux Killer – Still at Large'.

There was hardly any mention of the riots. No articles about rebuilding Ariesville or medical care for the injured civilians.

Burton folded the paper away and lay back in his bed.

Chapter Ninety

Burton was back on his feet after a few more days. He hadn't seen his daughter in person yet and it was driving him crazy. All he'd seen was pictures on Kate's cell phone screen. It didn't feel real. It gave him the motivation to push himself. He walked through the hospital, pulling his drip stand with him as he went. It took a lot of effort and the polished floor was cold under his feet, but it was worth it for the small freedom of getting out of his bed.

He pulled the stand down the corridor, past a small reception area between wards. It had a vending machine, three chairs and a small table with a plastic pot plant. An old man was leaning forward in one of the chairs, resting his hands on a walking cane in front of him.

'Hello, Detective,' he said.

He had a friendly half-smile and a Capricorn accent. Burton froze.

'I'm glad you're recovering,' said the old man. 'I've done what I can to help out. Within reason, of course. There are some things that even I can't fix.'

Burton tensed up. Rachel's sketch had been rough, but it matched. The greying hair. The cheekbones. He gripped his stand for support.

'Congratulations on your daughter,' said the man.

Burton looked around the hospital corridor. There was a man standing by the reception desk, not exactly looking in their direction but not looking away either. And another man sitting outside one of the wards with his hands in his coat pockets. Who would wear a coat in this heat? Burton looked back at the old man, who was still smiling faintly. He wouldn't be here without protection, and preparation. And Burton's daughter was at Hugo's house, which offered very little protection against someone determined, rich and insane.

'Calm yourself, Detective. I came to tell you that it's over.'

'It isn't,' said Burton.

The man shook his head.

'It is. Everything is back to the way it should be. The anger was purged. You played your part well and you've earned my thanks.'

Burton stared into the old man's face, memorizing every line on it.

'I'm doing my best to make things easy for you. I hear you're getting your old job back and your hospital bills are being paid for. Congratulations.'

Burton gritted his teeth. 'I don't want anything from you,' he said.

'That's too bad,' said the man. He got to his feet and stretched. 'You've already got it.'

'I'm not your pawn,' said Burton. 'If you're who I think you are, I'm going to take you down.'

'At what cost, Detective? People like me maintain the balance of society.'

'I'd rather see the city burn again than have people like you in it.'

The old man smiled. His jaw was lopsided.

'I'm very happy to hear that,' he said. 'Good day, Detective. And congratulations again on your beautiful daughter.'

His walking stick clicked on the hospital tiles as he walked away. Burton watched him push his way out through the revolving door and into the light of the sun.

Acknowledgements

This book wouldn't exist without the following people:

My wife, Dr Kerry Gordon, put up with a mentally absent husband for a whole year of writing, which is far too long. Thank you for not murdering me.

Emad Akhtar is a genius. He's the editor who picked out *Zodiac* from my list of story ideas and said, 'That's the one,' and then bounced the plot back and forth with me until it reached its final form. I have lost count of the number of times my jaw dropped at his story suggestions. Honestly, this book is as much his as mine.

My agent, Oliver Munson, did the dirty work. He worked tirelessly to promote me and opened doors that I didn't even know were there. Thanks, Oli.

The eagle-eyed copy editor, Lesley Levene, caught the weird sentences and non-Americanisms, and saved me from a lot of embarrassing mistakes.

My friend Sarah Lotz gave up her time to read a terrible early draft of the book and returned nothing but constructive criticism and undeserved positivity.

The trailblazing Lauren Beukes has been telling everyone to read this book well before I started writing it. Her constant support, encouragement, advocacy and friendship have been invaluable and generally awesome.

The great people at Sunrise Productions, particularly Philip Cunningham, Brent Dawes and Matthew Brown, gave me the time and flexibility I needed to write this book. They also provided the best working environment that anyone could ask for.

And many thanks to the early readers of the book, including Lauren, Sarah and Kerry (again), Danielle and Matthew Gair, and especially to my parents, Tony and Diana Wilson, who deserve a whole separate acknowledgements section of their own.